I0600306

the LEGACY *of a* LIE

A NOVEL

RON ELCOMBE

Author's Note: This story was first published under the title *Once Lost*. It has been rewritten, revised, and expanded.

Published by Windy Ridge Publishing
5328 Southwood Dr SW
Rochester, MN 55902

ISBN (print): 979-8-9930667-0-7
ISBN (ebook): 979-8-9930667-1-4

Book design and production by Domini Dragoone, Sage Folio Creative
Cover photos: Landscape courtesy of CC0 Colletion / 123rf;
    sheet music by Digital Classic Scores / MusicaNeo
Author photo by Drake Hokanson

In Memoriam

This book is dedicated to the memory of my good friend, Cheryl Caddy. Until her untimely death, Cheryl read almost everything I had written. Her always insightful comments and encouragement spurred me on in my writing journey. I owe her a huge debt of gratitude.

I miss her greatly.

Contents

ACT ONE

1996

CHAPTER ONE

Thursday, September 19

M aarit McDonough Malone backed the four-year-old black Impala into the street fronting her Stillwater townhome. The car radio crackled to life as the car cleared the garage.

"Top of the mornin' to ya! It's six fifty-two on this bright, sunshiny morning, and the temperature is fifty-nine, climbing toward a warm seventy-six degrees this afternoon. Stay tuned for news headlines at the top of the hour, followed by the weather forecast and sports here on WCCO-AM, *your* news talk radio channel. Now for this date in history, twenty-five years ago today..."

She turned the radio off as she pulled into the drive-through at the Coffee Stop. The attendant, too perky for the morning hour, wished her a great day and passed a medium coffee with cream but no sugar through the window. Only two meetings were scheduled for the day: the first with her boss at 11:00 a.m. and a division meeting at 1:00. With any luck, she'd escape the office early.

Instead of turning north to I–94 and Saint Paul, the car pulled out of the Coffee-Stop driveway onto the main street and turned south toward Red Wing. Maarit was surprised at the easy merge into the lighter-than-usual highway traffic.

"Why is the sun in my eyes today?" Maarit muttered. "It wasn't yesterday." Within a few minutes, where she expected stop lights, stop signs were spaced apart at irregular intervals. Long stretches of unfamiliar road stretched to the horizon. She looked at her watch and frowned. She should have been at work twenty minutes ago. The highway transitioned into a street with no curb or shoulder, then evolved into a narrow gravel road. She tried to turn around, but the car slid off the narrow shoulder into a ditch.

Confusion became fear. The front bumper hit an orange snow fence. The car shuddered. Forward motion ceased. Engine warning lights glowed red throughout the vehicle. Fear became panic. She tried to yell for help, but only a faint whisper escaped her lips. Her head throbbed. Everything blurred. Then, everything went dark as she lost consciousness.

～ ＝ ～

Police Log

8:17 p.m. The Stillwater police department received a call from Maarit McDonough Malone's boss. She had missed two meetings, and he couldn't reach her all day. Party stated he was worried.

9:24 p.m. Incoming 911 call from a concerned farmer who observed a car in the ditch a mile from his home. He reported that he spotted the driver slumped over the steering wheel.

9:36 p.m. First Responders and an ambulance arrived with flashing sirens and red lights. First Responders administered CPR, and victim was transported to the Ellston Community Hospital.

10:16 p.m. Maarit McDonough Malone was pronounced dead in the Ellston Hospital emergency room.

10:31 p.m. Law Enforcement called the phone number listed on the In Case of Emergency line in the victim's address book.

An autopsy later revealed that a series of strokes had resulted in her death.

Father Sean McDonough softly replaced the phone in its cradle. He bowed his head and let out a deep sigh. Fighting back tears, he crossed himself and whispered, "Rest in peace, Sis. Rest in peace."

Bending, he retrieved a small, brown paper package from the credenza's lowest drawer and placed it in the center of the desk. His desk chair groaned under the sudden addition of his weight.

The priest did not attempt to open the package. Instead, he reached for a family portrait, cradled it in his hands, and sat staring at the image. In the picture, his sixteen-year-old self was seated between his mother and sister while his father stood behind the trio. His father's chin jutted out and up, giving him the appearance of a diplomat. Instead of a friendly smile, he assumed the visage of a dignified and meaningful person.

His mother's kind smile, and the memory of her gentle hand on his shoulder, warmed the priest's heart. He smiled at the twinkle in his sister's eyes, recalling the giggles they had shared before the flash and click of the camera shutter. He chuckled out loud at the memory of boisterous laughter when the harried photographer told them the sitting was over.

He returned the photograph to the desk, picked up the package, and gently ran his fingers across the top. Two snips of the scissors and the string holding the wrapping fell away. Inside were two sealed envelopes: one addressed to him and a larger second envelope addressed to Allison Williams at the Williams-Laughton Law Office. Seeing his sister's delicate handwriting brought tears, blurring his vision.

Sean, please deliver this package to my attorney,
Allison Williams.

Thanks.
M.

The second letter was addressed to him.

Dear Sean,

If you are reading this, you know that I am dead. It feels very strange to write that sentence, knowing that you will only see it after I die. I know I have not been a very good sister, and I hope you will forgive me. There are probably a thousand psychological reasons for how I lived my life, all of which combined won't fully explain my choices. If I hurt you, I am genuinely sorry. Since you are in the forgiveness business, I count on your compassion.

I have three final favors to ask of you, dear brother. First, please call Kay and let her know. Tom won't care if I am alive or dead, but I hope that my daughter will want to know.

Next, this may come as a surprise to you, but I have a second child. Her name is Anna, born three years after Tom and I split up. She was adopted by a wonderful couple, John and Peg Jensen. They didn't know I was Anna's mother; the records were sealed. Please let her parents know that I have died. I leave it to them to decide the best way to tell Anna.

Lastly, please say a few prayers for the repose of my soul in a small, private wake. I know I haven't been a very good Catholic, but I'll rest easier if you will say some prayers for me. Please, ask Kay and Anna to attend; I hope they will agree to come. I don't want a public funeral with a lot of people looking at me lying in a casket, shaking their heads and saying, "Doesn't she look nice, so life-like, what a shame." Yuck.

Thank you, Sean. You and the two girls are the only family I have left. Please, think kindly of me, even though I don't deserve it.

Love,
Maarit

The second sheet, from May 1996, included the addresses and phone numbers for Kay Malone, John and Peg Jensen, and the Williams-Laughton law office.

Father Sean leaned back in his chair and reread the letter. He smiled again at the memory of posing for the portrait. It had been a hilarious session three days before Maarit left for college. It was one of the few times their father tolerated his children's shenanigans. As usual, his mother had laughed at their antics. Father McDonough shook his head and muttered softly. "That poor photographer had an awful time trying to get us to sit still and not wisecrack."

He reached for the phone and began to dial the first number on the list. He stopped mid-dial and slowly returned the phone to its cradle, touching the portrait and bowing his head. "Time enough to share the sorrow in the morning," he whispered.

CHAPTER TWO

Saturday, September 21

Thirteen-year-old Anna Jensen, all arms and legs, climbed onto her bicycle, waved at her piano teacher, and pedaled out of Mrs. Anders' driveway at full throttle. Tied in a ponytail, her nut-brown hair flew out behind her like a flag in a stiff breeze. Anna covered the three blocks to her home in record time and screeched to a halt at the top of the driveway. As usual, she left the bike on its side, grabbed her back-pack, and rushed through the front door.

"Mom, Dad! Guess what! Mrs. Anders wants me to play in a recital at the nursing home for Halloween. It'll be like, loads of fun—can I, can I?"

"Anna," Peg called. "We're in the kitchen. Come here, please."

Anna bounced through the kitchen door. "Can I, *please*? It will be so neat and cool. Mrs. Anders said I should memorize the music, but hey. What's going on? Is something wrong?"

Peg rushed to hug her daughter. "Come sit down; we have something to tell you."

Anna looked at her father. The last time she had seen that look was when he told her grandpa had died. She began to chew her lower lip nervously. "What's wrong? Did I do something wrong? I'm sorry. What did I do? I promise I won't do it again."

"Stop biting your lip," Peg gently corrected. "No, don't worry, you didn't do anything wrong. You're not in any trouble. But we do have something serious to talk to you about."

"Dad?" Anna let Peg steer her to the table. "I'm sorry, Dad. I know I left my bicycle in the driveway again. I promise I'll pick it up."

"It's okay, honey. This is not about your bike; we can move it later."

Anna began to bite her lip again.

Peg reached over and patted her daughter's hand. "Don't bite your lip, dear."

John pulled his chair closer to the table and leaned forward. "While you were at your piano lesson, we received a call from Father McDonough."

"Father McDonough? Who's that?"

"He's a priest at St. Francis," said Peg. "Sweety, there's no easy way to tell you this. On Thursday, your birth mother was found dead in a car a few miles north of town. The authorities think she died from a stroke while she was driving."

Anna frowned and looked at her Dad again. "My *birth* mother?"

"Yes, Anna, your birth mother. We don't have any details yet; they've started the investigation. I'm sure we'll know more later."

Anna shrank away from her father; her mouth opened, but no sound emerged. She wrapped her arms around herself like a cold wind had rushed through the kitchen. "Wha...uh...I...wha...who.... how..." Anna stammered and sputtered as she tried to find the right words.

Peg quietly walked behind her daughter and engulfed her in a reassuring hug.

"How?" Anna whispered. A million questions raced through her young mind, "How did you find out? Did she live here? What was her name? Did she know I lived here? I...I don't understand."

"We only found out when Father McDonough called us."

"How did he find out?" Anna asked.

"I'm guessing that the authorities must have called him. That's what he said, anyway. He said that the police called him late last night, and he waited to call us until this morning."

"Who was she? I mean, what was her name?" Anna slumped in her chair and clutched her stomach as if in pain.

Peg grabbed a chair and slid it next to Anna. She put her arm around her daughter and held her close. "Her name was Maarit Malone. We really don't know much more than that. We know a wake will be held at the church on Monday evening. We can go if you want to."

John cleared his throat. "There's one more thing we need to tell you. The priest said your sister…"

"My sister? *WHAT SISTER?*" Anna leaped to her feet so quickly that her chair toppled backward. The chair clattered to the floor, causing her to recoil at the sound. *What was happening?* With a flushed face and heaving chest, she stood shaking.

Peg grabbed Anna, afraid her daughter would collapse. "I know it's a lot to take in. Let's go into the living room and talk about this."

The three took a few minutes to settle into the living room. Anna curled up on the sofa in her mother's protective embrace while John prepared hot chocolate for everyone. After handing out the warm drinks, he sat in the recliner across from his wife and daughter. Speaking gently, Peg rested her head against Anna's and tried to calm her, whispering that everything would be okay. Gradually, Anna's rapid breathing slowed and became steady.

John smiled. "Are you ready to talk about it now?"

Anna nodded but remained in the safety of Peg's arms.

"Your birth mother's name was Maarit Malone. We don't know if she lived in Ellston or was visiting the area. I'm sure we'll find out more soon. All the priest said was that Maarit had died and that a wake would be held Monday evening at St. Francis church. I don't know how he knew that Maarit was your birth mother or that you have a sister. He said that Kay Malone, your sister's name, had agreed to come to the wake."

"This is weird." Anna shuddered. "Is this for real?"

"Yes, dear. I'm afraid it is. I'm sorry." Peg squeezed her daughter and ran her fingers through her hair.

"We don't have any details yet," John added. "I always hoped we would eventually find her, but it looks like she found us."

Anna wrinkled her nose. "Mom, did you know I had a sister?"

Peg looked over at John, the question in her eyes. He slowly nodded his assent.

"When we adopted you, we were told you had a sister. But there was no information on who she was or where she lived. The priest told us her name and that she is a student here at Milan College."

"Why didn't you *tell* me I had a sister?"

Peg sighed and wiped a tear from her daughter's cheek.

"Anna, you've known for a long time that you were adopted," John said. "We knew nothing about your sister except that she existed, and even then, we had no proof. The topic never came up because there was no reason to bring it up, and you didn't ask."

"No reason?" Anna wrinkled her nose in disdain.

John shrugged. "I'm sorry, kitten. We should have brought it up, but didn't think about it. I'm really sorry."

Anna frowned, then relaxed. "Do...do you think I should go? To the wake, I mean."

"Oh, honey. Only if you want to," said John.

"I don't...don't understand. If she lived close, why wouldn't she contact me? Why wouldn't she..."

Peg tightened her hug. "I don't know, child. I don't know what Maarit was thinking or why she did what she did."

Anna laid her head on her mother's shoulder, gathering strength.

"It's up to you whether or not you go to the wake, Anna," Peg replied. "You don't have to if you don't want to. But we'll be right there with you if you decide to go."

"You might regret it later if you don't," said John. "At least, by going, you would be able to see what your birth mother looked like and meet your sister."

"My sister will be at the wake?"

"Yes. Father McDonough said that Kay was planning to attend. But we can meet her, whether or not you attend the wake. We'll make sure that you meet."

"Can I think about it for a little while?"

"Sure."

⌇ ═ ⌇

With a deep sigh, Anna left the couch and trudged toward her bedroom. She stood at the bottom of the stairway to the second floor, and, at that moment, it felt like she was about to climb the highest mountain in the world. She took a deep breath and placed one foot in front of the other methodically. Her backpack, held by one of the straps, dragged on the floor behind her, thumping as she climbed one step at a time up the staircase mountain. The third step from the top groaned as always when stepped on.

"Dad," she yelled. "Will you please fix this step? It creaks every time I go up or down stairs. It's really annoying. Fix it." She knew she sounded demanding and bratty, but she didn't care.

Exhausted from the climb and the news that had just been dropped on her, Anna plopped the backpack on the floor by her desk, not willing to use the energy to put it in its proper place. She kicked off her shoes and fell onto her bed. Alfie, her beloved stuffed turtle and lifelong confidant, was just what she needed. She buried her face in his well-worn fabric and curled into a ball.

It didn't take long for her to realize she couldn't escape into sleep. "Alfie, we need to talk," she muttered, pushing herself against the headboard. Alfie assumed the place of honor on top of her knees—the spot of choice when his person needed him. "What should I do?"

Alfie's permanent smile showed he had no idea what his person was talking about.

"Should I go to the wake? I mean, I really don't wanna go. It's, like, too scary. I've never been to a wake. I've never seen, like, *a dead person*." Anna shivered at the thought.

"Oh, you want to know who died?" Alfie's smile showed that he did.

Anna whispered in her turtle's ear. "My birth mother died."

She slid off the bed and, with Alfie in tow, settled onto the bench below her window. Wedging herself against the wall, she tucked her knees to her chin and squeezed Alfie between her legs and chest.

The bench was her favorite spot—her safe spot. The curtained window kept the outside world away. She could sit and read or look out the window and make up stories about the people walking by on the sidewalk. Nobody would know she was there.

"Alfie, whaddaya think? Should I go to the wake? I don't really wanna. It's, like, kinda scary."

Anna straightened her legs and perched Alfie on her knees to talk to him face-to-face. "I'm not gonna go. It's too scary. I've never seen a dead person. Like, I don't remember ever seeing one. I would remember if I had…had seen one, that is. Alfie, what am I gonna do?"

Alfie stared back at her; his sweet face indicated that he understood her dilemma.

"Mom and Dad said they'd go with me. But, Alfie, they told me I have a sister. I didn't know why they didn't tell me about her before. Like, was it some deep, dark secret or something?" Anna sighed and pulled the stuffed turtle closer. "Dad's probably right. Someday, I might wish that I had gone, but then it would be too late. I wonder what she looks like?"

Alfie continued to smile.

"Why should I go? My birth mother didn't want me. She gave me away. So, why should I, like, care? I can always meet my sister at other times. I don't want to go, but…" Anna's voice trailed off as she looked out the window. "Maybe I should. It will be the only time I can ever see my mother."

Alfie smiled his approval.

CHAPTER THREE

Sunday, September 22

P eg placed the phone in its cradle and called her husband from the kitchen. "John, something is going on. I'm going to my sister's. It shouldn't be long."

John put his newspaper down and joined Peg in the kitchen. "Everything alright?"

"I don't think so. Allison was insistent that she talk to me right away. I asked if it could wait, what with the wake tomorrow and everything. It can't. I'll be back as soon as I can."

As Peg parked the car in the Williams' driveway, the house's front door swung open, and Allison motioned for her to come in. Peg followed her sister to the kitchen. "Okay, Ally, what's so important it couldn't wait? Are you in trouble of some kind? What's up?"

Allison silently poured coffee for each of them, lit a cigarette, and took a long drag.

Peg studied her sister's face. "When did you start smoking again? I thought you'd quit."

Allison turned her head and blew the smoke out of the side of her mouth, away from her concerned sister. "Since Anna's mother, Maarit, died."

"Maarit? What's she got to do with it?"

Allison put out her cigarette in the ashtray. "When I learned that she had died, I knew you and I would have this conversation." She paused and stared at the tablecloth under her cup, carefully choosing her words. "There's something you need to know before tomorrow."

Peg sipped her coffee and tried to ignore the tightening in the pit of her stomach. "Okay, what is it?"

"There's a lot I can't tell you because of attorney-client privilege. But I have been Maarit Malone's lawyer and friend since college. I felt you needed to know this now because I didn't want you to be surprised when I showed up at the wake tomorrow."

"You knew her from college?" Peg leaned in closer. "Did I hear you right?"

"Yes. We pledged the same sorority and later shared an apartment."

Peg took her glasses off, a scowl on her face. "Are you telling me that you and Maarit were far more than her lawyer over the years?"

Allison nodded.

Peg's flushed hot with anger. "I can't believe you waited until now to tell me. You kept it a secret!? Incredible. Don't you think I had the right to know? My god, Ally, what in the hell were you thinking?"

Allison raised her hands to fend off the verbal reprimand. "Calm down, Peg. I couldn't tell you for many reasons, most of which are related to being Maarit's lawyer. Allison paused. "And also, because I promised not to tell anyone."

"Ally, you're my sister. We're not supposed to keep secrets like this."

Ally looked down at the table to avoid her sister's glare.

Peg's voice turned cold. "You obviously knew Maarit was pregnant with Anna. What about Anna's father? Did you know him, too?"

"No, I didn't." Allison shook her head. "Maarit wouldn't tell me anything about him. I tried several times, but she wouldn't say anything."

"And I'm supposed to believe that?"

Allison's tone became very lawyer-like. "Yes, you are. Because it's the truth, you must understand that I am prohibited by law and ethics from disclosing certain things. But this is not one of them. I don't know who Anna's father is."

Partially mollified, Peg folded her arms over her chest. "So, she got pregnant, and you got her out of the jam by suggesting we take the baby."

"C'mon, Peg, you told me for years that you and John wanted a child. Maarit was going to have a baby, but couldn't keep her. It seemed like a no-brainer. Two problems solved. You don't regret it, do you?"

"Of course not. That's a dumb thing to say."

"Sorry," Allison said. "I thought I was doing the right thing."

The two women looked at each other across the table. "Peg, I'm so sorry," Allison said. "As her lawyer, I couldn't break her trust or confidentiality. As her friend and your sister, I tried to help everyone."

Peg stood. "Dammit, Ally. You've put us in one hell of a spot." She rubbed her forehead as if she were getting a stress headache. "Anna thinks we didn't know anything about her mother. She will think we've been lying to her all these years."

"You haven't been lying; you didn't know. And she's never asked me any questions, so I haven't lied either."

"Allison," Peg sighed as she rose from her chair. In exasperation, she began to pace the floor. "When this comes out, and it will, I don't know how Anna will react. She won't understand attorney-client privilege. Now, it turns out her aunt knew her birth mother. Not only knew her, but she was also a good friend. She's already upset that we waited until now to tell her she has a sister. This new revelation is not going to sit well."

Allison took a quick breath. "Oh, Sis, didn't you tell Anna she has a sister?"

"The topic never came up." Peg's eyes began to tear up.

Allison sighed. "Peg, I hate to ask you this, but can we not tell her about my relationship with Maarit until after the wake?"

"What, and compound the secrets?" Peg shook her head. "That doesn't sound like a good idea to me."

Allison paused to pour another cup of coffee and gestured toward the empty chair opposite her. "Peg, please sit down."

Peg did so reluctantly. The concern she had felt in her stomach had grown to fear.

"Father McDonough told me on the phone that Maarit had left a package with him last spring, and part of it is for me. Since I don't know what's in that package, could we wait to tell Anna until I've seen it and reviewed her will?"

"I don't know." Peg shook her head. "I don't think it's a good idea. This secret puts a lot at risk. It might be better to tell Anna right up front."

"I don't know what Maarit put into that packet," said Allison. "I'm honor-bound, if not legally obligated, to follow my client's wishes— even after death. I included in the adoption agreement that the files would remain sealed. The last time she and I talked was last spring. She was still adamant that I keep the secret. I need to know what Maarit included in that package before I can proceed. Please wait to tell Anna."

"I'm at a loss, Ally. I don't know what we'll tell Anna tonight." Peg slumped in the chair and shook her head tiredly.

Allison reached over and patted her sister's hand. "I know I'm asking a lot. But please. I must know what's in that packet before it all comes out."

"Okay," Peg agreed begrudgingly. "I don't like it, but it's probably best if we don't tell Anna until later. But Ally, we can't keep this under wraps for long."

"Thanks, Peg. As soon as I get that package, we'll talk and figure out the best way to handle this."

As Peg stood to leave, she turned to face her sister. "I suppose you knew Kay and her father, too?"

Allison hesitated. "Yes, I met Tom Malone in college and was maid of honor at their wedding."

Peg groaned.

Allison continued, "I haven't seen Kay since she was a small child. After Maarit and Tom divorced, he had full custody."

Peg cocked her head to one side. "Uh, Ally, did you say Maarit was in town last spring?"

"Yes?"

"Would she have known about Anna's choir concert?"

Allison shrugged her shoulders.

"I saw a stranger who looked a lot like Anna. Could it have been... Ally, have you been keeping Maarit informed all these years?"

Allison didn't answer.

"Tell me, Ally! Did you tell her Anna had a choir concert last May?"

Allison nodded. "I may have mentioned it."

"Did she attend that concert?" Peg asked.

Allison shrugged. "I don't know. She didn't say anything at the time."

The coldness in Peg's voice returned. "If the adoption was sealed, why did you inform her about Anna? Isn't that illegal or unethical?"

"I admit, I certainly got close to the line, but there was a loophole in the agreement related to the child's health."

"Didn't the judge see that?"

"He did and questioned me whether it was appropriate."

"What did you say?"

Allison flinched and tried to deflect the implied accusation. "I told him that the birth mother would only contact the family in case of a medical emergency involving Anna. Even though Maarit's medical history had been disclosed, she was concerned that a transplant of some organ or a blood transfusion might be needed if a donor couldn't be found. It was to protect the child, but other than that, the adoption was sealed."

She took a deep breath before continuing. "The judge had doubts about the clause, but at the time, the adoption laws were undergoing significant revisions in the legislature, and he allowed it."

"And you didn't think to tell us about that clause." Peg glared at her sister.

Allison exhaled loudly. "It seemed like a good safeguard at the time, especially since I was family and would likely know if any dire situation arose. I didn't want you and John to think that Maarit would come swooping in to take Anna back."

Allison leaned back in her chair. "If she had tried to insert herself, the law would have been on your side."

"Maybe, but it would have been an awful mess."

"It's a moot point now," said Allison.

Peg opened the front door. "I'd better get home and tell John about this. He and I need to talk. I think Anna was going to a movie with her friends. If I leave now, we'll have a little time to discuss this."

"Peg, I'm sorry. I probably should have told you years ago, but Maarit wanted it all kept secret, and I went along with it."

"I've got to go. John and I have to figure out what to say to Anna."

CHAPTER FOUR

Monday, September 23

"OMG. You'll never believe what happened at my house last night." Isabella Andresen leaned across the school lunchroom table to share some juicy teen gossip. Jordan Tyler, eager to hear about it, pushed her hair behind her ear and leaned in, too. Anna looked out the window, oblivious to the lunchroom commotion and her friend's big secret,

"Yesterday, a junior asked my sister, Tiffany, to go to the dance with him on Saturday," Isabella shared in hushed tones. "You guys know my sister, right? She just turned fifteen and has had a super crush on this guy for, gosh, I don't know, a long time. Like, *forever.* My sister couldn't believe that he asked her to go to the dance. She was so excited! I thought she was going to float away with happiness. When she told my Dad, he blew a gasket. I mean, *for real, Dad*, she's fifteen now. My Dad yelled that she was too young to go on a date alone with a boy in a car. He said he would take her to the dance and pick her up. Now it's a big mess. Anyway, Jason, that's the guy's name. He just got his license, and his Dad would let him take the car and everything. I mean, it's *totally* unfair. Parents can be so obtuse sometimes. Don't you just love the word 'obtuse'? Mr. Conley used it in English class on Friday. You were there, and we all went, 'huh?' Then he, Mr. Conly, said, 'Go look it up.' Chris was the first one to get to the dictionary in the corner. He's always trying to show how smart he is. Don't you hate it when he does that? But he is kinda cute…I mean Chris, not Mr. Conley. Anyway, when my sister told Jason about it, he called her a baby and said, 'Forget it.' What a jerk ….."

Jordan held up her hand to stop her friend's rant. "Geez, Isabella, take a breath! Anna, what's wrong? You haven't said anything all day and hardly eaten your lunch. Are you sick or something?"

Anna pushed her lunch tray away. "I'm just not hungry. Sorry, Izzy. What did you say?"

Isabella opened her mouth as if to speak, but she saw the sadness on Anna's face and stopped. "It's, like, okay, nothing, it's not important."

"Anna," Jordan said as she touched her friend's hand. "If you're not, like, sick, then something's bugging you. What is it?"

Anna looked down at the table and began twisting her hair around her finger. "You guys know that I'm adopted, right?"

"Yeah. You told us that forever ago. So?"

"On Saturday, my folks told me that my birth mother was, like, *dead*."

"Geez!" Jordan's eyes opened wide as she pressed her hands to her mouth in shock.

"They also said I have a sister who lives here in town."

Isabella gasped, "You….you're kidding, right?"

"No, for real," Anna picked at her fingernails. "My birth mother died, and I've got a sister I didn't know about. Besides that, I'm s'posed to go to a wake tonight."

"What's a wake?" Jordan asked.

Anna shrugged. "I guess it's sort of like a funeral, but not quite. My mom says the body will be there."

"Eww." Isabella wrinkled her nose.

"Mom said people come and tell the family they're sorry for their loss. Sometimes, prayers are said. Have you guys ever seen a dead person?" asked Anna. "I've never seen one."

"I saw my grandpa," said Isabella. "I was scared, but it wasn't a big deal except for all the crying and weird smells."

"Weird smells?"

"Yeah. Many people sent flowers, and among them were some unusual ones. I guess people send them to a lot of funerals. They're called gladiolus or something like that. Well, they have a strange, almost super-sweet smell. It's hard to explain, but they seemed to be everywhere. I had to leave for a while; the smell got to be, like, way too much. But I got used to it. The worst, I mean the absolute worst, was the crying. It'd get really quiet then someone would start to cry, and everyone would start. I mean, really."

"Isabella!" Jordan sighed. "Anna's got to go to one tonight."

"Sorry, Anna. Sometimes I get carried away and talk too much."

"It's ok, Izzy."

"Are you going to go?" asked Jordan.

"My dad thinks I should, and my sister's going to come." Anna absently drew circles on the table with her straw. The cafeteria crowd was more boisterous than usual, but she was too distracted to notice.

"That's neat; sisters are cool," said Isabella. "I've got a brother, and he's a pain in the—"

"Isabella, you shouldn't talk like that," said Jordan.

"Why not? He is."

Jordan rolled her eyes. "You just shouldn't. It's not nice."

"Whatever."

"Guys, would you go? I mean, if you were me?" Anna asked.

"I would," said Jordan. "It's the right thing to do."

"Me, too," Isabella chimed in. "Soooo, whaddaya think? Are you going to go?"

Anna stared out the window, not seeing the brilliant red and gold leaves on the maple trees lining the park next to the school. She reached into her jeans pocket for a tissue and dabbed her eyes to dry her tears. She whispered, "Yeah, I think I'd better."

The bell rang, signaling the end of lunch and the start of fifth hour. "Guys, please don't tell anyone about this, okay? I really don't wanna have to answer a bunch of questions."

"Sure."

"Okay."

Monday Evening

"Mom, I don't wanna do this." Anna clutched her mother's arm and tried to bury her face in Peg's coat sleeve. "Do we hafta?"

"No, my dear. We don't have to."

John, Peg, and Anna stood on the sidewalk, looking up at the towering façade of St. Francis Catholic Church. The twin towers flanking the lit, stained-glass window invited them to climb the steps to the entrance. The brilliant hues of reds, greens, browns, golds, and tans accented St. Francis' smiling face as he cared for the sheep and birds surrounding him.

"We don't have to go in," said Peg. "But before you decide, remember you came downstairs and announced you wanted to see your birth mother before it was too late. There's nothing in that church that can hurt you. Your dad and I will be with you the whole time."

Anna nodded, and the three began climbing the steps to the imposing wooden doors. "Mom, look at the carvings." She ran her fingers over the raised relief panels on the church doors. She pointed up, "They look the same as the window."

"They're lovely," said Peg as John opened the heavy door.

A priest appeared and extended his hand in a warm greeting. "Hello, I'm Father McDonough. We spoke on the phone. Thank you for coming. I wish our meeting had been under happier circumstances."

John returned the greeting. "Father, I'm John Jensen; this is my wife, Peg, and our daughter, Anna." Father McDonough shook hands with John and Peg, and when Anna extended hers, he cupped her small hand in both of his large ones.

"You look so much like your mother. I see her in your eyes and your smile."

Anna blushed.

Father McDonough turned to John and Peg. "The wake will be held in a small chapel to the right of the altar. I've invited a few of Maarit's close associates, her boss, her attorney, and several co-workers to attend the wake. They won't arrive for over an hour."

John and Peg exchanged glances at the mention of Maarit's attorney.

"I've reserved the first hour for the family," Father McDonough continued. "The rest will arrive at eight o'clock. Several sisters from the convent will join us to recite the rosary at 8:30. I understand you aren't Catholic, but please feel free to attend the prayers if you wish."

"Excuse me, Father," said John. "You said that Anna looks like her mother. Did you know her mother?"

"Yes. Yes, I did." Father McDonough looked directly at Anna. "Maarit was my sister."

Both John's and Peg's mouths dropped open in shock. Anna looked into Father McDonough's eyes, searching for understanding.

She nervously cleared her throat. "That's...I...What does that mean?"

"Anna, it means I'm your uncle." The priest turned to John and Peg. "I didn't mention it on the phone the other day. I wanted to tell you in person."

"Father...Uncle...I...how...uh...?" Anna stammered, trying to get her questions out at once.

"As you can see, we have many questions," Peg said.

"I'm sure you do, and I'll do my best to answer them, but Kay will be arriving shortly. Let's get together tomorrow night. Say, seven, in my study? We'll have more time and be a bit more comfortable."

"That will be fine," agreed John.

The priest led the Jensens into the sanctuary and down the center aisle toward the high altar. Anna craned her neck to look at the vaulted ceilings. She shivered at the sight of the crucified Jesus hanging over the altar and smiled at the cute cherubim and seraphim painted in fresco style around the crucifix.

Scattered throughout the sanctuary, individuals and small groups of people—some kneeling, some sitting, some talking in hushed tones—paid no attention to the group walking through the center of the church.

Anna tugged at her mother's arm. "What do those words say?" she whispered, pointing to the phrases in an unfamiliar language painted over the nave and above the marble columns flanking each side of the sanctuary.

Peg whispered, "They're all in Latin. *Agnus Dei* means 'Lamb of God.' *Qui Tolis Pecatta Mundi* translates to 'take away the world's sins.' *Dei Gratia* means 'Thanks be to God.'"

"How do you know that?"

Peg smiled. "Way back in the dark ages, I took Latin in high school. It used to be that all Catholic services were in Latin."

"That's weird."

"Well, the church used it as a universal language at the time. Services around the world were all the same."

At the altar, the priest genuflected, turned, and led the family into the small chapel next to the sanctuary. The light blue walls reflected the soft glow of the bronze wall sconces. The open casket sat opposite the door in front of a small altar and was adorned with sprays of beautiful flowers. Bouquets of roses and tulips rested on stands at the head and foot. Kneelers had been placed in front of the casket.

Anna stopped and grabbed her mother's hand. "Can we sit for a little while? Maybe wait for Kay?"

"Of course, dear." The Jensens slid into the last row of chairs. Father McDonough nodded his understanding and continued forward to kneel and pray in front of the casket.

Peg put her arm around Anna. "Whenever you feel like it, we can pay our respects at the casket."

Father McDonough finished his private prayers, crossed himself, and retreated to stand beside the door in the rear of the chapel.

Anna leaned closer to her mother. She tried, in vain, to avoid looking at the profile of her birth mother's face, which was visible above the edge of the bronze casket. Instead, she tried to distract herself by counting the rows of chairs and staring at the crucifix on the wall, anything to avoid looking.

She wrinkled her nose. "Mother, what's that smell?"

"It's the flowers," Peg said.

"Are they gladi...gladi...?"

"Gladiolas." Peg pointed to the flower stands in the chapel corners.

"That's what Isabella told me this morning. She said she didn't like them. I don't either."

"Neither do I." Peg kissed the top of her daughter's head.

The awkward silence suffocated the room. The flickering candle-light, the sweet smell of the gladiolas, and the ever-present weight of death stifled any conversation. Even the ambient sounds from the adjacent sanctuary did not lighten the heaviness permeating the small chapel.

A soft clicking sound of heels on the marble sanctuary floor began to grow. The sound stopped abruptly at the chapel door. Everyone turned to look.

Standing in the doorway was a raven-haired young woman dressed in a beige slip dress and a forest-green brocade jacket. Around her neck was a simple gold chain with a small round locket suspended from it. Her vibrant green eyes scanned the room before finally settling on Anna.

Anna nudged her mother. "Is that Kay?"

"I don't know." Peg and Anna rose to greet the newcomer. The two girls looked at each other.

"Kay?" said Anna.

"Yes. And you must be Anna."

Anna timidly waved her hand. Kay smiled, opened her arms wide, and enveloped the young girl in a warm embrace. "Hello, sister."

Father McDonough joined the group. "Hello, Kay."

"Father McDonough." Kay greeted her uncle without a smile.

"It's nice to see you again," the priest offered. "It's been a long time."

"Yes, it has."

Father McDonough introduced Peg and John to Kay before leading the group to the casket. Peg noticed that the shape of his chin and big, wide grin closely resembled Anna's. As Peg looked at Maarit's body in the casket, she had no doubt in her mind that the priest, Maarit, and Anna were kin.

When the group had gathered at the casket, Father McDonough started to speak. "My sister, in a letter which I received after her death, asked that this small wake be held and that I say a few prayers for the repose of her soul. With your permission, I'd like to lead those prayers."

Together, Kay and Father McDonough made the sign of the cross as the Jensens stood with heads bowed. "Hail Mary, full of grace, the Lord is with thee. Blessed art thou among women, for the fruit of thy womb is Jesus. Holy Mary, Mother of God, pray for us sinners, now and at the hour of our death. Amen in the name of the Father, the Son, and the Holy Spirit."

Father McDonough turned to face the small group standing in front of his sister's casket. "This is a sad occasion—sad because of Maarit's death. My faith, however, tells me this isn't the end but a new beginning. For those of us left behind, that is what we cling to. That is where our hope lies."

He continued. "There is also reason to rejoice. Through Maarit's death, her daughters have been brought together. Anna, John, Peg, I don't have the words to express how delighted I am to have met you. Already, I feel the bond of friendship and family."

Father McDonough looked directly at the older girl. "Kay, it's been a long time; I pray this occasion will bring reconciliation and peace."

Kay nodded politely but said nothing.

"Girls, when you think of your mother, I hope you will think kindly of her and not judge her too harshly. The reasons behind her choices may never be revealed. I hope that you will find comfort and joy in each other."

Father McDonough turned to face the casket, made the sign of the cross, and intoned, *"In nomine Patris, et fillii, et Spiritus Sancti. Amen."*

He then ushered John and Peg to the back of the chapel to let the girls have a private moment.

Kay and Anna stood by the side of their deceased birth mother, neither knowing what to say. Anna summoned up the courage to break the silence. "Are you really my sister?" she asked timidly.

"Yes, I believe so."

The silence returned.

Again, Anna spoke, "Did you know you had a sister? I mean, like before now?"

"No." Kay looked at Anna. "Not until the priest called the other day to tell me about my...I'm sorry, *our* mother. You?"

"Me neither 'til Mom and Dad told me I had a sister on Saturday. I guess they knew before, but didn't know it was you."

Again, the silence filled the church.

"Father McDonough said that I look like her. Do you think I look like her?"

Kay turned to look at Anna and then at the body in the casket. "You have her hair," Kay caressed Anna's head. "And the shape of your mouth is like hers, big and wide." Kay chuckled. "You definitely have her pointed chin. Yes, you look a lot like her."

Anna smiled and turned back to the casket. "I've never seen a dead person. I keep waiting for her to open her eyes, sit up, and laugh or something. But she's so still."

Kay nodded.

Anna hesitated, "Kay...is...is your father, like, my father, too?"

"No, I don't think so. It's been him and me until now. He would have told me if he had known I had a sister."

Anna slipped her hand into Kay's. "Was she nice?"

"I...don't know. I haven't seen her since I was a little girl. I remember she came into my room and tucked me in at night. She'd sing a little lullaby and lean over to kiss me. Her hair would tickle my cheek."

"Why haven't you seen her since you were little?"

"It's a long story. Perhaps we can discuss it someday. I can't today."

Kay put her arm around Anna's shoulder and leaned her cheek against her sister's head. The hand on Anna's shoulder tightened into a fist. Suddenly, Kay's forehead creased, and her mouth became a straight, hard line.

"Let's sit down for a minute," said Kay. The two girls moved to the front row of chairs. "Anna, I've been very angry at my mother for a long time. I thought coming to the wake would ease it, but it hasn't. I'm sorry, but I have to leave. I'm thrilled that I have a sister. Soon, we'll have a nice long talk. I want to know everything about you, but I need to leave now. I have your phone number. I'll call you."

"Do you have to go?" Anna asked, fighting back her tears.

"Yes, I really do. I'll call you."

Anna followed her sister to the chapel and watched as Kay hugged Peg, shook hands with John, and gave a nod of farewell to her uncle. The two sisters hugged, and then Kay turned and hurried out the door. The rapid sound of her heels clicking on the sanctuary floor faded into silence.

Allison arrived at the church shortly before the rosary was scheduled to begin. The only mourners who remained were Father Sean and three others, whom Allison assumed were Maarit's boss and coworkers. The three took their leave of the priest and quietly left the chapel. She approached the casket, pulling a handkerchief from her jacket pocket.

Father Sean let Allison stand alone at the casket for a few moments before joining her. "Ms. Williams?"

Allison turned to the priest.

"Hello, I'm Father McDonough, Maarit's brother. Thank you for coming. I'm afraid you missed the family."

"Yes, I know. I sat in the car across the street until they left the church."

"I don't understand?" said the priest.

"It's complicated, Father. Peg is my sister, and until yesterday, she didn't know that Maarit and I had been good friends since college. My niece, Anna, doesn't know either, and I'm afraid of how she'll react to all of this. Too many surprises, too many secrets."

"If I may," said Father McDonough. "It has been my experience that secrets have a way of surfacing at the most inopportune times."

Allison nodded.

"Ms. Williams, last spring, my sister visited me and left a packet in my care to be opened only after her death. Within the packet is an envelope addressed to you. I intended to deliver it tomorrow, but I'll retrieve it from my study now if you can stay for a few moments."

"Thank you. That would be fine."

"I'll only be a few minutes." The priest genuflected before the altar and left.

Allison stood looking at the body of her good friend. Memories of pledging the sorority, their first apartment, frat parties, concerts, deep late-night conversations, dinners over the years, vacation trips—all went through her mind like a grand parade. *Oh, Maarit. How I will miss you. We were closer than sisters. Closer than I am with my own sister.*

The soft rustle of rosary beads and almost-silent footsteps announced the nuns' arrival to recite the rosary. They patiently waited until Allison had completed her goodbyes before arranging the kneelers in front of the casket.

Allison waited by the chapel door for Father McDonough to return. "Sorry, I was detained. Here's the packet for you. If there's anything I can do to help, please let me know."

"Thank you, Father," said Allison. "Likewise, if I can be of any assistance to you, please call."

Allison handed Father McDonough her business card, took the package, and walked quickly through the sanctuary and the church's front doors. She ripped open the package in the car and found three envelopes, each addressed in the same calligraphic script. Each flap was sealed with wax and embossed with the script "*M.*"

Allison opened the one addressed to her and read.

Dear Ally,

Well, now you know. I died. As usual, I'm asking you to clean up after me. It doesn't matter how hard I try; I just can't make things work right. Hopefully, these letters will help to fix the lies I've told.

I wish I could have been more like you. Always doing the right thing at the right time, following the rules, and focusing on your goal. My life wouldn't have been such a mess if I had listened to you.

Allison paused and shook her head in remorse. "And all the while, I wished I could be more like you—full of life and fun, doing what you wanted regardless of what people thought." She sighed deeply and resumed reading.

Please deliver the enclosed letters in person and execute my will. You have all the account and contact information you need. I have also included documents that waive attorney-client privilege for the girls. You may tell them anything they want to know—everything except one last secret I want you to keep.

Anna's father is Derek Tyler. Yes, the same Derek we knew in college. He and I ran into each other at a conference in Paris. Anna is the result of a glorious lapse in judgment.

Please keep my secret unless it's absolutely necessary. Of course, if there's a health reason for Anna, you can share it, but other than that, please let it be our one last secret.

Thank you for being such a good friend for all these years. You are the sister I never had.

Love, Maarit

Allison reread the letter several times. "Girl," she said to the windshield. "You've been holding out on me." She put the letters back into the envelope and drove to her office. It was going to be a long, difficult week.

CHAPTER FIVE

Monday, Late Evening

There were few words meaningful enough to break the silence in the car on the ride home from the wake.

Anna sat in the back seat, hugging Alfie, staring out the car window, and occasionally sniffling. Peg reached into her purse, pulled out a tissue, and handed it over to the seat back. "Here," she said. "It's better than your sleeve."

A whispered "thanks" was all that the teen could muster. Anna wiped her eyes, squeezed the tissue into a tight ball in her hand, and tucked it into her coat pocket.

When the three arrived home, Anna still hadn't said a word. Peg hugged her daughter. "You've been really quiet since we left the church. Do you want to talk about it?"

"No."

"Sometimes talking about stuff makes it easier to understand."

"I know."

Still holding Alfie in her arms, Anna climbed the stairs to her room. A soft click signaled her bedroom door closing behind her. Peg started to follow, but John stopped her with a gentle touch and a slow shake of his head. "Give her time," he said. "She's got lots to think about. She'll be back when she's ready."

Grateful to be in the safe solitude of her room, Anna squeezed herself into as tight a ball as possible on the bench in the cupola. She tried to think about school, choir, piano lessons, anything at all, anything but the sight of her mother in the casket. But the vision of Maarit lying lifeless and the memory of how small she felt in the church wouldn't go away.

"Alfie," she said to her most trusted confidante. "It should be raining, or at least cloudy or something." She leaned her head against the drape covering the window. "The sun has shone all day as if nothing important has happened. My mother's dead, and the world didn't notice. Weird."

Well after midnight, John heard Anna's bedroom door open and the stairway's third step squeak. He reached over to touch Peg's shoulder.

"I'm awake," she said. "I'll check on her." Anna sat on the bottom step, clutching Alfie and looking distraught. Peg took her hand and led her to the couch. "It's okay, sweetie. Everything'll be okay."

Once on the couch, Anna lay with her head on her mother's lap. Peg caressed her daughter's head and carefully tucked Anna's hair behind her ear. In fits and starts, between sniffles, the question came: "Why didn't she want me? Was I too ugly?"

Peg kissed the top of Anna's head. "You were a beautiful baby. I almost entered you in the Gerber baby picture contest."

A half-hearted smile appeared on Anna's face. "But *why*, Mom?"

"I don't know why, honey. There are many reasons a woman will place a child for adoption. All I know is I'm glad she gave you to us. I can't imagine life without you. Your dad and I loved you as soon as the nurse put you in my arms. She pulled the blanket off your face, and we got our first look at you. In that instant, you became our daughter."

Anna snuggled closer to her mother.

"What did you think of your sister?" asked Peg. "She's beautiful. And so are you."

"I look like a dork. My braces make me look like a chipmunk."

"You won't when they come off."

Anna smiled.

Peg waited, gently smoothing Anna's hair. "Did something upset Kay when the two of you were talking? She seemed in a hurry to leave."

"She said she had been angry at her mother for years. Said she couldn't stay another minute." Anna turned to look up at her mother's face. "Did you ever meet her, my birth mother, I mean?"

Peg smoothed Anna's hair. "No, but I suspect that she knew about you."

"How?"

"I don't know, but there've been a couple of times, once at your fifth-grade graduation and then again at your spring choir concert, I noticed a woman I didn't recognize. She looked familiar; I thought I should know her, but I couldn't place her. She sat off in the back and left both times before the program ended."

Anna sat up. "Why didn't you tell me?"

"There was nothing to tell; it was only a suspicion." Peg pulled her daughter close. "At the wake, I recognized her. Your birth mother and the woman I saw were the same person."

Anna stood, put her hands on her hips, and faced her mother. "Why would she do that and not talk to me?"

"I don't know, Anna."

"Grown-ups, you're all alike. You don't tell us anything. I'm not a child. You should have told me my mother came to see me."

"Anna, I didn't know that it was your biological mother."

"You should've told me, anyway. Maybe we could've found out something. Now she's dead, we'll never find out anything."

"Why are you so angry?"

"I'm not!"

"You could've fooled me. You sure sound angry."

"I bet Father McDonough knows why she gave me away. Maybe he'll tell me the truth."

Peg stood and tried to hug her daughter.

Anna turned away. "Good night!" Anna grabbed Alfie from the couch and stomped up the stairs. The third step from the top protested, as it always did.

CHAPTER SIX

Wednesday, September 25

Paul Williams stood on the corner, waiting for the light to turn green. He unzipped his jacket, the autumn sun promising a good day. Between the light schedule for his last semester in college and the two part-time gigs—delivering documents for his mother's law firm and writing obituaries for the newspaper—he had plenty of time for late-season golf.

He was not an imposing figure. He had enough weight and was tall enough to play high school basketball, but not nearly big enough for college basketball. His field jacket hung comfortably on his shoulders and had enough roomy pockets to carry his ever-present reporter's notebook and a small Nikon camera, just in case he ran into something interesting.

Only three things left on today's to-do list: finish the term paper draft due next week, pick up his re-gripped golf putter, and deliver the package from his mother's law office to the bank, conveniently located next to the golf shop.

When Paul entered, the shop's golf pro waved, reached behind the sales counter, and laid a putter on its surface. "With that new grip, you should be all set for the 'Old Course' at St. Andrews."

Paul took the club and feigned a practice putt, testing the new grip. "Don't I wish. With my handicap, they wouldn't even let me on the course."

"Someday." The golf pro handed Paul's credit card back.

"One can only hope." Paul cheerily waved, left the shop, and walked next door to the bank to drop off the packet from the law office.

Distracted by his dream of sinking a forty-foot putt on the eighteenth green at Augusta, Paul tripped on the rug between the metal detectors at the bank's entrance. He tried to regain his balance but landed face down on the marble floor. The putter clattered to the ground and skittered across the polished tile, coming to rest at the feet of a tall, raven-haired girl at the teller's window. Paul found himself flat on the floor, at eye level, with a beautifully shaped pair of ankles clad in shamrock socks.

Even though he knew it was impossible to fall in love with a pair of ankles, having not seen or spoken to the woman attached to them, he was immediately attracted.

He stared at the shamrock-clad ankles as the guard and the bank manager struggled to get him to his feet. The raven-haired girl attached to the shapely ankles retrieved the putter and handed it to Paul. With twinkling green eyes, she greeted him. "Your club, sir."

Paul gasped and stammered, "Thank you." He turned a deep crimson and hastily moved to the manager's desk. He glanced over his shoulder at the raven-haired girl with the shamrock socks. He cringed and turned a deeper shade of red as she left the bank laughing.

After finishing his errands, Paul returned to the Williams-Laughton offices. The receptionist greeted him with a giggle and said, "Your mother would like to see you."

Paul shook his head and rolled his eyes. "You've all heard, haven't you?"

She giggled again. "Go on in, your mother is in her office."

Allison Williams leaned back in her chair and grinned at her son. She pushed a lock of premature grey hair off her forehead and said, "Are you getting clumsy in your old age?"

"Thanks, Mother. Love you, too."

"Are you okay?"

"Yeah, I'm fine. No injuries, just a little dented pride. At least I provide a little entertainment around here. Who called to tell you?"

"The bank manager. He wanted to be sure you were all right."

"Remind me to thank him." Paul rolled his eyes.

"He was concerned," Allison stood, drawing herself up to her five-foot height, which allowed her to look directly into her son's chin. She picked up a packet and handed it to Paul. "There's just one more delivery for you to make, then you can take the rest of the afternoon off."

Paul nodded. "Okay, anything to get me out of the office and away from the laughter."

"Deliver this packet to Dr. Keizer in the music department at the college. She needs to review some documents for the scholarship foundation. I need a signature on the receipt. Then go, enjoy the rest of the day."

Twenty minutes later, Paul was hurrying across the campus. He cut between the Humanities building and the library, took a shortcut around the back of the temple dedicated to students' political, spiritual, and social well-being, otherwise known as the Commons, and into the side door of the Performing Arts Center. The lobby directory indicated the music office was in Room G5.

"Can I help you find something?"

Paul turned to face the melodious voice offering help. Standing before him was the girl who had picked up his putter at the bank. His collar suddenly felt tighter, and his neck turned red with embarrassment. "Yes, I…I'm looking for the music department office."

"It's in the back of the building, down one floor. I work there. C'mon, I'll show you." The young woman led him to the corner stairwell, down the stairs, through the hallway that ran the length of the building, and turned the corner.

"A person could get lost in this building," said Paul.

"It's a big square," she replied. "You keep going around 'til you find the room you want."

Two-thirds of the way down the corridor, the two entered the Music office. "Now that we're here, how can I help you?"

Paul handed the young woman his business card. "I'm Paul Williams from the Williams-Laughton law office. I'm looking for Dr. Elizabeth Keizer."

She took the card. "I'm Kay Malone. Dr. Keizer's office is located in Room 318, three floors up, and is opposite the corner. Let me call her and see if she's in her office." Moments later, Kay returned and announced that Dr. Keizer was available. "She said she'd wait for you."

"Thanks," said Paul. "I have the strangest feeling that we've met."

Kay smiled at the line. "I don't think…" She raised her hands to her face and laughed. "Wait…you're the guy with the five irons at the bank this morning. Are you okay?"

"It was a putter, but I'm fine." Paul raised his eyebrows and cocked his head to one side. "Are you, by any chance, wearing shamrock socks?"

Kay laughed, held her ankle out, and pulled her slacks up, revealing the green shamrock-adorned stockings. "I'm sorry, I shouldn't laugh, but you were a sight down on the floor, wheezing and trying to say something."

Paul felt the crimson return to his neck.

"I'm sorry I laughed at you," Kay blurted. "Let me buy you a cup of coffee to make up for it. I get off in ten minutes. Can you meet me at the Roastin' Cup in thirty?"

Paul smiled and looked at his watch. "Sounds good. I'm done for the day, too. See you in thirty."

Like all coffee shops next to college campuses, the Roastin' Cup was crowded with rickety tables, a few high tops against a wall, a couple of overstuffed armchairs, and a couch that always seemed inhabited by someone deep in the pages of a classic novel.

Paul smiled at the intensity of the student studying in one of the chairs. Their expression said, *"I don't really understand what I'm reading, but it should expand my mind if I look at the words long enough."*

Most of the coffee shop's seats were occupied by students clicking and clacking away on laptops. To Paul, the atmosphere was a combination of fresh-roasted coffee, day-old pastries, and a hint of human desperation to meet the assignment deadlines. He claimed a small table in the back corner of the shop. From that position, he could observe the crowd's comings and goings.

He relished watching the activity: this girl flirting with that guy until another girl joined them, two guys surreptitiously checking out the girls at the high-top table across the room, and a small group engaged in a heated political argument. His vivid imagination conjured stories:

Was one girl trying to steal the boyfriend of the other?

Will those two guys gather enough nerve to approach the high top?

The small group consisted of political science majors arguing over the election.

Thirty minutes later, Kay entered, spotted him, and elbowed her way through the campus crowd. She stopped momentarily to greet this person and that, not tarrying long with anyone but not rushing to join Paul.

The get-acquainted dance began as usual: his major is English; hers is music and voice.

Her favorite sport is volleyball, while his is golf. His latest read is Ben Franklin's autobiography; hers is P. D. James' *The Black Tower*. Her favorite food is Italian, while his is Thai. He graduates at the end of the semester, and she finishes at the end of the summer.

For over an hour, they verbally danced.

"Kay," Paul leaned forward. "Why the shamrock socks? We're months away from St. Patty's Day."

Her eyes turned sad. "A long time ago, my mother gave me a gift of a shamrock encased in a plastic case. She said it was my good luck charm. I still have it on my…"

Kay stopped mid-sentence and turned away from Paul to look out the window. She brushed the corner of her eye to catch the tear before it could run down her cheek.

"Sorry," she said. "My mother died last week. This morning, I picked these socks out of the drawer. I don't know…" Kay's voice quivered.

Paul sighed. "I'm sorry. Are you okay?"

Kay nodded, averting her eyes to avoid the sympathy on Paul's face.

"Would you like to talk about it?" He waited for her to continue.

"The last couple of weeks have been strange."

"I can imagine," said Paul.

Kay held the coffee cup in her hands, warming them, before setting it back on the table without taking a drink. "I have a strange family. My folks split when I was a kid. I haven't seen my mom in years."

"That's hard." Paul locked eyes with Kay.

"Ancient history," she said. "Tell me about *your* family."

Paul shrugged. "Not much to tell. My dad died when I was very young, in a car accident. I'm an only child. Mom's an attorney. I've lived here all my life."

Kay nodded. "I thought I was an only child, too. Until my uncle, my mother's brother, a priest, called to tell me about my mother. It's weird. I haven't seen or talked to him in years, and out of the blue, he calls. It turns out I have a 13-year-old sister I never knew I had. All these years, I thought I was the only child. Now, all of a sudden, I have a sister. Met her for the first time at the wake."

Kay sighed, then shook her head. "I'm sorry, I don't know why I'm prattling on like this. I shouldn't be laying all this on you."

"It's okay. Sometimes, it's easier to tell a stranger something than it is to talk to someone close."

She smiled, "You are easy to talk to, you know?"

"I get that a lot. Especially from beautiful young women who wear shamrock socks."

"You do have a bit of the blarney in you, don't you?"

Paul laughed.

"Seriously," Kay said. "You are easy to talk to." She looked down and ran her finger around the rim of her coffee cup absently.

Seeing the pensive look in her eyes, Paul reached over and gently squeezed her hand.

"*C'est la vie,*" she said. "My dad's a great guy. I think he spoiled me a little to make up for Mom not being around."

Kay pulled her hand from Paul's and lifted the cup to her lips. The two sat silently, ignoring the hubbub surrounding them. Paul shifted in his seat, worried he had moved too quickly by reaching over to squeeze Kay's hand. As he began to move his hand away, it involuntarily jerked, hitting his empty cup and knocking it over. Kay grabbed the cup just before it slid off the table.

"Sorry." He turned beet red. "That's twice today you've caught something for me."

Kay laughed. "Don't worry about it. I've done that a zillion times."

Gathering his courage, he blurted out what was on his mind. "Kay, if I promise not to knock anything off the table, would you have dinner with me Friday night?"

Kay hesitated, searching his eyes. "Yes, I'd like that."

"Great. How about that Italian place on Franklin? Luigi's?"

"I love Luigi's. I'll meet you, say, at seven."

"It's a date."

Thursday, September 26

The music department chairperson looked around the table. "This late in the meeting, I hesitate to address this last item, but we are facing a deadline and a dilemma. A decision has to be made today. Two of our students have applied for the same internship with the Atlanta Opera Workshop. Both are seeking the department's endorsement. Did everyone get a copy of the resumes I sent out with the agenda?"

Half the department pulled out their copy around the conference room table, and the other half looked at each other, totally uninterested in the topic. Only a few nodded.

"As you can see, there is very little difference between the two. Both have starred in productions and have been active in the department and the community. Both are very talented and work hard. Unfortunately, the workshop requires a departmental endorsement. What's your pleasure?"

The orchestra director looked at Dr. Elizabeth "Liz" Keizer.

"Liz, aren't they both students of yours? Which one do you recommend?"

"From my point of view, both are excellent talents and have earned this type of opportunity. The problem is that the Atlanta folks require a departmental endorsement."

"Let's endorse the two of them and let the workshop choose. Why do we have to play Solomon and make the choice?"

Dr. Keizer shook her head. "We tried that the last time we had this situation. I got the feedback that if we, who know the students best, can't make a choice, how can we? They passed over both students that time because we wouldn't choose."

"As far as the workshop is concerned, these two candidates are tied. Their audition tapes and application materials are great. They have room for only one in their program."

From the other end of the conference table, the oboe instructor spoke. "What can we use as a tiebreaker—flip a coin?"

The department chair shook her head. "And how do you propose we tell the students that a coin toss decides their futures? That won't fly at all."

"What about grade point average? GPA would be at least somewhat objective."

The department chair checked the students' transcripts. "Very close. One has an overall 3.79, and the other a 3.83. Each earned a 4.0 within the department. There is not enough difference to base the decision on."

"Are we back to the coin toss?"

The murmur of side conversations threatened to derail the discussion. "Folks, we've got to decide today. Any other suggestions?"

"Does anyone know which of the two has attended Milan the longest?" asked the theory instructor. "I've had them in class. Both aced the courses."

Keizer answered, "Kay started as a first-year student right out of high school, and Ansel transferred halfway through his sophomore year."

The theory instructor said, "Since all other things appear equal, I move that we endorse Kay Malone for the workshop since she has been part of our program for longer. And, I nominate Ansel Donaldson as the alternate if Kay can't accept the appointment for whatever reason."

"Is there a second?"

"Second."

A chorus of *ayes* rose from around the table.

"I move that we adjourn."

"Second."

"We stand adjourned."

The department chair motioned to Dr. Keizer. "Liz, got a minute?"

She resumed her seat at the conference table. "Do you want to tell the students, or should I?"

"I'll be glad to tell them," Dr. Keizer replied.

"Do you think Ansel will react badly?"

"He'll be okay with it. He was also considering grad school, and that's where he belongs. I've written a couple of letters on his behalf. He won't have trouble getting into one of the top programs."

The professor stood. "Kay concerns me a little. She's quite naive about the professional world, but who isn't at the beginning of a career?"

"Did we make a mistake recommending her? The Atlanta Workshop can be a tough place. Will she survive it?"

"She's got all the tools to be a success. The only question is: Can she develop toughness without losing her sensitivity? She'll take a few bumps and bruises but will do fine. I wouldn't have encouraged her to apply if I thought it would destroy her."

"Okay. Thanks, Liz." The department chair rose to leave. "How we chose isn't that different from flipping a coin, is it?"

"That may be true," replied Dr. Keizer. "But it will be a whole lot easier to explain."

CHAPTER SEVEN

Tuesday Morning, September 24

"Would you like some toast, Anna?"

"No."

"Some juice?"

"No."

"Perhaps some escargot?" Anna met John's friendly teasing with silence and a scowl.

Peg tried the cheerful approach. "Are the tryouts for the musical today?"

"No."

"When are they?"

"Next week."

"Are they after school?"

"I guess."

"Are you planning to try out?"

"No."

"But you were looking forward to the musical," said John.

"Don't want to."

"But, dear…"

"Don't want to."

"Honey, I know you're upset, but don't let this stop you from doing something you will enjoy."

"Leave me alone."

"Okay."

The squeal of the school bus brakes broke the silence.

"The bus is here. Or do you want me to give you a ride to school?"

"No."

"I can pick you up this afternoon. Remember, we are meeting with Father McDonough tonight."

"I know. I'll walk home."

Anna bolted out the front door and sprinted to catch the school bus. In her distracted haste, she left the front door wide open.

John looked at Peg. "What was that all about?"

"She's scared. And I can't explain why her birth mother gave her up. She's mad at me because I didn't tell her I suspected Maarit attended last spring's concert."

"Mad at you? You didn't know for sure who it was."

"John, you're looking for logic where there is only confusion and emotion. The problem is that we know it probably was her mother, and we can't say anything until we hear from Allison. Anna's in shock, and she's only thirteen. I'm unsure; maybe I should have shared my suspicions with her last spring."

"She'll calm down." John took another swig of coffee.

"I'm not so sure." Peg put the breakfast dishes in the dishwasher and left for work.

Tuesday, Noon

Isabella and Jordan ate their lunch while surreptitiously glancing at Anna. No one had spoken more than three words since they had met, as usual, for lunch after their fourth-hour classes. Occasionally, Anna would look up, but not at her friends. Instead, she would stare out the window, completely unaware of anything around her. The birds fluttering by, searching for a place to land, didn't catch her attention.

Isabella opened her mouth as if to speak, but Jordan's head shake prompted her to remain quiet. Lunchtime was almost over when Anna finally broke the silence.

"I'm sorry," she said. "I'm not very good company today. I have to do something tonight, and I'm scared."

"What do you have to do?" Jordan asked.

"I have to go back to the church tonight, and all I can think of is my birth mother lying in that casket. I keep seeing her face, and I get scared."

"Last night was pretty bad, huh?" Isabella's lips turned down with a sad smile. "Why do you have to go back? Is there another service?"

"No," said Anna, "My uncle's going to tell us about my mother."

Deep furrows appeared on Jordan's forehead. "What happened last night? You haven't told us anything. We've been waiting for you to tell us."

Anna took a deep breath. "We got to the church before anyone else. I remember seeing those large doors with carvings on them. There was a beautiful stained-glass window high on the church front."

"What church was it?" Jordan asked.

"I think it's called St. Francis. It's a Catholic church."

Jordan smiled. "That's the church I go to."

"Wow," said Isabella.

Anna looked at her friend. "Wow, is right."

Jordan took a sip of her milk. "What happened at the church that has you so scared?"

Anna rubbed her hands on her jeans and avoided looking at her friends' faces. "After we climbed those big, long steps and went in the door, a priest met us..."

"Who was the priest?" Jordan interrupted.

"He said his name was Father McDonough. He told us he was my birth mother's brother. He's my Uncle."

"Father Sean is your uncle," Jordan smiled. "He's cool and tells funny stories during the homily."

"Homily?" Isabella tilted her head quizzically to one side.

"It's like a short talk the priest gives during Mass."

Isabella rolled her eyes. "A sermon."

"Yeah," said Jordan. "It's a fancy word for a sermon."

"Did you meet your sister?"

Anna nodded. "She's gorgeous. She has dark hair and really pretty green eyes. I really liked her, but she left almost right away."

The bell rang, signaling the end of the lunch break. Anna stood, picking up her tray of uneaten food. "I'll see you guys later."

Tuesday Evening

Father McDonough's study was what the Jensens expected: nicely appointed but not lavish. Shelves were lined with books and souvenirs from South America, Ireland, and Italy. On the wall to the left of the desk, a kneeler rested in front of a small altar. To the left of the altar stood a small statue of Mary, and to its right, a statue of Joseph. Over the altar hung a crucifix.

"Welcome." Father McDonough gestured to a low table surrounded by four wing-back chairs. "Please, make yourselves comfortable." A pot of tea and a plate of scones awaited his guests. John and Peg took chairs on each side of their daughter.

Father McDonough sat opposite Anna. He took a wrapped package from the table and handed it to her. "I have a gift for you. Please open it."

Anna slid her thumb under the taped wrapping and carefully unfolded the paper to reveal a framed family portrait. "Is this my mother?"

"Yes, it's your mother and your grandparents and me." Father McDonough pointed over his shoulder to the opposite side of the room. "I keep it on my desk. I thought you might like to have a copy. This was our last family portrait. It was taken just before Maarit left for college, and your grandparents were posted to Argentina. Your grandfather was a diplomat for the Irish Ministry of Trade. He always assumed the 'official' dignified look whenever his picture was taken. Your grandmother was full of fun and life."

Anna showed the photo to her parents. Gently, she placed it on her lap and caressed the glass protecting the photograph. "Thank you," she whispered.

"That's very kind of you, Father." Peg looked at the portrait over her daughter's shoulder. "It's lovely."

"You're welcome," Father McDonough said, studying Anna's face. "I can't believe how much of my sister I see in you. I can't tell you how happy I am to meet you."

"Father McDonough," began John. "Do you have any idea what the circumstances were that prompted Maarit to place Anna through adoption or who her birth father was?"

"I'm afraid I can't be of much help with that. Once she divorced Kay's father, my sister and I had minimal contact. I'd get an occasional Christmas card or a postcard from somewhere in Europe. She loved to travel."

The priest paused, and the corners of his mouth twitched upward as if recalling a distant memory. "To my surprise, last spring, mid-May, I think, Maarit called one day and wanted to stop by. She told me she had quit the State Department and was working as a translator for a medical research firm in Saint Paul. She gave me a package to be opened only if she died. It was in that package that I found out about you, Anna."

Anticipation and curiosity hung in the air. Father McDonough cleared his throat and shifted in his seat before continuing. "She assured me she wasn't sick; she just wanted to 'cover the bases,'" Father McDonough made air quotation marks to emphasize the odd statement. "I felt there was more to the story at the time, but she wasn't ready to talk about it. She didn't mention you, Anna, or ask about Kay, which surprised me a little. I let her take the lead, and she didn't broach the subject. I guess she couldn't bring herself to tell her brother, the priest, about her indiscretions."

Anna clutched the photograph to her breast. "Father McDonough, what was my mother like?"

"She was smart and beautiful. She could always make me laugh, sang like an angel, and played the piano. She was tall, like you, and slender. Her hair was the same shiny brown as yours, and if she leaned over, it would fall on each side of her face."

Anna brightened. "I play the piano and played in a recital last year and won a bust of Chopin. It's on the piano at home."

"Looks like you inherited your musical talent from her."

Anna smiled.

Father McDonough continued. "Katy-did was a lot of fun…"

"Katy-did?" Peg interrupted.

"Sorry," Father McDonough laughed. "That was her family nickname. Katherine was her second name. My parents gave her four names: Maarit, Katherine, and Elizabeth McDonough. I liked Katherine better than Maarit, so I always called her Katy. One time, when I was around four or five, she was tickling me on the couch in our apartment. I struggled to escape, knocked over a lamp, and broke the shade. Mother asked who broke the lamp, and I said, 'Katy did.' From then on, if something got broken, which seemed to happen frequently, I said, 'Katy-did.' It became a family joke, and she eventually liked the nickname."

Father McDonough looked down at the table with a wistful smile. "I think the last time I called her Katy-did was when that portrait was taken."

The priest paused to pour another cup of tea for the Jensens and himself.

"My sister was also a rebel. She would openly break any rules that she considered 'stupid.' She and my dad would get into it over almost anything. After a big fight, she would turn on the charm and get my dad to agree to whatever she wanted. Thinking back on it, she didn't pick on weak people. It was always a fight with the authority figures. Nuns, priests, our father: it didn't matter. She made sure you knew if she didn't like something."

Father McDonough stopped and looked directly at Anna. "This must be quite a shock for you. New sister, new uncle, and your birth mother...all at once. How are you doing?"

"Okay, I guess."

Peg sighed. "It's been a tough few days. I think it's thrown Anna for a loop."

Anna bristled. "It has not. I'm fine. It's no big deal."

"Anna!" Peg exclaimed. "It is a big deal."

Anna glowered at her mother.

Father McDonough cleared his throat. "Sometimes, unexpected events can upset anyone. I suspect it has thrown all of us for a loop. It takes time to put everything in perspective."

Anna slumped in her chair, avoiding eye contact with her uncle. "Father McDonough, why did my mother keep Kay and give me away? Didn't she want me?"

He paused. "In some ways, my sister also gave your sister away. Her father raised Kay. I don't know all the circumstances; my sister never told me about it. Over the years, Anna, I have counseled several women who placed their babies for adoption. The one thing their stories had in common was that they couldn't care for the baby and wanted the child to have a chance for a better life. I don't know what my sister was thinking, but I believe that whatever the circumstances were, she wanted the best for you."

Peg reached over and took her daughter's hand. Anna pulled it away.

John leaned forward. "Father, is there anyone you can think of who might have known Maarit and could shed some light on this?"

Father McDonough rubbed his forehead before answering. "Perhaps her attorney? Maybe someone over at the college?"

Peg lowered her eyes at the mention of the attorney.

John stood. "Father, I think we've taken enough of your time tonight. Thank you so much for the photo and everything. We have a lot to digest. Perhaps we could get together again soon and discuss the family history?"

"Of course." Father McDonough wrote a phone number on the back of two business cards. He gave one card to Anna and the other to Peg. "If you ever want to talk, here's the number at the rectory, and my cell phone number is on the back. Someone will always answer the rectory phone. If I'm unavailable, leave a message, and I'll call as soon as possible."

Father McDonough shook hands with Peg and John. Impulsively, Anna put her arms around Father McDonough's waist in a tight hug. He returned the hug. "Anna, we're family now."

CHAPTER EIGHT

Wednesday, September 25, 5:30 P.M.

John entered the kitchen from the garage and peeked through the door that led to the living room. "What's with Anna? I've never heard Mozart sound angry on the piano before."

"She's been playing that way since I got home." Peg touched John's elbow and led him back to the kitchen table. "I asked her how school went, and all I got was a shrug and a grunt. She clearly doesn't want to talk."

"She's got a lot to process."

"I know, but it isn't healthy for her to keep it all bottled inside."

"Maybe she's taking it out on the piano," John said with a wry smile.

The angry Mozart simmered into a soft, melancholic piece. John looked toward the front room. "I haven't heard Anna play that before, have you?"

"No, that's new. Maybe it's for the recital on Halloween."

John and Peg stopped and listened briefly; a mournful Mozart replaced the angry one.

"By the way, have you heard anything from Allison yet?"

Peg shook her head. "Talked to her on the phone this morning. She's reviewed the will but has to verify a couple of things. She wouldn't tell me what. Something to do with the terms of the will that can't be resolved until she has the death certificate."

Anna appeared in the doorway. "The death certificate? What are you whispering about?"

"Nothing," said Peg. "We didn't want to disturb your practice."

"Were you talking about Aunt Allison and my mother?" Anna shoved her hands into the pockets of her jeans. "Why are you keeping secrets from me?"

"No secrets," said John. "There are always legal things that need to be taken care of when someone dies. We're waiting for your aunt to tell us if we need to do anything."

Anna looked from one parent to the other, scowling.

"Supper will be ready soon," said Peg. "Why don't you play some more until it's ready?"

"I'm not hungry." Anna turned and pounded up the stairs to her room. Skipping over the third step from the top.

Peg started after her, but John put his hand on her arm. "Let me," he said.

John gently knocked on Anna's door. "Kitten, can I come in?"

A faint "Okay" came through the door.

~ ═ ~

John entered, picked up the box of tissue on the nightstand, and joined Anna, curled up like a ball on the window bench. "Here, use these instead of your sleeve."

Anna made room for him on the bench. "Th-thanks."

John sat beside Anna on the bench under the window and put his arm around her. She leaned against her father. "Dad, can I ask you a question?"

"Sure."

"What happens when a person dies? After they're buried."

"Over time, the flesh decays and eventually the body turns to dust."

"Am I only a body? What will happen to *ME* when I die? What happened to my mother when she died?"

"Is that why you're scared?"

"I am not scared!"

"Oh, I see," said John. "What would you call it?"

"Confused?" Anna looked at the floor.

"About what?"

"Everything?"

"That covers a lot of territory. Be a little more specific."

"All day, I couldn't think about anything but the wake. I kept seeing the casket and her in it. I kept thinking I should be sad, but I'm not. It was strange seeing a dead person, but I couldn't imagine her alive. I get scared 'cause what if you and Mom die, and I'll be all alone?"

John squeezed his daughter's shoulder. "Kitten, listen to me. Yes, someday, a long time from now, both your mom and I will die. But you'll never be left alone. Someone will always be around to love you. When you became our daughter, we arranged for you to be cared for. If something happened to us, your Aunt Allison would step in. If, for some reason, she couldn't, our good friends, the Johnsons, would. Besides that, in a few years, you'll be quite capable of caring for yourself."

"But what happens to *Me* when I die?"

"That's a pretty big question." John leaned back against the window. "Philosophers and theologians have been arguing about that for thousands of years. Whole religions have been formed to try to answer that question. Some people think we have an eternal soul that never dies and is rewarded or punished for all eternity. Others are convinced that after we die, there's absolutely nothing. They think that when life ceases, it's all over, and nothing happens. Some people believe that we are reincarnated and live many lifetimes."

"I read that. I guess people in India believe in it," said Anna. "I kinda like that idea."

John smiled. "No one knows the answer. The only people that do are dead, and they're not talking."

"Dad, I'm serious."

"I know you are. I'm sorry, I shouldn't make a joke, but sometimes that's the only way I can get through difficult times."

Anna turned to look at her dad. "What do you think happens?"

"I think a part of us survives—the '*Me*' part. But what happens to it, I don't know. It's one of the great conundrums of this existence."

"What does Mom think?"

"That, Kitten, you will have to ask her." John patted Anna's arm. "Supper? It's probably getting cold by now."

John stood, leaned over, and kissed his daughter's head. He took her hands as she stood. "C'mon, let's go eat."

"Can I skip supper? I'm not very hungry."

"Okay."

John returned downstairs to report on his conversation with Anna. Peg fixed a plate of food from the leftovers, poured a glass of milk, and brought it to Anna's room. She knocked gently on the door, didn't wait for a response, and opened the door, placing the tray on the desk. Nothing needed to be said.

Thursday, September 26, 1:00 P.M.

Throughout Thursday morning, Anna took notes and wrote down the day's homework assignments—later, they looked like gibberish. She didn't participate in the class discussions or raise her hand to answer questions. At the end of second-hour English, her teacher called her aside to ask if she was okay.

"I'm fine," Anna mumbled.

"If you want to talk…"

Anna made it through half of the fifth-period choir before a flood of tears overcame her, and she ran for the door. Mr. Larson motioned for Isabella to go after her. She found Anna in the corridor, sitting against the wall, hugging her legs, her forehead buried in her knees.

"You stay here," said Isabella. "I'll be right back." She returned with Ms. Jenkins, the principal's secretary. Ms. Jenkins took Anna by the hand. "I know. This has been a huge shock to you. Let's call your mother."

Anna nodded.

"What classes do you have this afternoon?"

"Ch...choir and Hi...history," Anna stammered. "And study hall."

"Okay, I'll take care of telling the teachers that you aren't feeling well. You'll have an excused absence."

The ride home was quiet. Upon arriving, Peg stopped Anna from escaping to her room and led her to the sofa, cradling her in her arms.

The two sat for nearly an hour without saying a word. "Mom, I'm scared."

"I know, honey."

"She was so still. I wanted her to move, but she didn't. It was weird."

"You saw death, and it scared you?"

Anna nodded.

"Death is as much a part of life as living is," Peg said, squeezing her daughter gently. "But no need to worry."

Anna looked at her mother. "I can't stop thinking about Maarit."

"What do you think about when you think of her?"

"You know. *Things.* Like, what was she like? What did she do? Who was my father? That kind of stuff."

"I wish I could give you answers, honey. But I can't."

"Mom, what do you know about my mother?"

"Not a lot. We know that she went to college. We know you had a sibling, but we didn't know who it was. We knew she was Irish. We knew she had no major health issues that would affect you."

"How did you know she was Irish? Did she tell you?"

"We didn't meet her, so it must have been your aunt who told us." Besides, her brother's name is as Irish as it gets, so she had to be Irish, too.

"How did you pick me to adopt? Did you go to the hospital, point at me, and say, 'I'll take that one?'"

Peg laughed. "No, sweetie, it didn't work that way. Your aunt knew we wanted a baby. She said she had a colleague who had a client who was pregnant and couldn't keep the baby. So, Allison arranged the adoption and handled the legal matters. We like to think that somehow, you chose us to be your parents. However it happened, the minute you were put in my arms, you were my daughter."

"Did Aunt Ally know my mother?"

"I don't think so," Peg lied. "I mean, I'm sure your aunt met Maarit to get the adoption papers signed, but I don't think Allison actually knew her."

Anna frowned. "Why did you think my mother attended my concert last year?"

"Anna, we've been through this already. Let it go. I told you. She looked familiar, probably because you look a bit like her. I wish I had told you then, but I didn't. I'm sorry."

Friday, September 27

Anna trudged out of the choir room on the first floor to her sixth-hour class on the third floor. Halfway up the first flight of stairs, a small rebellion began to bubble in her stomach. On the second-floor landing, the rebellion grew into a full-fledged revolution. She rushed to the bathroom.

By the time she recovered, the late bell had rung, and classes had started. She stood at the stairwell, looked to the top floor, then down to the first; both were deserted. Anna tiptoed down the steps to the first floor and slipped out the side door unnoticed without a permission slip.

The school door closed and locked behind Anna. The only way back into the school was through the front door, which would require explanations. She took a deep breath and ran down the lawn to the nearby park. On the walking path, she looked back to see if anyone had spotted her. No one had. For the first time in her life, she was utterly alone. No one knew where she was. She was free, ecstatic, and *petrified*.

Halfway around the park, Anna slipped into a gazebo set back from the main path, slung her backpack onto the picnic tabletop, and climbed over the seat to sit next to it. On the other side of the park, she saw two young mothers leaning against a swing set, watching their children play. The rest of the park was deserted.

Anna propped her backpack on her knees and hugged it. The vision of Maarit in the casket returned. *Why can't I stop thinking about her?* Hunched over, trying to make herself as small as possible, she rocked back and forth, willing the visions to stop.

She opened the backpack, rummaged through it in search of a pencil, and retrieved a notebook. She began to draw patterns and doodles. The random squiggles became the shape of faces. The first face had long hair, closed eyes, and lips set in a rigid line. The lips neither smiled nor frowned, forming a motionless straight line. Under the face of one of the drawings, she wrote *Maarit.*

Anna drew a second face with open eyes, a small nose, and a mouth with downturned corners. She twisted her hair before drawing furrowed lines on the portrait's forehead. She titled this one *Kay.*

The third face had short hair, a man's haircut, and a big, broad smile: *Uncle Sean.*

She drew one more, larger than the others. It had long hair in a ponytail. Instead of features, she drew a large question mark covering the entire face. *Me,* she wrote.

Visions of Maarit in the casket, Kay walking out of the chapel, and Father Sean hugging her pushed all other thoughts out of her mind. She made a pillow from her backpack, lay her head on it, and cried bitter, salty tears.

CHAPTER NINE

Friday, September 27

At 2:15 p.m., the telephone rang on Peg's desk.

"Hello, Mrs. Jensen?"

"Yes."

"This is Alice Johnson, attendance secretary at Wizzyington Middle School. Did you or your husband pick Anna up for an appointment this afternoon?"

"No, why?"

"Anna didn't attend her last two classes. I thought I'd better check; she's had a tough week. I tried calling your house, but no one answered. I hope everything is alright."

"Thanks, Ms. Johnson. I appreciate the call. I'll go home and check on her."

"Shannon, I've got to go home," Peg said to her assistant. "I've left a message for John to call me there. Please tell him I've gone home if he should call here."

"Is everything okay?"

"I'm sure it is; I've got to check on Anna. Have a good weekend."

"You too," Shannon responded to her boss' retreating figure.

On the drive home, Peg reminded herself to slow down twice. "There's no sense getting a ticket or getting into an accident."

As soon as she swung the front door open, she called out calmly, "Anna, are you here?"

No answer.

Peg climbed the steps to the bedrooms, knocked on Anna's door, and peeked in. "Anna?"

The room was empty.

"Where is that girl?" Peg muttered.

The telephone in the master bedroom rang. She hurried to answer it. "No, John, no sign of her. I didn't see a note downstairs. Nothing in her room...I'm scared...this isn't like her...she always lets us know where she is. This is different. God only knows what's going on in her head... What do you mean, be calm? Come home as soon as you can. Take a look at the route she usually takes home from school, okay? She could be lying in a ditch for all we know...okay, okay, I've calmed down. I'll call her friends. Maybe she went somewhere with them...come home soon, okay? Bye."

Peg dialed Andresen's phone number. "Hi, Isabella, this is Anna's mother. Have you seen her since school got out?"

"No, Mrs. Jensen. She usually walks with us after school. When she didn't show, Jordan and I left. Is everything okay?"

"I'm sure it is. Thanks."

John arrived home at 4:55 p.m. "Any luck, Peg?"

"Nothing. None of her friends have seen her. I've talked to Kay, Father McDonough, and Allison. No one has seen her today. Allison said she would call Paul to come over and help her search. Father McDonough said he was on duty at the rectory until eight. If she hasn't been found by then, he'll come over, too."

Peg paced back and forth in the living room. "Should we call the police?"

John looked at his watch. "It's only 5:10. She hasn't been gone long enough to warrant a missing person's report. Let's wait until the others arrive, and we'll devise a search plan."

"John, I'm scared. What if she's been hurt, what if...?"

"I know, honey. It's okay." John put his arms around his wife and held her close. It was enough for one of them to show fear. It wouldn't help to reveal his own.

Friday, September 27, 5:30 P.M.

Paul's cell phone rang.

"Paul, it's Kay. I'm sorry, but I have to ask for a rain check. Could we go out some other time?"

"Sure. No problem. Something wrong?"

"Yeah, my sister is missing."

"Missing?"

"No one's seen her since lunch," said Kay. "I'm going to her house to see if I can help."

"I'll pick you up. I'll help, too." Paul jotted down Kay's address. "On my way."

As soon as he hung up, his phone rang again. "Hi, Mom, can I call you back? I've got to run."

"Anna's missing," Allison said. "Can you come over to help search for her?"

"She's what?"

"She skipped school this afternoon; no one has seen her since."

"Oh my god." Paul's voice shook.

"What?"

"Mom, I had a date with a girl tonight who just called to cancel because her sister is missing. I was getting ready to pick her up to help with the search."

Allison demanded. "What's her name? Your date?"

"Kay, Kay Malone." He heard his mother gasp. "Mom, are you alright?"

Allison said softly, "Kay Malone is Anna's half-sister."

"Wait, *what?*"

"That's a long story," said Allison. "I'll explain later."

"Okay, but I'll want that explanation sooner rather than later."

"I'll see you at Peg and John's." Allison hung up.

Ten minutes later, Kay slid into Paul's Mazda. She started to say, "The address is—"

He interrupted her. "What's your sister's name?"

"Anna—"

"—Jensen?" Paul finished Kay's answer. "Anna is my cousin. I was leaving to pick you up when my mother called to tell me she's missing. Anna's mother is my mother's sister."

"You've got to be kidding?" said Kay.

Paul smiled. 'I didn't make the connection the other day, but it appears you and I are related by adoption."

Kay laughed. "At least we're not related by blood."

CHAPTER TEN

Friday, September 27, 5:55 P.M

The girl walked into a small room through an open door. Each of the three walls facing her had a closed door and no windows. A cold breeze fluttered her ponytail with a faint rustling like the sound of leaves on a windy day. She shivered.

She turned around in time to glimpse the back of someone walking through the doorway. The presence closed the door behind it. The girl tried to follow the apparition, but the doorknob wouldn't turn. She shook the door, but it refused to open. She called out, "Who's there?"

No answer.

In a panic, she rushed to the other three doors. The first one was locked. No amount of pushing, pulling, or twisting affected it. She managed to pull the second door open a crack. She pulled hard, but it felt as if someone, or something, was playing tug-of-war with her from the other side.

It was stronger than her, and the door instantly slammed shut again.

The girl sank to her knees in front of the last door. "Let me out!"
she cried. "Please, let me out." The last door squeaked as it slowly
opened on its own. She saw a group of people walking away from
her through the open door. She tried to join them, but an invisible
barrier stopped her. She could see outside, but couldn't get through
the doorway. The girl screamed, but no one turned around.
She screamed again.

Then, a hand gently shook her. "Are you okay, child?"

Anna jolted awake from her dream only to see an unfamiliar face
peering down at her. For a moment, she forgot where she was.

"Are you okay?" the woman asked again.

Anna sat up. "Yes, I'm okay. I, like, must've fallen asleep."

"We heard you scream. It must have been a bad dream."

"It was," Anna answered as she sat up and swung her legs around.
She slid off the picnic table and planted her feet on the hard ground,
hoping its stability would help her recover her bearings.

The man accompanying the woman asked, "Can we call your parents or someone to take you home?"

Anna looked at her watch. "No, I'm fine. Thank you so much for
checking on me. I can walk home on my own." Cheeks burning with
embarrassment, she scooped up her backpack and almost ran out of the
gazebo and up the path. Out of sight of the couple, Anna collapsed on
a bench and opened her backpack to pull out the notebook. A business
card fell out and fluttered to the ground.

On the back of the card was a phone number and a message: *Anna,*
call me anytime.

In the distance, the bells from a downtown church tower rang
six times.

At 6:16 p.m., the rectory doorbell rang. Father McDonough swung open the door to reveal a shivering Anna standing on the stoop. "Hi, Uncle Sean."

"Thought you might come here," he said. "C'mon in."

"Thanks."

"So, do you want to call your folks, or should I?"

"I'd better do it."

Father McDonough led her into his study, handed her the phone, and left the room.

"Hi, Mom…I'm at Uncle Sean's…I'm okay…no really, I'm alright…I know…I'm sorry…can we talk about it at home…I know…I said I'm sorry. Uncle Sean will give me a ride home…Okay. I love you, Mom. No, you don't need to pick me up. I'm sure he'll give me a ride home. I'm in his office…wait a minute, I'll get him."

At the office doorway, she called, "Uncle Sean, my mom wants to talk to you."

"Hi, Peg. Yes, she's here…looks a little cold, but none the worse for wear. Yes, I'll bring her home. Not a problem. I think she wants to talk, so it may be a little while…Okay, yes. I'll bring her home soon. Bye." Father McDonough turned to his niece. "Have you had anything to eat?"

She shook her head.

"Come on, let's see what we can find in the kitchen."

Anna sat on a bar stool at the kitchen center island. Her uncle rummaged through the refrigerator and cupboards to see what the housekeeper might have left.

"Uncle, can you cook?"

"Well, my repertoire is limited. Your choices tonight are scrambled eggs and toast or a peanut butter and jelly sandwich."

"What kind of jelly?"

"Grape or strawberry, or we may have some bananas. Have you ever tried a peanut butter and banana sandwich?"

Anna wrinkled her nose. "I'll take a peanut butter and strawberry."

Father McDonough pushed the peanut butter jar across the counter. "Here, you spread the peanut butter, and I'll put on the jam. Make one for me, too. I'll get us some milk."

Anna nibbled on the bread until only the crusts were left, then devoured them, too. "That's an interesting way to eat a sandwich," said her uncle.

"I, like, always eat them this way. Don't know why, just do."

"I've only seen one other person eat a sandwich like that."

"Yeah, who?"

"My sister...your birth mother"

"Are you kidding?" Anna's voice wavered.

"Nope. It didn't matter what kind of sandwich she ate; she would always nibble on the inside and then eat the crust. Apparently, you inherited that from Maarit as well as the music." Father McDonough looked past Anna's shoulder as if trying to remember something. "You know, I think my mother, your grandmother, did the same thing. Must be something in the genes."

Anna became quiet. Father McDonough waited for her to resume the conversation.

"I s'pose you heard that I skipped school."

Father McDonough nodded. "Your mother mentioned it when she called three times to look for you. The last time, half an hour ago, she said they were organizing a search party. You gave them quite a scare."

Anna winced. "I know. I'm prob'ly grounded for life."

Father McDonough leaned his elbows on the center island. "Want to talk about it?"

"Uncle Sean, I'm all mixed up. I can't think of anything 'cept the wake. I keep thinking of the casket, you, my sister, and...it's like a movie that won't quit. It goes over and over again in my head." Anna leaned on the counter, supporting her head with her hand and elbow.

"That was a difficult day. It's not surprising it affected you," said Father McDonough. "What is it that has you all mixed up?"

"Can I show you something?"

"Sure."

"Don't laugh at me, okay?"

Sean raised his right hand. "I promise."

Anna stood to retrieve her backpack and searched for her notebook. She opened it to the drawings and pushed it across the table to her uncle.

The priest took several minutes to study the drawings. "I see the confusion," he said.

Anna twisted her hair. "I, like, always knew I had a birth mother somewhere, but she wasn't real, ya know. I hoped I'd meet her someday, but she didn't seem real."

Father McDonough looked at the drawings again.

"Now, I've seen her; she's dead, and I'll never get to talk to her." Anna looked down at the countertop, furiously twisting her hair. "Uncle Sean, I've, like, got two mothers, which is my *real* one?"

Father Sean hesitated, searching for the right words. "That's an interesting question,' he said. "Legally, since the adoption, Peg and John are, in the eyes of the law, your mother and father. They are responsible for you."

Anna nodded.

"Aside from the holes in your jeans, it looks like you are well clothed and fed."

"Uncle Sean, I mean, like, everybody wears ragged jeans."

"Oh, I see. It's a fashion statement."

"Well, duh, yeah." Anna rolled her eyes.

"Your mother lets you wear ragged jeans in public?" Father McDonough's eyes twinkled.

"Now you're teasing me, Uncle Sean."

"I guess I am. Tell me, do Peg and John take care of you if you're sick?"

"Of course."

"So, they feed you, clothe you, and care for you when you're sick. I guess you could say they act like real parents."

Anna lowered her eyes. "But what about your sister? Isn't she my mother, too? I mean, she did give birth to me."

"Yes, she did. There isn't any doubt about that. So, my sister and your biological father, whoever he may be, gave you your genetic makeup."

"So?"

"So, from a biological perspective, my sister is your mother. And, for the adoption to be legal, she had to agree to it. Therefore, before you were adopted, she was also your legal mother."

"Uncle Sean, which one is my real mother?"

Sean reached across the table and placed his hands on his niece's. "Anna, does it have to be one or the other? Can't it be both?"

Anna looked up, her eyes wide, the corners of her mouth turned up in a large grin. "Yes, it can. It is! It's both."

Paul and Kay excused themselves after Anna was safe and sound and all the thank-yous were exchanged. "It's still time for dinner," he said. Luigi's may be packed, but we should be able to get a table."

"Paul, I'm beat, maybe another time."

Neither spoke much on the short ride to Kay's apartment. Before she exited the car, Kay leaned over and gently kissed Paul. "You are a sweet guy."

Paul grimaced. "But..."

"Yes, *but*." Kay laced her fingers with his as she struggled to find the right words. "You see, I'm leaving for Atlanta next week. As much as I enjoyed meeting you, I don't think I can start a relationship when moving so far away. I don't know if I'll ever move back. It's not fair. I wish we had met sooner."

Paul shifted to face Kay. "Atlanta? Why Atlanta?"

"I found out yesterday that I won an internship with the Atlanta Opera Workshop. They said that if I can start by October 5th, I can be part of the Christmas production, or I can wait until the new year. This could lead to a professional career. I can't pass it up."

"Of course, you have to take it. When do you leave?"

"I'm flying out on Wednesday to find a place to stay and get settled. The internship starts the week after."

Paul nodded. "I understand. Don't like it, but I do understand. Kay, I hope the career you are chasing works. Promise to send me a postcard when you reach the top."

"Will do," Kay smiled. "What are your plans?"

"For the past year, I've been writing obituaries and movie reviews for the newspaper. They said I could go full-time if I wanted. Since nothing else is on the horizon, I'll do that."

"Obituaries? That sounds depressing."

"Actually, it isn't. Mostly, the family writes them, and I edit them. Often, the obit gives a sense of who the people are and their lives. It keeps their memory alive and tells their story to the world. That's important, not depressing."

"That's a neat way to look at it," she said.

"I don't expect I'll do it for the rest of my life, but I love to write. I'm sure it will lead to something else."

"No real plan for the future, go with the flow, eh?" Kay shook her head. "I couldn't live like that. I know what I'm aiming for. I'm not sure of the route it will take, but I know where I want to go."

"You're the 'set a goal and go for it' type."

"'Fraid so."

Paul took her hands in his at the door to her apartment building and pulled her close for a kiss. "Good luck, Kay. Send me tickets for your opening at La Scala."

CHAPTER ELEVEN

Sunday, September 29

"MOTHER!!"

The scream, followed by a loud bang and a dull thud, woke Peg and John. A glance at the clock on the bed stand showed 2:28 a.m. Peg raced across the hall, only to discover her daughter lying on the floor sobbing, "Mommy, make it st-stop! Make it *stop*!"

Peg knelt beside Anna, gathered her into her arms, and rocked back and forth. "It's okay, it's okay, it's just a bad dream, you're safe now, shhh. Nothing in the dream can hurt you, it's okay, it's okay."

"She was chasing me. I couldn't get away. I ran and ran, but she was always right behind me. Wherever I turned, she was there. Then I saw the casket, but it wasn't Maarit in it—it was…you." Anna gulped, half-choking on her sobs.

"It's okay. It's just a dream. I'm here. It's all right." Peg held Anna tightly in her arms. "You're safe. It's only a bad dream. It's just a dream. You're okay. Come on, let's get you back into bed." Peg stood and helped her daughter climb into bed.

"Don't leave me."

"I'm not going anywhere. You're safe." Peg sat on the edge of the bed, tucked the covers around Anna, and gently stroked her hair. "Shhh, everything will be fine. Try to go back to sleep."

John stood by the bedroom door. "Pretty scary dream."

"Sure is," whispered Peg.

John restored the clock radio Anna had knocked off the table to its proper place. "I think we need to find a way to get rid of that 'movie' and these nightmares. I'll brew some tea."

"I'll be down as soon as she falls asleep."

John paced aimlessly around the kitchen, making as little noise as possible until Peg entered the kitchen. "Is she alright?"

"It took a while, but she's back asleep. Is the tea ready?"

"If I had known it would affect Anna this way," John mused as he poured his wife a hot cup of tea. "I would never have let her go to that wake."

Peg clutched the mug in both hands as she sipped the hot beverage. Worry lines creased her forehead as she spoke. "She had to face this sometime. If we had known more, maybe we could have prepared her for this, but we didn't."

"I know. You're right. I hate to see her in such pain. She's still a child. She shouldn't have to deal with life and death yet."

"In your eyes, she'll be a child when she's thirty-five and has kids of her own," Peg teased.

"That's a dad's prerogative. The other day, I told her she could start dating when she's thirty or older. I got the expected *'Oh, Dad!'*"

"I thought that we had turned the corner after her escapade on Friday and the talk with Father McDonough. She was so happy; I couldn't even get mad at her for skipping school. Now this."

John stood and leaned against the counter, "I think the real key to this is helping her come to terms with the reasons Maarit placed her for adoption. For that to happen, we need to know more about Maarit."

"But how're we going to do that? Father McDonough doesn't seem to know much more than we do."

"Maybe Kay has some information that would be helpful," Peg said.

John ran his hand wearily through his disheveled hair. "You know, the priest said something in passing the other night that might be a clue where to look next."

"Where?"

"The college. Maarit went to school here."

"I missed that completely."

"Tell you what," John said. "You call Kay and find out what you can. I'll nose around at the college on Monday. I know the folks in the admissions office. In the meantime, let's try to get a couple more hours of sleep."

"Okay, I'll go check on Anna first."

Monday, September 30

Kay sat across from Peg at Tom's Diner on Ellston's main street. The clinking of coffee cups and plates amid the lunch crowd's buzz gave the illusion of privacy.

"I know you mean well," Kay said. "I'm sorry that Anna is upset, but I don't want to discuss my mother. She left, and I barely heard anything from her until the day she died. I was dead to her, and she to me, before she died. That's the end of it. I don't care to hear anything more concerning her. I don't know what she did after she left. It's a matter of complete indifference to me. It's a waste of time to try to find out. She's dead. I don't want to have anything to do with trying to find anything out."

The venom and anger in Kay's words made Peg instinctively press herself against the backrest of the booth. "I didn't realize that you were so deeply hurt. I'm trying to keep Anna from the same kind of pain. Please, if not for your own sake, for hers, tell me about your mother."

Kay's face softened. "Peg, I don't know much. I was very young when she left. My Dad always avoided questions. If I thought I could help, I would, but I can't."

Peg patted Kay's hands reassuringly. "It's okay. I understand. Do you want me to keep you informed if we find anything?"

"No, I want to let that part of me stay dead." Kay took a sip of coffee and set the mug on the table. "On a different topic, you were on my list to call today."

"Oh?"

"I'm leaving for an internship in Atlanta this week. I fly out Wednesday."

"Whoa, that's quick," Peg said.

"I applied months ago and found out a few days ago that I was accepted. They want me to start as soon as I can. Will you tell Anna for me?"

"Of course, but you need to call her, too."

"I'll do that tonight."

"Are you flying out of LaCrosse or the Twin Cities?"

"LaCrosse. 5:00 p.m. flight on Delta."

"If it's okay with you, I can see if the three of us can join you at the airport for a proper send-off."

Kay's face brightened. "That would be great."

"A bon voyage party at four, it is then!" As the pair rose to leave, Peg paused and looked deeply into Kay's eyes. "I have one last question: why are you so angry if she's dead to you?"

Kay stopped in her tracks, and her stance became stiff and defensive. "Leave it alone, Peg. Leave it alone." Without another word, the young woman turned and left the diner.

⌒ ═ ⌒

John shouldered through the jumble of students scrambling to get to their next class as he left the visitor parking lot on his way to the Admissions Office. Fortunately, the office was located directly across from the parking lot, so he didn't have far to go.

The Director of Admissions had been sympathetic, but she had no information for him. Their electronic records didn't go back that far. She suggested he try the business office because they could provide more assistance. The office was in the administration building, opposite the commons, right next to the new library. The director had looked at her watch and added, "Classes should have begun by now. You shouldn't have to fight the crowds."

The commons had been almost deserted except for a small group of students playing Frisbee on the lawn. The business office receptionist was equally unable to help. The secretary had not been able to confirm that Maarit had attended the university because their records from that far back were stored off campus. John had voiced the urgency of his inquiry, but the business office personnel's hands were tied. The chance of accessing the records he needed was slim, if they even existed.

John next visited the registrar's office at the business office's urging, and they were slightly more helpful. Yes, Maarit McDonough had graduated cum laude with an American Studies major. Her concentrations were music, languages, and political science. The office staff apologized for not providing John with a transcript without Maarit's approval. Even though Maarit was deceased and unable to approve, privacy laws prevented them from sharing the information. Their suggestion was to make John's next stop at Alumni Association.

"It's in the little yellow house on the corner. You can't miss it."

The Alumni Association office was a block off campus behind the science building, and the staff was gracious and helpful. Their records showed Maarit's address following graduation and stated that she had married Tom Malone. Maarit had not updated her address since then, but she had answered a survey indicating that she had sung in the concert choir. Someone in the music department may remember her. They wished him good luck.

John walked the familiar path to the Performing Arts Center. He had spent considerable time there as an undergraduate, and the familiar sounds emanating from the building were wonderfully chaotic.

Inside, on the recital hall stage, a string quartet was working its way through a Beethoven piece, while in the orchestra rehearsal room, a pair of trumpets was making a valiant effort to master a Vivaldi concerto. *Keep at it*, he thought. *It'll be worth it.* He walked through the halls to the music office, a nostalgic relief from the past few days.

"I have a strange request," he told the young woman sitting behind the receptionist's desk. "I'm looking for a faculty member who would have been teaching here about twenty years ago. I'm hoping they might remember a student, Maarit McDonough. She might have been a voice student; I understand she sang in the choir."

At the sound of the name, a middle-aged woman at the table turned abruptly. "Excuse me, sir, did you say, 'Maarit McDonough?'"

"Yes, did you know her?"

"I did. She was my advisee and took voice lessons from me. I haven't heard her name in years. Why the interest in her?"

"Maarit died a couple of weeks ago," John replied. "We just learned that she is our daughter's birth mother. We're trying to find out any information we can, hoping to learn why she placed her daughter for adoption."

The woman held out her hand, "I'm Dr. Elizabeth Keizer. She was an up-and-coming talent. I'm unsure how much help I can be, but I'd be happy to tell you what I know. Unfortunately, I have to teach a class now. Could we meet in, say, an hour and a half?"

Ninety minutes later, John sat attentively in Dr. Keizer's studio office. As college offices go, it was relatively spacious. The studio had enough room for two chairs, a small grand piano, a desk with stacks of music scores, and two music stands. The walls were adorned with autographed pictures of Keizer posing with various conductors and composers. Over her desk hung a small, framed copy of her Doctorate of Musical Arts from the Juilliard School of Music.

"The news of her passing is so sad. How did it happen?"

"She suffered a series of strokes while driving," John replied. "She was found in a ditch near a farm north of here, but it was too late."

"Was she living in Ellston?"

"From what we can tell, she was working in the Twin Cities and, for some reason, drove down here that day."

Dr. Keizer shook her head. "Back in the day, she was one of my most promising students."

John nodded. "Maarit's passing has hit Anna, our daughter, very hard. She's having nightmares, and during the day, her thoughts are dominated by visions of the wake. It's turned her from a happy, exuberant child into a sad and angry girl. I'm afraid that she might be sinking into a depression. We're hoping you can shed a little light on who Maarit was and maybe an insight into why she placed Anna for adoption."

Dr. Keizer paused. Her face gathered in a slight frown. Her fingers rubbed her throat as she summoned a collection of dusty memories. "It's been a long time since I've seen Maarit," she said. "Our last meeting ended badly. She was one of the most talented students I've ever had, but had a temper and didn't accept critiques easily. Following a run-in with the orchestra conductor, she came to me during an opera rehearsal. The maestro had wanted a particular phrase done one way, and Maarit had a different interpretation. The conductor, an old-school German, didn't tolerate being challenged in front of the entire cast and told her they would do it his way since *he* was the conductor."

Dr. Keizer signed deeply and shuffled the papers on her desk before continuing.

"Maarit came to me, and I backed the conductor. She was furious and stormed out. The next thing I heard was that she had changed her major, quit the choir, and left the opera cast. The faculty's opinion was split on the issue, as they hated to lose someone with as much talent and potential as Maarit had. But musical organizations are not typically democracies." Keizer shrugged sadly.

"Sounds like a pretty ugly scene," John offered quietly.

"It was. Maarit was mercurial. One minute, she was flying high, had the world by the tail, and was an absolute delight to be with; then, almost instantly, she could become quiet and almost morose. She was both a delight and a challenge. The problem was that Maarit was very talented but not very disciplined. To make it in the music world, you need both."

"Anything else you can tell me? Anything at all?"

Dr. Keizer thought for a moment. "I think she did have one very close friend. Her name was Ellie or Molly, something like that. I don't remember exactly. Maarit would occasionally mention her in a conversation. I think they belonged to one of the sororities, but I'm afraid I can't remember what the connection was. If I think of it, I'll let you know."

John stood to leave. "Thank you for your time, Dr. Keizer. This has been a crazy roller coaster ride for all of us. In addition to Maarit's death, we discovered that Anna has a sister who's a student here and an uncle who's a priest at St. Francis."

"What's her sister's name? We could find her in the student directory."

"Kay, Kay Malone."

Dr. Keizer's mouth hung open. "Kay Malone is Maarit's daughter?"

"Yes, do you know her?"

"Indeed!" exclaimed Dr. Keizer. "Kay is one of my students. In fact, through a contact of mine, I helped her get an internship in Atlanta. I think she leaves this week. Unlike Maarit, Kay has the talent and the discipline to succeed."

She shook her head in disbelief. "My word, Kay Malone is Maarit's daughter."

"Thank you again, Dr. Keizer," John said, handing her a business card. "You've been most helpful. Please let me know if you need anything else to help us."

"Of course. I'd like to meet Anna if you think it is appropriate and helpful. Maybe she'd like to hear a few happy stories about her birth mother."

"I think that might be an excellent idea; we'll see how this all works out."

ACT TWO
1996 – 2016

CHAPTER TWELVE

Wednesday, October 2, 1996

Paul flopped onto his favorite living room chair. He sat sideways, both of his legs hanging over the armrest.

"Kay's off to Atlanta. Her plane took off a couple of hours late," he shared, trying his best to look aloof.

"When will you ever learn to sit properly in a chair?" his mother chided him.

"When I'm old and grey like you."

"Love you, too." Allison grinned at the easy banter as she sipped her steaming coffee.

"You promised me a story about Maarit, Kay, and Anna," Paul reminded.

"Not much to tell. Maarit was pregnant. She couldn't keep the baby. John and Peg had wanted a baby for a long time. End of story, happy lives all around."

"That's not a story; it's a summation of the facts. Stop being a lawyer. What's the story?"

"There's not a lot more to tell," Allison retorted.

"Mom, there's a lot more to tell. Maarit was more than just a client, wasn't she?"

Allison paused. "What makes you say that?"

"It stands to reason. Maarit could have given the baby to an agency. Instead, she trusted you to find parents for her baby."

Allison did her best to deflect her son's line of questioning. "Was it hard to say goodbye to Kay at the airport?"

Paul rolled his eyes. "Nice pivot, Mom, but it won't work. Why would Maarit trust you to find good parents for Anna rather than an agency?"

"You'll make a great reporter someday, kid," Allison said. "You keep asking questions even when there seem to be no more answers. That's a good skill."

"Mom?" Paul was getting exasperated by his mother's attempts to be vague.

Allison sighed and threw up her hands in mock despair. "Alright, Maarit and I have been friends since college. I've been her attorney all these years, and she came to me for help when she got pregnant. Her religion forbade an abortion, so that option was out of the question. John and Peg had wanted a child for many years. I put two and two together, and it all added up. Now, you have to answer a question for me. Was it hard saying goodbye to Kay at the airport?"

"Yes, it was. We'd only met a few days ago, but it could have developed more if she had stayed around."

"Was Kay the girl at the bank?"

Paul nodded. "She worked at the music office at the college. I met her there when I delivered the packet to Dr. Keizer, and we went for coffee."

"She seemed like a nice girl. Did she say anything about Maarit or the wake?"

Paul's eyes narrowed. He looked at his mother over the top of his glasses.

"I know that look," Allison said. "You get it every time you think someone is hiding something."

"We didn't really talk much about Maarit. When we had coffee the other day, she seemed quite upset and sad about her mother. She didn't seem comfortable with the idea of having a sister."

"Interesting," Allison said.

"Mom, you've gone into lawyer mode, prying for information. What's going on here?"

"Nothing, I'm just curious." Allison pretended to study the design of her coffee cup.

"On the way back from the airport, I thought about this whole situation. There seems to be a missing piece in all this. It doesn't add up," Paul said.

"Let's change the subject," Allison said. "Have you heard anything about that reporter's job at the *Herald-Review*?"

"Not yet. The editor said the decision will be made next week."

Allison smiled. "I have a good feeling about this; I think you'll get it."

Wednesday, October 2

Passengers jockeyed for position around the baggage claim carousels at the South Terminal of Atlanta's Hartsfield-Jackson airport. Nikki Aronson stood by Carousel #6, holding a sign with *K. Malone* printed on it. She smoothed her skirt for the umpteenth time while scanning the wall of monitors for the arrival time of Delta Flights from Minneapolis. The flight was on the ground two hours late.

"Hi, I'm Kay Malone. Are you here to meet me?"

Looking in the opposite direction, Nikki nearly jumped. She composed herself and extended her hand. "Hi, welcome to Atlanta. I'm Nikki Aronson. Did you have a good flight?"

Kay shook her head. "It was only the second time I've flown. It was bumpy, and the pilot had to fly around a storm. Nerve-wracking, to say the least."

"I've flown dozens of times," Nikki offered. "Eventually, you get used to it."

Four inches taller than the petite blonde, the raven-haired Kay felt comfortable but underdressed in her blue jeans, tennis shoes, and a simple blouse under a maroon and gold sweatshirt. Nikki, in contrast, looked like a bronzed fashion model, with long blonde hair tucked behind her ear and clothes almost certainly bought on Rodeo Drive.

Waiting at the carousel, the two women glanced sideways at each other as awkward silence filled the air. "By the way," said Nikki, breaking the tension. "I have an extra bedroom in my apartment. You're welcome to stay with me until you get settled or stay at the dorm. They have a wing reserved for grad students and interns."

"That's very kind of you," said Kay. "Thanks, I'll take you up on that offer. Dorms aren't my favorite."

"Great, it'll be nice to have a roommate."

"Are you part of the workshop staff?" asked Kay.

"I'm an intern like you. I work in the office part-time. It helps to stretch the budget."

"How long have you been in the program?"

"This is my third year. I'd be glad to show you around."

"That'd be great. New places are always a little intimidating."

After Kay's luggage finally slid down the chute onto the circular carousel, the two women elbowed through the crowd to catch the tram that looped continuously between the terminals and the parking ramp.

"I was told that the Christmas show auditions start soon. Have you heard anything yet?"

"Auditions on Monday and Tuesday. Rehearsals start on Friday," said Nikki. "I think they're likely to put you in the chorus. That's what they typically do with first-year interns. I'm expecting to get a solo role this year. You're a mezzo-soprano, right?"

"Yep."

"Me, too." Nikki glanced at Kay, wondering just how strong a voice she might have. "I've been studying voice, just forever. I love being on the stage. Have you had a lot of experience with opera?"

"Some. I sang the lead in *Madame Butterfly* last spring," Kay replied as she adjusted her hair in a ponytail. "Have you seen the script for the Christmas show?"

"Not yet. They don't release it until the auditions are over. They want to test sight-reading and interpretation on the fly."

Kay wrinkled her nose. "Nothing like starting with a trial by fire."

"Welcome to the professional world. It's going to be fun. I love to sight-read."

Nikki chattered on her way downtown, pointing out landmarks here and there. She made sure Kay understood that the internship was challenging, that the coaches and conductors were highly demanding, and that the music was difficult. "But I'm sure you'll do fine," she added. "I hope your technique is strong enough and you have a lot of endurance. This isn't college."

Nikki pulled into the underground parking garage of her apartment building. Together, the two carried Kay's luggage to the elevator. "My apartment is on the third floor. The view isn't much, but it's only two blocks from the opera house. It's well-lit, so the walk home from a late rehearsal is okay, and the building has a security system."

Nikki leaned against the bedroom door while Kay began to unpack. "You're lucky to have an apartment this close to the school!" said Kay. "It must cost a fortune."

"Daddy helps, and I usually have a roommate to share the rent. If you decide to stay, Daddy pays a third, and I'll split the rest with you. You can stay till the end of the month, before I'll need help with the rent."

"That's very generous of you. Let's see how it plays out."

"We'd better get you checked in at the Workshop. Have they told you who your main voice coach will be?"

Kay pulled out a packet of information. "It says Mateo DiPorta."

Nikki let out a derisive snort and rolled her eyes. "Yuck. I took lessons from him in the first quarter. Didn't like him at all. Always waving his arms around and yelling, *'No, No, No. Land on top of the pitch. Don't reach for it.'* I couldn't stand him, so I changed coaches at the end of the term. You'll do the same if you're smart."

"Thanks for the tip. That's funny. My voice teacher in college always yelled the same thing. Sounds like he has the same pet peeve."

Monday, October 7

"Ms. Malone, you're next. You'll have five minutes to review this score. Mr. Eckart will play the accompaniment for you. You may study the music together." Mateo DiPorta was a portly man who looked as Italian as his name suggested. His glasses, as usual, rested on the top of his head, except when he looked at music. His thick fingers were constantly busy flipping his glasses from his head to his face. "Any questions?"

Kay took a careful look at the music folder that had been given. "Excuse me, Professor," she said. "I was told this audition was to test my sight-reading skills. I know this exercise; I have sung it many times."

"Interesting, not many vocal coaches use this. Who was your teacher?"

"Dr. Elizabeth Keizer. Milan College."

DiPorta laughed. "I should have known. Liz loves this exercise."

"You know Dr. Keizer?" Kay's eyes widened in surprise.

"We were at Juilliard together. Let's try this one instead." DiPorta handed Kay and Brian a different set of music exercises. "Brian, do you know this accompaniment?"

Standing beside Kay, beside the piano, Brian opened the score and played the first few measures. "No," he said. "I'll be sight-reading it, too."

"Good, let's see how you both manage it."

Kay and Brian huddled around the piano, pointing out various points in the music to each other.

"Okay, we're ready," Kay said.

Five minutes later, Brian played the last chord of the exercise. The three members of the auditioning team leaned toward each other, whispering.

"Tell me, Ms. Malone," DiPorta asked. "Do you know the spots that caused you trouble?"

"Yes," Kay looked down at the music. "In measure twenty-six, I sang a G-sharp instead of the E, and I missed the diminuendo and ritardando in measure forty-three."

Brian spoke. "That last one was my fault. I kept the volume and didn't slow the tempo in measures forty-two through forty-four."

"You both are correct. Thank you. We'll be having a cast meeting on Wednesday. We'll let you know our decisions then."

Wednesday, October 9

Wednesday morning, Kay and Nikki joined the rest of the Christmas festival cast and sat in the auditorium's back row. Brian spotted them and slid in next to Kay. He leaned forward. "Nikki, how'd your audition go?"

"Quite well. I think I nailed it."

"Wish I could say that," said Kay. "I missed two spots."

"Yeah, but one of them was my fault, and the wrong note was within the chord; only the judges would notice it."

"Unfortunately, they did," Kay shrugged.

Nikki smiled.

The auditorium became quiet when Dr. DiPorta took the stage. "Ladies and gentlemen, as a reminder for those of you who have been around awhile and as a heads-up for those new to our program, this is the second of three major productions here at the Atlanta Opera Workshop. Major music critics review the major productions from around the country. Careers have been made and broken by these reviews."

Nikki whispered to Brian and Kay, "Last year, two soloists were offered contracts based on those reviews. This is so exciting. I was an understudy last year, so this year, I should get a solo spot."

DiPorta continued. "As is our custom, this year's Winter festival features music composed especially for the show by the students in the theory and composition track. They are under the guidance of Dr. Connors."

Polite applause. A murmur of anticipation spread through the auditorium. The announcement of the soloists came next.

"This year's theme is 'An American Christmas.' All of you were invited to this announcement and will play a role in the production. The soloists were chosen for their fit for a specific role. You all are good musicians, or you wouldn't be here. At this level, the fit for the role is the most important consideration."

Nikki crossed her fingers.

"The program will be structured around four regions of the country: east, south, midwest, and west, with one soloist representing each region. The finale will feature the four soloists as a quartet, the chorus, and the full orchestra, symbolizing the country's unity. The soloists are…"

Kay leaned over to Nikki, "Breathe."

Nikki audibly exhaled.

"Soprano Kay Malone—Midwest, Alto Cindy McKnight—East, Tenor Phillip Alexander—West, and Bass Alan Smithson—South. Brian Eckhart, Monica Lester, and Melanie Lee will serve as rehearsal accompanists. Maestro DeVeaux will conduct. Rehearsals begin tomorrow; please take a copy of the schedule. Soloists, I'd like to meet with you briefly following this meeting. Thank you all."

Nikki sat perfectly still, her mouth slack, her face expressionless.

"Nikki," Kay asked. "Are you alright?"

"How did that happen? This was supposed to be my turn for the solo. I don't understand. You haven't even been here for a week, and you're already getting the solo. This doesn't make any sense. It was supposed to be mine."

Nikki's shocked face worried Kay. "Brian, will you stay with her? I have to meet with Dr. DiPorta. I'll be back as soon as I can."

"Sure. I'll take her home."

"Okay, but don't leave until I get there."

The four soloists joined Professors DiPorta and DeVeux on stage.

"In addition to the regular rehearsal schedule," DeVeux began. "We'll meet twice a week on Tuesday evenings and Sunday afternoons. I don't think any of you have classes at those times. Please clear your personal schedules. Any questions? Okay, good. See you on Sunday afternoon at two."

Kay caught DiPorta at the stage door. "Professor, do you have a minute? I have a question for you."

"Sure."

"Why did I get the role?"

The maestro raised an eyebrow. "You cut right to the chase, don't you?"

"My dad taught me it was the best way."

"Okay. Three reasons. First, your audition tape was excellent. Liz Keizer doesn't send me people who aren't ready. Second, you admitted to two mistakes at the audition and didn't blame Brian for them. Lastly, you let us know you are familiar with the vocal exercise. Didn't try to snow us with your sight-reading. I know the materials that Liz likes to use with her advanced students. It was a test, and you passed. Any other questions?"

"No, I guess not." Kay shook hands with the professor. "Thank you for your candor."

"My father taught me it was the best way," he responded with a wink and a smile.

"One more thing, Dr. DiPorta."

"What's that?"

"Nikki Aronson took it pretty hard. She seemed to think the role was hers because she had been here longer than me."

"Ah, yes. Ms. Aronson." DiPorta paused. "I understand you are currently rooming with her."

"That is correct."

"If I may give you a piece of advice, Ms. Malone. You should move sooner rather than later."

"That's a strange thing to say. Is there something I should know?"

"Let's just say that you can fix some things, but you cannot fix others."

"I see. Thank you for your time. I'll think about it."

"You do that. Good evening."

Brian sat in Nikki's living room while she ranted and raved. "That role was mine!" she thundered. "She stole it from me!"

"Nikki, come on. She couldn't do that. You both auditioned well. It's like DiPorta said. She's the right fit for the role. You are an excellent singer; there'll be other roles."

"Don't you dare take her side! She stole the role. This was supposed to be my turn to be the star. She must have cheated."

"How could she cheat?" Brian shook his head. "Look, I accompanied her. She didn't cheat. She is the better fit for this role. Besides…"

"Besides what?"

"Nothing, never mind."

"Come on, besides what?"

Brian went mute.

Nikki stormed across the room. "Listen, asshole! Don't take her side. What did she promise you? Maybe a little extra on the side? Aren't I enough for you?"

Brian rose, standing toe to toe with her. His face softened. Silently, he took her hands and sat her down beside him on the sofa. In a quiet voice, he answered. "Nikki, Nikki, come on. Let's not go down into the gutter. You and I haven't been together for over a year. We both knew then it wouldn't work out between us. I love accompanying you. Your voice is pure and clear when you're not angry or scared. But you don't handle the pressure of the solo. It causes you to freeze, and your voice becomes shrill. You are best suited to lead the section. The other singers follow you. That's your strength."

Nikki's shoulders slumped. She turned her face away from Brian, hiding her watering eyes. The sound of Kay's key entering the door lock and the sight of her entering the room sent a cold wave of anger through her. Her face reddened, veins pulsing in her temple. "How dare you come here? You stole my part!"

Kay raised her hands, palms open. "I didn't steal the part; they chose me for the role. I auditioned the same way that you did."

Brian moved to stand between them. "Nikki." His voice carried a warning.

Jaw clenched, Nikki spat, "I think it best if you find some other place to live. It's clear we're not going to get along."

"I agree," said Kay. "I'll move out tomorrow."

"The sooner the better," Nikki snarled. "This clearly isn't going to work out.

Kay signed sadly. "Brian, will you give me a ride to the housing office? Hopefully, there will be a room open."

"Sure." Brian felt Nikki's icy stare on the back of his neck as he followed Kay out the door. He didn't want Nikki to feel betrayed, but Kay needed the ride, and Nikki was in no mood to listen to reason. He hoped he would be able to calm her down later.

During the silent drive to the housing office, the silence inside the car felt deafening. After a few blocks, Kay finally spoke. "Brian, I have two questions for you."

Brian nodded. "Okay."

"I overheard you and Nikki through the door. What did you mean when you said there were other reasons Nikki didn't get the part?"

He sighed. "Last spring, she did a solo recital. Her nerves got the best of her. She missed entrances, and her voice lost its warmth. I overheard the faculty talking; I don't think they trust her under pressure."

"Is this her third year as an intern? I thought it was a two-year program."

"It is. They hired her in the office—she's a great organizer. And they're allowing her to take classes and audition for roles."

Kay hesitated. "I...uh...guess I have one more question."

Brian smiled. "You want to know if Nikki and I are dating?"

"Uh...well...yeah."

"We were. Last year, but it didn't work out."

"Oh, I'm sorry. I'm so nosy."

"It's okay." Brian parked in front of the student center. "Here we are, let's find you a place to live."

CHAPTER THIRTEEN

November 1997

A knock on the practice room door in the Atlanta workshop basement interrupted Kay's warmup exercises.

"Ms. Malone? Ms. Kay Malone?"

"Yes."

A woman in a business suit stood in the doorway, clutching two tan envelopes and a brown leather briefcase. She paused briefly before stepping forward and offering Kay a crisp, glossy business card.

"I'm an attorney with the Williams-Laughton office in Ellston, Minnesota. We're representing the estate of Maarit McDonough Malone; I believe she was your mother. Is that correct?"

"Yes. But I really don't…"

"This will only take a few minutes," the woman interrupted. "But we need to speak. We can talk here, or if you prefer, we could go somewhere more private."

Kay shook her head. "Here is fine. I have no…"

"I normally would do this in an office, but you are a hard person to track down. One of the professors in the administration office suggested I check here. He said it was the best place at this time of day."

"Ms…" Kay glanced at the stiff business card. "Laughton, I'm pressed for time today. Let's talk here."

The lawyer set her briefcase on top of the piano. "I have two things for you. The first is a check for your share of your mother's estate. The estate has been divided between you and your half-sister, Anna Jensen."

"The second item is this letter from your mother. Her will stipulated that it be delivered in person. Please sign this document to acknowledge receipt of these two items so we can conclude our business today."

Ms. Laughton handed Kay two envelopes. The first contained a check representing her share of the estate, and the second was a creme-colored linen envelope with hand-written words in an elegant calligraphic style.

Eager to be done with anything to do with her deceased mother, Kay quickly signed the document. Without hesitation, she tore the linen envelope into pieces and handed it back to the lawyer. "I'm not interested in anything my mother has to say. Ever."

"As you wish, Ms. Malone." The lawyer took the torn pieces and put them back in her briefcase. "Thank you for your time." The sharp tap of her high heels echoed in the hallway as she disappeared.

Kay sighed and began a series of deep breathing exercises; the same exercises Dr. K. had taught her to control her nerves before a performance. *I have work to do, I'll deal with my mother later.*

Before the lawyer had reached the end of the hallway, she heard Kay's soprano voice begin singing strong and clear.

〜 ═ 〜

Allison's official tone on the phone put John and Peg on edge. "I need to talk to all of you tonight, including Anna," Allison stated. "I'll be by after dinner, about 7:30."

At 7:30 sharp, John, Peg, and Anna nervously watched Allison pull a legal pad and a thick folder of documents from the briefcase.

"Anna, I'm not sure if you know this," began Allison. "But I arranged your adoption. It was a private adoption, meaning an agency wasn't involved. The court typically is cool toward private adoptions because of the potential for insufficient background checks and safeguards for the child. But, because of certain special circumstances at the time and the fact that adoption laws were changing at the legislature, Judge Henley, with some reservations, approved your adoption."

"Allison, you're making us quite nervous," John said. "Is there a problem with the adoption? Are we in danger of losing Anna because of some legal technicality from thirteen years ago?"

"No! No, not at all!" Allison hastily reassured. "Anna is your daughter in all respects. No legal problems exist."

"Then why is there an urgent need to talk to us tonight?"

"I'll get to that," Allison said, turning to Anna and taking her niece's hands. "Your birth mother, Maarit, was my best friend in college. We remained friends all her life. When she became pregnant with you, she asked me to arrange an adoption. I knew your Mom and Dad wanted a baby, so I arranged for them to adopt you."

Anna was already feeling tense, but her aunt's revelation caused the muscles in her neck to tighten even more. Anxiously, her finger twisted her dark hair repeatedly.

"Stop that, you'll get knots in your hair," Peg gently chastised as she put her hand over Anna's. Anna pulled her hand away.

"You did know her," Anna snarled at her mother in an accusing tone. "You lied to me. I could have met my mother when she was alive. And you did, too, Aunt Ally. You all lied to me."

"Anna." John's face was stern, and his voice serious. "First of all, we're your parents, and you don't talk to us in that tone. Secondly, there are reasons you weren't told about Maarit. You need to hear what they are before you get all high and mighty."

Anna looked down at the table, unwilling to abandon the start of a good sulk.

"In the legal world," Allison began. "What a client tells her attorney is a secret. It's called attorney-client privilege. And, usually, the attorney cannot tell all that she knows."

"That's dumb," said Anna.

"That can be argued another time. The point is, I couldn't tell any-one, including your mother and father, everything I knew. It was only after Maarit's death that I told your mother about my friendship with your birth mother. I asked Peg to keep my secret until I could review several documents."

"Have you had a chance to look at them?" asked Peg.

"Yes. Father McDonough gave me a packet containing several documents, signed by Maarit, that waived most of the attorney-client privilege, and I've reviewed her will. I had to wait until the death certif-icate was official before executing the Will."

"Aunt Ally, I'm, like, really confused…" Anna's nervous hair twist-ing started up again.

"I know, honey. I'll answer your questions. As I said, after Maarit died, your uncle, Father Sean, gave me a package."

"I remember," said Anna. "He told us that he had delivered it to my mother's attorney, but he didn't say it was you."

"Father McDonough didn't know we're related, nor did he know the contents of the package."

"What was in the package?" asked Peg.

"There were legal documents related to a trust fund for Anna's edu-cation, affidavits freeing me from attorney-client privilege, and, most importantly, there were two letters—one for you and one for Kay. My colleague delivered her letter yesterday. She agreed she wouldn't speak to you until I had delivered your letter. She will call when I tell her we have talked."

Allison reached into the folder, pulled out a thick cream-colored linen envelope, and placed it in front of Anna. The envelope's simple inscription, handwritten in exquisite calligraphy, read, *For Anna*.

"Please, read this letter, which I have not seen, and then I'll try to answer your questions."

Anna's hands trembled as she broke the seal, unfolded the contents, and began to read silently.

Dear Anna,

I want to say much to you, and I expect you will have many questions you'd like to ask me. But if you are reading this letter, then you know that I have died.

I have watched you grow up through my friend, Allison. She told me what a wonderful singing voice you have, how beautifully you play the piano, and that you love to play soccer. I am sorry I couldn't be a part of your life. I did go to your 5th grade graduation ceremony. I sat in the back of the auditorium and cried as you walked across the stage. I was very proud of you. I was also at your choir concert last spring. Seeing you accompany the choir for one of the selections was wonderful.

Allison has been my best friend since we were roommates in college. I have given her permission to tell you everything that she knows about me. Ask her anything you want.

I'm sure that one of your biggest questions is about your father. I wish I could give you a lot of information about him, but I can't. You were conceived in Paris, France. I was alone, tired, and very lonely on a business trip. I met Andre, and we spent a weekend together. I never saw him again. All I can tell you is that he was handsome, bright, and fun to be with. He never knew about you. If he had, I believe the situation would have been different.

When I found myself pregnant with you, I decided to place you for adoption. I knew I couldn't raise you by myself, especially since my career had me traveling to all parts of the world. Besides, I had already failed at marriage and wouldn't likely be married again. I thought it best that you be raised by special people, which I know John and Peg are.

Allison knew how much they wished to have a child to love. She arranged the adoption and kept me informed about you. I have many regrets in my life, Anna, but you are not one of them.

I haven't contacted you until now because I didn't want to confuse you or interfere in any way. I hope that you won't hate me. I love you, and I know that Peg and John love you as much as anyone possibly could.

Your mother,
Maarit

Peg, John, and Allison sat, waiting for Anna to finish reading. Allison and Peg exchanged furtive glances, trying to read their daughter's expression. Anna read and reread the letter while wiping her eyes with her sleeve. She hugged the letter to her breast before handing it to her mother. "Mom," she said, "Maarit did love me."

As Peg began to read it aloud to the others, Anna stood and silently left the room. She lay on the bed upstairs in her bedroom, hugged Alfie tightly, and whispered to him, "She loved me, but she didn't want me."

Anna pretended to be asleep when her mother peeked into her room and softly called her name. When no answer came, Peg rejoined the others in the kitchen. "She's pretending to be asleep," she reported. "I think it's best if we give her some space to process all this."

CHAPTER FOURTEEN

Spring 2002

N ikki Aronson stopped in the doorway of Dr. DiPorta's office and knocked on the glass of the open door. "You wanted to see me, Dr. DiPorta?"

Professor DiPorta looked up from the music score on his desk and stood to welcome her with a sweep of his hand. "Yes, thanks for stopping by. Please, sit down."

Nikki cleared her throat and moved across the room to sit at his desk. She smoothed her skirt and looked up at the professor. "How can I help you, sir?"

"Nikki," he said. "As you know, internships here at the Workshop are a two-to-three-year program. In your case, we extended it by an additional year and asked you to take on some office duties, which you excelled at. Especially in your interactions with new interns and faculty."

"Thank you. I enjoyed that part of my job."

"That was clear." He paused. "That brings me to why I asked you to meet me. Unfortunately, we cannot have you remain an intern in the program. The faculty feels that you have progressed as far as you are likely to progress here."

Nikki felt the blood drain from her face. *This couldn't be real, could it?* "If it's a matter of tuition, I'm sure that it will not be a problem for me to pay my own way," she sputtered in response.

"It's not the tuition."

"What is it then?"

DiPorta rubbed his fingers across his brow. "I understand you tried out for the Atlanta Opera; is that right?"

Nikki lowered her eyes. "Yes, it is."

"How did your audition go?"

"I thought it went well, but they didn't offer me a position."

"It's pretty tough competition," the professor noted.

"Yes, but if I could get one more year of training here, I believe I could make it next year."

DiPorta paused to consider his words carefully. "Nikki, I don't think another year would make any difference," he added gently.

Nikki's shoulders fell forward, her body shrinking into her chair.

DiPorta continued. "You're a good musician, but your singing technique isn't strong enough for the professional ranks."

"Sir, I promise I'll work extra hard this year."

"Nikki, you've been working hard for four years. Look, you'll always be a strong singer; any amateur chorus or symphony chorale would be delighted to have you sing with them. You'll have many opportunities to make music, but I'm afraid it won't be as a professional soloist."

Nikki buried her head in her hands. "But I so want it."

"Desire and hard work are not sufficient. One more year is not going to have a different result."

Nikki stood to leave. "Is that all?"

"No, not quite. I'd like to offer you a full-time position in our advancement office."

"Fundraising?"

"Yes."

"I'm not sure I could do that."

"The administration has been watching you and your interaction with our donors, other faculty, and colleagues for the past year. We think your personality is ideal for the position. We've seen you charm our donors and noted you have a knack for writing presentations." He paused again. "Are you interested?"

"What about my music? Could I still participate and take lessons?"

"Yes, that could be arranged. But you wouldn't be eligible for any starring roles; those will always go to an intern. But, as a member of a production's chorus and in the Workshop choir, I see no reason you couldn't participate when it didn't interfere with your primary duties."

Nikki shifted her weight from side to side. "Do you really think I'll never make it as a soloist? It's been my dream since I was a little girl when my dad took me to see *Carmen*."

"Let me tell you what I see," he said. "You clearly understand music. Not everyone is cut out to be a soloist. That doesn't mean you have nothing to contribute. Over the last four years, the faculty has seen a hardworking, talented individual who can't handle the pressure put on a soloist. You excel in a small group or a large section where the pressure is spread around. Your charm and grace, and the ability to make others feel comfortable, are ideal in the role I'm offering."

Nikki met DiPorta's gaze. "I really do love it here. If I can continue taking voice lessons, I may prove you wrong in a year and get a position with an opera company. I accept your offer."

"Splendid." DiPorta slipped a paper across the desk to her. "We'll start you on a salary and bonus system. You'll be working directly with our Advancement Director, Leslie Robb. Have you met her?"

"Yes, several times."

"Good, I'll let her know you've accepted the position. You can start as soon as the summer term begins. Please make an appointment to see Leslie next week. Welcome aboard. By the way, nothing would please me more than to be proven wrong."

Nikki left DiPorta's office and stopped at the desk to schedule Ms. Robb's appointment. "Have you heard?" the receptionist asked.

"Heard what?"

"One of our interns landed a spot with the Atlanta Opera Company. Isn't that fabulous?"

"Yes, that is impressive. Who was it?"

"Kay Malone."

A familiar chill crept up Nikki's neck. Her nostrils flared in anger. "That bitch," she muttered.

"I'm sorry," said the receptionist. "Did you say something?"

Nikki shook her head. "No, nothing."

"Okay, would Tuesday morning at 9:00 work for you to see Ms. Robb?"

"That would be fine," Nikki growled through gritted teeth before swiftly leaving the office.

Kay sat alone at Buck's Diner. She had taken the last booth in the back and now sat mindlessly stirring the coffee before her. Two menus remained unopened. It didn't matter. She knew it would be French toast and bacon for her, an omelet for Brian—a breakfast they had shared on many early mornings after a late rehearsal. They had tried kissing once, but shortly after they met, they looked at each other and laughed. They were musical soul mates, not destined to be lovers.

She looked at her watch again and peered through the cafe's front window. Annoyance gave way to relief as she spotted Brian entering the café. He was twenty minutes late.

Brian waved and joined her in the booth. "Relax, Kay," he said. "You're going to like the review. The performance was spectacular." He placed a newspaper on the table and shoved it toward Kay.

"Did you look at it? Is it good?"

Brian shook his head. "Nope, didn't read it. I wanted to see your face when you saw it for the first time."

She scanned through the paper and found the Arts and Theater section. The review was on the last page, tucked above the fold, and she quickly scanned it.

"Go on. Read it to me," he said.

"Okay." Kay nervously started to read the printed page out loud. "*The highlight of The Atlanta Opera Workshop's annual performance featuring its interns was Kay Malone, singing the role of Marguerite in Charles Gounod's Faust. The warmth of her voice, perfect intonation, and nuanced expression combined to make a wonderfully moving experience for one so young. She has a marvelous future ahead of her."*

Kay squealed. "They loved it."

She continued reading, *"Alan Jackson as Faust and Jonas Simmons as Mephistopheles perfectly portrayed the struggle between good and evil, love and hate. The chorus was well rehearsed and did an admirable job, although at times the sopranos seemed to be rushing a bit."*

"That's going to upset Nikki," said Brian. "She was leading the section. Go on, what else did they say?"

"The Soldiers' Chorus, ably performed by the men of the chorus, is always a thrilling part of the opera. Overall, it was a very satisfying production of the Gounod classic. These young artists are destined to delight audiences for years to come."

Kay carefully refolded the Arts and Theater section and set it beside her on the bench. "My first professional review," she murmured proudly.

"Congratulations. You should frame it."

"Naw, just a scrapbook page, I think."

"Better get a big scrapbook. You're going to need it."

"What's next for you? Have you decided?" Kay asked.

"I've gotten offers from both Eastman and Berkeley. I'll probably go to Berkeley. I like the West Coast. You?"

"Staying right here. The Atlanta Opera has offered me a position in the chorus, with the chance to play some minor roles next year. I also signed with Sarah Tomlinson Talent Agency. Sarah got me the gig in Atlanta and wants to start planning a regional concert tour. Now I really have to start expanding my repertoire."

"Double hit for Nikki," Brian mused.

"How so?"

"She's staying in Atlanta, too. The Workshop offered her a position in the Advancement Office and promised she could sing occasionally with the chorus. She also tried out for the Atlanta Opera, but didn't make the cut. You're moving up to the professional ranks, and she's staying behind with the interns."

"She'd make a great fundraiser," said Kay. "It's a real opportunity for her."

"That's what I told her, but she has dreams of being a big star. Unfortunately, it's just not going to happen. Nikki's problem is that she tends to blame others instead of realistically evaluating herself. It's sad. She has a lot to offer, but not on the stage."

"Well, I hope she does well," said Kay.

"Me, too. But watch your back. If she gets a chance to stick a knife in, she will."

CHAPTER FIFTEEN

Spring 2002

J ordan sat on the deck glider, her head in her hands. Anna stood with her back to her best friend. "Is it true?" Anna demanded.

She couldn't hear the whispered response. "Well, is it?" Anna turned on her heel to face her friend.

Jordan nodded without lifting her head.

"Why? I could see Isabella flirting and doing it, but you? How could…"

"Anna, I'm so sorry. Rob showed up at the party without you. We were dancing and drinking, and the next thing I knew, we were making out in the car, and…well…you know."

"You've been my best friend since forever. How could you do that to me?"

"I was drunk, Anna. Please, please, forgive me."

"I think you'd better go. We're done." Anna watched her friend run off the deck and disappear around the corner of the house. She felt, rather than heard, Jordan's car drive away.

Half an hour later, Anna heard the doorbell ring, but she didn't move to answer it. The doorbell rang again, demanding acknowledgment. She stormed through the house, ready to tell whoever it was to buzz off.

She opened the door and stood face-to-face with her boyfriend, Rob. His hands shoved deep in his jean's pockets, he stood straight and tall, doing his best to maintain a facade of confidence. In contrast, the realization that he had messed up big-time was all over his face. He was remorseful but still couldn't bring himself to look directly at his girlfriend.

"Anna..."

"Go to hell," she yelled and slammed the door in his face.

"What's going on?"

Anna turned to see her mother at the foot of the stairs. "Let's not tear the door off its hinges," said Peg.

Anna ran past her mother up the stairs to her room. Peg heard the door to the upstairs bedroom slam shut.

The doorbell rang again. Peg opened the door to find herself face-to-face with Rob. "Mrs. Jensen, please, I need to talk to Anna."

"She's really upset, Rob. What's going on?"

"Ask her if she'll talk to me."

"Alright, do you want to come in?"

"No thanks. I'll wait out here."

Peg climbed the steps to Anna's room and knocked.

"Go away!"

"Anna, he's waiting. Will you talk to him?" Peg said through the closed door.

"Tell him to go away. I never want to talk to him. Ever."

Peg returned to the front door. "I don't know what's happening, but she refuses to see you. I think letting her cool down for a while is best."

Anna suddenly appeared behind her mother. "Meet me on the back deck," she snarled at Rob.

Anna settled on the glider couch and held up her hand to stop Rob as he moved to sit beside her. "Stay standing. You won't be here long." Righteous anger boiled inside her. She felt her face turn red. She crossed her arms in front of her, a shield against a lover who had become an enemy.

Rob moved to the side of the deck and shrank under his girl-friend's venomous stare. Despite his discomfort, he gave reconciliation one last shot. "Please, let me explain. I'm so sorry. I got drunk. It won't happen again."

"Doesn't matter," Anna shot back angrily. "I don't care if it happens again. It happened once, and that's enough for me. It's too bad I spent all those years with you. Time wasted. I know Jordan can't drink very much, but you can. I guess that you got her drunk and took advantage of the situation. I've heard rumors about you. Now I know there's truth behind them. In time, I'll forgive Jordan, but not you. Leave now. Don't come back." Anna turned sharply on her heel and left Rob standing alone on the deck.

Peg waited for her in the kitchen. "Do you want to talk about it?"

"Not much to say really. He cheated. I found out about it and sent him packing. End of story."

"Was that what you and Jordan were talking about before he got here?"

"Yep."

"Oh, Anna. I'm so sorry. You two have been friends for a long time."

Anna rubbed her eyes and swallowed hard. It felt like an elephant was standing on her chest. In the course of a few hours, she had lost a boyfriend and a best friend.

"I'll probably call her up in a couple of days and we'll work through it."

"Do you think you can get past what she did?" Peg poured two glasses of iced tea and rummaged in the cupboard for some cookies.

Anna shrugged sadly. "I don't know. You know, actually, she did me a favor. When she gets drunk, she's an easy target, which confirms what I had heard. The last thing I need is a man who does that."

"Your dad will be pleased."

"Dad?" Anna's forehead furrowed in confusion. "What do you mean by that?"

Peg's cheeks reddened, and her body language became flustered. "Uh…Oops, I think I spoke out of turn. You'll have to ask him about it."

Anna shook her head. "The last thing I want to do is talk to my dad about my love life. Somehow, I don't think that's a good idea."

"Probably not," Peg chuckled. "I'm a little surprised you're taking this so well. How are you *really* doing?"

"Bummed. Angry. And plenty of other mixed-up feelings. I'll probably cry myself to sleep tonight. I'm more relieved than sad. Hurt that the jerk seduced my best friend," Anna shrugged. "But, Mom, this really sucks."

"Yes. Yes it does."

"How many times have I broken up with that jerk?"

"At least once a year since you were in high school. All told, probably five or six times."

"Why do I always take him back?"

"That's the million-dollar question. Why do you?"

Anna twisted her hair, slumped onto the couch, and looked at the door. "I think I'm scared."

"Scared? Of what?"

"Of being alone."

"Is that why you didn't move into the dorm or go away to college?"

"I...I don't know. I've never made that connection."

"Your father and I were delighted you stayed around and went to college here, but we were surprised when you decided to live at home. Your first year."

"I thought of moving out, but this was easier."

"Took the easy way, huh?"

"I guess."

"When did you become afraid of being alone?"

Anna thought for a long moment. When she spoke, the words came out in a whisper. "When Maarit died. I think that's the first time I realized that, someday, I would be alone."

"So, you always take Rob back because you don't want to be alone. Look, you're an attractive woman. You're bright. You're talented. You have friends."

"Yeah, friends that sleep with my boyfriend."

Peg laughed. "Yeah, but you know you two will get to be friends again. Maybe not best friends, but certainly not enemies."

Anna smiled, "Yeah, I know. That's not the real issue, is it?"

"No, it's not."

"Mom, what should I do?"

Peg reached over and tucked her daughter's hair behind her ear. "Be yourself."

"Easier said than done."

"Yes, it is. But true nonetheless." Peg paused. "And don't take that jerk back. He's not worth it."

CHAPTER SIXTEEN

April 2002

Peg and Anna sat arm-in-arm in front of John's casket. Peg had arranged for a private time for the two of them to say their private goodbyes before the visitation and funeral began. The serenity of the empty chapel took Anna by surprise. She felt the weight of sadness but also gratitude for the intimacy of the moment with her mother.

"The first time I noticed your father," Peg said. "He was wearing tights and a doublet with a ruffle around his neck. We were in college. He was recruited for *Romeo and Juliet*, as well as other fencing team members. I forget which of the feuding clans he was part of."

She paused to dab her eyes with a crumpled tissue.

"I don't think he had ever been in a play. He was like a kid in a candy store. Everywhere he looked, he saw something new. He was always craning his neck to see what was in the rigging or behind a curtain. I was a first-year student and part of the stage crew. In the green room, at dress rehearsal, he finally noticed me. I'd seen him at the first run through. God, he had such scrawny legs."

Peg's voice wavered. "Did I ever tell you where your father and I went on our first date?"

"Yes, many times, but tell it again; I love the story." Ann rested her head on her mother's shoulder.

"We were at the cast party. He finally got enough nerve to come over and talk to me. He was still halfway in character, so he swaggered a bit. He wasn't obnoxious, just a guy trying to impress the girls, especially me."

A gentle rain started outside, and the patter on the church's roof was oddly comforting.

Peg continued. "He asked me if I would go on a date with him. I thought he'd take me to some nice, romantic place for dinner, but no, he asked if I'd like to go to a fencing competition. I was dumbfounded. Before I could recover from my surprise, he hemmed and hawed, said we could go somewhere else if I liked. I told him that I would be happy to go with him. I didn't know anything about fencing, but it was clearly something important to him."

Thunder rumbled in the distance, and the rain intensified. She smiled at the memory of her husband standing at the kitchen window watching it rain. "He loved the cliche *'April showers bring May flowers.'* He always followed that comment up with 'Besides, we need the rain.'"

"So, we went. It was fascinating. He gave a running commentary describing the thrusts, feints, parries, and ripostes. It was a world I hadn't known existed." Peg sighed heavily. "The best part was your dad. He showed me something he loved on our first outing as a couple. Before the date, I was interested; after the date, I was smitten. From that point on, we were always together."

Anna wiped a tear from her eyes.

"He was really proud of you, Anna, always telling people about your latest exploits."

Anna's eyes welled up with new tears. "Really? He never told me he was proud of me."

"Typical," Peg said. "I thought he would burst his buttons after your high school musical."

Anna smiled. *"Marian the Librarian.* That was a fun time."

Minutes passed in silence. "The flowers are sure nice," Peg noted. "Did you see the bouquet Kay sent?"

Anna nodded. "That was thoughtful of her. It was so nice of her to come from Atlanta for the funeral."

Peg rose and went to stand by her husband's casket. Her hands lightly rested on the edge as she spoke. "I can't believe how fast the cancer took him. Oh, John, I still need you."

Anna stood and put her arm around her mother's shoulder. "You're strong. You'll do fine, and I'll be around to help you. I'm going to stay in Ellston. I'll try to get a job at the college."

Peg glanced at her daughter with a mixture of surprise and concern. "You've got your own life to live. You don't have to stay here."

"I hate the Metro Area," Anna said. "Too much noise, too much traffic. I'll also be able to study with Dr. Keizer. It's what I want to do."

"You've got to fly the coop someday, Anna. Don't let me keep you here. The world's a great big place."

"Ellston is a big enough world for me." Anna looked at her watch. "It's time, Mom. Are you ready?"

"Give me a moment alone with your dad, okay?"

Anna nodded and slipped from the chapel into the lobby, where Paul and Allison were waiting. "He was a good man," Allison said as she embraced her niece.

Anna buried her head on her aunt's shoulder and let new sobs flow freely. Izzy rushed to her friend's side and hugged her. Several of John's friends and coworkers stood in quiet, respectful conversation.

The funeral director approached the group. "It's almost time to begin." He led the small group to an adjoining room for a few quiet moments. After Father Sean's short meditation, the visitation began. Outside, Mother Nature voiced her disapproval and sorrow.

~ ═══ ~

After the funeral concluded, a sober procession of cars and mourners made their way to the gravesite. Tears were shed as the casket was lowered into the ground. Then, it was over. Not yet willing to face the empty house, Peg went home with Allison. Flanked by Paul and Kay, Anna leaned against Paul's rental car, not quite ready to leave but unwilling to watch the cemetery workers fill in the grave site.

"It was a lovely service," Kay said.

Paul nodded and murmured his agreement.

"Bullshit," Anna exploded unable to hold back her anger and grief any longer. "It was horrible."

Paul took his cousin in his arms and let her bury her face in his broad shoulder as her fists pounded his chest. "I want my daddy," Anna wailed. Sobs racked her body as Paul held her tightly, each sob stabbing his soul. Kay wrapped her arms around them, and the three cried together. Each cried for Anna's loss. Each cried for their lost parent.

When no more tears were left to be shed, Paul helped Anna into the car. "I'll take her to Mom's house. She and Peg are staying there tonight." He turned to Kay, "Are you staying at the Riverside?"

Kay nodded.

"I'll meet you there, in the lounge."

She nodded again and leaned in to kiss her sister. "I'll see you tomorrow before I leave."

Anna hugged her sister. "Thanks."

When Paul joined her in the Riverside lounge, the glass of wine in Kay's hand was still half-full. Not waiting to take his order, the waitress brought his usual Glenlivet on the rocks.

"I'm surprised they remembered," Paul said, answering the unspoken question on Kay's face. "I used to come here before I moved to Kansas City last year."

"Do they have you writing obits down there?" Kay's voice was teasing.

Paul grinned. "No, I actually was promoted from that. After you left for Atlanta, the *Herald-Review* moved me to general reporting and feature writing. That's what they hired me to do in Kansas City."

"Congrats. Sounds like you're moving into the big time."

"Just like you. Anna told me you're now singing with the Atlanta Opera."

"I'm in the chorus and get a few minor roles here and there. My agent also has me doing some touring around the country. It's great."

They each sipped their drinks to avoid an awkward silence.

"Anna sure took it hard today. Is she okay?" Kay asked.

"She's only nineteen, that's pretty young to have to deal with losing a parent."

"It's not easy at any age."

"No," Paul said. "It's not."

The two sat in thoughtful silence. The usual soft chatter between the waitress and bartender and low voices from nearby tables strangely enhanced their contentment in each other's company. Neither felt compelled to speak, and neither wanted the moment to end.

A boisterous group of hotel guests entering the lobby ended the moment. The group's loud laughter at the jokes they told amid the shouts to the bartender to turn on some dancing music instantly changed the atmosphere in the room. Kay looked at Paul and shook her head. They quickly finished their drinks and went to the lobby.

The pair hugged, said their goodbyes, and promised to keep in touch, knowing it would not happen.

CHAPTER SEVENTEEN

August 2005

Hi Brian,
What's new in California? I'm getting some guest soloist shots
here in the Southeast. I've been to Florida twice and landed
a supporting role with the Atlanta Opera. Sarah keeps telling
me to be patient and develop the repertoire. She thinks I
have a couple more years of seasoning before the big break.
—K

> *The solo shots sound like fun. Would you be interested in*
> *doing a recital with me in San Francisco? It'd be fun to work*
> *together again. Maybe Sarah can get you a couple of gigs out*
> *here to make the trip worthwhile. What do you think?*
> *—Brian*

I talked to Sarah. She's got an idea for some guest gigs in Monterey and
Sacramento. She'll contact you to arrange dates and so on. She says it's
about time for me to get a little exposure on the West Coast. Besides, I
can stop in Phoenix and see my dad. He got tired of the cold and moved
to Arizona. How about some Dvorak and Britten for the recital?
—K

Sounds good. Any ideas for a theme we could use?
—B

How about Legends? Britten wrote an opera
based on Paul Bunyan. There are all sorts of
music we could tie to Legendary Songs.
—K

I like it. We could do songs about legends, as well as music
that has become legendary. Both approaches would work. I
could try out some new material I've been working on.
—B

Sounds like a plan.
—K

September 2005

The day after Brian and Kay's recital, Kay and her agent, Sarah Tomlinson, sat in the conference room of the San Francisco Plaza Hotel. The windows, more like walls than windows, provided a view of the bustling downtown and mid-morning activity. The two women, both preferring their casual attire to the formality of a business suit, sipped the tea and enjoyed the scones Sarah had ordered from the hotel catering service.

"I was totally shocked to see you last night," Kay remarked. "What brought you across the country? Surely not just my recital?"

"No, not just that. I was scouting some new talent over at the San Francisco Opera. They have a finishing school, which is not unlike the one you went to in Atlanta. Your recital was a bonus."

"Did you like what you heard?"

"Absolutely. You and Brian make a great team. It's always fun to listen to the two of you." Sarah paused. "How's it going with your new business manager?"

"Couldn't be better. My God, Sarah, he's become so much more than my business manager. I never thought I'd feel this way about anyone. Syd makes me feel like a…I don't know what. It's been a whirlwind. It's so nice not having to worry about paying bills or balancing the checkbook. He takes care of all that. It's wonderful."

Sarah pulled out a notebook. "I do have a few things we need to talk about. A little business mixed in with the pleasure. I got a strange request from Syd the other day. Thought I'd better make sure it's what you want."

"Oh?"

"Last week, he sent me an email indicating that in the future, I should send the invoices directly to him instead of you. Since it was a change in procedure, I wanted to know if that was what you wanted."

"I didn't ask him to do that, but it makes sense. I've turned all the business affairs over to him. He's managing the money for me."

"I see." An unsettling silence fell over the room.

Sensing Sarah was holding back, Kay pressed for more details. "Is that an unusual request?"

"It is. Typically, this early in an artist's career, they want me to send the invoices to them directly. Helps them get a feel for how the business works."

Kay sat back in the chair and crossed her arms across her chest. "You didn't fly all this way to ask about that. There's more to it."

"There is." Sarah looked at her friend and client with concern in her eyes. "Syd had a second request that really did bother me. It was a request I wanted to discuss with you face-to-face, not through email or a phone call."

A chill ran through Kay's body. She cleared her throat, laced her fingers tightly, and fought to calm her voice. "Sarah, do we have a problem?"

"Potentially, yes. Syd wanted me to clear all future bookings with him first. He said that, as your manager…"

"My manager?"

Sarah nodded and paused for a sip of tea. It was clear that the conversation made her uncomfortable, but she was determined to be heard.

"That's the word he used. He indicated that he would organize the information, consult with you before committing to any gigs, and then inform me of your decision." Sarah leaned forward and looked directly into Kay's eyes. "Did you ask him to do that?"

Kay bit her lip. "No, I didn't. I don't understand."

"That's what confused me. All of my clients want me to contact them directly with any potential gigs. That's the way I've always worked with you. Together, we've mapped out a strategy to advance your career and prepare you for the big opportunity. I thought we had a good working relationship, so I had to check it out with you directly."

Kay shook her head. "I don't know what to say. I've not instructed him to change how you and I work together. I'll get it straightened out. I don't want to change a thing."

"I'm very glad to hear that. I don't think I can be effective if everything has to go through a third party before it gets to you." Sarah pulled more papers out of her briefcase. "There is a third issue."

"Oh?" *What's going on? I've never had trouble like this.* Kay frowned, afraid of Sarah's following statement.

"Was there something wrong with my last two invoices?"

Kay's brow furrowed. "Not that I saw. I approved them both for payment as soon as they arrived."

Sarah slid photocopies of the bill and check across the table. "Well, the checks for each invoice were several hundred dollars short of full payment."

Kay's face flushed. "I...uh...I don't know what to say. I approved them for full payment. I'm sure there must be a mistake. I'll check into it right away. I'm so embarrassed."

"No worries," Sarah said. "I'm sure it was just a mix-up, but I thought I'd better check."

Anxious to forget the unpleasant revelations, Sarah switched to business mode and opened the folder she had placed on the table.

"I've been putting some ideas together for you. It may be time to relocate from Atlanta to the West Coast. It's time to move you up a notch and build a more substantial reputation. I've been in touch with the Seattle and San Francisco Opera companies. They are interested in jointly offering you a two-year contract, with the option to extend. Two operas a year, one in each location, combined with a few solo engagements with West Coast symphonies. You could even squeeze in a recital or two with Brian, if you wanted to. What do you think?"

Grateful to talk about more positive topics, a smile tugged at Kay's lips. "That's interesting. But since I live in the East, why not move to New York? My dream is to one day sing with the Metropolitan Opera company."

"I thought about that, but I don't think you're quite ready. The New York establishment is a tough nut to crack. You don't have enough experience yet. The East Coast opera companies are traditional, and they like seasoned professionals. Frankly, you need the seasoning. This move would give that to you."

"Seattle and San Francisco? I don't know much about them."

"By opera standards, they're relatively young companies. Seattle has been around since the 1960s, while San Francisco has been around since the 1920s. Both like to do newer works."

"That's appealing."

Sarah continued. "Given last night's program, I thought it might be. By the way, I loved the Ives next to the Dvorak, what a combination."

Kay laughed. "That was fun, a little quirky, but fun."

"That's why the West Coast would be a good idea. San Francisco and Seattle programs present two or three works by contemporary composers and librettists each season. Could be interesting. And, you could unpack your suitcase for at least a couple of years. You'll want to make San Francisco your home base. More centrally located."

Kay nodded. "Okay. Can you set up a meeting with them?"

Sarah grinned. "I took the liberty."

Kay laughed. "I should have known. When is it?"

"Two weeks."

"I'd like you to be there for those meetings," said Kay.

"I was planning on it."

─── ══ ───

Syd strode into the Plaza Hotel suite late in the afternoon, looking the part of lord of the manor. He adjusted the cuffs of his shirt to show just the right amount of sleeve at his wrist under the sports coat. He was a tall, meticulously groomed man who projected an image of competence and high status, with a touch of arrogance.

At the sound of the door opening, Kay looked up from the music score she was studying and checked her watch. "I've been waiting for you. What held you up?"

"Sorry, I met some people, and we got talking. The contacts I made are very valuable for the future," Syd said. He leaned over to kiss Kay and then sat on the small couch in the corner of the suite. "How did your meeting with Sarah go this morning?"

"Fine. She had some interesting ideas."

"I've been wanting to talk to you about her," Syd said. "I'm not sure she's the right agent for you."

"Oh, why not?"

"She should be pushing you faster. You should be singing at the Metropolitan Opera, not these small regional gigs. I think she's holding you back."

"What are you suggesting?"

"I should handle all the bookings for you. I should be your agent as well as your business manager."

Kay's throat tightened as she braced herself for a fight. "Have...have you ever been an agent for anyone?"

"No, not exactly, but I've watched how your career has been managed. I can do it. And do it better."

"I see. Do you have contacts in the music world?"

"A few." Syd moved across the room and took Kay's hands in his. His pale blue eyes looked deeply into hers. "Kay, we can zoom to the top. We don't need Sarah."

Kay pulled her hands free. "An interesting choice of words. Don't you mean 'me?'"

"Yes, of course I do," Syd hastily backpedaled and smiled disarmingly. "Besides, haven't I freed you up to concentrate on your singing? We can make a great team and soar to the top. I think it's time to make a bold move to New York."

"New York?"

"That's where the action is. That's where we belong."

"We?" Kay felt a flush of anger creep into her cheeks.

"I mean you."

Does he really think I'm foolish enough to turn my career over to someone who isn't a professional agent? I may be from a small town in Minnesota, but I'm not a rube.

Unwilling to stay silent, Kay spoke quietly. "That's an interesting idea, Syd. What do you know about the opera scene in New York?"

"Well, I know the Metropolitan Opera is where you belong."

Kay barely concealed her anger. "Tell me, do you know Beverly Sills, or Maria Callas, or Birgit Nilsson?"

"I think so. Didn't we meet one of them a couple of months ago?"

"That would have been quite a trick. All three of them are dead. You don't know anything about arguably the best three sopranos of the twentieth century, and you think you're ready to tackle New York?"

"I can learn anything I need to know."

"Is this why you told Sarah Tomlinson that all future bookings should go through you first?"

"I didn't."

Kay stifled the urge to jump up from her seat. "Then why would she tell me that you did? One of you is lying."

Syd's perfectly manicured hands fidgeted with his cuffs to buy time. "Well, she may have misunderstood. I just said that if I could organize the proposals, I could make your life easier if she sent the information to me first."

Kay rose from the desk where she had been studying the music score. She moved to stand directly in front of Syd, still seated on the couch. She stood close, leaving no space for him to stand. She leaned over him and wagged a finger in his face.

"That's not the way I want it," she spoke calmly, but her words were forced and tense. "I'll deal with my agent directly, not through you."

"Okay. Okay. Fine." Syd sputtered defensively as he tried to slide to the opposite end of the couch to escape Kay's anger. "If that's what you want. I just think we could be moving faster than we are."

"*We*, again?" Kay's voice was icy cold.

"You know what I mean." Syd tried to placate and soothe Kay's temper. He rose to his feet and attempted to massage her shoulders. He leaned in to kiss her neck, but she stepped away and turned to face him, brushing aside his clumsy attempt.

"Sarah tells me the last two invoices were not paid in full. There were several hundred dollars deducted from the payment."

Kay's glare further unsettled Syd. He winced and backed away. He turned to face Kay and tried to take the offensive and bluff his way out of the trap. "Kay," he raised his voice. "She charged you too much, so I reduced the payment."

"Syd." Kay's voice matched Syd's intensity. "I approved the full amount. The invoices were consistent with the terms of my contract. You had no right to change those amounts."

"I'm sorry. I probably should have talked to you first. But as your business manager, I thought it was in your best interest." Syd hung his head in a weak attempt to act humbled.

Kay's body was rigid with anger, and her eyes snapped with fury. She moved one step closer to Syd, a move that caused him to lose his balance and topple onto the couch.

"Here's what's really interesting," she added. Her tone was calm, but her body language said otherwise. "I checked with the bank today, and there were two cash withdrawals from the checking account, dated the same day as the checks for the invoices. When I added the withdrawals and the checks and compared them with the invoice amounts, lo and behold, they matched exactly. I didn't take any cash out at that time. The only other person who has access to my checking account is you. Explain that."

"Well, I—"

Syd's guilty expression was all the confirmation Kay needed. *How could she have been so blind?* Resigned to the fact that she had been deceived, it took every ounce of remaining strength not to throw something at the person she had once trusted. Quietly, she voiced her final blow to the relationship.

"There were also three other cash withdrawals from the checking account that I did not authorize. Explain those."

Syd didn't answer. His bluff hadn't worked. His attempts to distract and deflect had failed. He looked at the floor, his shoulders slumped, and all the bluster and bravado drained out of him.

Kay shook her head. "You've been stealing from me in the most inept way imaginable. You're fired as my business manager. Go back to Atlanta. Pack your stuff and get out."

"Kay, don't I mean anything to you?"

Kay pointed at the door. "I've already talked to the apartment building superintendent in Atlanta. He's changing the locks on my apartment. He'll let you in and stay with you while you get your stuff. You can consider the amount you stole as your severance pay."

CHAPTER EIGHTEEN

November 2011

Hi Anna,

I'm going to be in Duluth on Saturday, February 4, for a gig with the symphony. Can you come to the concert? I've got an extra day in my schedule. We could hang out on Sunday, go up the shore a bit. Please, try to make it.
Love, Kay

> *Count me in. Where, when, etc.*
> *Love, Anna*

The concert is at 7:30 p.m. at the Duluth Entertainment Convention Center (DECC). I'll leave a ticket at the box office. You can stay with me in the suite at the Fitgers, an old brewery converted into an elegant hotel. Meet me backstage after the concert. We'll go to the reception together, then make our escape. Can you stay until Monday?
Kay

> *Sis, I'll have to leave Monday morning. Got a meeting late in the afternoon in the Twin Cities. See you on the 4th. This is going to be great. BTW, what brings you all the way to Duluth from San Francisco? Are you on tour?*
> *Anna*

Yep, the Tour starts in Fargo, then Duluth, then on to Madison, Kansas City, and ends up in Toledo. My first tour in the Midwest. See you in February.
Kay

February 4, 2012

Anna made her way backstage after Kay's curtain calls and encore. A group of musicians and society elites, dressed in furs, tuxedos, and finely tailored suits, stood in a semicircle facing Kay and the maestro. Anna watched the courtiers gently jockeying for position before the star and conductor. One woman had positioned herself at the front and center of the circle. None dared elbow her out of the way. She clearly had clout, expected deference, and had enjoyed it for many years.

Reluctant to insert herself into the scene, Anna waited in the wings, watching the crew clear the stage. In short order, the chairs and music stands were in racks, and the conductor's podium was on a cart. Only the acoustic panels were left in place for tomorrow's performance.

Kay spotted Anna, excused herself, and rushed to embrace her. She took Anna by the hand and led her back to the courtiers. "Maestro Hochstein, everyone, I'd like you to meet my sister, Anna Jensen. She drove up today from Ellston for the concert. I think it's the first time she's heard me perform."

The maestro took Anna's hand, bowed to her, and crooned in a thick German accent, "My dear, it's delightful to meet you. You are as radiant as your lovely sister."

Turning to Kay, without letting Anna's hand go, he said, "She must join us at the reception."

Anna blushed. "Thank you. That's very kind of you. I'd love to."

Kay turned to the assembled group, "Thank you all for coming tonight. We'll see you at the reception. Come on, Anna. Help me change."

Safely in the dressing room with the door closed, Anna burst into laughter. "Is he for real?"

"Oh yes. The accent is real, and so is the old-world charm. Especially when pretty young girls are around, he's quite harmless and an excellent musician. This is my first time working with him. It's been fun."

Kay quickly changed out of her formal gown and into an elegant suit for the reception. "I'll have to mingle tonight. I'm afraid you'll have to pretty much fend for yourself. Sorry. It comes with the territory for me."

"Don't worry, I can amuse myself. Who's all going to be there?"

Kay smiled and shot a playful look at her sister. "The maestro, of course. I'm sure he'll pay attention to you. Most of the people you met backstage were members of the orchestra, especially those holding endowed chairs, other major donors, and honored guests, such as the mayors of Duluth and Superior. Food and wine, the usual stuff."

Kay checked her appearance in the full-length mirror before continuing. Her forest green pantsuit made her eyes even more vibrant.

"A small combo from the orchestra will provide music. You may meet a cute trumpet player but watch out for the oboe players. The back pressure on those double reeds wreaks havoc with their brains." Kay winked.

Anna shook her head and rolled her eyes. "Will you have to stay late?"

"Until close to the end. Probably eleven or so."

~ ═══ ~

At the reception, Anna lingered off to the side of the room, nursing a glass of wine and sneaking peeks at her watch. Several guests had stopped by to welcome her and then gone off to the cocktail schmoozing. The maestro had stopped to make polite conversation before he left to flatter the ego of the symphony board president.

"My dear, you look absolutely bored to tears." An unfamiliar voice startled Anna, and when she turned, she immediately recognized the woman who had been at the center of the backstage entourage. "Oh, I hope it wasn't too obvious," she joked.

"I'm bored to tears, and I know everyone. I'm Ellen Jacobsen." The woman positioned herself directly in front of Anna.

Though the same height as Anna, she projected authority and competence. Her dress was made of tailored linen and was accompanied by a cream-colored jacket. The flawless fabric was adorned with a brooch that must have belonged to the woman's grandmother, and it spoke of an elegant, refined, and timeless style. But her eyes, crystal clear despite the age suggested by her weathered face, projected her strength and determination.

"It's a pleasure to meet you." Anna offered her hand.

"Come on, let's sit down over there. Whoever thought that heels should be part of a woman's couture had to have been a man or a masochist."

Anna laughed. "You are so right."

The two found a comfortable settee in a corner overlooking the harbor and the Aerial Lift Bridge. The light snow glowed and sparkled under the bridge lights and a full moon.

"I love this view of the harbor," Ellen said. "Even with the cars crossing the bridge back and forth, there's a peacefulness this late on a winter's evening."

"I've never been to Duluth in the winter. Our trips were always to visit the state parks up the shore during the summer."

"Which one is your favorite?"

"Oh, Gooseberry Falls, without a doubt. Kay and I are planning to go there tomorrow."

"Be sure to wear ice treads on your boots. The trails can be treacherous. Winter and early spring are my favorite times to visit Gooseberry. There is something magical about the sound of water rushing behind an icy curtain. Ellen paused and looked directly at Anna. "May I ask you a personal question, my dear?"

Anna nodded.

"Backstage, your sister said this is the first time you ever heard her perform. Is that true?"

"Yes, it is."

Ellen waited, silently asking for further clarification as her perfectly manicured nails gently drummed on her champagne glass.

"We're half-sisters. She's a few years older than me. We were raised in different households."

"She's very talented."

"I agree. I'll be sure to tell her you think so."

"Did you inherit musical talent as well?"

"I play the piano and sing, though not nearly as well as Kay. Mrs. Jacobsen..."

"Please, call me Ellen." Her warm and sincere voice was an invitation to friendship rather than a command of authority.

"Ellen, you seem to be probing for information. May I ask why?"

"I'm sorry, my dear. Just being nosy. I'm very impressed with your sister and curious about you." Ellen brushed a non-existent piece of lint off her skirt.

"I'm afraid I'm not terribly interesting. Kay is the one going places. I live in my small town, work, care for my mother, and write an occasional ditty."

Ellen perked up. "Write?"

"Oh, it's nothing really, and please, don't mention it to anyone. Especially to Kay. I wouldn't want to be compared to her."

Ellen removed her glasses and let them hang from the chain around her neck. "I have a feeling about you. If you ever find enough courage to step out from under your sister's shadow—and I grant you it's likely to be a very big shadow—you will do amazing things."

Kay approached the settee. "Are you two solving all the problems of the world? You seem to be having a very serious conversation."

Ellen and Anna stood to include Kay in the conversation. "I was telling Anna that I think you will have a fabulous career, and we in Duluth will one day say, 'We heard her when.' It was a wonderful concert. Thank you for braving our northern Minnesota winters. You brought warmth to our frozen city," Ellen shared as she perched her glass back on her slender nose. "Safe travels."

Sunday, February 5

The sisters followed the waiter across the diner's black-and-white checkered floor. Lake Superior's expanse of open water, beyond the icy shore, stretched beyond the horizon. The sun, barely above the invisible tree line of Wisconsin's western edge, sent a line of light dancing on the waves.

"Bring a pot of hot coffee, please," Anna said to the waiter as they sat on the crisp blue and white booth seats. Each looked over the other's shoulder at the lists of fresh pies on the reader board dominating the opposing walls.

"French toast and bacon, without a doubt," Anna said as she returned the menu to the waiter.

"Me, too," Kay said. "And let's order a fresh apple pie for later!" She wrapped her hands around the warm white mug.

"I'll bring the pie out when you've finished breakfast." The waiter collected the menus and returned to the kitchen.

"Gooseberry Falls is fifteen minutes up the shore, and you'll need the calories and caffeine for the hiking we're going to do," Anna noted as she watched another group of hungry diners file in.

"At least the sun is shining, and with no wind, it will be a pleasant walk." Kay laughed. "Notice I said walk, not hike."

The two devoured the food and settled back into the booth to enjoy a last cup of coffee. The sun, now higher in the sky, cast a wider line across the open water. The ice shelf stretched a couple of hundred yards beyond the shore. It would still be a month or two before the ore ships ping these waters again.

Kay leaned back and blissfully sighed before turning her attention to her sister. She couldn't help but notice how much she had changed from the awkward thirteen-year-old she had met so many years before.

"Whatever happened to you and Rob. You dated for years, and then suddenly, he wasn't mentioned in any of your emails. I don't remember seeing him at your dad's funeral."

"That's because he wasn't there. We broke up. Ages ago."

"That's not the first time. You always got back together."

"Not this time." Anna let out a snort and shook her head.

"C'mon. *Details.*" Kay teased as she refilled their coffee cups.

"Long story short, he seduced my best friend after a party, and I told him to get lost, permanently."

"Your best friend?"

"Yeah—Jordan. I don't think you ever met her, but we'd been friends since second grade."

"That's awful."

"Strange thing is, I miss her more than him."

"Can you and she get past this?"

"I don't know. We'll see. How about your love life?" asked Anna. "Anyone on the horizon?"

Kay shrugged and fiddled with her fork. "I thought I had found 'the one,' but turns out he was stealing from me. Since then, I've never in one place long enough to develop any relationships. Someday, maybe."

Anna looked out the window at the lake. "Do you remember the first time we met?"

Kay averted her eyes. Her jaw tightened. "Yes. At the wake." The emotions of that day flooded Kay's mind. The joy of meeting Anna for the first time. The surprise of loving Anna the moment she hugged her. The coldness she felt toward her uncle, the priest. The sadness combined with rage at seeing her mother's body, so still. The regret of not having had a mother when growing up. The love a six-year-old girl had for her mother, leaning over to kiss her good night. The instantaneous combination of emotions overwhelmed her.

"We had started talking about mother, and suddenly, you tensed up and needed to leave. Do you remember?"

Kay nodded, almost imperceptibly.

"You said that one day we'd have a nice long talk. Is today that day?" Anna's face could not hide her hopefulness.

Kay ran her finger around the rim of the coffee mug. "This has been such a wonderful weekend. It's the first time you and I have spent any real time together., Let's not spoil it by talking about her."

"Okay. But someday?" Anna hid her disappointment by picking up the cup to finish the last of her coffee.

"Yes. Someday."

The parking lot at Gooseberry Falls was only half-full, so Anna had no trouble finding parking near the visitor's center. The snow and ice crunched under her tires, and she swung her car into the spot.

"Here," Anna said, handing a box to Kay. "I brought an extra pair of ice treads for you. Put these over your boots. The ice can be dangerous."

Kay slipped the treads on and pulled the coat hood over her head. "Tell me again," she shivered. "Why did I leave warm, sunny California to do a concert here in February?"

Anna laughed. "C'mon. Once you get over the shock, it's not so bad. It's like jumping into a lake. Once you start to swim, you forget about the cold."

"You've lived up here too long. I think your brain's frozen."

The sisters picked their way up the ice-covered path, past the visitor's center, toward the upper falls. The winter silence grudgingly gave way to the occasional car rumbling across the Gooseberry bridge, and then quickly returned. The crisp winter air filled their lungs with freshness, and the birds happily sang their approval.

Abruptly, Anna stopped and held up a mittened hand. "Listen. Hear it?"

Kay slipped the hood off her head. "Is that the falls? I thought they'd be frozen solid."

"I did, too. Last night, Ellen told me to stop before we got to the falls and listen. They're frozen over, but the water continues to flow under the ice. She was right. The sound is magical."

The two picked their way gingerly across the ice patches under the bridge. A few steps further, they stood opposite the upper falls. The muted roar of the water rushing under the ice cut through the cold air. They stood silently awe of the shrouded falls and snow-covered banks. Below the falls, the moving water had not frozen over and spilled out from under the ice.

Anna broke the spell. "Why don't you ever come home?"

Kay pulled her hood back on. "Too many memories. Couldn't wait to get out of there."

"Was it that bad?"

"It was."

"Why didn't you go away to college instead of staying home?"

Kay shrugged. "Money, and my father. Dad wanted me to stay, and I loved Dr. Keizer's music lessons. When I got the chance to go to Atlanta, I jumped at it. I love the big city. You can go anywhere and be unknown."

"That's ironic, Sis," said Anna. "Now you're building a career that will make you a celebrity. You'll be known wherever you go."

"That's different. I may be known, but I'll be in control. People won't know my private life and my history. That'll all be hidden. They'll only know what I let them know."

"What's so bad about people wanting to know your history? That's small-town life. It's like being wrapped up in a big, comfortable quilt in front of a fireplace in the middle of a snowstorm." Anna shivered and crossed her arms for extra warmth.

"Precisely," said Kay. "That's small-town life. I hated it." She kicked at a snow clump and watched it scatter across the ground.

Anna shoved her mittened hands deep in her coat pockets. "I guess I just don't understand wanting to leave and never return. I was delighted to get a job and stay in Ellston. Everywhere I go, people smile and say '*Hi.*'"

"What I remember," said Kay. "Was the scandal my mother caused. Wherever I went, I could feel people's eyes looking at my back and whispering, 'What a pity her mother left. Shameful.'"

"That must have been hard."

Kay turned to her sister, her face a dark cloud. The sting of the shame she had felt then began to return, fueling her resentment toward Anna for bringing up the topic. "I don't want to talk about it. I've already said more than I wanted to."

"You've got to talk about it someday."

"Maybe, but not today. Let's go."

Neither sister spoke on the walk back to the parking lot, the silence punctuated by the crunch of the ice treads on the path. Anna touched her sister's arm while in the car. "Kay, I'm sorry. Don't be angry with me. You're my only sister; sometimes my nosiness gets in the way."

Kay hugged her sister warmly and lovingly. "It's okay. Every time I think of Ellston, the first thing that comes to my mind is my...*our* mother lying in that casket, and all the gossip that went around town when she left. I used to get teased about it at school. The only things I remember fondly are my music, Dr. K., and you."

She tipped her head back, drew a deep, calming breath. The cold air stinging her lungs was invigorating, but a reminder that she wasn't used to the frigid temps. "C'mon, it's cold and I'm hungry, let's head back for dinner."

CHAPTER NINETEEN

July 2013

T he house was finally quiet.

The last mourner and well-wisher hugged Anna and left. The ladies from the church had cleaned the kitchen and put the remaining dishes in the dishwasher. The rhythmic swishing of the water against the machine walls was oddly comforting to her.

"Mom, I remember," she said to the empty room. "You always told me helping others was a blessing."

Her late mother had been one of the church ladies who considered it one's human obligation to ease the burdens of others. This time, the church ladies came to her daughter's aid in a time of need.

Anna wandered around the living room. She couldn't bring herself to sit in the recliner, her father's favorite chair, or settle on the couch where she and Peg had cried, fought, and laughed. She wandered the room, picking up random items from the shelves and the cases her father had built to hold her mother's treasures.

She teared up at the memories evoked by the teaspoon collection gathered from places friends had visited. Her mother had been particularly fond of delicate blown-glass figurines of ballerinas, swans, and skaters on mirrored ponds. They remained lined up proudly on a shelf but were now slowly collecting a fine layer of dust. Next to them was the Cyprus creche from the holy land that her mother kept out all year.

My parents loved this house, thought Anna. *They never saw a need to move. It was home, and home was where they stayed. Dad would sit in his recliner, and Mom on the couch in the evening, and one would say to the other, 'There's no place like home,' and then laugh as if it were some kind of inside joke.*

"I remember, Mom," Ann spoke again to the empty room. "I remember the day that I cried so hard when I broke up with my first real boyfriend in high school. I was sixteen and sure that the whole world would shut down and take note of my broken heart. You didn't laugh at me. Instead, you sat with me on the couch and let me cry it out."

Anna sniffled and smiled faintly at the memory of her mom's favorite catch phrase when times were tough.

The sun will shine again tomorrow.

When boy trouble led to tears, Anna remembered how her dad would come into the room to discover what was happening, only to be shooed away by her mother. Matters of the heart could usually only be soothed by maternal love.

Anna scooped up Alfie from the couch and gazed into his one remaining eye. Even though she was no longer a child, Alfie remained her favorite confidante.

"She told me I should go and clean my room and punch my pillow," Anna shared with her stuffed friend. "Then she would smile, and that made me smile, and before we knew it, we were laughing. That was pretty much what she did: got everyone to smile."

Anna's voice cracked with sorrow as she asked Alfie, "What will I do now? I'm all alone."

Alfie just smiled.

Slowly, Anna climbed the stairs; the third step from the top squeaked, as always. Her father never got around to fixing that step, making it impossible for her to sneak in from a late date. Like clockwork, the step would squeak, and her dad's voice could be heard saying, "Good night, kitten. Glad you're home safe."

She would give anything to hear those words again.

At the top of the steps, Anna stopped to gaze at the open door of her parents' room. Instead of entering their room, she walked to her old room at the end of the hall. It was much as she had left it when she moved to her first apartment. The room hadn't been kept as a shrine, but there had been no need for an extra guest bed.

Mom had her hobby room downstairs, and Dad had turned half the garage into a workspace and his "man cave." Her mom had often reminded her that her old bedroom was ready and waiting if she ever needed a place to stay.

"Think of it as a back-up plan," she would add, then laugh.

Anna turned in a slow circle and scanned the room. Her memory conjured the old posters that papered the walls when she was fourteen: Britney Spears, Captain Kirk with Mr. Spock, and the *Baywatch* crew, with that cute Parker Stevenson. The posters had long since been taken down and the walls repainted, but the small busts of Bach, Beethoven, and Chopin, prizes she had won at piano recitals, still sat on the shelves above her desk.

Not searching for anything in particular, she opened and closed the drawers in the desk and dresser. They were all empty, cleaned out.

The tour around her bedroom brought her to the closet, which was empty except for a couple of boxes sitting on the top shelf. She pulled one down and blew the dust from the top of the carton. The tape sealing the boxes showed no signs of having been opened.

Inside were her diaries, all carefully placed in chronological order with the dates clearly displayed on the spines. Still sealed, her teenage thoughts had remained private. "Just a little OCD," Anna muttered.

She smiled at the memories contained in the diaries: her first real date, getting her driver's permit, junior and senior proms, coming in second at the state soccer tournament, and failing the driver's exam the first time because she couldn't parallel park. Rob moved in next door.

Her smile faded as memories of Maarit's wake came back. She brightened at the thought of her Uncle Sean and her sister, an almost complete birth family. "Someday," she said. "Maybe I'll be able to find out who my birth father was."

Alfie's usual resting spot was in the corner of the second box. Anna hugged her favorite toy before tucking him back in his seat of honor. She then lightly ran her fingers over the collection of diaries before returning the boxes to the shelf. Then, she closed the closet door and left her childhood on the shelf.

When she began her descent back down the stairs, the third step squeaked once again, and it was enough to trigger her grief. Anna collapsed onto the top step, buried her face in her hands, and sobbed.

Finally, the tears subsided. She felt, rather than heard, a voice that seemed to come from her parents' bedroom.

"It's okay, kitten. Everything is okay."

Anna stood and dried her eyes with the back of her hand. She descended the stairs, looking over her shoulder until the half-open door to her parents' bedroom disappeared from sight. At the front door, she paused long enough to turn off the living room light. In the darkness, there was only the sound of the sunburst clock's tick-tock on the far wall.

Anna closed the door behind her, slipped the key into the lock, and turned it. The lock clicked with finality.

CHAPTER TWENTY

September 2015

The medevac helicopter flew level with the tree line through the Afghan valley, barely out of range of rifle and machine gun fire on the hillside. This flight was the one thing Paul had not done during the six months he had been embedded with the troops. His assignment had been straightforward: observe and write about the military's support for the non-governmental agencies' humanitarian efforts.

He had watched the construction of schools, followed soon by their destruction. He had seen roads built, bombed, and built again, only to be booby-trapped with IEDs. Now, less than a week before he was to leave, he found himself in a contraption that common sense told him couldn't possibly fly, swooping down into a valley, dodging bullets to save the life of a soldier. He wondered what fateful force had put these young men and women in a country four thousand miles from home, away from everything they knew and loved. Paul shook his head and muttered, "What the hell am I doing here?"

The pilot's voice crackled through the intercom in Paul's helmet. "The same thing we're all doing: our duty." The rest of the crew laughed. Paul could be interviewing this crew over a drink in some fancy bar about the latest play, novel, or pop group in another time and place.

He looked out over the mountain valley. The sides were steep and rocky. Sun-baked huts, shimmering in the summer heat, seemed glued to the mountain sides. Six months ago, he remembered seeing a haze over those same buildings from the dung that residents used to heat them in the winter.

For the last nine days, a U.S. combat group had been attacking a Taliban regional command center. The operation was nearing its conclusion, but not without casualties.

Ping, Ping…Ping.

Paul ducked and cringed at the unmistakable sound of bullets hitting the side of the helicopter. The chopper turned quickly in a defensive maneuver, trying to avoid the gunfire before the enemy on the ground could zero in. The medic next to him sat grim-faced.

In a sudden lurch, the helicopter began a dive, heading for a small clearing on the valley floor. Before the copter touched down, still feet above the ground, two medics jumped from the helicopter and rushed to meet the soldiers, carrying a wounded comrade between them.

The pilot applied the power with the soldier strapped onto a stretcher and the medics safely back aboard. The bird roared and flew out of the clearing. It took less than an hour to run the gauntlet to surgery for the bleeding soldier lying in front of him.

The two medics shouted at the young man; the words were barely audible above the sound of the rotors.

"Stay with me, man. Stay with me. We're almost home."

They worked feverishly to staunch the bleeding from the soldier's side. The wound was too large and too deep, but they kept at it. An ambulance met the helicopter at the pad, and the young man was quickly loaded into it. Paul watched the ambulance until it turned the corner out of sight. The pilot tapped him on the shoulder and held out her hand.

"A souvenir for you." In her palm rested the remains of a bullet. "You were our lucky charm today," she said. "This narrowly missed you and the fuel line. Keep it."

"Will he make it?" asked Paul.

"He was dead before we landed."

Paul looked down at the jagged metal and then back into the pilot's eyes. "How do you keep doing this, day after day?"

She smiled. "It's my job. It's what I'm good at. I do it for them. They're family," she added, pointing at the crew. The pilot took off her helmet and shook out her red hair. "I could ask you the same question."

"It's my job," he replied. "It's what I'm good at. And I hope it will make a difference."

"It does," she said.

Three days later, Paul was ushered into the base commander's office. "Thank you for keeping me safe over the last six months. I can't say that it's been a pleasure being here."

The Commander chuckled. "Glad we could be of service. I understand you had a close call the other day."

Paul fished the shell fragment out of his pocket. "This didn't have my name on it, but it sure seemed to have my initials. It's a souvenir I'll keep for a long time."

"We all have those souvenirs. And still, we stick our necks out."

"That's one of the amazing things I saw out here. Day-in, day-out, you all do exactly that."

The Commander handed a folder to Paul. "Arrangements for your transport home have been made. Your flight leaves at 0500 tomorrow. You'll stop in Germany for a couple of weeks to decompress and make sure you haven't picked up some exotic disease, then on to the States and home. I've read the reports you've written, and no, I didn't censor anything, but tell me, what have you learned that didn't get into the reports?"

Paul thought for a moment. "You guys are caught in an impossible situation. I know the military's mission isn't nation-building, but that's what you must do. I came here with a preconceived notion that we needed to get out. Now, I look at it and think we both have to stay and get out. I don't know which is the right path, but eventually we will have to leave."

An aide appeared at the door, "It's time, sir."

The Commander looked at his watch and stood. "There is one more thing I'd like you to see before you leave. Come with me."

Paul was escorted to a tent where a large company contingent was assembling. He was given a seat along the tent's back wall and instructed not to take pictures. At the front of the tent were five rifles with bayonets stuck into the ground. A photo of a soldier hung from each rifle stock. On a small platform in front of the gun was an empty pair of boots facing the assembly.

The soldiers in attendance were eerily silent. A sergeant major strode to the front, saluted the officers, and turned to face the assembly. In a loud voice, he called out the names of various platoon leaders. From the assembled troops, answering calls came:

Here, Sergeant Major.

Here, Sergeant Major.

Here, Sergeant Major.

The Sergeant Major paused briefly before calling out the next name. There was no answer.

He paused again and called out a name.

Again, no one answered.

Five different times, the officer called out a name, only to be answered with silence.

After the last name was called, the Sergeant Major moved down the center aisle to stand at the rear. The company stood at attention as comrades of the fallen soldiers came to stand in front of the rifles, boots, and pictures. Some knelt and crossed themselves. Most cried. All executed the slow salute given to the dead.

When the company had departed and those who had come to salute their comrades finished their goodbyes, the Sergeant Major returned alone to the front of the tent. He knelt before each rifle and cried for the loss of their lives.

Paul slipped silently out of the tent. The Commander came up beside him and held out his hand. "When you get home, tell the truth."

Paul shook his hand. "I will."

CHAPTER TWENTY-ONE

September 2016

"Y ou have one crazy sense of humor, Anna." Dr. K. handed Anna's composition assignment back to her. "Really? A song cycle based on the life of St. Urho and his wife Sinnika? Where in the world did this idea come from?"

Anna's eyes twinkled. "I was hiking the Superior Hiking Trail last summer and stumbled on a booyah in the little town of Finland."

"A booyah?"

"It's a stew of sorts. An authentic booyah is cooked over an open flame outdoors. They make it in huge quantities, at least 200 gallons, and stir it with a canoe paddle. Some say it makes lutefisk taste good. Best of all, it's always an excuse for a party."

Dr. Keizer laughed and shook her head in mock disbelief.

"I went to the Booyah Festival. I heard a storyteller spinning yarns about St. Urho and his long-suffering wife. I couldn't resist the idea of creating a song extolling the virtues of his wife—she's the main character—as Urho drove the frogs, or, depending on who's telling the tale, the grasshoppers out of Finland. Getting rid of the grasshoppers saved the vineyards and the Finnish wine industry. St Urho's day is March 16, giving both the Finns and the Irish a reason to celebrate for an extra day."

"It's great fun, but you've stuck a message underneath the fun. She's the hero, not him."

"Dr. K., there's one more piece I'd like you to look at." Keizer played through the next piece. Anna sat beside her, turning pages.

"This quartet is hilarious," Dr. K. said. "The tenor is singing in the style of Mozart, the soprano is Wagnerian, the alto is imitating Debussy, and the bass is trying to bring the logic of Bach into the conversation. The four of them are talking over each other, and no one is listening to anyone else. The clever part is that the astounding thing is how seamlessly the music goes from one to the other. And yet, musically it holds together beautifully. Is this going to be part of a larger work?"

"I think so. Not sure what yet, but it could be the start of a musical." Anna turned to her mentor and smiled. "I've been hatching a little plot for your retirement."

Dr. Keizer cocked her head to the side. "What mischief are you up to?"

"Talked to my sister a couple of weeks ago. Floated the idea past her to come home and do a benefit concert for scholarships in your honor. Last night she called. Kay has a three-week break in March, and her favorite accompanist is available as well. They both have penciled in the date."

Dr. Keizer, for once, was speechless. The thought of Kay coming back for a recital was astounding.

"I've also talked to the Foundation office and the music department chair. They are willing to sponsor and publicize the concert. The Foundation president is sure some donors will match the concert proceeds."

Anna grinned. She could tell by the stunned and speechless professor that she had caught she completely by surprise.

"Kay does have a stipulation," Anna added as she gathered her music sheets. "She will donate her services and her accompanist's expenses, if all proceeds from the recital go directly to the scholarship fund."

"That's incredibly generous. Thank you." Dr. Keizer's face lit up with genuine gratitude.

"It will be a lot of fun. All you have to do is show up and enjoy the concert."

"I don't know what to say, Anna. Thank you so much," Dr. Keizer replied as she hugged Anna. "Now, I have a question for you."

"Okay. Shoot."

Dr. K. and Anna moved to sit around the small conference table in the corner of her office. "When will you admit that your real passion is music?" she cocked her head to one side. "You have a significant gift that needs to be developed."

As she waited for a response, Dr. K. leaned back in the chair and tossed her glasses onto the stack of music piled on the desk corner. She folded her hands on the table as if she were about to pray, and leaned closer to her student, a quirk she always did when posing a penetrating question.

"I've told you many times, I can't take you any further. What you need, you won't find in Milan. It's time for grad school. Anna, when will you admit that music is your passion?"

"Dr. K., it's just a hobby," Anna insisted. Whereas her mentor's formidable body language would rattle newer students, Anna found it amusing and endearing.

"Sorry, kid, not buying it. It's more than a hobby when you go on a hike, wander into a 'booyah,' and come home and write a fun and excellent song cycle. You've developed your talent as far as you can here at Milan. You need more than you can get here. You need grad school."

Anna shook her head. "What would I do with a doctorate? I don't want to teach, and I'm not a performer like Kay. Music is a hobby that keeps me sane. Besides, I love working in the admissions office. I'm good at it, too."

"You have as much talent as your mother and sister. And are just as stubborn as well. You don't have to choose Anna. You can do both; you can have a career outside of music. Consider Charles Ives; he was a highly successful insurance executive. Very creative in that field, and his music 'hobby' changed Western music forever. Your talent needs to be developed, or it will waste away. What does Kay say about your music?"

The seriousness on Dr. K.'s face stopped Anna from joking about what Kay would think. Honestly, she wasn't sure how her sister would feel about her musical ambitions.

"Oh, she doesn't know I write music. And that's the way I want to keep it. Dr. K.," Anna's voice was firm and filled with resolve. "The only reason to go to grad school would be if I wanted to be a professional musician. I'm not good enough as a pianist or a singer."

Dr. K. nodded. "I agree, you wouldn't make it as a performer, but with more training and the right environment, you would do quite well as a composer or arranger. Look, I've taken you as far as I can. You have the basic tools you need and the imagination to go with them. You are already writing music at the Master's level; you need more than Milan College or what I can provide."

Dr. K. leaned back and studied Anna's face. Her student's eyes were downcast, and she couldn't tell if Anna was upset or considering attending grad school. *So hard to read,* she thought, *just like her mother.*

Dr. K.'s face softened, voice tender. "Let me send some of your work to a friend of mine at Juilliard. I told her about you, and she's willing to do an unofficial evaluation."

"I don't know," Anna answered meekly as she anxiously picked at the hem of her shirt. She sighed softly. *Dr. K. isn't going to stop until I give in and let her send the music to her friend. Do I dare?*

"You'll never know unless you try," Dr. K. said, sensing Anna's silent musings.

You'll never know unless you try. That sounds like something my mom would say...

Anna threw up her hands in defeat. Dr. K. could be *very* persistent. "Fine. You can send her a sample if you want. But please don't say a word to Kay."

"If that's the way you want it, okay." Dr. Keizer drew an imaginary cross over her heart. "I promise."

December 2016

TO: Elizabeth.Keizer@MilanCollege.edu
FROM: TBaxter@JulliardMusic.edu

Liz, great to hear from you. Heard you were about to retire.
Now, maybe you'll have time to visit me!

I reviewed the score by Anna Jensen. She's clearly talented, with
an interesting and even quirky imagination. She should definitely
pursue an advanced degree to develop her compositional skills. It
would take a complete evaluation by the admissions committee to
determine if she would be a good fit for Juilliard. I encourage her
to apply here and elsewhere.

By the way, let me know if you'd be interested in giving a guest
lecture series here after you retire. I think it would be fun.

Best, Terri

Anna handed the copy of the email back. "I can read between the lines, Dr. K. I told you that Julliard wouldn't be interested. I'm just not in that league."

Liz Keizer let out an exasperated sigh. "Let's look at this logically. First, my friend acknowledged that you have a talent worth developing. Secondly, she can't commit to anything on behalf of Juilliard. She's not even a member of the admissions committee. Lastly, Juilliard only admits five to six percent of those who apply. Last year, they had over 2,700 applications. You do the math. She suggested you not limit your applications to one school."

Anna's hands suddenly felt clammy, so she nervously wiped them on her jeans. "You may be right. I just don't want to leave Ellston. I'm safe here."

"It's a big, wide world out there, Anna," Dr. K said. "Maybe it's time you ventured out into it."

Anna blinked back a tear. "That's what my mom said to me when my dad died. I'll think about it."

Dr. K looked over her glasses at Anna.

"*Really*, I will."

They both laughed.

CHAPTER TWENTY-TWO

November 2015

T he warmth of a soft evening breeze carried the happy sounds of a mariachi band to the Santa Fe Plaza. Paul and his editor sat in an outdoor café, finishing dinner. When he signaled the waiter for another round of drinks, his editor covered his glass with his hand. Undeterred, Paul ordered his fourth of the evening.

"That was nice work you did in Afghanistan," the editor commented. "Corporate is quite pleased with your in-depth reporting, both on the misery of the people and on what the military tries to do. The articles had just the right mix of emotion and objective practicality. Well done."

The waiter arrived with Paul's drink. "I'm glad that Corporate's pleased, but I could do without another assignment like that. Six months in a war zone was quite enough, thank you."

The editor studied Paul's face. "Your recent articles don't have the fire of your earlier work. Somehow, they seem to be lacking something. Can't put my finger on it, but something's missing."

Paul reached into his pocket and pulled out a twisted piece of metal. He slid it across the table to his friend.

"What's this?"

"The remains of a bullet that came within inches of my head."

The editor examined it before pushing it carefully back across the table to Paul. "The helicopter in Afghanistan?"

Paul nodded and slipped the bullet fragment into his pocket.

"Why show this to me now?"

"That's the *zing* that's missing."

Paul's boss nodded. "I hate to bring this up, but Corporate has another story they'd like you to do. After this one, I want you to take a vacation. Go on a cruise or go hide in a cabin in the woods, anything to get your head back on straight."

Paul downed his scotch but didn't answer. The lilting sound of the Mariachi band and soft conversations drifting from the other tables filled the silence.

His editor leaned in closer. "This one should be easier. They want you to do a follow-up on the tornadoes that went through Oklahoma and Kansas last year. It should be an uplifting story of reconstruction and putting lives back together."

"What am I, the go-to-guy for wars and disasters?" Paul frowned. *I don't know how much more of this I can take.* "This will be the fourth assignment in a row, and the seventh or eighth in the last four years."

The editor leaned back in his seat. "The problem is, Paul, you always approach these stories with a midwestern naivete. You look for good amid the chaos. If something to celebrate can be found amidst the horror, you find it."

Paul signaled for another scotch.

"That's not going to help, you know."

"Do I ever show up at the office drunk?" Paul couldn't keep the irritation out of his voice.

"No."

"Am I on the clock now?"

"No," said his editor. "That's not my point."

"It helps me sleep."

"Maybe, but it won't help you forget."

"It does for a little while." Paul glanced up to see if his drink was coming. "I don't want to go to Oklahoma. Corporate said I could have input on my assignments. I don't want to do that one."

"Okay. There's one other story they suggested. If you take this one, I can talk them out of Oklahoma."

Paul sighed. *Well, I do have to earn a living.* "Where is it?"

"Montana."

Paul pursed his lips thoughtfully. *This one could be so much better for me.* "At least it's pretty countryside. What's the story?"

"I'm not sure of the details, but I think it's about a young man who survived a suicide pact. The local paper ran an article on it, but the corporation would like to do a syndicated feature on it. You know, an uplifting story of overcoming hardship from the depths of despair. Your name came up."

Paul fidgeted in his chair. *Where was his damn drink!* "Okay, I'll do it, but then I'm going to take some time off."

"Fair enough."

Paul's eyes locked on his editor's. "No, I mean it. I want some real time. I want a leave of absence for at least a year."

"What are you going to do?"

"Undetermined." *I'll figure it out later. Right after, I have one more drink.*

As if on cue, their waiter appeared with another scotch.

March 2016

A blast of cold air swept across the Shelby, Montana, train depot platform. Paul put his back to the wind and turned up the collar of his bomber jacket, but it did little to ward off the sharp spring wind. Shivering, he pulled out a pocket watch, the silver-plated case worn smooth from years of being pulled out and pushed into jean pockets.

The watch indicated 3:10 a.m., and his train, interestingly named *The Empire Builder*, was now six hours and thirty-seven minutes late. According to the ticket agent, the train was only ten minutes away. Heavy mountain snow had once again slowed James J. Hill's signature train.

"Not much of an *Empire Builder*. I should have flown," Paul grumbled. He wasn't worried about being overheard by anyone because a cold wind gust immediately obliterated his words. But he also hated flying. *Too noisy, no time to think in that damn flying cigar,* he had once told his mother. The thought of the wheels clicking and clacking, the drafty but warm observation car, and the bottle of scotch safely tucked into his knapsack brought a smile to his face.

Paul traveled light: a knapsack to carry the necessities slung over one shoulder, and his laptop case over the other. He had chosen to wait outside; the red and white linoleum squares pattern on the depot floor made him dizzy. Outside, the streetlight cast barely enough light to show the depot's clapboard siding in desperate need of paint.

He shuddered and pulled out his cell phone to snap a picture of the train depot. The photo would remind him of the place's emptiness and loneliness, a perfect setting for the story he should write. Even if he could write it, he wouldn't publish it. He knew he couldn't do it justice.

He had committed the unforgivable journalistic sin of becoming personally involved with a story's subject. He tried to help the kid find a solution, but the kid was now eighteen, and social services programs were nonexistent.

He clenched his fists and screamed at the mountains. "Why am I always Don Quixote? People read my stories and cry, but the situation doesn't change. Promised help doesn't arrive, and the headlines are soon filled with the next disaster. Misery never ends. It only moves from place to place."

The platform was empty; no one had heard his outburst. He checked his backpack to be sure the bottle of Glenlivet was still intact. He was counting on the trip home and the scotch to erase the memory of the kid's face. He feared the kid's next suicide attempt would be successful.

The train whistle signaled the *Empire Builder's* arrival for a fifteen-minute stop, taking passengers for the 1,250-mile trip to Chicago. But he wouldn't be traveling that far. His hometown in Minnesota was a little over a thousand miles away. With any luck, he would be home in twenty hours. The number of freight trains that would force the *Empire Builder* to wait on a siding would determine his arrival time. As always, commerce took precedence over people. Freight trains had priority; passenger trains had to wait.

~ ══ ~

The train slowed and stopped. The sign on the depot, which looked much like the one in Shelby, Montana, read Ellston, Minnesota—population 21,349. According to the clock under the sign, it was almost noon. Paul's stomach confirmed the time. *Only three hours late,* he thought bitterly. Amazing, they made up nearly three hours in the past twenty-four.

Halfway through North Dakota, he had texted his mother to say he was on his way home. The spare bedroom would be ready for him. He put his laptop in its case and discarded the remnants of his lunch. The train ground to a stop at the edge of the platform. It was a short platform, only two car lengths long. Through the window, he waved at his mother and cousin, Anna.

Anna was the first to hug him as he stepped off the train. "Why don't you let a person know you're coming home? And what did I read in the paper? You're the new managing editor of the *Herald-Review*? Why didn't you tell us this was in the works?"

"Whoa, give a guy a chance to get off the train at least before the cross-examination starts," he teased his younger cousin.

"Welcome home, son." Allison kissed him on the cheek.

Arm in arm, the three crossed the red pavers and onto the crumbling asphalt of the parking lot. "There's my car," said Anna, pointing to the red Mazda at the end of the row.

"We're all going to fit in that?"

"Sure, plenty of room for us if you sit in the back." Anna giggled, and Allison rolled her eyes.

Paul sighed. It was good to be home.

ACT THREE

2017

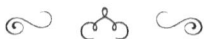

CHAPTER TWENTY-THREE

Wednesday, March 15, 2017

Exhausted, Kay stood in line at the gate to check in for the flight from Chicago to LaCrosse, Wisconsin. The "red eye" from San Francisco to O'Hare had been late leaving, so the connection to the LaCrosse flight had been tight. She checked her boarding pass for the third time—seat 12C. *At least it's an aisle seat,* she thought.

At seat 12C, Kay dropped her handbag on the seat and began to lift her carry-on. A voice behind her said, "Please, let me help you with that."

Kay turned. "Gladly," she said. "Thank you." A thirty-something-year-old man, dressed in a comfortable yet stylish sports coat, hoisted her carry-on and then his into the overhead storage bin.

"It looks like we're in adjacent seats, I'm in 12A," he said. She stepped aside to let the young man slide into his seat before settling into hers. "These early morning flights are a killer," he added.

"Try an overnight flight before, that's a real killer," Kay joked. "At least this flight..." Her sentence was interrupted by the attendants' pre-flight routine.

"You were saying?" her seatmate prompted.

"Only that this flight isn't a long one." Ordinarily, Kay avoided conversations in airplanes, preferring to be immersed in her thoughts. However, the warmth of his smile charmed her. *He has the bright eyes of a young soul.* "Are you going to LaCrosse on business?"

"Partly," he said. "And partly for pleasure. I'm heading upriver to Ellston." He pulled a grey striped necktie out of his pocket. "I have a meeting later this morning, then I will stay for the weekend. There's a concert Saturday night, I'm attending."

"Concert?" *A fan?*

"It's a recital honoring a favorite college professor of mine. The recital features a mezzo-soprano I've wanted to hear for some time. My parents are into opera, and I've caught the bug."

The young man paused and looked intently at Kay. "Please, forgive me for staring, but you look quite familiar."

She reached out her hand. "I'm Kay Malone."

He gasped. "Kay...*the* Kay Malone?"

"That's me." Kay chuckled.

He heartily shook her hand. "It's such an honor to meet you. I heard you sing two years ago at the Lyric Opera in Chicago. When I heard you would be in Ellston, I couldn't pass up the opportunity." He leaned back in his seat in shock, his eyes wide as if he had just received news that he had won the lottery. "*Wow,* I can't believe..."

Kay smiled at his enthusiasm. "And you are...?"

"Jim...Jim Tiegen."

The rest of the flight passed quickly, with conversation about Tiegen's family's architectural firm and the opera scene in Chicago, the college classes they had both taken at Milan College, and the quirks of their professors' teaching styles.

To pass the time, they discussed Greek architecture, the influence of Frank Lloyd Wright, and how music trends shifted from ornate to simplistic and back again, paralleling similar trends in art and architecture.

"Thank you for the conversation," Jim said. "It's been a treat to meet the legendary Kay Malone."

Kay blushed. "A legend? I hardly think I'm old enough to be a legend. But thank you."

"You have been legendary in Milan's music department for some time. You know, hometown girl who made it big."

Kay laughed and shook her head.

Teigen continued, "I remember being a freshman and going into Dr. Keizer's office for my first choir audition. That morning, a signed poster from you arrived. Dr. K. was so delighted that she showed it to everyone walking by. I was in her office again a week later, and the poster was framed and hung on the wall. Legendary in her mind, for sure."

"That's very kind of you to say. Dr. K. was my voice teacher, and I'm proud to say, a good friend. It's strange, though, even after all these years, I still can't call her by her first name. It's always Dr. K. or Dr. Keizer, never Liz or Elizabeth."

"She's an amazing person. Friendly and warm, but a force to be reckoned with." Teigen leaned back in his seat as the plane banked one last time in preparation for the final landing. Kay gripped the arms of her seat so tightly that her knuckles turned white. *Next time, I'll take the bus*, she silently lamented.

The aircraft's wheels hit hard against the pavement before settling onto the runway. The pilot engaged the reverse thrusters, dramatically reducing the speed and pressing the passengers into their seatbelts. When the plane finally settled, Kay relaxed, let the air out of her lungs, and shot Tiegen a side look. "Must be a rookie pilot getting some experience in the backwaters. But, as the old saying goes, any landing you can walk away from is good."

The plane lurched to a stop at the terminal, prompting the hurry-up-stand-and-wait ritual to begin. Like a wisp of smoke, the intimacy developed between confined strangers vanished. Standing beside each other in the crowded aisle, Teigen politely cleared his throat. "I have a rental car reserved. May I offer you a ride to town?"

"Thank you. That's very kind, but my sister is supposed to be meeting me. I'll take you up on your offer if she isn't there."

Teigen nodded. "Like the old saying goes, 'Break a leg.' I'm looking forward to the concert."

Kay and Teigen walked out of the security area together, angling toward the baggage claim carousel. "Looks like someone important is arriving," he said. "See the microphones at the end of the terminal? Even the TV station is here."

Rushing across the terminal, Anna waved and called, "Kay! Kay! Wait 'til you see the welcome they've arranged. The university's president, mayor, Dr. Keizer, and the dean of the music school are here. Your homecoming is a big deal."

"I guess no sneaking in and out of town this time," Kay said wryly. "Anna, this is Jim Teigen. We met on the plane. He's here for my recital. Jim, my sister, Anna Jensen."

"Very nice to meet you, Jim."

"You as well," he replied with a cordial nod. "I guess you won't need that ride, Kay."

"Guess not. Thank you for the conversation; I enjoyed talking with you. I look forward to seeing you at the recital."

"Come on," said Anna, tugging at her sister's sleeve. "They're waiting for you. We'll get your luggage later."

The two sisters walked toward the welcoming party at the other end of the airport lobby. To Kay, it seemed as if Anna glided across the terrazzo floor rather than walking. From the waist up, her sister was the image of efficient motion. Her posture was perfect. Her head and shoulders swayed neither side to side nor up and down. Even her not-quite-shoulder-length hair remained perfectly in place. Her little sister had evolved into a fine young woman.

Kay was utterly different from Anna to the casual observer, but had a commanding presence that no one could deny. In any room she entered, her mere presence would be felt. She punctuated the conversation with laughs and large sweeping motions of her hands and arms. Her whole body reacted to the conversation; her expressive movements were designed to convey stage action to the last row of a concert hall's balcony. Her confidence was evident in everything that she did.

As the sisters walked, Anna said, "Jim looks very familiar to me. Can't seem to place him, but I think I met him somewhere."

"He said he graduated from Milan about a dozen years ago, maybe you met him in college?"

"Maybe." Anna shrugged. "Anyway, he's kind of cute."

When Dr. Keitzer welcomed Kay with open arms and a warm smile. "Welcome home. Welcome home." After exchanging hugs, Dr. K. led her to the group assembled in front of the TV camera. After the formal greetings from the mayor, who gave Kay a key to the city, the university president, and Dr. Keizer, Kay took center stage.

"First, let me say how happy I am to be home to present a recital honoring Dr. Keizer. She has profoundly influenced me and thousands of other students musically and personally. I feel honored to be asked to present this program. All the proceeds from this recital will be donated to the university to establish an endowment that funds music scholarships in Dr. Keizer's name."

The small gathering applauded. Casual onlookers stopped briefly to gawk before going on their way.

Kay continued. "This will be the first time I have performed in Ellston since my college senior recital some twenty years ago. All you music critics, please be gentle."

Chuckles rippled through the crowd, followed by polite applause. Kay nodded her thanks and stepped back to allow the university president to resume his position behind the microphone. "I see we have a question from the editor of our local newspaper."

Paul, dressed in his usual jeans, plaid shirt, and tan field jacket, not looking the part of a city editor, asked, "What's going to be on the concert program?" A wink accompanied his impish grin.

Kay noticed the wink but maintained her professional expression. "It will include a set of select arias from one of my favorite operas, *Faust* by Gounod, selections from a Schubert song cycle, plus a little Jerome Kern and Frank Loesser," she responded crisply.

Paul nodded and then tapped his pen on his lip, considering his next question. "A follow-up question, Ms. Malone. Do you still own a pair of shamrock socks?"

"Would you repeat that question? I'm not sure what..." A laugh escaped Kay's throat. With a smile of recognition, she added, "I'll answer that question with one of my own. Do you still send five irons skittering across bank lobbies?"

"Actually, it was a putter, and I still own that club, but haven't taken it to a bank in a long time."

Kay addressed the audience: "Sorry for the inside joke. Mr. Williams is an old friend with a good, slightly mischievous sense of humor. Thank you all for this warm welcome. It's good to be home again. I hope to see you all at the recital on Saturday night."

Paul leaned against the wall, patiently watching Kay charm the gathered well-wishers. After the room had cleared, Kay approached him. "It's good to see you again, and a big surprise. What are you doing back in Ellston?"

"It's a long story. By the way, you work a room better now than you did in that coffee shop twenty years ago."

Kay's eyes twinkled. "And when did you last visit Cork and kiss the stone? It must have been last week with all the blarney you throw around."

"I only wish," he said. "Haven't been to County Cork in years." *It's been twenty years since that sweet kiss.*

"Will you be covering the recital as well as this shindig?"

"No, as soon as the news of your recital was announced, Brad Quinn, our arts, music, theater, dance, and movie critic, was in my office begging to cover the performance. He will do those honors, but I reserved your homecoming for myself. Welcome home." The corners of Paul's eye crinkled with genuine delight.

"I can't get over the surprise of finding you here," Kay said. "The last I heard, you were off gallivanting in Africa or somewhere exotic." She reached out and touched his arm, shaking her head in disbelief. "And that crazy question about shamrock socks in a press conference. Only you would do something edgy like that."

Paul laughed. "I noticed you couldn't resist returning with the golf club thing. I'm amazed you remembered it."

Kay nodded in agreement. "It's funny the things that stick in one's memory." Paul pointed to where Anna and Jim Tiegen were talking. "Anna and I would like to take you to dinner on Friday night, if it fits your schedule. Sort of a mini reunion."

"I'd love that. Give us all a chance to catch up. Is Luigi's still open?"

"Luigi's it is. Anna and I will pick you up at the hotel at seven."

During the press conference, Jim Teigen joined Anna, standing at the edge of the press pool. "Your sister is quite impressive."

Anna, surprised by his reappearance, faced him. "Thanks. I'm amazed at how comfortable she is in front of an audience. I wish I could do that but never will."

"Why not?"

"Oh, I don't know. I always hated speech class. Everybody is looking at me, expecting me to say something interesting. It always made me nervous. Too afraid I'd make a mistake, I guess."

Anna and Teigen fell silent, their eyes on Kay and Paul, who were just out of earshot. Their conversation was getting animated, and the pair seemed comfortable in each other's presence. Anxious to fill the awkward silence, Anna saw the chance to say what was on her mind. "Mr. Teigen, I have the strangest feeling we've met before."

Tiegen laughed. "Call me Jim, and you stole my line! I was about to say the same thing. We may have met, but I'm drawing a complete blank on where or when."

Anna twisted her hair. "It's been bugging me for the last twenty minutes, too. Kay said you went to Milan College, and I went there, too. Maybe it was back then."

Jim shook his head, his brow furrowed as if trying to recall a memory. "I can't seem to make the connection. What was your major?"

"I had a double major: History and Music. Sang in the choir and occasionally accompanied it on the piano."

"That's it." Jim's face brightened. "Watching you walk away from the baggage claim. I noticed how you glide across the floor. You did the same thing on the stage, walking to the piano. Now I remember."

Anna shook her head. "I wish I could say the same, but I'm sorry, I don't remember you."

"That's okay. I was only a face in the tenor section. We never met or talked, so it's no surprise you don't remember me. In any case, it's a small world."

"Yes, it is. What brings you to Ellston? Anna flashed a flirtatious smile.

"Two things. I have a business meeting in Ellston this afternoon, and then I plan to attend your sister's recital on Saturday."

Anna's face lit up at the mention of her sister's event. "Wonderful. Maybe we'll see you at the concert."

"I'll look forward to that." Jim took his leave. He turned at the airport exit, looked over his shoulder, and waved.

That was interesting, Anna thought. She had watched him walk away and returned his wave as he left the airport.

～ ═ ～

After the welcoming party at the airport dispersed and the ceremony concluded, the two sisters retrieved Kay's luggage and climbed into Anna's car for the half-hour ride through the river valley to Ellston.

The sun, still a week from the spring equinox, had slipped below the western ridge, placing the highway in the shadow of the bluff. The river channel and the bluffs on the eastern shore remained bathed in the golden light of the afternoon. Kay adjusted the seat to lean back, relax, and enjoy the scenery.

"Have the first two ships of the season come through the lock and dam yet?"

"Not yet," replied Anna. "It's usually the first week of April before the ice is out of the locks."

"That was a big deal when I was growing up. We used to ride our bikes down to the levee and wave at the tugboat's crew. Sometimes the captain would blow the horn and wave. We'd yell and wave harder." Kay smiled as she remembered simpler times.

"I remember doing that. Mom didn't like it. She thought the river was too dangerous. But Paul would let me tag along, and we'd stand on those floating docks by the levee and watch the boats go by. The docks attached to poles would move up and down as the river rose and fell. I always thought they were cool."

The sisters drove in silence for several minutes. Kay leaned forward and squinted into the distance. "Are those fishing boats out in the channel?"

"Looks like it. A few die-hards always don't let a little thin ice at the boat launch keep them from being out on the water."

Kay smiled and nestled back into the seat, "I remember fishing early in the spring with my Dad. I'd be all bundled up and could hardly move. He'd put me in the boat while he pushed it off the trailer and into the water."

Kay shook her head at the memory. "I still remember the sound of the ice cracking under the boat's weight. I would squeal, 'Don't let go of the rope,' and he'd laugh. Fun to remember now, not much then." Kay leaned back against the headrest and closed her eyes.

Anna glanced at her sister. "Tired, Kay? Long flight?"

"Had to take the red eye from San Francisco to connect through O'Hare. Didn't get much sleep on the plane." Kay gazed out the passenger window at the river. "It's beautiful. I'd forgotten how majestic the valley is. That water has flowed for centuries."

Anna glanced over at her sister again, her eyebrows raised in curiosity. "I'm happy you decided to do this recital. I know coming home is not high on your list of favorite things to do."

"If it weren't for Dr. Keizer, I wouldn't have the career I've got. I owe her this much. Besides, we don't often get to see each other."

"Well," said Anna. "I'm grateful you decided to come home."

Kay became silent, her eyes focused on the river. "I took a philosophy class in college," she finally said. "One day, the professor asked us if we could step into the same river twice. The class was divided on the question...actually, almost everyone said yes. Only one girl said no, reasoning that even if you stepped into the same spot, the place was changed forever, however minutely. The water you stepped into had flowed down the river. It wasn't the same river."

"A matter of perspective, I guess."

"That was the professor's point. The river's timeless, always the same, and never the same. Funny the things one remembers."

"You're waxing philosophical today," said Anna, a hint of worry in her voice. "Anything special on your mind?"

"Just a little tired." Kay changed the subject. "Tell me, any new relationships in your life?"

Ann shook her head without taking her eyes off the road. "Nope. And you?"

"Ditto, I'm never in one place long enough to develop any."

The sisters laughed. "What a pair of sad sacks we are."

"Speaking of relationships," Anna said. "Did I sense an undercurrent of something at the airport?"

"What do you mean, an undercurrent?"

"Oh, I don't know. Maybe something about shamrock socks, putters, and bank lobbies. You and Paul? I've never heard that story."

"Nothing to tell."

"Nothing to tell? Let's see: a reporter, in a public press conference, asks an opera star if she still owns shamrock socks, opera star responds with a comment about banks and golf clubs, and the two of them laugh at a private joke while the rest of us look at each other and wonder what the hell that was all about."

The car glided to a stop at a traffic light, and Anna used the opportunity to side-eye and playfully nudge her sister.

Kay shook her head.

"Now, the opera star's sister hadn't heard the story about her sister and her cousin but remembers seeing a kiss between the two when the older sister got on the plane to Atlanta. Come on, girl, what's the story?"

"Oh, that."

"Yes, that."

"It was all your fault." Kay shot back teasingly.

"My fault?" Anna's tone was incredulous. She couldn't tell if her sister was joking or not.

"The day before you caused a hullabaloo by skipping school and not coming home until after dark, causing all sorts of panic and commotion, including searches by Paul and me, not to mention the police."

Anna rolled her eyes and remained silent, keeping her sister talking.

"Anyway, I was in the bank downtown the day before, and this guy, Paul, came in carrying a golf club. The bank had installed a new metal detection system. Paul tripped over the alarm mechanism. He and the golf club landed at my feet. It was bizarre."

Anna laughed, imagining the sight of Paul on the floor, wheezing.

"Later that day, Paul delivered some legal papers to the college music office. We went for coffee and arranged a date for the next night. Then you pulled your stunt. Paul, I, and others all arrived to look for you. You turned up at the rectory, but it was too late for our date. He took me home, kissed me, and I left for Atlanta. End of story."

"I was right," said Anna. "I think he sort of kept track of your career through me. Have you two kept in touch?"

"Not really. We exchanged emails a couple of times. We had a drink after your dad's funeral. He called me once for an interview after I was in Atlanta. I think it was for an article he wrote at the time."

"Hmm...interesting." Whimsy danced across Anna's face.

"Anna, you are a hopeless romantic. There wasn't enough time for anything to develop between Paul and me twenty years ago, and nothing's going on now."

Anna steered the car into the hotel driveway and found a parking spot near the entrance. "You know, you could have stayed with me. I have plenty of room, which would be much more comfortable than the hotel."

Kay smiled and patted her sister's shoulder. "I know, and I'm grateful for the offer, but I have a set routine before a performance. It's best if I keep that routine. Tell you what: there's a break in my schedule, two whole weeks before I need to be in Salt Lake. Why don't I spend some of that time with you?"

"Perfect. I'll take some vacation time, and we can roam around. Do whatever we want, whenever we want. No schedules."

Kay sighed blissfully. "No schedules. That sounds like heaven."

"Paul and I will pick you up for dinner Friday night at seven."

CHAPTER TWENTY-FOUR

Wednesday Evening, March 15

With a sigh, Kay tried to make her hotel suite less institutional. *Hotels all look alike*, she thought. *Some are more comfortable than others, but still all the same.*

In addition to the bouquet of spring flowers she had requested, two more bouquets flanked hers on the desk. The first, an arrangement of peach-colored roses, with a card that read:

Welcome home, Fuzz Top. Wish I could be there for your triumphant return.

Love, Dad

Sweet as usual, thought Kay. A card attached to the second arrangement of tulips, daisies, and lilies read:

Looking forward to your recital.
The Milan College Music Faculty

The contrast between the warmth of her father's greeting and the impersonal note on the department's card brought a smile to Kay's face. *A nice gesture from the department. But it is a typical institutional response.*

She unpacked her suitcase, placed her folded clothes in the dresser, and carefully hung her concert attire in the closet. *One last touch*, she thought as she placed the picture she had taken of her father in front of the Grand Canyon on the nightstand. She liked it to be among the first things she saw in the morning and one of the last before falling asleep.

Kay opened her computer, sent a quick email to her father thanking him for the flowers, and then reviewed the itinerary for the rest of the week:

Thursday 7 p.m.—vocal exercise with Dr. K.
Friday 2 p.m.—final rehearsal with Brian
Friday 7 p.m.—dinner with Anna and Paul
Saturday 5 p.m.—light vocal warm-up
Saturday 7:30 p.m.—recital

The pattern of her life had become a marathon from one hotel to another, another stage, another appreciative audience. Once in a while, she might stay a few weeks in one place for a role in an opera, then she would be off to somewhere new. But the theme was always the same: another opening, another show. The never-ending routine was beginning to lose its charm.

"Why in the world do you do this?" said Kay to the room's walls. "Why do you put up with this grind? How long can you keep doing this? I can't even get to a grocery store and back without a taxi. It used to be more fun."

With a deep sigh that felt like it came from her soul, she picked up her purse, double-checked that she had the key, and exited her temporary home. The secure click of the door latching behind her was strangely comforting. It was one of the few small things she had control over these days.

She turned to her left and walked a few steps, only to stop and turn on her heel. The elevator was in the opposite direction. Even trips to the elevator felt like the "same old, same old" lately.

Thursday, March 16

The portico covering the hotel's entrance provided enough shelter from the light spring rain for Kay to stand outside while waiting for the taxi. The last winter snow, shaped like mini mountains by the plows, ringed the parking lot.

Typical weather for this time of the year, she thought. *I'd forgotten the crispness and freshness of the early spring.*

"Hello, Kay." An unexpected voice startled her deep thoughts. She turned to see a priest quickly climb the steps leading from the parking lot to the portico's shelter. Kay inwardly cringed. *This was yet another reminder of my mother.*

"Father McDonough," she acknowledged. Her hands closed into a fist, belying the professional smile she had developed over the years. She hoped a practiced smile would hide her resentment toward her uncle.

It didn't. Father McDonough had spent years reading people. He recognized the smile for what it was: *subterfuge.*

"It's been a long time," he said politely, undeterred by his niece's standoffishness. "I'm looking forward to your recital tomorrow night."

Kay's eyebrows rose in surprise. "You're planning to attend?"

"Wouldn't miss it. It's not often I get to hear the great Kay Malone sing, who also happens to be my niece."

"I hope you enjoy it," Kay said crisply as she ended the conversation by moving toward her waiting taxi.

The priest opened the taxi door for her. No eye contact was made. No further conversation was offered.

Thursday, 7:00 P.M.

Dr. Keizer met Kay on the main stage of the Milan College Performing Arts Center. "I see you remembered the way," she chuckled.

"The old place hasn't changed much in the past twenty years." Kay stood center stage, looking out at the auditorium. "This place feels like my second home. I loved sitting on the balcony but avoided sitting under the balcony during a concert; the sound didn't reach those seats, either."

"No, it hasn't changed much. A few cosmetic panels to help under the balcony, an upgrade to the seating and acoustics, but essentially the same. This is like old times, a little *'Deja vu all over again'* to quote my favorite baseball player."

The two walked to the grand piano in the center of the stage. Dr. K. lightly touched her former student's elbow. "Thank you for doing this recital. It means so much to me and our students."

"It's a little payment forward for all the help you have given me."

Dr. Keizer sat on the piano bench and positioned her hands above the keys. "Where do you want to start?"

"I still use the scale, arpeggio, and melodic exercises you drilled into me twenty years ago. Let's start with the scales."

Dr. Keizer began the introduction. Kay's voice reverberated throughout the empty recital hall. Per powerful voice, trained to fill spaces twice as large as the Milan College auditorium, exuded a warmth, vibrancy, and clarity achieved by few sopranos.

"Your technique has greatly improved," Dr. Keizer said. "You used to have some trouble with that last scale exercise."

"The vocal coaches in Atlanta were a big help. They pushed, pulled, and cajoled until I managed to master it. Thanks to you, I had the fundamentals down cold."

"Okay," said Keizer as she readied her hands again. "Ready for the melodic vocalise?"

Kay grinned. "These are my favorite parts of the warm-up," she said. "They're pure music. No words, only the vowels' sound and the melodies' shape to convey the meaning."

The exercise demanded that her voice reach for the highest stars, the loudest volume, and the softest, gentlest emotion. If there had been one present, the sounds she produced would have moved an audience from joyful exuberance to the quietest of tears.

Dr. Keizer laughed. "For an old teacher like me, hearing you sing those exercises is worth the price of admission."

Kay beamed at her mentor's praise.

"Okay." Dr. Keizer twinkled with mischief. "Let's play stump the star. Remember this one?" She began playing the introduction to an old standard from the solo repertoire.

Kay laughed. "I do! It's Schubert's *Ich wollt, ich wär ein Fisch*." No further prompting was needed as she broke into song.

At that moment, the two women were no longer a teacher and a student, but peers making music together for no reason other than the pure joy of it. For over an hour, they traded songs, covering opera arias, solo literature, and musical theater until, in a fit of laughter, it was time to stop.

In sharing the music, the two had become one, two instruments, blended to perfection. The moment passed, and the two became individuals again, their bond cemented by the shared experience.

"Maarit, that was great fun. Thank you."

Kay's expression moved from surprise to confusion and then to consternation. "Dr. K., did you call me Maarit?"

"Did I? I'm sorry—a slip of the tongue."

"Dr. Keizer, that was my mother's name."

The teacher hesitated. "Yes, Kay...I know it was your mother's name."

"How could you possibly know that?" Kay gasped. "I don't think we ever talked about my mother."

Dr. Keizer took a deep breath and answered simply. "Your mother was a student of mine."

Kay gripped the edge of the piano; her knuckles turned white. It felt as if all the air had been forcefully pulled from her lungs.

Seeing her friend's distress, Dr. Keizer rose from the piano and took Kay's hands in hers. Kay started to speak, but Dr. Keizer raised her hand to halt the questions.

"Please, let me tell you the story."

Kay, still unable to speak, nodded. Her emotions bounced between disbelief and shock.

"It was in my first year teaching at Milan, more than forty years ago. Your mother auditioned for the choir and registered for voice lessons. Twenty years later, you did the same thing. At the time, I didn't make the connection, different last names, years between you and your mother, it didn't dawn on me that you were related."

Kay leaned against the piano. Her breathing was shallow, and her pulse was racing.

"You had already left for Atlanta when Anna's father came looking for information about your mother. That's when I learned about the relationship. Learning that mother and daughter were the two biggest talents I had ever coached was a shock. The connection is obvious when I hear you sing and see your stage presence. You are what she could have been."

Kay backed away from her mentor, putting physical distance between herself and the story.

Keizer continued, "There is, however, a huge difference between the two of you. Your mother was undisciplined. Took any critique as a personal affront. By the time she was a junior in college, she had fought with most of the music faculty and several students." She paused to give Kay a moment to absorb the story before continuing.

"The final straw was a confrontation with a guest conductor for an opera production. That incident ended badly. Music productions aren't democracies. Open rebellion over interpretation, especially in front of an entire cast, is not appreciated by any conductor. This particular conductor was a German autocrat. He didn't mince words or tolerate insubordination, especially from an undergrad."

Kay continued being silent, her eyes downcast and her face pale.

Dr. Keizer continued. "I supported the conductor. Your mother exploded, quit the opera cast, dropped out of choir, and changed her major. At that point, I lost track of her. Later, in a casual conversation with a colleague, I heard she had married."

Keizer turned to look out at the empty auditorium. "What wonderful sounds this auditorium has heard. I shall miss it."

She turned back to Kay. "Your mother sang on this stage. Her voice was beautiful. She could sing with great power and with delicate nuance. You have the same ability. Your voice is richer, more mature than hers was then. The big difference is that you were willing to take criticism as a means to improve, not as a personal insult. You worked at it. She didn't."

Dr. Kaiser paused as if remembering the past. A faint smile tugged at her lips.

"Your mother could be fun, witty, and charming. But she'd quit and run away when the dark moods overtook her. I don't know what happened in her marriage, but I suspect her mood swings had something to do with it."

Kay blinked tears from her eyes. "I never knew she could sing. I remember her singing lullabies to me when I was a child. I never imagined she would've sung on this stage, or in an opera."

"Such a waste of talent." Dr. Keizer shook her head sadly.

Kay took a deep breath. "Dr. Keizer, I've hated her since she left, and I realized she was never coming back. Hated her for the scandal she caused when she left. My dad tried to tell me that my mother loved me, but that they couldn't live together. I was young and I didn't understand. Still don't, for that matter."

"I've never believed in coincidence," said Dr. Keizer as she slowly walked back toward the piano. "Somehow, the apparent randomness of everything seems to make sense when considered retrospectively. I'm sorry. I didn't mean to revive old hurts with my slip of the tongue. But, perhaps it's for the best. Now it's out in the open."

Kay leaned against the ebony concert grand piano and stared at the backstage rigging, losing herself in the ropes and pulleys that controlled the stage. Slowly, she hunched over the piano, her head cradled in her hands.

Dr. Keizer moved to stand beside her protégé. Gently, she put her arm around Kay's shoulders. "It's okay."

Kay managed a weak smile. "It still hurts. I can't forgive her for leaving me."

"Kay, you've had a very long day. Come on, I'll give you a ride to your hotel." Kay nodded in response. She felt too emotionally drained to form words.

Early Morning, Friday, March 17

Kay screamed, leaping out of the bed to stand in the middle of the hotel room, heart pounding, her body shaking uncontrollably. The clock on the nightstand read 3:10 a.m. on Friday.

Still in that space between sleep and wakefulness, she climbed back into bed and burrowed under the blankets into the fetal position, trying to regain the warmth of the bed. She was glad to have escaped the unreality of the dream and returned to the reality of the hotel room. It was clear sleep wouldn't return for a while.

I've had this dream before, but this time, it's different. Kay tossed the bed covers off in frustration. She wrapped her robe tightly around herself, took out her journal, and started writing. She needed to get this awful dream out of her head and onto the page. It may make more sense then.

An awful dream. I'm standing at the edge of a river. The water is flowing very fast and wildly. On the other side are Peg and John. I think they are waiting for someone. I call to them, and they smile and wave at me. I try to get to them, but the river is too fast. I try several times. I yell to them to wait for me, but they just smile and wave.

They don't call back to me. I don't think they are waiting for me, but I want to talk to them. They continue to smile and wave.

I'm being chased in a house that is crumbling around me. Don't know who is chasing me, but I have to get away. Someone, I can't tell if it is a man or a woman, is watching me run around the house. It's a friend. I feel I'd be safe if I could get to them, but I don't know who it is, and no matter how hard I try, I can't get to them.

Next thing I know, I'm awake. I have the strangest feeling that Peg and John were waiting for my mother.

A soft knock on the hotel room door startled her. "Hotel security," a deep voice came from the other side of the door. "Are you okay, Ms. Malone?"

"I'm fine," replied Kay through the door. As a precaution, she called the front desk. "Did you send security to my room?"

"Yes," the voice on the other end of the line said calmly. "A guest reported hearing a scream come from your room. We thought we'd better see if you were okay."

"Thanks for your concern. I'm okay now. I had a bad dream and woke up screaming. Didn't mean to disturb the other guests."

"No problem, Ms. Malone. I'll tell security everything is alright."

Kay stumbled back to bed, still shaking from the nightmare. She sat on the edge of the bed for several minutes, trying to make sense of the dream and the 'ghosts' that had haunted this trip, beginning with thoughts of her mother on the flight from California. Emotionally and physically exhausted, she pulled the covers up to her chin and slept fitfully.

CHAPTER TWENTY-FIVE

Friday, March 17

K ay stepped out of the elevator in the hotel lobby as Paul and Anna walked through the entrance. Anna laughed, and Paul shook his head when Kay pulled her trouser leg up a little to expose the shamrock socks she was wearing.

"I couldn't resist," Kay said. "After all, it's St. Patty's Day. And we must honor the saints. Besides, I'm ready for a good party."

Anna hugged her sister. "So am I."

"And that makes three of us," Paul interjected.

Paul and Kay exchanged cheek kisses, and the three left the hotel arm in arm. The short three-mile drive south of Elleston to Luigi's was filled with happy chatter about nothing and everything. Pulling into the parking lot, the three pointed and laughed at the green lights shining on the brick exterior of the restaurant. "Even the Italians are Irish today," Kay noted.

"Last year," Anna said. "On Saint Patrick's Day, I chided Uncle Sean for not wearing a single green thing. He straightened to his full six feet two height, looked at me over the top of his glasses, and said in the deepest bass voice with a hint of disdain, "Anna, I'm Irish, Irish, not American Irish." Then he laughed that wonderful deep, melodious chortle of his."

"That sounds like him," Paul said with a chuckle. Kay put on her best pasted smile and said nothing. Only Paul, the professional observer of human reactions, noticed the subtle change in Kay's facial expression.

As the trio walked through the parking lot, Kay nudged Anna, "Is that Jim Tiegen going into the restaurant?"

"It looks like it?" Anna replied.

Paul looked at Kay, "Jim Tiegen?"

"Kay met him on the plane from Chicago, and I chatted with him during the press conference," Anna said. "We were in the college choir together, but I didn't know him then. He seems like a nice guy."

Kay smirked. "And he's kind of cute." Anna shook her head and rolled her eyes.

As Paul held the door for his companions, Jim almost ran into Anna as he stepped out of the restaurant's front door. "Leaving so soon? We just saw you walk in," Anna remarked.

Jim shook his head in frustration. "I forgot it was St. Patrick's Day and didn't make a reservation. The wait for a table is too long, I'll have to eat here another time." Dressed in a light spring jacket and jeans, he shivered and pushed his hands deeper in the jacket pockets. "Brrr. I should have worn my coat. I forgot how cold that wind can be coming up the river."

Paul noted the disappointed look on Anna's face. "You'll have to join us, then. I've reserved a table and am sure there will be room for an extra setting. Besides, it will keep these two from ganging up on me. Let's get inside. We don't want you to freeze."

"I don't want to intrude."

"Nonsense," Kay and Anna said simultaneously. "Please, join us."

The maitre'd led them on a winding route through tables covered with red and white checkered tablecloths to a booth at the back of the restaurant. The booth afforded a view of the entire restaurant, including the vine-covered trellis covering the small stage and dance floor. Above the booth, typical of American-Italian restaurants, was a large picture of the Italian countryside. Similar photos adorned much of the room's wall space.

"I saved your favorite booth for you, Paul," the maître d' said as he handed each of them a menu. "Your server will be here shortly."

"Thanks," Paul said. "I appreciate it."

Kay and Anna slid into the booth first. To Anna's delight and Kay's amused grin, Jim slid in next to Anna. Without complaint, Kay joined Paul on the opposite side. The jazz trio, setting up at the edge of a small dance floor, recognized Paul as a regular and waved.

"Is there anyone in town that you don't know?" Anna asked. "It never fails. Whenever I'm with you, it seems you know half the people we see. I've lived in Ellston my entire life, and most of those who greet you are strangers to me."

Paul grinned, "It's a friendly town."

"I suspect it's more like the newspaper editor cultivating sources," Kay said. "The more people you know, the higher the chances of running into an interesting story. Isn't that true?"

Paul shrugged. "What can I say?"

"I was surprised to see you at the airport," Kay said. "And to hear you're managing the *Herald-Review*. Last I heard you were somewhere in Africa. Didn't you get a Pulitzer for something?"

"And, a Peabody," Anna added.

"Impressive. Congratulations." Jim raised his glass and nodded to Paul.

"Thank you." Paul acknowledged the toast. "So, Jim, what brings you to town?"

"Two reasons, I have a business meeting next week, and Kay's recital tomorrow."

"Are you an opera fan?"

"Yes, it's a family thing. My parents were big fans, and I caught the bug. My dad always said that the way opera combines theater and music is the pinnacle for both art forms."

Kay nodded. "A smart man, your father."

"Anna doesn't remember me," Jim teased. "We sang in the choir together in college."

Anna's face turned a light shade of pink. "It was a large choir. And, we didn't officially meet until Kay introduced us at the airport," she sputtered.

Kay reached over to touch Paul's coat sleeve. "Jim and I met on the airplane from Chicago."

Paul looked at him. "You live in Chicago?"

"I'm a partner in an architectural firm there." Jim spread his arms, indicating the two women. "How did you manage to have two such charming companions as dinner partners?"

"The three of us go back a long way," replied Paul. "Anna is my cousin, and I met Kay in a bank over a mishap with a golf club."

Jim laughed. "Hence the exchange at the press conference."

"You should have seen him," Kay said. "He tripped and ended up wheezing on the floor. His golf club skittered across the lobby and almost hit me. You could say he got my attention by attacking me with a deadly weapon. We've been friends ever since, though rarely in the same town at the same time."

"That's an innovative way to meet a girl. I've never tried to meet one by throwing a golf club at her," Jim smiled and shook his head. "I have to say, it's original."

"No," Anna playfully shot back. "You do it the conventional way, by starting conversations with young women on airplanes and at airports."

"One of the few times I've met with success and ended up having such delightful dinner companions."

Through dinner, the conversation flowed easily. The four traded stories of college days in Ellston, classes they had suffered through, and the characters that seem to populate small towns everywhere.

"I recall reading a nationally syndicated newspaper column written by Paul Williams," Jim said as he pushed his nearly clean plate away. "By any chance, are you he?"

"I had a syndicated column for a few years."

"I also remember reading that the column had won several awards?"

Paul nodded. Even after all his years as a journalist, he still felt awkward and uncomfortable talking about himself. "One of them was for some reporting I did in Afghanistan, and the other was on how aspiring arts professionals prepare for professional careers."

Kay's eyebrows lifted in surprise. "Was that the result of the interview you did with me?"

"Partially," said Paul, his eyes briefly locking with hers. The moment was broken by a loud crash in the kitchen. "Some poor staff member would clearly be sweeping up glass for a while," he said.

Undeterred by the crash, Jim leaned in toward Paul. "One of the Chicago papers carried your column. You wrote about some pretty intense topics, as I recall. I thought you were working out of the southwest."

"I was at the time. Now I'm here," Paul answered flippantly as he fidgeted in his seat. It was time to shift the focus *off* of himself. "Kay, I was in London just before your debut there. What was it, six or seven years ago? I was passing through the week before the show opened but unfortunately couldn't stay."

"Oh, too bad we didn't connect. I was in rehearsal for three weeks before the opening."

"That would have been fun," said Anna wistfully. "Rome, Paris, Milan, where haven't you two been? You guys get to see the world, and I'm stuck here."

"It has been fun, but the glamor soon wears thin," Kay said

Anna wrinkled her nose. "Yeah? Maybe. But all I've managed to accomplish is to stay in this small town in the middle of nowhere, while the two of you have great careers that take you to all sorts of exotic places."

Paul nonchalantly placed his elbows on the table. "There are worse fates than staying in the old hometown. Like Kay said, the travel glamor soon wears off. Many of the places I've seen have been dirty and dangerous. They never appear in travel brochures."

Anna sat back, her eyebrows pulled together, forming a crease across her brow. "I know, but at least the two of you have done interesting things, making you interesting people with stories to tell. I'm only a boring girl next door."

Kay reached over to gently squeeze Anna's hand. "You could have moved away. Why didn't you?"

"After Dad died, I moved back to help Mom."

"Your mom's gone now," said Paul. "What's keeping you here?"

"I don't know." Anna shrugged her shoulders. "I'm not sure where I would go. It doesn't seem to make sense to go to a new place just to do something different. There'd have to be a reason for that drastic change. Besides, I like my job in the college admissions office. I think what I'm doing is useful. It's hard to give that up."

Kay turned to Jim, "I'm sorry, we must be boring you to death. Tell us about Chicago."

"Not bored at all, Jim smiled reassuringly. "I see three people who love each other but rarely have a chance to talk. The conversation naturally turns into important topics because time together is rare. I feel privileged that you are comfortable enough to have this conversation around me."

He paused to finish his glass of wine. The jazz trio's rendition of Hoagy Carmichael's *Stardust* filled the silence.

"My life in Chicago centers around work and the arts scene. Our company supports the Lyric Opera and several small, yet excellent, amateur choirs and orchestras in the Chicago area. Other than that, life is pretty routine."

The arrival of coffee and dessert and the strains of a lively tune from the jazz trio lightened the mood.

"Anna," Jim leaned toward the young woman. "The dance floor looks like it has room for another couple. Would you care to dance?"

Anna smiled at him, "I'd love to."

Jim touched Anna's elbow and gently guided her to the dance floor.

Paul relaxed against the chair back. "You've made quite a career for yourself. London, Paris, New York, San Francisco. Even La Scala, for which, by the way, you did not send me an invitation."

"Would you have come?"

Dang! Still as direct as ever! "I would have tried," Paul answered truthfully.

"Next time for sure." Kay glanced up from her coffee and looked directly at Paul. "Have you been keeping track of my career?"

He blushed. "Anna has made a point of keeping me informed. I'm curious about one thing, though."

"What might that be?"

"Why did you come home for this concert?"

"To honor my friend and mentor, Elizabeth Keizer, and to spend some time with my sister."

"I know that's the published reason," Paul replied, not buying into her evasiveness. "I can't help feeling there's more to it than that. Anna tells me you rarely come home, and you've been distracted most of the evening. You keep looking around as if expecting something bad to happen."

Kay took a deep breath and shifted in her seat. An up-tempo song cut through the momentary silence as the couple on the dance floor spun around happily. She hesitated, not sure how much to reveal.

"Off the record?"

"Yes, of course."

Kay's eyes narrowed at Paul. "No, really. Fully *off* the record?"

"We're old friends having a conversation. I'm not looking for a story."

Kay hesitated and stared at her old friend briefly before letting down her guard. "Paul, it's been a strange few days."

Paul's forehead furrowed. "How so?"

"Between you and me, only?"

"Kay…" Paul began with exasperation, but when he saw the concern in Kay's eyes, he simply replied, "Yes. Just you and me."

"This town has very bad memories for me. Mostly tied to my mother. It's been like she's haunting me since this trip began."

Kay nervously picked at the fancy lace tablecloth and glanced over her shoulder as if unwanted ears were listening. "On the red eye out of San Francisco, I dreamed about her. In my dream, she was leaning over me. I could feel her hair tickling my nose. Then, when I arrived, one of the first people I met was my mother's brother. Haven't seen him in years."

"Your uncle?"

"Yes, Father Sean McDonough. My mother's only sibling."

"You mean, Father Sean, over at St. Francis?"

Kay silently nodded her confirmation and glanced at her sister and Jim, who were still dancing up a storm. *Why do I feel so exposed here?*

Paul leaned back in his chair and waited for her to continue.

"Do you know much about my mother?" Kay asked.

Paul ran his fingers through his already tousled hair. "Anna has told me a little bit, but not much. I know you weren't close to her. You told me that when we first met."

"Not even *slightly* close to each other." Kay laughed, but it sounded forced and without humor. "Last night was a real shocker. Dr. K. and I met to do some vocal warm-ups, and it was just like old times until she dropped a bomb on me at the end of the session by telling me that my mother had also been one of her students.

Kay drained the remainder of her drink and signaled the waiter to bring another. She wasn't much of a drinker, but the subject of her mother was one of her least favorites. "It affected me way more than I wanted it to. I swear it felt like a body blow that I still haven't recovered from. Every time I turn around, I fear I'll see someone or something that will remind me of her."

Concerned, Paul reached out to Kay's hand. This time, she didn't pull away. "I don't know what to say. Have you told Anna yet?"

Kay sighed. "At this point, it's just my own paranoia, so I don't think there's a need to say anything to her. It's not like there's anything wrong, I'm just struggling with some old ghost of my past. I just needed to tell someone…" her voice trailed off.

Paul gave her hand another gentle squeeze but said nothing. He was pleased that she confided in him but was unsure what she wanted or needed next.

The pair sat in silence, watching Jim and Anna on the dance floor.

"They look good together, don't they?" Kay murmured.

Paul nodded. "Yes, they do."

Kay turned back to the table. "Does Anna seem nervous to you?"

"A little."

Did you notice she kept turning her knife over and over and twisting her hair?"

"I've seen her nervous like this a couple of times. When I've asked her about it, she pooh-poohs it and tries to laugh it off. Once, she admitted that she occasionally has these episodes. Calls them premonitions. She claims that something bad happens to one of her friends within a few days. Nothing disastrous, like a death, but something serious. She can't predict who will be affected, but it upsets her and makes her a little nervous."

On the dance floor, Jim and Anna fit together perfectly. He expertly led, while she anticipated his steps, moving as a unit to the beat of the music. When the music drew to the final cadence, they executed a twirl and dip to the delight of those sitting around the dance floor.

Back at the table, Anna said, "That was fun. You are an excellent dancer."

Jim mocked bowed. "It was clearly my partner who made me look good."

"Oh, God," snorted Kay. "Another one who has kissed the Blarney Stone." The foursome shared a laugh.

Anna fanned herself with a napkin to cool down. "That is more exercise than I have had in ages. It was great fun. Thank you, Jim."

"My pleasure," Jim turned to Kay. "Are you all ready for tomorrow's recital?"

"I put the final touches on the music with Brian this afternoon."

"Brian?" Paul inquired.

"Brian Eckhart, my accompanist. I've worked with him for years. We know each other's foibles and idiosyncrasies. He brings a *joie de vivre* to all he does. It's infectious."

"It must be strange to sing for the hometown crowd," Paul remarked. "I know it was disconcerting for me to walk into the newsroom where I had started my career...especially since I was coming in as the new boss. I worried that the staff would resent me coming in from the outside."

"I am a little apprehensive," Kay admitted. "I didn't think much about it until I got on the plane to come here. I always get a few performance butterflies, but being back home is different."

"How so?" asked Jim.

Kay picked at the checkered tablecloth as she pondered her answer. "I have sung on the major stages around the world, in front of royalty, in front of the most musically sophisticated audiences, and the harshest critics. The nerves are different this time. The problem is I haven't sung for friends, family, and people who've known me since college. I'm a little nervous. Will the hometown crowd expect more than I can deliver?"

Only Jim noticed the tightness in Anna's face and the nervous wrapping of her dark hair around her fingers. "Kay, I'm really looking forward to your recital. I'm sure it will be thrilling for the audience."

"Come on, gang. It's time for one last dance," Paul said as he stood and gestured for his new friends to follow. The band's last song of the night was a peppy, upbeat number perfect for dancing.

Anna held out her hand to Jim just as Paul offered his to Kay. She smiled, took his hand, and moved toward the dance floor.

CHAPTER TWENTY-SIX

The Night of the Big Performance

After the standing ovation, Kay returned to the stage for an encore. She thanked the audience for the warm welcome home they had given her. She paid homage to her mentor, Dr. Elizabeth Keizer, who had inspired her and so many musicians, students, and faculty during her forty-year career at Milan College. She announced that for an encore, she'd perform one of her favorite pieces, a lullaby by Johannes Brahms. She nodded to Brian Eckhart to begin the introduction.

As she filled her lungs to begin singing, a movement in the audience distracted her. A young woman in the front row had bent over to retrieve her program from the floor and sat upright. Kay blinked at the sight, coughed, and missed her entrance. Her accompanist expertly tried to cover the mistake by smoothly repeating the last few measures of the introduction. Kay opened her mouth to sing, but no sound came. She had no choice but to clear her throat, apologize to the audience, and ask Brian to begin the introduction again.

Brian smiled, nodded, and began again. As her entrance to the song drew near, Kay felt a surge of panic in her stomach. When her cue to join in arrived, she began to sing, but her voice faltered and then stopped altogether. A third attempt failed completely. Her voice would not work at all.

Kay fled the stage in a panic. Brian followed her. A moment later, he returned to inform the stunned audience that Ms. Malone would not be able to complete the concert. He apologized and left the stage.

CHAPTER TWENTY-SEVEN

Sunday Afternoon, March 19

Anna sat beside Kay on the couch in her apartment. The folder containing the review of last night's concert rested on Kay's lap. Paul handed it to her when he arrived. He sat across from the two sisters, waiting for Kay's reaction.

"Anna, please," whispered Kay, pushing the folder away from herself. "I can't bear it." Anna took the folder and began reading:

Music Review for Monday, March 20, 2017
Brad Quinn, Music Critic, Herald Reporter

MALONE'S VOICE FAILS AT RECITAL
Concert Cut Short by Apparent Strained Vocal Cords

The benefit recital on Saturday evening by international opera star,
Kay Malone, ended in a shockingly dramatic failure of her voice
at the end of the performance. As she started to sing the encore,
Malone's voice cracked at the entrance to a lovely Brahms lullaby.
After clearing her throat and apologizing to the audience, she
asked her accompanist, Brian Eckhart, to begin again. No sound
emanated from her throat the second time she reached her entrance.
A third attempt had the same result. Ms. Malone left the stage,
followed by her accompanist.

*A few minutes later, Eckhart returned and informed the
audience that Malone could not complete the recital. He apologized
for the failure, thanked the audience for attending the performance,
and left the stage.*

*Until her voice gave out, the program was excellent. Malone
executed the subtle nuances of the music with great skill. The
selections from the Schubert song cycle "Winterreise" (Winter
Journey) were of particular note in the first half of the recital.
Malone's command of the music was unparalleled; her intonation
was perfect, and the tonal warmth of her voice highlighted the
music's subtleties.*

*In the first half, Malone included arias from the opera "Faust"
by Charles Gounod. While the overall effect of the music was
emotionally satisfying, it seems that in the "Spinning Song,"
Ms. Malone was unsure of one of the entrances. Mr. Eckhart, her
accompanist, expertly covered for her. I'm sure most audience
members were unaware of the mistake. This was particularly
surprising because Ms. Malone has sung the role of Marguerite on
many occasions.*

*As an accompanist, Eckhart is a consummate artist. His
technique is flawless, and his stage presence exudes a joy that
enhances the performance experience. His innate sense of when
the accompaniment should be brought to the fore and return to its
supporting role is without equal.*

*The program's second half featured show tunes by Jerome Kern,
Frank Loesser, Rodgers and Hammerstein, and George Gershwin.
The selections were a delight, and the standing ovation and
demand for an encore were well deserved.*

*We hope that Ms. Malone's voice will heal quickly and allow
her to return to her very successful career.*

Anna leaned back on the sofa in her living room and put her arm
around her sister. Kay tried to speak, but her voice refused.

"Paul, can this review be killed?" Anna's eyes pleaded with Paul.

Paul shook his head grimly. "Afraid not. Brad accurately reported what he heard and saw. The review of the performance itself is very complimentary. I've already approved it to run in tomorrow's paper."

Kay whispered, "Paul's right."

Suddenly, the melodious tones of Rossini's *Lone Ranger Theme* interrupted the conversation. Kay handed her cell phone to Anna. Glancing at the caller ID on the screen, Anna said, "It's Dr. Keizer."

"Hi, Dr. K. This is Anna. Kay can barely speak above a whisper." Anna signaled for paper and pen, which Paul quickly supplied, and began to write. "Yes, I'll tell her. Thanks for calling."

Kay moaned, struggling to talk. "I've let her down, after all she's done, I couldn't even finish a recital for her. Did they have to refund the money?"

"That's not it at all," Anna gently patted her sister's hand in comfort. "Dr. K. has made an appointment for you with her personal physician. He'll see you at eleven tomorrow morning. She says he specializes in voice ailments. She said she has referred several students with voice problems to him in the past, with excellent results. She'll pick us up at your hotel at 10:30, and then take us out to lunch after you see the doctor. Typical take-charge by Dr. K. Classic."

"How do you know that's typical of Dr. K?" Kay whispered, her eyes registered surprise even when her voice couldn't. "You're not wrong, but how do you know that?"

"Didn't I ever tell you that I took piano lessons from her in high school, and voice lessons in college?"

Kay shook her head, her brow furrowed slightly.

"In any case, she'll pick us up tomorrow. Now, you need some rest," Anna shifted and looked at her cousin. Paul, thanks for bringing the review by. Call me tomorrow night, and I'll tell you what the doctor says."

Taking the hint, Paul went to Kay and wrapped her in a comforting hug. It took every ounce of energy he had to resist the impulse to kiss her. "It'll all work out, Kay," he murmured. He wanted to stay, but this was a time Kay needed her sister.

Monday, March 20

Anna paced back and forth in the doctor's sterile waiting room. The receptionist busied herself at the desk, ignoring Anna's treks across the office. It was a small room with only a dozen chairs to accommodate patients and their families. The worried Anna didn't notice the series of Norman Rockwell prints meant to amuse both old and young patients.

Liz Keizer sat patiently, paging through a two-month-old issue of *People* she found buried in the middle of a neatly arranged stack of out-of-date publications. She glanced at her flustered student as she pretended to read an article.

"Anna, please sit down. Pacing won't make her exam go any faster."

Anna sat beside her teacher, but her fingers continued twisting her hair nervously. "Dr. K., what do you think is going on? What could have caused Kay to lose her voice like that? Has she just been working too hard? Or could it be something else?"

"Dr. Samuels will be doing a thorough exam. We'll know in a few minutes. I don't think it's something physical. Her voice was strong throughout the recital. Other than the missed entrance in the Gounod aria, her performance was flawless until the encore. If the problem is physical, there would be some indication: a sore throat, a cough, something concrete."

"I hope you're right. It would be a shame if this ended her career." Anna grimaced at the thought.

"It won't end her career, but it will certainly change it. She can't walk away from the music more than you can."

"I can't sing or play like she does. I'm an amateur pretending to be a musician."

"We've been through this before," Dr. Keizer said. "I know you don't believe it, but you are as talented as she is. Are you an amateur? Yes, but only because you don't get paid for your music. You are a musician, not a pretender. The songs you write and the unusual combination of instruments in your orchestrations are among the best I've seen. By the way, have you shown your music to Kay yet?"

Anna slid forward in the chair, aching to pace. "No, I couldn't do that. She might laugh at them."

Dr. Keizer laid her hand on Anna's arm to calm her nerves and stop the endless hair twisting. "Tell you what. I want to show Kay some of your songs, without telling her you wrote them. Trust me, the only thing Kay will laugh at will be the musical jokes you love to hide in the middle of a song. Okay?"

Anna squirmed. "Oh, I don't know..."

Dr. K. nudged her playfully. "Come on. Let me show them to her. You have nothing to lose."

"Alright. But don't you dare tell her that I wrote them."

A squeak of a door hinge and soft, muffled voices let Anna and Dr. K. know the exam had ended.

Kay entered the waiting room from the clinic's exam wing. She said in a soft, scratchy voice and a stony demeanor, "Dr. Samuels says there is nothing physically wrong with my voice. No damage to the cords, no nodules, nothing. He saw no physical reason that I couldn't talk or sing. He had me try a few soft scales, three or four notes, and my voice quit. He's scheduled a battery of tests for tomorrow."

Slowly, Kay's façade of control began to crumble. "What am I going to do? My voice is gone. My career is gone. What will I do?" Sobs wracked her slim body.

Anna rushed to embrace her sister, while Dr. Keizer stood quietly off to the side, tears flowing freely. When the raw emotions began to fade, she spoke in her usual confident way.

"The first thing we're going to do is get some lunch. Food always makes things seem a little better. After lunch, we'll figure out what to do next."

The two sisters smiled, nodded, and wiped their eyes.

Dr. Keizer continued, "The fact that there's nothing physically wrong with your voice is good. Now we can look in other directions for an answer. The tests tomorrow will tell us how to proceed. Where do you want to eat?"

"Does the Roasting Cup, down near the University, still serve those wonderful, old-fashioned caramel malts?" whispered Kay.

"Yes, they do," replied Anna.

Dr. Keizer laughed. "Nothing like an old-fashioned malt to bring perspective to the world. However, I think chocolate is better than caramel. The Roasting Cup it is."

"After that," said Anna. "We're going to get you moved into my house. It'll be much more comfortable than the hotel."

Kay started to protest, but the words caught in her throat.

"No point in arguing. I've already decided," Anna declared firmly.

CHAPTER TWENTY-EIGHT

Tuesday, March 21

Jim Teigen poked his head into Anna's office. "Got time for lunch?"

"Jim?" At first, Anna didn't recognize the tall man, dressed in a tailored business suit and vest. "Oh! What a surprise!"

"A good one, I hope." Jim stepped into the office, a boyish grin on his face.

"A delightful one." Anna pushed away from her desk and checked her watch. "Yes, I have time for lunch, but it must be quick. I have a meeting at 1:30. We can eat at the college cafeteria since there's not enough time to go off-campus."

"Works for me," agreed Jim. "I had hoped to take you to a little fancier place."

"That, I'll take a rain check on," Anna answered with a wide smile.

"You look beautiful today." Jim turned a light shade of pink, embarrassed at his awkwardness.

Anna, full of mischief as always, replied. "You clean up pretty good, too. I almost didn't recognize you in that suit."

The noontime lunch crowd filled the college cafeteria with laughter and banter. The delicious smells of pizza, roast beef, and grilled chicken punctuated the festive and noisy atmosphere. Anna and Jim weaved their way through the crowd and managed to snatch a table on the upper level.

"At least, it's a little quieter here," Jim noted. "Not much privacy, but with the hubbub, no one will pay any attention to us."

"Thanks again for stopping by. This is a treat. What brought you to campus today?"

Jim finished chewing before answering. "Had a meeting with President Anderson. Thought it would be fun to have lunch with you, if you were available."

Anna grinned. "Did the president have anything interesting to say?"

Jim shrugged. "Not really."

Anna leaned forward and lowered her voice. "I know he has a big project in mind. We've been raising funds for it for the past year. I also know you're a partner in a Chicago architectural firm that works with colleges. Two plus two still equals four. Or a hundred, if you prefer to use binary."

Jim raised his eyebrows.

Anna leaned back in her seat with an impish smile. "I Googled you on Saturday."

"That's okay, I Googled you Friday night!" Jim took a bite of his hamburger and continued. "I can't talk about the president's project yet, so we'll have to find a more interesting topic...like, oh, I don't know, maybe...*you*?"

Anna laughed and feigned innocence. "Little ol' me?" she added, batting her eyes playfully.

"Little ol' you," Jim grinned.

"What do you want to know?"

"Oh, the usual stuff."

"Let's see...I have a terrible temper."

"I'll have to be sure not to get you angry. And?"

"And...I hate pickles and sauerkraut." Anna wrinkled her nose.

"I guess German restaurants are out of the question. And?"

"And I've never tried sushi!"

"*That* we can fix," Jim said. "Will you make me dig for all the vital information?"

Anna paused. "I guess the most important thing right now is I'm not married or in a relationship."

A bright smile lit up Jim's face. "That is the most important piece of information. Thanks for not keeping me guessing."

Anna looked at her watch. "I'm so sorry. I've got to get back to work. Next time, we'll talk about you."

Jim raised an eyebrow. "Next time?"

"Yes, next time. Which will be tomorrow night when you take me to dinner."

"That's a date."

At the cafeteria entrance, they exchanged phone numbers and arranged to meet at Luigi's the following evening. Anna thought she heard Jim humming a tune as he left for the parking lot, and she walked down the hallway toward her office.

Wednesday Evening, March 22

Jim and Anna sat next to each other in an intimate booth at Luigi's. Typically, there were few diners on Wednesday nights, and they were relatively subdued, unlike the usual crowds on weekends. The jazz trio only played on weekends, so the dance floor was dark and empty.

"You are an absolute delight," Jim said. "Charming, witty, great dancer, but I don't know much more about you than when we started dinner, other than Kay is your sister."

"Not much to tell. My childhood was pretty normal. I played soccer, took piano lessons, went to college, fell in love, or at least thought it was love. We broke up shortly after graduation. Both my folks are gone now. So, I'm thirty-three years old, and I own a house and a car—a new one at that. I work in the admissions office at the college. That's it. Pretty standard story," Anna folded her hands on the tabletop and quizzically tilted her head to the side. "Now it's your turn."

Jim folded his napkin and leaned forward. "Very succinct recitation of the facts. That fits what I've seen of you, but it hardly tells me who you are, which I suspect was on purpose."

"As I said," Anna replied firmly. "*Your turn.*"

"Okay," Jim was surprised by Anna's directness and serious tone. "Turnabout is fair play. Born and raised in Evanston, a northern suburb of Chicago. Dad was an architect, and Mom is a lawyer. Prefer baseball to football, especially the Cubbies, though I am delighted when the Bears beat the Vikings. I graduated from Milan and attended the Architecture School at Northwestern. Became a partner in my father's firm when he retired. Mom is still practicing law. Never been married, have a sister and a brother, don't own a house, but do own a car. I'm thirty-four and, as you already know, love music. See, I can be succinct, too."

Anna laughed. "What else do you want to know about me?"

"Politics?"

"Independent, lean left. And you?"

"Independent, lean right," Jim confidently replied.

"That's tolerable, should make for interesting conversations," Anna said. She found herself thoroughly enjoying their back-and-forth exchange.

"Agreed. How about religion?" asked Jim.

"In Protestant jargon, a C and E'er."

Jim paused mid-drink. "'C and E'er?'"

"Christmas and Easter. In other words, there's something out there, but I don't know what it is."

"Catholic by family tradition. Can't say I'm practicing. Is that a problem?"

Anna smiled. "Not for me."

Jim leaned back in the booth and took another sip of wine. "Tell me, what do you do when you're not working?"

"Oh, I like to hike and sing in the Chorale. Love jazz. Sometimes, I think I work to support my music habit." Anna paused and began to twist her hair. "Can you keep a secret?"

Jim's eyes twinkled. He leaned closely and whispered. "Is it a deep, dark, juicy one?"

"Silly. We don't have to whisper!"

Jim threw up his hands in mock exasperation. "Oh, I thought the best secrets were the ones you had to whisper. What's your deep, dark secret?"

"You have to promise not to tell anyone, especially my sister."

"I promise." Jim raised his hand in the three-fingered Boy Scout salute.

"Were you really a Scout?"

"No. But Scout or not, I promise."

He's so easy to talk to! Anna leaned closer and whispered, "I write music."

"You write music?" Jim repeated, slightly baffled at her revelation.

"Ssshhh," said Anna, pressing her forefinger to her lips. "It's a secret."

Both leaned back and laughed.

"Seriously?" Jim said. "You write music? What kind of music?"

"Mostly choral and orchestral."

"That's cool. But why the secrecy? Especially from your sister?"

"That's hard to explain. Mostly, I think it's because I don't want to be compared to her. I'm not nearly as talented as she is. Besides, if it were to become known, I'm afraid I'd be a disappointment. Does that make any sense?"

"Yes, I get it," Jim nodded. "I promise to keep your secret, but someday, I think you will need to summon the courage to tell Kay."

Anna shrugged. "Maybe, but I doubt it." The confused look on Jim's face prompted her to add, "I know it seems weird, but Kay is so good. I'm just not in her league."

Jim felt flattered that Anna had confided in him. It increased his curiosity about the mystery surrounding her. He paused, asking, "Will you play your music for me?"

"It depends."

"On what?"

"On where this goes." Anna felt a nervous flutter in her chest. *I hope that's what he wants, too.*

"Are we on a path to somewhere?" Jim's gaze was bright and direct.

Anna cocked her head to one side and began twisting her hair. "I don't know exactly, but it's not nowhere."

Saturday, March 25

"Ten serving nine, match point."

Thwaunk.

Thwaunk.

Thwaunk.

Thwaunk.

Thwaunk.

Thwaunk.

Thwaunk.

Thud. The racquet ball hit the corner of the sidewall, six inches above the floor, ricocheted to the front wall, and rolled past the service line. The melodic back-and-forth *thwank* of the ball ended abruptly.

"That's two games to one. Game and Match!" Jim said, raising his racket victoriously.

"No defense for that corner shot. Nice hit," Paul commented as he wiped the sweat from his forehead. "Great game. Thanks for the work-out. Lunch?"

Jim, hands on his hips, tried to catch his breath. "Good idea."

The two men cooled off on the short walk to the club cafe. They opted to sit on the sunlit veranda. Protected from the spring breeze, they basked in the March sunlight that hinted at an early spring. "I understand you visited the paper's morgue on Friday," Paul casually commented. "Did you find what you needed?"

"Some of it." Jim fiddled with the coaster under his cup of coffee.

"I grew up in Ellston. Maybe I can help you find whatever you're looking for."

"Just trying to get a feeling for the town and its history." Jim wiped the perspiration from his forehead and looked off into the distance.

Paul looked at his new friend, shook his head, and raised his eyebrows. "Not buying it."

Jim laughed. "Are you always this skeptical?"

"Always. Both by nature and by training. My gut tells me there is more to this than meets the eye."

Jim smiled disarmingly. "Your gut?"

Still not buying it, dude. Paul put on his friendliest smile, the one meant to disarm a potential source. "You have to admit it's a little curious. An architect from Chicago comes to this little town for a concert. He stays around for several days longer than expected, makes friends with the town's newspaper editor, and asks to look through old issues in the paper's morgue. It's quite surprising that an architect would even know, let alone use, the jargon term 'morgue.'"

Jim shrugged and smiled.

But Paul wasn't ready to drop the subject. "Now, this architect is a nice guy, plays a mean game of racquetball, and begins to take an interest in the editor's cousin. The cousin can take care of herself, even if the editor thinks she's still thirteen."

Jim continued to fiddle with his coaster and feign interest in what the other diners were doing.

Paul continued, "The editor runs into the architect at the cemetery and begins to wonder what grave he's visiting, since there's no known connection to the town. The editor's gut begins to get an old familiar twitch, and he wonders if maybe he's smelling a story. The more the editor ponders it, the curiouser and curiouser he becomes."

Jim sat silently, looked around the room to see who might be within earshot, and leaned across the table.

"Actually, I do have connections to this town. I went to college here. As for the cemetery, the parents of a college friend who was very kind to me are buried there. The concert was a good excuse to check out a couple of locations I might be interested in acquiring. My firm has a division that restores and repurposes old buildings."

Paul interrupted, "That, I know. It's on your company website."

"You've been checking on me?" Jim wasn't sure if he should be flattered or annoyed.

Paul smiled. "You'd have been disappointed if I hadn't."

"That's true." Jim laughed. "As far as the cousin goes, she's quite a charming woman, and I think we both enjoy each other's company."

"In other words, mind my own business?"

Jim shrugged his shoulders and nodded his head.

"I can do that," said Paul. "What you say is plausible, and it may even be true. What buildings are you interested in? Maybe I can help."

"It's a pretty competitive business, I don't want to disclose the properties I'm researching, especially to the press. I'm sure you understand." Jim deflected his friend's prying by looking at his watch and grabbing the receipt for their drinks. "Gotta go. I have to run several errands before I pick up Anna. This round is on me. I'll catch you later."

Paul watched Jim walk out the cafe door, and when he was out of sight, he pulled out his cell phone and called the morgue manager at the paper.

"Jake, this is Paul. Has Jim Teigen asked you for copies of any articles from the morgue?" Paul waited a few seconds. "Okay. If he asks, go ahead and copy them for him, but let me know what he asks for. On the Q.T. Thanks."

Monday, March 30

"Hey, Paul," Jake called from across the room as Paul was leaving the newspaper morgue. "You asked me to let you know if Teigen made any requests for articles. I copied four for him today."

"Oh, which ones?"

"Let's see, an article about the armory, another about the construction of the Adams house from forty years ago, an article on architectural firms in the area, and an obituary."

"Did you notice whose obit?"

"It wasn't a name I recognized, so I didn't pay it any mind. I think it was from around twenty years ago."

"Thanks. Keep me posted."

"Will do."

CHAPTER TWENTY-NINE

Thursday, March 23

D r. Samuels rose to greet Kay when the nurse escorted her into his office. A second man, somewhat portly and dressed in a finely tailored, three-piece suit, rose from his chair in front of Dr. Samuels' desk and stood to greet the young woman.

Dr. Samuels introduced his colleague. "Kay, this is my associate, Dr. Alan Phillips. Dr. Phillips is a psychologist who has worked with many artists and musicians over the years. I consulted with him after the tests you underwent showed no physical or neurological issues that would explain the loss of your voice."

Kay struggled to speak. Her voice was still strained and raspy, but not as weak as before. "Do you think it's all in my head?"

Dr.Phillips chuckled and waved a plump hand toward a vacant chair in the office. "I wouldn't phrase it quite that way, Ms. Malone."

The warmth of his smile and his kind demeanor surprised her. Kay immediately felt comfortable in the doctor's presence. The tension in her shoulders eased slightly as she sat in the second chair next to the two men.

Dr. Samuels began. "First of all, the fact that your speaking voice has returned, albeit distorted, is quite encouraging. Based on the tests you took yesterday, we believe we can rule out any physical condition, disease, injury, or neurologic cause as the problem."

"What concerns us," Dr. Phillips added. "Is that when we asked you to try singing even a few notes of the simple tune, 'Happy Birthday,' your voice refused to respond. No doubt that your condition is real. We also believe that whatever causes your voice to refuse to sing, even as your speech improves, must be found for you to heal."

Kay turned to Dr. Samuels. "Do you agree with Dr. Phillips' assessment? Could something physical have been missed by the tests?"

"We didn't miss anything physical, Ms. Malone. I scrutinized your throat and vocal cords and saw nothing wrong. I was surprised there were no signs of strain after singing a recital less than a week ago. The MRI indicated no abnormalities, and the EEG showed no neurological issues. Yesterday's tests ruled out any physical or neurologic cause."

Kay sat quietly, absorbing Dr. Samuel's description of the test results. *Am I going crazy?* "What's next? She asked as calmly and confidently as she could. In reality, she felt anything *but* calm and confident.

"We think you have what is termed a Conversion Disorder," replied Dr. Phillips. "For some people, the symptoms include speech problems such as the inability to speak. In your case, it manifested as the inability to sing. Typically, a physical manifestation of a Conversion Disorder is triggered by some stressful or traumatic event. Ms. Malone, has something happened to you recently? A car accident or near miss? Something that scared you?"

Kay shook her head. "No, life has been hectic, but not anything unusual. I occasionally have a bad dream that wakes me up, but it's nothing of consequence. I had a weird one the other night."

The doctors exchanged a glance. "What was in the dream?" Dr. Phillips eyed Kay's reactions carefully.

There was a long pause before she began to speak. The doctor sensed the dream affected her more than she let on. He noted the twitching muscles at the corners of her mouth and chin. Just when he was certain she would decline sharing, she sighed and began to tell the dream.

"I was at the river's edge and couldn't get across. People I knew were on the other side, waiting for someone. In the dream, I knew they weren't waiting for me. I had the strangest feeling they were waiting for my mother. Then I ran, trying to get to someone. Not to the people on the other side of the river. I felt like I knew him, but I couldn't reach him. Knew I'd be safe if I could."

Dr. Phillips pursed his lips thoughtfully. "There are some interesting images in that dream. What was your relationship to the people on the other side of the river?"

"They were very dear friends." Kay's body relaxed briefly, and she smiled at the memory of Peg and John. "Both are gone now. I would've loved to talk to them."

"What about your mother? In the dream, did you try to talk to her?"

"She's been dead for twenty years." Kay's lips tightened from a warm smile to a thin, grim line.

"Dr. Phillips observed the change in Kay's expression. "I'm sorry to hear that. The recital, did anything unusual happen before, during, or after? Abnormal stress or an event connected to it?"

Kay shook her head. "It was unusual because I haven't performed at home in twenty years. But it has been a treat to visit with my sister, see old friends, and honor Dr. Keizer. The recital itself went very well until my voice gave out." Kay paused. "Dr. Phillips, is my singing voice going to come back?"

"Yes, I believe it will, but I can't predict when or to what degree."

"Doctor, my career is on the line here. What can be done to fix this?"

"We have several options for you to consider. First, it is possible that with rest, your voice will return on its own, so we could wait and see if that happens. Secondly…"

Kay interrupted. These were not the answers she was hoping to hear. "I don't have time to wait and see. I begin rehearsals in Denver in three weeks. I can't just sit and wait."

"A more proactive course would be several sessions of psychotherapy. Such therapy could help discover the root cause of the voice loss. Or, we could try a course of Valium to help you relax."

Kay's expression turned from desperate to shocked. "Valium?"

"Perhaps, the relaxation and respite from stress would induce the singing voice to return. However, I'm not sure that it would, at this point, help all that much, but it is an option." Dr. Phillips leaned back in his chair, the wood creaking in protest.

"Frankly, the idea of going on Valium isn't appealing, unless necessary. Would psychotherapy help to discover the cause?"

The doctor shrugged slightly. "No guarantees, but I think it gives us the best chance to find out what's going on."

Kay sighed. *Is this really happening?* She turned to face the other physician. "Dr. Samuels?"

His answer was immediate. "My advice would be to try psychotherapy."

Kay looked at each of the doctors in turn. "If the therapy sessions will help find out what may be causing my voice to quit, then let's try them. I have to be able to trust my voice, or my career is over."

"Very good," said Dr. Phillips, handing Kay his business card. "Call this number to arrange an appointment. My office is on the seventh floor of this building. Let's see if we can't get you back to singing Ms. Malone."

Sunday, March 26

Anna stood leaning against the kitchen counter, her hands jammed into her jeans, her shoulders hunched, veins pulsing in her neck. Kay sat ramrod straight at the table, her fists tightly closed around the coffee mug before her.

The sound of the automatic ice maker dropping a tray of ice cubes into the freezer's ice tray, the drone of the after church traffic, all ignored by the sisters. All the sounds inside and outside the house were ignored. The tension between them was palpable.

"I don't get it," said Anna.

"What don't you get?" Kay snapped. "It's quite simple. She abandoned me, and by the way, abandoned you, or have you forgotten?"

The sharpness in her sister's voice stung enough to trigger Anna's anger. "I haven't forgotten anything! But, Kay, it's been thirty-five years since she left, and you're still so angry that the mere mention of her name sets you off. I'm walking on eggshells around you whenever Maarit or Uncle Sean are mentioned. That's what I don't get."

"What I don't get is why you insist on defending her. She was a hateful, nasty woman." Kay's throat tightened, and angry tears formed in her eyes.

Anna bristled. "I'm not defending her. But isn't it time you got over it?"

"'*Got over it!*' How can you say that?"

Anna, exasperated, grabbed a kitchen chair, turned it around with the back facing the table, and sat leaning toward Kay. "And how, exactly, do you know she was nasty? You, yourself, said you hadn't had any contact with her from the time she left until she died. How do you know she was a bitch? Maybe she had grown. Maybe she had changed. Maybe she was ashamed. Maybe a lot of things. You can't possibly know, but you won't even give her memory the benefit of any kind of doubt."

Kay vehemently shook her head. "No doubt in my mind. Only a horrible person would abandon her child and not have any further contact with her. No birthday cards, no phone calls on graduation day. Nothing."

Anna lowered her voice. And increased the intensity. "She didn't exactly leave you on a stranger's doorstep. She left you with your 'sainted' father."

Kay stood, leaned across the table, the palms of her hands flat on the tabletop. "You leave my father out of this. He sacrificed a lot to raise me. Including marrying again." Her eyes snapped with a mix of anger and hurt.

"That was his choice. Who knows what role he played in the divorce?"

"None of it was his fault."

Anna's voice softened as she rose and returned the chair to its proper position. "There are always two sides to any split. I still regret the way

I reacted to my split with Rob. I tried to take revenge. In the process, some people got hurt who didn't deserve it. I still wonder how much it was my fault."

"My God, Anna! He slept with your best friend. Of course, you'd be angry."

"The question is, my role in the fiasco."

"Yeah, well, maybe your reaction was problematic, but my anger is justified," Kay said.

"That may be, but anger is anger. It's eating you up. Look at what it's costing you. You suffered the embarrassment of not being able to complete a concert. You can't do what you always loved to do: sing. Your career is in jeopardy, and we're fighting."

The two sisters glared at each other. Anna's hands balled into fists while Kay's face was as rigid as stone.

Anna's shoulders began to shake. Slowly at first, then more quickly, her jaw quivered as she tried to suppress a laugh.

Kay tried, also without success, to stop the corners of her lips from turning upward in the beginning of a smile. "What's the use of having a sister if you can't fight with her?"

"Agreed," said Anna. "Still friends?"

"Well, I'm stuck with you as a sister. We might as well be friends, too."

The two of them collapsed into their chairs, laughing, tears streaming down their faces. After wiping her face, Kay's expression softened. "I'm sorry about the breakup thing. I didn't know it was such a mess. How did you manage to get over it?"

"I can't say that I'm over it. Rob hurt me, but I turned around and hurt more people than he did. I spread rumors about my best friend. They caused a breakup with a boy she had just started dating shortly after the infamous party. That's the hardest part to live with. What kind of person seeks revenge and doesn't care who gets destroyed in the process? Now I'm afraid of relationships. I have trust issues that make it difficult for me. And that's a problem because I'm starting to like Jim. It's not him I don't trust. It's me."

Kay sat quietly looking at her sister. "Have you told him about all this?'

"I told him I had been in a relationship, but not the whole story."

"Do you think maybe you should?"

"Kay, I can't," Anna said. Her fingers began busily twisting her hair. The whole topic made her uncomfortable. "It's better to let the past die a natural death. Let the dead bury the dead."

Monday, March 27

Anna and Father McDonough drove up the cemetery service road to John and Peg's grave. They sat in the car for a moment while Anna gathered the emotional strength to stand before her parents' graves. "Thanks for coming with me, Uncle Sean. I like visiting them in the spring, and I didn't want to do this by myself today."

Sean put his arm around his niece and squeezed her shoulders. "How long have they been gone, now?"

"Over fifteen years," Anna's voice cracked. "It still seems like yesterday. I asked Kay to come with me, but she refused. She got angry and we had a good old-fashioned sister fight."

Sean chuckled in his deep bass voice. "I'm having trouble imagining the two of you arguing. It seems quite out of character for both of you."

"I probably overstepped my bounds. Never could keep my mouth shut. My mouth disengages from my brain sometimes, and I don't think before I speak." Anna sighed. "Basically, I told her to stop being angry at Maarit. Told her it was time to 'forgive and forget.' She didn't take my suggestion too kindly."

The priest nodded grimly. "She wasn't quite ready to hear that. How did you two leave it?"

Anna laughed. "We decided that having a sister to fight with was good."

— 208 —

Sean nodded approvingly as they stepped between a row of gravestones and paused to read the inscriptions.

JOHN ALLEN JENSEN: 1952–2002
MARGARET 'PEG' JENSEN: 1951–2013
TOGETHER AGAIN

Anna knelt to place a bouquet of tulips on her parents' grave. An early spring breeze carried the warmth of the sun away. Blades of new grass and tender new sprouts bent under the gust. She pulled her jacket tightly around her.

"Mom loved tulips. She would laugh when a spring snow covered the flowers' stems after their heads had poked above the ground. Within a day or two, the snow would melt, and the tulips would still be there, little green sprigs against the white of the snow. Mom would say, 'A little snow can't stop spring.'"

Anna leaned in, adjusted the flowers, and stood up straight. "I can't believe they're both gone."

"Your mom was quite a lady," Father Sean noted. "I loved visiting with her and John. I remember the first time I met them. They understood my grief even as they tried to figure out why Maarit placed you for adoption."

"Every once in a while, I take out the letter Maarit wrote to me," Anna said. "I think when she found out she was pregnant, she must have been scared and lonely. She did the only thing she could think of: give me a life and a family. I was lucky. John and Peg were wonderful parents."

The two stood quietly for a few moments, wrapped in the warmth of memories. Together, they walked silently a few rows away to Maarit's grave. The priest made the sign of the cross over the grave and knelt. The ritual was a prayer for the repose of a soul, one that was close to his heart. He knelt, bowed his head, and placed a bouquet of daisies on his sister's grave. Anna stood, waiting for the prayer to come to a close.

The cold spring breeze that had chilled her earlier suddenly faded, and the sun's warmth returned to comfort her. She slipped off her light jacket and draped it over her arms, holding it loosely in front of her. Red-winged blackbirds happily babbled in the background as if announcing their pleasure at the season's arrival.

As her uncle concluded the prayer, Anna felt a familiar shiver at the nape of her neck. "Uncle Sean, do you ever feel her presence?"

"Occasionally...but not frequently."

"I stop here every time I visit my parents' graves. I don't know why; I never knew her. I just feel like I have to."

Sean stood and brushed dirt and grass clippings from his trouser leg. He said nothing, hoping his silence would encourage his niece to continue.

"It's strange," Anna said. "Every time I stand here, I *feel* a presence. I don't feel it at my mom's grave, but I do here. It's weird."

"You've never mentioned that to me before." Sean smiled gently, his eyes filled with a hint of sorrow.

Anna shrugged. "I was afraid you'd think I was crazy."

The priest looped a reassuring arm around his niece's shoulders. "Does it happen every time?"

"Every time." Anna paused, her brow furrowing. "I get this tingling at the back of my neck and a feeling like I'm not alone. Sometimes, it's so strong I look around to see if someone is standing behind me. I'm never scared, but it is creepy."

"You feel it now?"

"Yes," Anna nodded. "She's here."

"She?" The priest glanced at his niece.

"It's got to be Maarit, doesn't it? It's not my mom. I don't know how I know, but I know." Anna turned to face her uncle. "Do you feel it, Uncle Sean? The presence?"

"No, not at the moment, but that doesn't mean it's not here." Sean glanced at Anna and silently thought, *Did she inherit the fey spirit that Maarit had?* "Have you ever felt a presence somewhere other than here?"

"Yes," Anna admitted. "Several times over the years."

"When?"

"The first time was at my high school graduation. Walking across the stage, I felt a tingling, and it felt like she was walking beside me."

"Is an emotion always tied to the presence?"

"Beside her grave, it's always loneliness and sadness. Sometimes yes, other times no."

Sean smiled. My darling niece, you have inherited a touch of the *fey*. You see things and feel things others don't. For the Irish, it's not strange, but it is unusual. Very few have been given that gift."

"*Fey?*"

"Fey are Fairies; mythical creatures that live in the forests. We Irish like to blame them for things we do not understand. It appears that you have a mystical awareness that most people don't have or dismiss out of hand."

Anna shivered and slipped her jacket over her shoulders.

Her uncle paused before continuing. "Maarit had a touch of the fey, too. She was always seeing things and feeling things that others didn't. She learned quickly not to tell what she was seeing. It got her into trouble a couple of times in school. I was the only one, besides Mother, that she would talk to about it."

Anna took out a handkerchief and wiped her eyes, struggling to gain control of the emotions coursing through her. She laid her jacket on the ground and knelt next to the grave. Sean joined her, waiting for her to continue. Anna let out a deep sigh.

"I felt that same kind of sad presence the day Mom called to tell me Dad had died. The two of them had been joined at the hip since they married. Rarely did either of them go very far without the other one. I remember when Dad had to go to a meeting in St. Louis. Usually, Mom went along on such trips, and I would stay with a friend, but this time she had to stay home. He would call her at night, and they would talk for hours, filling each other in on the details of what had happened that day. It was like they were the breath of life for each other."

Anna closed her eyes. The warmth of the sun, the gentle breeze, and the songs of the birds enveloped her. A peaceful calm settled her anxiety.

"When Dad died," she continued. "I could sense a deep sadness and loneliness in her. I think my staying here instead of moving away helped, but she never fully recovered."

"Perhaps that is why you don't feel Peg's presence at her grave. She has reunited with your dad. No reason for her to linger," Sean noted.

With a final glimpse at the gravestone, Sean helped Anna to her feet, and the pair turned to leave the cemetery. "I don't know what to say to you, Anna. The only thing that comes to my mind is that some unfinished business is connecting you and Maarit, and perhaps Kay."

Anna said nothing, and the tingling on the back of her neck began to disappear. The presence was fading. *Goodbye*, Anna thought. *Maybe I'll see you someday.*

⁓ ═ ⁓

Kay and the psychiatrist settled into the overstuffed chairs in his office. She always felt a little intimidated by the surroundings. Maybe it was the fact that it was so quiet and neat. No clutter anywhere. No clock ticking, no music, only a faint sound of the heating and cooling system as it worked to keep the room comfortable quietly.

Dr. Phillips began Kay's third session with a simple directive. "Tell me about your mother."

Kay's reaction was swift and to the point. Her body became rigid, her breathing shallow, and her voice angry. "No way in hell I want to talk about that bitch."

Dr. Phillips had no intention of letting her off the hook. "Nevertheless, you must. What is the last thing you remember about her?"

Kay bristled. Her neck bulged and turned bright red. *Why did I ever agree to this?* After her outburst subsided, she dug deep to find the strength to answer. After all, she was here to heal and get her career back on track.

"She left me and my father and never looked back. She's horrible, and I hate her. I've hated her since..." Kay stopped.

"Since?" Dr. Phillips prompted.

"Since I realized she was never coming back," Kay slumped. The revelation left her nearly breathless with shock.

"Tell me about the day she left," the doctor quietly urged.

"No," she whispered. Her eyes stung, and her nose itched. Telltale signs that she was about to weep. *For God's sake! Be strong!*

Dr. Phillips' voice turned gentle. "Yes."

Kay composed herself, smoothed her hair, and began. "I was six. I remember being in the car. Mommy and Daddy didn't say a word to each other or me. They started fighting once they were in our driveway and out of the car. I remember that they each held one of my hands, and I was stretched between them like a rubber band. I pulled away from them, ran to my bedroom, and hid under the covers. I prayed, *'Dear God, make Mommy and Daddy stop fighting... please make them stop.'* But they didn't. I think that's when I stopped believing in God."

"What happened then?"

"I remember waiting until the house was quiet before going to sleep. It took a long time. Sometime in the middle of the night, the yelling began again." Kay shivered at the memory of hiding under the covers when the fighting began again.

"Then it got real quiet. My mother came and sat by my bed. She leaned over and kissed me. I remember her hair tickling my ear. She said, 'Punkin, please wake up. I have to leave for a while. Daddy will be here when you get up in the morning. He'll fix you breakfast and take good care of you while I'm gone.'"

Kay felt a familiar deep ache in the pit of her stomach. In a feeble attempt to keep her composure, she twisted the strap of her purse tightly around her hand.

"I asked her where she was going; she just said she had to leave for a while, but Daddy would take care of me." Tears of sorrow began to trickle down her cheeks. The emotional dam that had been holding back two decades of hurt was starting to crack.

Kay dabbed at her eyes with a crumpled tissue. "I begged her to stay, but she pulled my arms from around her neck, tucked the covers under my chin, told me she loved me, and left the room. I ran across the bedroom floor and opened the door in time to see her walk out the front door and close it behind her. I tried to run after her. My father grabbed me and held me tight. He kept telling me that everything would be all right, that he wasn't going anywhere."

The sigh that left Kay's body sounded like it came from her toes. "She never came back. I didn't see her again until she was in a casket."

"Did you ever ask your father why she left?"

"Many times. He would say that sometimes people who love each other can't live together."

"Kay," Dr. Phillips began, "I think this is the breakthrough you've been hoping for. It may be the nub of the problem with your voice. It will take a while to understand what you've just said. When you do, the singing voice may begin to return. I'll see you next week."

Thursday, March 30

After dinner, the two sisters settled into the living room, Anna in her favorite wingback chair, and Kay, as usual, on the couch. Throughout dinner, Kay had been distracted, unwilling to talk about anything beyond tomorrow's weather forecast. Anna refreshed Kay's coffee, settled back, and waited.

For several minutes, neither sister said anything. Instinctively, Anna knew that Kay had to begin this conversation. Any attempt to pry information out of her would result in avoidance and the erection of a silent wall. Kay fidgeted with the decorative pillow on the couch, running her fingers over the stitched pattern on its face. "I sure like what you have done to this old house," she said. "You managed to update it and keep it comfortable. It's beautiful."

"After mom died, I redecorated the whole house. I think it took me six months to complete the job." Anna took another sip of her decaf coffee and waited. Kay stood and restlessly wandered the room. She stopped in front of the mirrored wall hanging, her back to Anna. "Life takes some weird twists and turns."

"How so?"

"I always knew I'd retire from the stage someday, but not this way."

"Is that what you discussed with Dr. Phillips today?"

"That, and…" Kay's voice trailed off.

"And?" Anna carefully prompted. She could feel the tightness of anxiety in her chest starting, so she resorted to her favorite calming habit: twisting her hair.

Kay continued to wander the room, as if seeking the perfect place to find comfort. Stopping at the grand bay window, she stared through the glass for a long time before settling on the couch again. Finally, the words came out. "Our mother," she whispered.

Anna pushed her thick hair behind her ear and remained silent.

Kay leaned forward and set her cup on the coffee table. "Dr. Phillips is an excellent therapist. The first two sessions were more of a get-to-know-each-other. We talked about my dad, growing up in this town, high school and college stuff, my career. It was almost as if he was listening to what I didn't say and what I did. Today, Dr. Phillips started the session with a directive."

"A directive? What did he say?"

"Tell me about your mother."

Anna wasn't sure whether to cringe or applaud. Instead, she softly responded, "Oh."

Kay's jaw tightened, then relaxed. She struggled to remain calm while telling her sister about the session. *Breathe, Kay. Breathe.*

"First, I said I didn't want to talk about her. I couldn't bring myself to call her mother. She was never a mother to me as a child."

"What did he say to that?"

"He said, 'Nevertheless, you must.' I started to cry, then I got angry. I couldn't believe the venom that came out of my mouth. It was a torrent. I used words that I would never use in public. I called her every derogatory name in the book. Even now, I feel the anger rising again."

Anna waited. The setting sun cast a warm glow on her sister, but it was clear she was feeling anything *but* warm and cozy.

"Finally, my anger and tears were spent. I collapsed, drained." Kay twisted her hair into a knot before combing it with her fingers.

"What was Dr. Phillips' reaction?"

Kay wadded up her napkin and tossed it next to her now-cold coffee. "First, he let me compose myself, then asked, 'When was the last time you let yourself go like that?'"

"My guess would be decades, if ever," Anna said.

"That's about it. I haven't let myself think seriously about my mother in a long time. And I never let myself get that far out of control; it's too dangerous."

A small smile tugged at the corners of Anna's lips.

"At the end of the session, he looked at me with such kindness and understanding. 'I think,' he said, 'we have finally gotten to the crux of the problem. Now, we can make progress. I'll see you next week. For now, go, enjoy your visit. Get your mind off your voice.'"

"I think this is the breakthrough you've been looking for," Anna added encouragingly.

Kay smiled a tiny, but hopeful, smile. "That's exactly what Dr. Phillips said."

Anna jumped up, took Kay's hand, and pulled her sister up off the couch. "This calls for a celebration. Let's go down to the Den, there's a great jazz group playing that I want to hear."

Kay waved a hand dismissively at her sister. "Oh, I'm beat, you go. I'll stay home."

"Nonsense. You need a night on the town. Let's go."

CHAPTER THIRTY

Friday, March 31

T he school board meeting adjourned two hours past the scheduled
ending time.

It wasn't a contentious meeting; there was just a lot of business to
conduct. As a newspaper editor, Paul Williams dutifully interviewed
the board president to clarify several issues that had been raised during
the meeting. Father McDonough, the priest responsible for the local
Catholic schools, routinely attended the meetings. Both men also used
every opportunity afforded by their respective professions to observe the
pulse of Ellston.

The two finished their obligatory schmoozing of the crowd and
stopped to chat in the lobby of the school administration building.

"Another routine board meeting." Paul shoved his notebook into his
ever-present backpack.

"Routine," agreed the priest. "Better than school board fights I
have seen."

"That's for sure." Paul adjusted the straps on the backpack. "Ale
House is right around the corner. Time for a nightcap?"

"Lead the way." Father McDonough exaggerated his Irish brogue.
"It's been a long day, a bit o' Irish whisky would be welcome."

The Ale House, a comfortable small-town bar, was often used by
locals for quiet conversation. Paul, a regular, was greeted with a cheery

wave from the bartender and several regulars. The presence of Father McDonough, while not a surprise, elicited a respectful "Good evening, Father," from several patrons.

Comfortably settled in a booth, Paul spoke first. "I'm curious about something. Father McDonough, what's kept you in this small backwater town? You're the son of a distinguished Irish diplomat with great connections, you've studied canon law in Rome, graduated from Notre Dame, doctorate from the University of Chicago, and yet you remain a priest in this small town, I would have figured you'd be at least an auxiliary bishop in a major diocese."

The corners of Father McDonough's eye crinkled with amusement. "You've done your homework."

"I like to know who the movers and shakers are. It's an occupational hazard. Seriously," Paul said. "You have not risen in the church hierarchy as expected with your background."

"It's simple, really; the bishop likes me."

Paul raised a skeptical eyebrow. "He likes you?"

"Yes, after I returned from Rome, I requested a small parish in Minnesota, and he granted my wish. He hasn't seen fit to send me anywhere else."

"I find it somewhat hard to believe," Paul said. "With the sophistication of your family, your education, and having served in Rome, a small town like this would be enough."

"Is your cynicism an occupational hazard as well?"

Paul laughed. "Definitely." A keen observer with a disarming smile, Paul saw himself reflected in Father McDonough's face. Each man studied the other for a slight change in expression or posture that would hint at the other's thoughts without betraying their own.

"Let's turn the tables for a moment. Why are you hiding here in your hometown? After being an international correspondent, two major journalistic awards, that I know of, you've more than seen Paris, you've covered it, not to mention Rome, London, Los Angeles, and God knows where else. It doesn't seem like a newspaper with a circulation of, what, maybe eighteen thousand doesn't seem like much of a challenge for someone like you."

Paul shrugged disarmingly. "You've been checking up on me."

"I do my homework, too," Father McDonough said.

Paul took a leisurely sip of his scotch on the rocks before answering. "You know, Father, my career has taken me around the world. Over the years, I've encountered many priests. I can tell you this with certainty: *you* are a rarity. Most priests I have met are more concerned with following the rules than understanding and interpreting the meaning of things."

"In defense of my fellow priests, there is a proper time to follow the rules. But I find it easier to obey if I can understand the reason for the rules in the first place. I always want to know the reason for imposing a rule. The problem comes when the rule continues, but the reason for it is long since gone."

"You're training as a lawyer is showing through."

"One of my occupational hazards."

"You haven't, however, answered my original question. Why stay in such a small town?"

"The answer is pretty straightforward. I like being a priest. I like knowing my parishioners. I don't like the administrative tasks at the diocese, and politics at that level are insane. I looked closely at that level and became a priest in a small town. My bishop understands this and leaves me here. And, I have the added personal level of being in the town where I have family. A most unusual circumstance for an ordained minister."

"As I said, you are an unusual priest."

"I've also been around long enough to know that this invitation to have a drink had an ulterior motive. McDonough smiled politely before leaning forward, forearms crossed on the tabletop. "What's on your mind?" His volume was soft, but his tone invited whatever type of confession Paul would share.

Paul absently spun his empty glass before him, signaling the waitress to bring another round. The priest shook his head at the server, indicating he didn't want another.

"I had the most disturbing conversation with your niece the other day."

Sean chuckled. "Which one? They both can prompt disturbing and delightful conversations."

"That is most certainly true."

Father McDonough grinned at the line from Luther's Small Catechism.

"This time it was Anna. The gist of the conversation was that I drink too much, don't see much beauty in the world, and have become a cynic."

"Is she correct?"

Paul shrugged and took a deep gulp of his fresh drink before answering. The liquor warmed him to his core, like a hug from an old friend. "Largely," he admitted.

Sean said nothing in hopes that his silence would encourage Paul to continue.

"Father, clergy and journalists encounter the evil part of human nature regularly, probably more than any other group. How do you keep from sinking into despair? You see the same evil happening again and again and again. Doesn't the human species ever learn? How often do we have to make the same mistake before realizing our actions are destructive?"

Sean nodded. "The world seems to be bleak at times."

"Bleak!" Paul set his drink down with force. For a split second, his calm demeanor vanished, and his green eyes snapped with anger. "That is a gross understatement," he snorted.

"Perhaps."

Paul shook his head in frustration. "*Perhaps?* Father, I know you see the evil. How can you ignore it?"

"Is that what you think I'm doing?" Father McDonough gently smiled. He could sense that Paul was desperately seeking answers and some sort of relief from internal turmoil. "What has led you to conclude that all is lost and hope is futile?"

Paul pushed the nearly empty liquor glass in a circle. "Father, I have reported on wars, on natural disasters, on murders, on politicians who can't tell the difference between a lie and the truth, and worse, don't care. I've visited regions two years after a major earthquake. I found the will to rebuild, but the hope and zeal to reclaim their lives had evaporated. The publicly pledged aid never arrived. Despite all the rhetoric, the rubble in the streets wasn't cleared."

Paul seemed to shrink in his chair under the weight of his memory. He steeled himself by draining the last of the scotch in his glass. Sensing Paul had not finished, Father McDonough waited for him to finish his drink and continue.

"My last assignment was the one that destroyed the last of my illusions. I was sent to do a story on a teen suicide pact out in Montana. Six of seven teens succeeded in taking their lives. Can you imagine anyone saying that a person 'succeeded' when they killed themselves? But that's exactly what the editor said when he sent me on the assignment."

Paul desperately wanted another drink but fought the urge to flag down the waitress.

"The young man, seventeen years old, who had 'failed' in his attempt, was the only survivor of the pact. I still don't know why he agreed to talk to me. We talked for three days. His story was tragic. Orphaned at eight, parents dead from a drug overdose. In and out of foster care, he became angry and withdrawn. Finally, an aunt and uncle took him in, but they would beat him when they got drunk. He began hanging around with a group of teens whose stories were similar and equally tragic."

Painful memories washed over Paul like a wave; he paused to gather himself, drained the remaining scotch, and signaled for another. *Screw it. I need a drink.*

He continued. "The kid was a gentle soul. Lost in a sea of hopelessness. At one point, I told him he was a bright, pleasant young man and that he could have a great future ahead of him. That he was lovable. He said I was the first to tell him he was lovable. The thing that tore me up the most was the matter-of-fact tone of his voice. Even though I had said it, he didn't believe it. He didn't think it was even a possibility."

Paul stopped; the memory of the young man overwhelmed him. The heaviness in his chest was almost unbearable. "I tried to find resources to help him, but they were rapidly drying up. He was almost eighteen. On his birthday, all juvenile programs that might help him disappear."

The sharpness of the liquor flowing down his throat was comforting.

"Father, I do not doubt that he will attempt suicide again. And, I fear that he will succeed." Paul hung his head, and his shoulders slumped. He had no more fight left in him. He was defeated.

"Why did you decide to come home?" Father McDonough's voice was soft and soothing. "You could have gone anywhere in the world if your goal was to drink and forget. Why home?"

Paul shrugged. "I had nowhere else to go." The words caught in his throat.

Father McDonough waited until Paul regained control. The few minutes it took would have seemed an eternity to an outside observer. But the priest had been in these situations many times and knew when it was the right time to speak.

"So, you returned home to escape the evil you saw elsewhere. Did you find evil here?"

Paul sighed and raised his head. "I had hoped it wouldn't be."

"But..."

"But yes, I found it. Not as tragically obvious, but still..." Paul's voice faded.

"Your newspaper reports on such evils when you encounter them. Doesn't it?"

"Of course, Father, that's the job of the paper."

"And, as managing editor, it's your job to ensure that the content is accurate and meets the community's needs. Correct?"

"Yes, we try."

"Are all the stories you publish about evil in the world?"

Paul hesitated as he searched his memory. "No," he said. "Not all."

"Oh? Why not? If evil is all that exists, and you are the final arbiter of the newspaper's content, what else would you publish?"

Paul looked up at the priest. "It's a small town. I'd lose readers if I didn't do human interest stories. It's hard enough to keep circulation these days. Small town papers need a strong local content or are doomed to extinction."

Father McDonough straightened in his chair. He spoke quietly, as a lawyer would when beginning a cross-examination: "Paul, is economics-readership the only reason?"

Furrows appeared on Paul's forehead. "Never thought about it any other way."

The priest continued, "What criteria do you use to include a story in the paper? Space is expensive, no?"

"The usual ones," Paul folded his arms across his chest. A faint smile tugged at his lips. "This feels like I'm back in first-year journalism school."

"Humor me."

"Okay. A story should inform the public and empower them to make good decisions about their lives and the community. It has to be recent and important. It's the old cliché. Dog bites man is not news. Man-biting-dog is news, especially if it happens to be the mayor."

"That doesn't seem to be a very cynical criterion."

"It's not."

Father McDonough couldn't suppress a twinkle in his eye. "What was the news value of the story you ran two weeks ago about the high school coach who, in the last game of the season, put a girl with Down syndrome into a basketball game, both teams, and the officials helped the young woman score a basket?"

Paul smiled and shook his head. "Father McDonough, you are one tricky priest. I'm hoisted on my own petard."

Father McDonough smiled, "There's an old Cherokee legend. A grandfather is talking to his grandson. 'There are two wolves,' he said, 'on each of my shoulders.' These wolves sit on everyone's shoulders. One wolf is mean and nasty. He is greedy, selfish, hateful, lazy, and all bad things. He loves to fight and bully anyone. The other wolf will fight if he has to, but he is kind, generous, and loving. Those two wolves fight inside me every day.

The grandson was silent for a moment, then he asked his grandfather which wolf will win. The grandfather smiled and said, 'The one that I feed.'"

Paul sat silently for several minutes. "I see your point. The question is, which wolf do I feed?"

"Precisely," the priest said.

CHAPTER THIRTY-ONE

Tuesday, April 4

Brad Quinn, the arts and entertainment reporter for the *Ellston Herald-Review*, dropped a folder on Paul's desk. "There you have it," he declared. "After I wrote the review of Malone's voice quitting in her recital, I investigated her career. I found out that the great Kay Malone got her first big role by screwing the voice coach in Atlanta."

Paul picked up the folder and read the first page. His eyes narrowed, and the corners of his mouth were decidedly downturned. "That's quite an accusation. What do you have to back it up?"

Brad leaned forward, unable to contain his excitement. "I was looking for background, hoping to get a follow-up interview with Ms. Malone. It took some digging to find someone who knew Malone back then. I talked to Nikki Aronson. She worked at the Workshop for several years and was also an intern there, alongside Malone. Aronson claims it was common knowledge that Kay received the starring role because she was having an affair with the vocal coach. The coach persuaded the conductor to cast Malone as Marguerite. That launched her career.

"I see," Paul said. "Is Aronson still at the Workshop?" *Oh God, here we go again. I researched this years ago.*

Brad dismissed the question. "No, it doesn't matter."

"Where is she now?"

"I found her in Wichita doing something with the orchestra there. We can use this information to run a feature on Ms. Malone's career, exposing her private life and how she slept her way to the top. Send me to Atlanta, and I'll interview the staff and faculty and find former students. I'll get the inside story. We'll confront Malone and get her reaction to the story. Her response will put the icing on the cake. A story like this would put this Podunk paper on the map."

Paul tugged on his lower lip. "And it wouldn't hurt your career as an investigative reporter, would it?"

"My career isn't the important thing. It's telling the truth that's important." Brad leaned back and put his hands behind his head, satisfied with his triumphant declaration.

Paul glared at the junior reporter over the top of his glasses. "Of course not, we must tell the truth. Tell me, what exactly is the truth?"

"That's clear. Malone used sex to get ahead. That's morally reprehensible; everyone should know her for what she is."

"Are you sure of these facts? Is your source reliable? What's her name again?"

"Nikki, Nikki Aronson."

"What do you know about her?"

Brad's tone changed from excitement to grating irritation. His breathing became louder. "Don't you get it? There's enough here to publish. My source has worked in the Opera Workshop office for several years. She was a student there at the same time as Malone. She's still involved in the national music scene. She has all the connections to know what's going on."

Paul dropped the folder on his desk. "What would prompt Aronson to share that information about Malone with you during a phone call? She doesn't know you from Adam."

Brad scowled. "Does it matter?"

"A source's motivation always matters. Did she give you this information on the record?"

Brad looked sheepish. "Off the record. She didn't want her name to be used."

Paul shook his head. "That's a big red flag. She has something to lose if she doesn't want to be named as a source. Any idea what that might be?"

"No, I suppose it would cause her embarrassment. Who cares?"

Paul fought to hide his irritation. "Journalism 101, Brad. Who, what, where, when, how, and why." He looked down at his desk and read more of the document Brad had given to him.

"Do you know who the voice coach was that supposedly had an affair with Ms. Malone?"

"Aronson wouldn't give me his name, but I discovered three vocal coaches on staff at the time, only one of whom was a male."

"You are assuming that he was the person, without any proof, and that the affair was with a man." Paul's tone was getting sharper.

Oblivious, Brad couldn't contain his excitement. "Oh, that would be even more delicious if it were with a woman!"

Paul took his pen, underlined a phrase in the draft, and wrote a note in the margin correcting a grammatical mistake. He noted another error and wrote a second note before asking. "In your conversation with Ms. Aronson, did you have to press her to get this information? Did you get any direct quotes?"

"Not exactly, but Aronson sure gave a lot of hints. It was easy to connect the dots."

"What exactly did she tell you?"

"She said that Malone isn't the innocent that her reputation would have you believe. She also indicated that rumors about Malone and the vocal coach have been around for years."

"Did you try to contact the vocal coaches?"

"Yes, I talked to two of the three there when Malone was an intern.

Brad rolled his eyes and shuffled his feet on the weathered tile floor. His patience with the questioning was quickly evaporating.

"Did you ask them about the rumors?"

"Of course I did!" Quinn couldn't control his edgy tone. "They both laughed at me. They said it was professional jealousy."

"And the third coach?" Paul made another note in the margin.

"Couldn't find him. I believe he left the workshop several years ago and moved back to his home in Italy. Seems to have lost contact with the school and the other coaches."

"And the conductor? Did you talk to her?"

Brad shifted in his chair. "No, I couldn't make contact." Suddenly, his face lit up. "Wait a minute. How did you know the conductor was a woman?"

"Because I have followed Malone's career since she went to Atlanta. I heard these rumors fifteen years ago and checked them out as part of a series on arts professional finishing schools. I was freelancing at the time. The article was published in *Arts News*."

Paul tossed the manuscript Quinn had given him on the desk and tossed his pen on top of it. He leaned on his crossed arms on the desk. With great difficulty, he kept the anger out of his voice.

"I also followed the careers of a painter, an actor, an orchestral conductor, a violinist, and a sculptor, all at various stages of their careers and training. Malone even gave me a telephone interview. It turns out that your source was a rival of Malone's back in the day. Ms. Aronson and Ms. Malone frequently auditioned for the same role, and Ms. Malone usually won the role. Aronson was often relegated to singing minor roles and serving as understudy to Malone's lead. I think Aronson is suffering from a bit of the 'green-eyed monster.'"

Brad scowled, chin jutting out. "Regardless, the fact remains that Malone won the role by having sex with the vocal coach."

"Have you been able to corroborate…"

"No," Brad interrupted. His enthusiasm was quickly giving way to impatience. "But it's clear what happened."

"No, it's not clear." Paul stood. *It's idiots like this that make me want to have a drink.* "You don't have anything. You have a series of assumptions based on conjecture and an accusation by a rival. In addition, you have an indication, from individuals who would be in a position to know, that the rumors result from professional jealousy."

Paul picked the document up from his desk and tossed it back to

Quinn. "Do your homework, Brad. Don't bring me half-baked assumptions and innuendos and try to pass them off as facts. I haven't got time for that shit."

Thursday, April 6

Paul joined Jim Teigen on a bench in Central Park. "What's with this cloak-and-dagger stuff? My office is a whole lot more comfortable than here."

The call from his new friend had come as a surprise. The air of mystery surrounding the request to meet had the newspaperman both intrigued and suspicious. His gut churned.

Jim looked around to see if anyone was in earshot. "I wanted to have a private and personal conversation. You must admit, your office is Grand Central Station, with people coming in and out constantly."

"A park bench in the middle of the day is more private?"

Jim nodded. "Less chance of being overheard." Jim zipped his jacket and raised the collar to block the early spring wind. It was still too cold for many people to be out walking in the park. In shaded spots, around bushes, and under trees, bits of snow had resisted the melting sun.

"What's going on? I have an edition of the paper I've got to get out today."

"First, a personal question," Jim glanced over his shoulder again, shifting slightly to get a better view of his friend's face. "What's your relationship with Kay Malone?"

Paul frowned. "That's a strange question."

"Is your connection with her professional or personal?"

Paul was beginning to regret agreeing to the meeting. "What bearing does that have on this conversation?"

Jim frowned. "I need to know if I'm talking to the journalist or Kay's friend."

Paul didn't answer, instead focusing on a fat robin hopping across the damp ground in search of worms. He hoped his silence would either end the conversation or make Jim get to the point.

Jim's throat tightened, and he averted his eyes downward. "I hesitate to ask this, but did you send one of your reporters to talk to me about Kay?" Jim raised his head to hear Paul's answer, knowing that his friendship with Paul, possibly Kay, and certainly Anna, hung on Paul's response.

"No," Paul said. "I didn't." *What in the world was Quinn up to now?*

Jim swallowed hard and lowered his voice. "One of your reporters called me a couple of days ago. He insinuated that you had given him the assignment to investigate Kay's career, and how can I put this delicately, her romantic entanglements. He also told me that he had heard that Kay had worked as a stripper in Atlanta."

Paul shook his head in disbelief.

Jim continued. "He wanted to know what Anna might have mentioned to me. He said he was 'doing his homework.'"

"What did you tell him?" Paul leaned against the back of the park bench and rubbed his fingers on his furrowed forehead.

"I said that Anna and I haven't talked much about Kay. She's obviously sad that Kay lost her voice. By the way, I know Maarit's story and why she left the family, but I didn't mention that to him."

"Wait a minute. You know about Maarit's family?" Paul leaned closer to Jim. Jim's revelation caused Paul to drop his usual affable smile.

"I have sources in the Chicago Diocese. They knew the family," Jim said. "I don't know the details, but I understand Maarit's family was unhappy about how her marriage broke up."

Paul nodded. "Go on. What else did you tell the reporter?"

"I also told him that I didn't think Kay and Anna had spent much time together over the years." Jim paused.

"And?" Paul prompted.

"Your reporter insinuated you and Kay are lovers. He said you refused to run a story he had written. He all but accused you of burying a scandal."

"Jim, why are you telling me this?"

"We don't know each other well, but you are a straight shooter. I want to protect Anna if I can. I know you two are close, almost like brother and sister. She adores her sister. I'm not sure she would react kindly to your reporter's insinuations."

Paul sighed and shifted on the park bench. "It's Brad Quinn who talked to you, right?"

Jim nodded, his lips forming a grim, straight line.

"I take it you haven't told Anna any of this?"

"That's correct."

"Good." Paul mentally ticked through the options—*tell Kay— violates ethics concerns. Same with Anna. Relationships are at risk, both for Jim and himself.* No clear answer appeared.

"Have you told Kay?"

"No, I wasn't sure of the best way to deal with this. That's one of the reasons I came to you. You're the only one I know who knows both sisters."

Paul sighed and tiredly ruffled his hand through his hair. "Jim, this puts me in a very awkward position. If the reporter has news about a public figure, I have to publish that information, regardless of the consequences. I don't know what to tell you. What is it you want from me?"

"I guess I was hoping you would take me off the hook and talk to Kay."

Paul shook his head. "Sorry, but that isn't going to happen. It would cross a journalistic boundary for me to talk to the principal subject of one of my reporter's stories."

"I understand."

"What does your gut tell you to do?"

Jim sighed. "I think I have to tell either, or both, about the dirt your reporter is trying to dig up. I think I'll probably talk directly to Kay. Anna would explode, and that's not necessary at this point."

Monday, April 10

Kay stormed into Paul's office, leaving a trail of shocked expressions in her wake. If the lightning in her eyes could have wreaked havoc, the office would have been burned to a crisp.

Paul stood and extended a welcoming hand. "Kay, what an unexpected..."

Kay slammed the door behind her so hard the glass rattled in protest. "You know bloody well why I'm here. Your reporter is starting to piss me off. Sorry for the vulgarity, but it wouldn't take much for me to wring his neck right now. He's been digging into rumors debunked many times in the past twenty years. The story seems to have a life of its own, and it's come around again."

"Kay, calm down. What are you talking about?"

"Calm down, that..." Kay swallowed hard and did her best to censor her language. "*Weasel* was trying to worm his way to Anna through Jim." Her words may have been tamer, but the venom in her tone was still there.

"Yes, I know."

Kay's face turned beet red. "*You know?* You knew and didn't tell me!"

"Now just a minute, calm down. Let me explain."

Kay defiantly leaned over Paul's desk and glared. "I will *not* calm down. I want to string Quinn up right here in your office. If you publish a story along the lines that he was questioning Jim about, I will sue you for slander and put this pitiful little paper into full receivership. That isn't an idle threat. I have the clout and the resources to do that to him personally and you."

Paul, overwhelmed by the barrage, held up his hands in surrender. "Okay, I get it. Now, please, let's talk without yelling at each other. I'll tell you what I know."

He stood and steered Kay to the conference table in the corner and poured two coffees. Kay's anger began to dissipate. *I need to remember not to get on this girl's enemies list. I can just imagine what the office is saying to each other now.*

Kay finally calmed down and was able to talk normally, though it was clear the volcano could erupt again without warning. The usual hum of a newspaper office returned.

Here's what happened," Paul said. "A few days ago, Brad told me a story about your time in Atlanta. I told him we wouldn't run the story; he had made too many assumptions that hadn't been verified. I told him that before he made those kinds of allegations, he had better do his homework."

Kay's eyes darted between Paul's face and the door to his office. Given any provocation, she was still ready to wring Quinn's neck.

"I thought I had effectively killed the story," Paul explained. "He apparently took it as encouragement to keep digging. He doesn't want to ferret out facts to support his conclusions; hearsay and juicy speculation were more fun."

Kay slumped in the chair. Her fiery bravado faded, replaced by worry and weariness. "I'm so tired of this. Someone talks to Nicole Aronson every few years, and it surfaces again."

Paul rubbed his fingers across his brow as if trying to rub out the wrinkles that always appeared when stressed. "Forget about Aronson. Her bitterness will eventually catch up to her. But, if you're game, I know how we can teach Quinn a lesson or two."

Kay cocked her head to one side; a glimmer of hope appeared in her eyes. "What do you suggest?"

Paul took a sip of his steaming coffee and then continued. "I've been trying to figure out how to teach the young man about the real world. Let's invite Mr. Quinn into the office and have him ask you directly about the rumors. Make him face that when writing an exposé, he is talking about real people, and his words have deep consequences. What do you think?"

Kay twisted her hair around her finger and combed it out while considering her friend's idea.

Paul broke the silence with a chuckle. "You know, your sister does that same hair-twisting thing when thinking."

Kay laughed; it lightened her mood. "I know. It must mean that we come from the same gene pool."

"What do you think, Kay? Should we give Brad a taste of facts?"

"Yes, let's."

Paul picked up the phone. "Brad, could you please come to my office for a minute? And bring a notepad with you."

"What's up, boss?" Brad swaggered into the room, but his steps faltered, and his face couldn't hide the shock of seeing Kay seated at the conference table. "Ummm, Ms. Malone. How nice to see you again."

"Sorry, I can't say the same, Mr. Quinn."

Brad's Adam's apple visibly bobbed as he swallowed nervously, his brain scrambling to find a calm and professional comeback. When his mouth went dry and no words came, he turned red like a tomato.

"Please, sit down," Paul instructed Brad, pointing to an open chair at the conference table. "Ms. Malone came to see me to protest your contact with Mr. Teigen. He told her about the questions you've been raising."

"I...uh..." Brad stammered.

Paul continued, his face stoic. "She is aware of the story you showed me the other day. No, I have not shown it to her, nor, to my knowledge, has she read it."

Brad squirmed in his chair.

"Furthermore, Ms. Malone has graciously agreed to be interviewed by you regarding the issues you've raised. Proceed. And yes, I'm staying in the room to listen to the interview to corroborate the contents, should the need arise."

Paul and Kay looked expectantly at Brad. The silence was deafening.

"I...I'm not sure what to say." A small bead of sweat appeared on the young man's brow.

Paul glared at him. "You had plenty to say the other day. Go ahead. Ask her about the allegations you shared with me."

Kay nodded and said, "I'm prepared to answer any questions you want to ask."

Brad began to rise in an attempt to escape the room.

In a quiet voice, Paul commanded, "Sit down, Brad. Begin the interview."

Brad nervously cleared his throat. "Uh, Ms. Malone."

"Please call me Kay."

"Uh, okay." Brad looked down at the table and opened his notebook while struggling to gather his thoughts. "Kay, is it true that you had an affair with one of the voice coaches in Atlanta and that he persuaded the conductor to cast you as the lead in an opera?"

"No and yes. No, I didn't have an affair with Dr. DiPorta, and yes, he did persuade the conductor that I should be given a lead role."

"Why would people think that you had an affair with him?"

"Besides being my coach, I became close to his entire family. I babysat his two young children. His wife, Gina, and I were great friends. I spent a lot of time with his family. They sort of adopted me. Some people were jealous of the relationship I had with them."

Kay took out her phone, found the contact information she was looking for, and wrote it down for Brad. "If you want to confirm this, Dr. DiPorta can be reached at Tanglewood."

"Do you remember Nicole Aronson?"

Kay nodded. "Yes, I do."

"What was the relationship between the two of you?"

"We were at the Atlanta Opera Workshop at the same time. I understand that she is no longer there."

"Were you friends?"

Kay smiled grimly. "I wouldn't say that. We knew each other and often auditioned for the same roles."

Still unsure of the situation and nervous about interviewing Kay under his boss's scrutiny, Brad continued, "Did you usually win the role, or did she?"

"I did. She often had a secondary role or served as understudy for the role I sang."

"Did that cause friction between the two of you?"

"Not on my part, but I understand she didn't agree with the casting decisions."

Quinn hesitated, embarrassed to ask the next question. "Uh, Ms. Mal...Kay, did you work as a stripper in Atlanta?"

"What?" Paul exclaimed. "Brad, what kind of question is that?"

Kay threw her head back and laughed. "Mr. Quinn, are you familiar with Richard Strauss's music?"

"Vaguely."

"One of his compositions is a one-act opera version of Oscar Wilde's story 'Salome.' It's infamous for its iconic scene, 'The Dance of the Seven Veils.' We staged that in Atlanta, and I sang and danced in the role of Salome."

Kay paused long enough to sip her coffee before continuing. "The role called for me to strip, and I did. I was twenty-three or twenty-four at the time. Did I strip? Yes. Was I a stripper in a club? No."

"Any more questions?" Paul looked directly at Quinn.

The young man sheepishly closed his notebook. "No, I don't think so. Thank you for your candor, Ms. Malone. I apologize if I caused you any difficulty."

"Mr. Quinn, please do me a favor. The next time you run into allegations like this, check out all the facts. Don't report only the rumors."

"Yes, of course."

Paul and Kay stood simultaneously, signaling the end of the interview. With one hand on the doorknob, Brad turned back briefly. "Um... one more thing, Ms. Malone."

"Yes?"

"I hope your voice heals quickly. The beauty of your singing is greatly missed."

Kay allowed a small smile to tug at her lips. "Thank you for saying that I truly appreciate it."

With that, Brad quickly retreated to his office

"Now that was fun," laughed Kay. "He is young, naive..."

"...and ambitious," finished Paul. "He wants to leap to the top without paying the necessary dues. Thanks for making him pay. Maybe he won't be so quick to jump to conclusions next time."

Kay and Paul sat quietly for a minute. She took one last sip of coffee. It had become cold, and the taste was bitter. "Whatever happened to those young, fresh-faced, naive kids we once were?" she murmured ruefully.

"Twenty-plus years of life, I'd guess," Paul answered. "It's been a tough couple of decades. But you have done quite well for yourself, even if you did have to strip to make it to the big time."

Kay shook her head and laughed. "Sorry to disappoint you. I wore a bodystocking, and the lighting was designed to protect my modesty. It was fun, though. It felt just a little naughty without actually being naughty."

Paul chuckled, and his eyes twinkled. "If you don't mind, I will keep that fantasy alive in my imagination. You, as Salome, modestly stripping, is too delightful an image to let go."

"You're welcome to it, if it makes you happy," Kay said playfully. She paused and glanced at her old friend, her mood turning serious. "Whenever the topic of you coming home is broached, you always steer the conversation away. People like you and I don't quit and come home for a rest. Will you tell me what happened or avoid the topic again?"

Paul avoided Kay's eyes. Undeterred, she continued. "When we first met, you were the most upbeat, optimistic, and idealistic guy I had ever met. In the past twenty years of traveling the globe and meeting all types of people. Few of those I met have had that quality of idealism that you wore like a comfortable old shirt. It was who you were. Now, your smile has become inscrutable. It's still friendly. It's not fake, but it's changed. It seems like it's part of a facade that shields you and keeps the world at arm's length. That's sad to see."

Paul sat in stone-faced silence, his thumb and forefinger absentmindedly tapping on the sides of his mug.

Sensing her friend's discomfort, Kay backpedaled. "I'm sorry. I've overstepped my bounds. It's none of my business. I had better get going. Thanks for helping me with the Quinn situation."

Kay stood and walked around the table to stand behind Paul. Gently, she rested her hand on his shoulder, leaned over to kiss him on the top of the head, and stepped toward the door.

"Kay, wait a minute. I want to show you something." Paul abruptly stood up and retrieved a sheet of paper from the top drawer of his scuffed metal desk. The words *Good and Evil* were centered in the middle of the page in a 36-point bold New York Times font. Flanking the words were faint images of two wolves snarling at each other.

Superimposed over the wolf on the right was a headline, *Six Teens Succeed in Suicide Pact.* Over the wolf on the left was a partial box score of a high school basketball game. One player's name was bold and larger than the others, though she had scored only two points.

Kay looked at Paul, "What's the story?"

Paul ran his fingers gently over the drawing. "The headline on the right was the last story I covered before I quit and came home. The details aren't important, but the proverbial straw broke the camel's back. I couldn't stand another look at the evil and horror in this world."

Paul's expression softened as he handed the drawing to his friend. "On the left is the name of a young girl who scored only two points in a basketball game. She has Down syndrome. At the urging of her teammates, the coach put her in the last minute of the last game of the season. Her team, the visiting team, the coaches, and the officials cheered her on and helped her score."

"That's a marvelous story," Kay said. "Why the poster?"

"Your uncle reminded me that both good and evil, ugly and beautiful, all exist in the world simultaneously."

Moved by Paul's vulnerability, Kay quietly studied the art before asking, "The wolves? How do they fit?"

"In an old Cherokee legend, a grandfather, teaching his grandson about life, tells the boy that a terrible fight between two wolves is happening inside him, and everyone. One of the wolves is evil. He is angry, envious, regretful, greedy, arrogant, filled with lies, false pride, and ego. He will fight all the time because of his anger and hate."

She studied the evil wolf illustration more closely. The artist's attention to detail in the wolf's snarling lip, bared fangs, and angry eyes elicited a visceral reaction. She felt a slight shiver tickle the back of her neck.

"The other wolf represents good. He is joy, peace, love, hope, serenity, generosity, truth, and compassion. He only fights if it is absolutely necessary. The grandson thinks for a moment and asks, 'Which wolf will win?' The old Cherokee replies, 'The one I feed.' In the news business, one constantly finds evil, making one quite cynical. I spent years feeding the evil wolf. I've asked the paper's graphics department to make a poster of this. I hang it in all the departments in the paper and my office."

Paul took the paper back from Kay, cradled her face in his hands, leaned in, and gently kissed her as he had done at the airport twenty years before.

Kay returned the kiss. "It's time to feed the good wolf," she said.

CHAPTER THIRTY-TWO

Tuesday, April 11

Anna reached the highest point in Perrot State Park, the lookout on Brady's Bluff, before Jim. "C'mon, check out this view."

Jim stopped twenty yards behind her and fifteen feet below the summit to catch his breath. "Be right there," he puffed. Five minutes later, he reached the top and collapsed on the polished, split-wood bench in the clearing. "That's one steep hike," he groaned. "How high are we, anyway?"

"About five hundred feet above the valley floor." Anna stood, hands on hips, at the edge of the lookout, admiring the view.

Jim sighed. "Glad someone thought to put a bench up here."

"You can thank the Izaak Walton League for that. There's a plaque on the back of the bench. Take a look."

Jim pulled himself off the bench and read.

SO THAT ALL MAY KNOW THE BEAUTY OF NATURE,
WE WORK TO PRESERVE THE HERITAGE OF
PURE WATER AND CLEAN AIR.
IZAAK WALTON LEAGUE
LA CROSSE, WISCONSIN
1953

After reading the plaque, he went to stand behind Anna. He put his arms around her, and she leaned back against him.

"I love this spot," she said. "Have you ever been up here before?"

"No, didn't do much hiking when I was in college here."

"I come here several times yearly to sit and look across the river valley. Helps me clear my head."

"It's breathtaking."

Sitting shoulder to shoulder, they looked out across the four-mile-wide span of the valley. The sun, reflecting off the rock outcroppings on the bluffs on the Minnesota side of the river, created a patchwork of glowing brown. Against the early spring green of the trees. Rounding the bend, two tows, one heading upstream, the other down, each pushing eight barges, saluted each other with horn blasts.

Anna pulled a small binocular out of her daypack, looked through them momentarily, and handed them to Jim. "See those large white birds making circles over the river?"

Jim took the binoculars to look at the birds. "What are they?"

"They're American white pelicans. See the black wingtips? And the long necks doubled back against the shoulder? They're one of the few birds that fly that way."

He took her hand and led her to the bench. "That's amazing. What are you, an ornithologist?"

Anna chuckled. "No, but I have over a hundred and fifty bird species on my birding life list."

"Really?"

"Yes, really," she said.

For several minutes, they sat quietly on the bench. She snuggled beside him, took his arm, and wrapped it around her shoulders. Puffy white clouds played tag with the sun, alternately cooling and warming them.

"This valley is a major flyway," she said. "I spend a lot of time in this valley during the spring and fall migrations. The pelicans are among my favorites. When they return in the spring, it gives me a sense of balance. The natural rhythms of nature are still in place, so to speak."

Jim murmured. "I can see why. I liked watching the river when I was here but never found this place."

Anna rested her head on his shoulder. "Can I ask you a personal question?"

"That depends."

"Upon what?"

"Upon what is it you want to know?"

A chipmunk scooted up a bench leg, sat on its haunches holding a nut in its paws. He considered having his picnic, saw the couple on the other end of the bench, and scampered away.

Anna looked up at him. "You know, you are a bit of an enigma."

Jim smiled, leaned over, and kissed her. "I've been called many things, but never an enigma."

Anna blissfully smiled. "That was nice. Again, please." He kissed her a second time.

"Don't misunderstand, I'm pleased you're still here, but…it's been a couple of weeks since the recital, and…" She let the question hang in the air.

"That's the same question my business partner asked me yesterday," he said.

Anna sat up to get a better look at Jim's face. "What did you tell him?"

"It's a *her*, actually."

"Oh…what did you tell her?"

"I told her there's a property we should pursue as a restoration proj-ect, and a local company here that we should consider partnering with on the project."

"And…" Anna put a fake scowl on her face, silently demanding an answer.

"And…I told her I met this strange girl, who glides when she walks, laughs a lot, loves jazz, writes music, counts bird species, and exhausts me with hiking in the bluffs."

Anna gave him a playful shove. "No, *really*. What did she say?"

Jim grinned. "Well, she's very interested in the property."

"Stop teasing, you know what I'm asking. By the way, are you close to your partner?"

Jim looped his arm around her shoulders. "You could say that. Besides my mother, she's probably the person I'm closest to."

Anna twisted her head to try to read Jim's expression. *Why are you putting your arm around me if you're close to another woman?*

"I've known her a long time. We lived together for years."

Anna pulled away from him.

"She's my sister."

Anna gently punched Jim on the shoulder and returned to his embrace. "You are a brute, you know that?"

"Yeah, I know."

"What did your 'sister' say?" Anna used air quotes to emphasize.

"She said I've been working too hard and should take a vacation to keep in touch. She also said that if I want to work remotely for a while, that would be okay, too. And…she wants to know when she gets to meet you."

"Do I get to meet your sister?"

"Would you like to?"

"Yes, I would."

"Then come with me to Chicago this weekend."

Anna grinned. "That sounds like fun."

Tuesday, April 18

Paul casually leaned on the doorframe of Anna's office in the college Admissions department. "How was your weekend in Chicago?"

"Chicago?" Anna feigned innocence.

"Yes, Kay told me you were gone for the weekend, and Jim was also mysteriously gone. It doesn't take a genius to figure that one out."

"No secrets in a small town." Anna rolled her eyes.

"Nope. My question stands. How was the weekend?"

"Still playing the big brother, Paul? I could tell you it's none of your business."

"Yes, you could, but..."

Anna knew there was no point in trying to deflect her cousin's questions. "It was very nice. Chicago is a wonderful place to visit, but..."

"I know, you wouldn't want to live there."

She motioned for Paul to close the door. "That's the problem. I like Jim, and his family couldn't have been sweeter, but his life is in Chicago, not mine. I can see myself with him, but not in the city."

Paul obliged and sat on the edge of her desk. "Anna, what are you afraid of?"

"Jim loves the city. He loves the energy of it. We went down to the Loop to a wonderful steakhouse for dinner on Saturday. While we were walking around, a storm rolled off the lake. You should have heard the thunder echo through those buildings. It was as if the city were a huge canyon. It rolled around and around. We must have heard that one clap of thunder a half-dozen times. He loved it. Me, not so much. I need to break it off before it goes any further." Anna began fretfully twisting her hair around her forefinger. Her anxiety was not lost on Paul.

"Why would you do that? The city isn't the problem, and you know it."

Anna bristled. "It is the problem!"

Paul shrugged his shoulders. "I don't buy it. Blame the city, blame the weather, blame anything you want, but that's not what you are afraid of."

"I am not afraid," she shot back, trying to hide the fact that Paul was exactly right.

Paul had no intention of letting up. "What would you all call it then?"

"Cautious."

Paul shook his head in genuine despair. "Yeah, right. That's just another word for being afraid. So, you had a bad romance. So, what? Jim's a nice guy. Please don't cut it off before it even gets started."

"I've got to get back to work." Anna dismissed Paul with a wave of her hand.

CHAPTER THIRTY-THREE

Thursday, April 20

The William Tell Overture, better known as the *Lone Ranger* theme song, signaled an incoming call from Kay's agent, Sarah Tomlinson. Feeling slightly more ornery than usual, Kay pushed the *answer* button and greeted her agent dryly. "If you're calling with more cancellations, I don't want to hear about 'em."

Sarah's voice was neither surprised nor offended. "What, no pleasantries?"

Kay sighed and settled into a seat at her sister's kitchen table. "It's been pretty intense the last few days."

"Any progress?"

"Hard to say." Kay sighed loudly enough for Sarah to hear her exasperation. "Dr. Phillips is optimistic my singing voice will return, but there is no timetable or guarantees. I can finally talk, but I sound like an old frog."

"My phone has been ringing off the hook about you," Sarah said. "Venues are calling, concerned about your future bookings. The press wants an interview, including the New York Times and Opera News, just to name a couple. Are you ready to do one?"

Kay cringed. "Not yet."

"Kay, you can't hide forever. We have to do something."

"I know."

"What would you think about putting out a press statement acknowledging the voice problem. Based on your doctor's advice, we can say that you are taking a six-month rest to allow your voice to recover fully. We'll indicate that a full recovery is expected, and you will return to your California home to rest and recover."

"You're right. Let's do a press release. Better add the Ellston paper to the list. Their music critic wants an interview, too."

"Will do. Anything else I can help with?"

"No, but I think I'll hide with my sister for a couple of weeks. Don't want to be alone."

"Sounds like a plan. I'll send a draft to you later today. By the way, there may be an interesting development within the San Francisco Opera organization. I'll keep you posted."

"Really?" said Kay. "That's intriguing. And encouraging. Thanks, Sarah."

Friday, April 21

Kay entered the lobby of the Performing Arts Center. She stood facing the double doors to the recital hall. She closed her eyes to heighten the memories of her college days. The comforting smell of the freshly waxed floor prompted a memory of almost falling while rushing through the lobby to avoid being late for a Tuesday noon student recital.

With a sigh, she returned to the present, walked up the stairway to the second level, and the row of faculty offices. Entering the office marked Dr. Elizabeth Keiser, she greeted her mentor.

"Same office as twenty years ago," Kay noted as her eyes scanned the modest office. "Dr. K., you've collected more autographed photos from former students than you had the last time I was here. Looks like you're running out of wall space."

Dr. Keizer laughed. "I started this collection years ago. I think it has taken almost forty years to fill the wall."

Kay moved closer to the wall to study the photos more clearly. "I recognize some of these folks. I've been in productions with several of them."

"I'm not surprised. All of these folks became professional musicians in one genre or another. Like you, the music drove them." Keizer smiled. "I promised myself that I would retire when that wall was filled, or I'd been here forty years, whichever came first."

Kay ran her fingers over one of the polished wood frames. "Since your wall still has four or five spaces left, it must have been the forty years that came first."

"Yes, it was. I think a couple of those spaces will likely be filled by the end of the year." Dr. K. waved a hand toward a vacant chair. "Please, have a seat."

Kay sat in the chair next to the desk, facing her former professor. "There's quite a history on that wall. It's a remarkable tribute to you."

"More of a tribute to the department than to me." Dr. Keizer took a moment to appreciate the awards and memorabilia that covered most of the walls in her office. "The department chair was in my office the other day. She wants to put the pictures on the wall between the entrances to the recital hall."

"What a great idea."

Turning back to her former student, Dr. Keizer's tone turned serious. "Kay, how are you doing?"

"Dr. Phillips thinks we've had a breakthrough. He's calling it a Conversion Disorder and thinks it's a result of anger at my mother for her leaving all those years ago. The singing voice hasn't returned yet, though my speaking voice is getting better. It's still a little raspy, but at least I can talk."

"Interesting. Isn't it strange what effects something can have years after the fact?" Dr. Keizer paused for a moment before getting right to business. "I want to show you several compositions by one of my students."

The two women moved to the piano in her office and sat side by side. Dr. Keizer explained the setting for the music: "This quartet for soprano, alto, tenor, and bass is part of an operetta set in the Roaring 20s. She, my student, wrote the outline of the libretto first and is now two-thirds of the way through setting it to music."

Dr. Keizer began to play while Kay looked intently at the music score. Five minutes later, when Kay started to laugh hysterically, she smiled. "You got it."

"This is clever," Kay said. "The four of them are talking over each other, no one listening to anyone else. The clever part is that the tenor is singing in the style of Mozart, the soprano is Wagnerian, the alto is Debussy, and the bass is trying to bring the logic of Bach into the conversation. The astounding thing is how seamlessly the music goes from one to the other. What else has she written?"

Keizer pulled another piece from the stack on the piano and began to play and sing.

Kay sat in enchanted silence. "What a lovely ballad. This is her own style, isn't it? She's not trying to imitate anyone."

"That's right. This is all hers."

Keizer played through several more pieces. Finally, she said, "There's one more I want to play for you. It's a lovely, whimsical lullaby."

At the end of the song, Kay was unable to say anything. The melody's simplicity and the words' tenderness contained a depth of emotion that only music could express. Words alone were inadequate.

Dr. Keizer looked at Kay, handed her a tissue to wipe the tears, and softly said, "Do you realize you were humming the melody as I sang it? Let's try it again."

Keizer began the introduction. At the beginning of the melody, Kay hesitated and began to hum, first hesitantly, then more confidently. At the end of the song, neither woman said anything. Keizer started to play the intro again, "Try the words this time."

Kay nodded. She hesitated where the words and music started, opened her mouth as if to sing, but her voice was silent. A low guttural sound of frustration came from deep within her soul. "Why won't it come out?"

Dr. Keizer smiled and gently replied. "One step at a time. One step at a time."

Kay smacked a hand angrily on the piano's polished veneer. Frustration made her face flush, and her throat feel dry. "I know, I know! But why won't the voice sing? It will talk, but it won't sing? It's being stubborn."

Keizer suppressed a laugh. "Being stubborn has occasionally served you well. I remember a particular passage in *Madame Butterfly* that gave you fits. You couldn't master it no matter how hard you tried. But you were too obstinate to quit until you could sing it perfectly."

This was not the first time in Liz Keizer's career that she had had a student whose voice, for one reason or another, typically due to a nodule on the vocal cords or a severe sore throat, refused to work. This was different, unusual. A voice simply refusing to sing when it could still hum was a mystery.

"Look, we now know that your voice will match pitches. You hummed that melody. Whatever is blocking your singing hasn't been found yet. I'm betting the singing will return when you resolve that issue, whatever it is."

Kay forced a grim smile. "You have more confidence than I do, and certainly more patience."

"In fact," Keizer continued. "I'm willing to bet that you will figure this out and be able to sing at my farewell recital next month. I want to hear you sing one of the pieces we looked at today. We'll decide which one later."

"You've got to be kidding." Panic crept across Kay's face. "There's no way that's going to happen. No way."

"I'm not kidding. We've got to get you back on the horse."

Kay looked at her mentor, doubt and fear speaking louder than any voice could. "I don't think I can commit to that."

"I understand, but the longer you put off singing in public, the harder it will be to get back on that stage. We won't publicize it, so there won't be the pressure or expectation of the voice being back to full strength. We'll announce your presence from the stage, not in the program."

Kay shook her head.

"We'll choose music within whatever range and technical ability you have regained by that time. In the meantime, you and I will get together for an hour every day, including weekends, to gradually get your voice back in shape. We know you can hum a melody; we'll start with that and gradually add vowels."

Kay looked doubtful. "I don't know, Dr. K."

"You have to decide whether you *want* to return to the stage. You have to decide whether you ever want to make music again, at any level. Regardless of how much your voice has returned, if you don't get on that stage, you will never sing in public again. The odds are you won't ever make music again. You will waste the talent, and that would be a tragedy."

Kay bristled, "How can you say that? I've dedicated my life to making music. All for what? My voice gives out at the top of my career. A career that now lies in shambles. Future bookings are canceled every day. I'm afraid to answer calls from my agent. Every time I do, my 'rest' gets longer. I gave my life to music. What did I get in return? More nights in a hotel room than in my own bed. A couple of short-term relationships that couldn't mature because the next month I was off in some other part of the world. And irony of ironies, I sing a performance, a performance for you, that destroys me. Now you want me to add 'star pizzazz' to your final recital."

Her rant over, Kay took a deep breath.

Dr. Keizer looked at Kay with gentle eyes. "Tell me, why did you get that major singing role at the end of your internship in Atlanta?"

"I worked hard for it."

"So did everyone else."

Kay stood, turning her back on her mentor. "I knew the music. I had it nailed."

Keizer nodded. "No one gets that internship without 'nailing it.' What set you apart from all the other very talented, hardworking interns who wanted that singing role? What made them choose you?"

Kay sat down on the piano bench and looked at the keyboard. Her hands went to the keys and began to play the *Chopin Etude Opus 10 No. 3.*

Dr. Keizer sat back, transported to the first time she heard Kay play. It had been that etude that convinced her to take Kay on as a private student. She had seen the potential, had seen it in the nuance, in the technique. However, the one intangible that most convinced Keizer to become Kay's teacher was the depth of emotion that she brought to life. She had never seen a sixteen-year-old who, instinctively, understood what Chopin was saying.

The tender notes at the end of the etude floated into the air as Kay lifted her hands from the keyboard and placed them in her lap.

"I vividly remember the audition for that singing role. I stood alone on the stage before the auditioning committee and began to sing. The aria lasted only two or three minutes, but I was that character for that period. Every fiber of my being was engaged. For a little while, Kay Malone didn't exist. Only the character did. I was Marguerite. It wasn't Kay Malone playing a part. It was Marguerite, alive."

Dr. Keizer placed her hands on Kay's shoulders. "*That* is why you got the part. And that is why you must sing again."

"I've spent my career seeking those moments; moments when the music gives me a glimpse of pure joy, beauty, and truth. I've only had three or four times when everything came together perfectly. They are rare and beautiful." Her voice dropped to a whisper, "I haven't felt one of those moments in a long time."

"It is not only you who have experienced those moments," Keizer said. "Many of those in the audience have experienced them while you were singing, even if at that moment you didn't. Even if you can never perform in public again at the level you did, the music will live through whatever you do. But if you don't try to get back on the hypothetical horse, the music within you will die. I've seen it happen. It happened to your mother."

Kay sat silently at the keyboard, absent-mindedly stroking the keys. Finally, in a whisper, she murmured, "What time do you want to meet?"

"Four p.m. every day, after my last class, and one on weekends."

CHAPTER THIRTY-FOUR

Tuesday, April 25

The sound of the choir and orchestra rehearsing on the Performing Arts Center's main stage was an irresistible magnet for Kay. She slipped into a seat in the back row of the auditorium. Given a choice, she would always choose to observe a rehearsal. It fascinated her to watch a conductor work with an ensemble.

When the choir entered, she was amazed at the sound filling the auditorium. The simple, direct power of the music sounded vaguely familiar. The harmonies were fresh and new, but not strident. The pulsating, driving, rhythmic pattern, constantly repeating itself, reminded her of Ravel's Boléro. It wasn't a copy, but more of an homage to a great composer. The syncopated, rhythmic pattern was a fresh take on an old idea.

The conductor stopped the ensemble to ask for more balance between the brass and the choir. Kay shook her head and thought, *It's always an overly zealous trumpet section with trouble hearing anything around them.* She nodded in approval when the conductor asked the sopranos to use a little less vibrato, and the tenors to land on top of the E-flat instead of reaching for it from below.

He didn't chastise the sopranos by demanding they stop wobbling, but instead asked them to smooth out the tone, and then complimented them on the purity and intonation of their singing, a carrot on the end of a very gentle stick. Both the trumpets and the sopranos responded favorably, with the result being satisfactory.

The alarm on Kay's watch reminded her of her appointment with Dr. Keizer. She left the auditorium and went down the hall to Keizer's studio. Progress had been frustratingly slow.

The transition from humming to vowels on the exercises worked well, but her voice refused to work as soon as she tried to sing the words. What had once been her trademark—clear, bell-like high notes—had disappeared. Attempting to sing only served to heighten her frustration.

Dr. Keizer kept emphasizing the positive, encouraging her that she was making excellent progress and insisting that the high notes would come back. Kay wanted to believe, but she doubted she would ever sing again. What had once been as natural as breathing now brought anger and fear. Kay knew today's session would be more of the same.

Halfway to the studio, she stopped. The joyous music from the rehearsal hall had faded away, and only her footsteps were heard in the empty hallway.

"Who am I trying to kid?" she muttered. "It's over. I'm a has-been. The career is over, gone." She stopped, hesitated, turned, and shuffled toward the exit.

"I never figured you for a quitter," called Dr. Keizer from the music office door.

Kay stopped, just a moment from leaving.

"I watched as you passed the office. Each step you took became slower, more labored. I could almost see the wheels in your mind grind to a halt."

Kay's hand clutched the door handle as she turned to face her mentor. "I think we need to face the facts. I'm never going to sing again. Will never dare go on a stage again. It's over."

With a subtle gesture, Dr. Keizer beckoned her to the conference room next to the music office. Kay followed, but avoided eye contact, and her arms hung limp at her side. She chose a chair at the far end of the conference table. She looked down, hair falling in front of her face, hiding the redness of her eyes.

Dr. Keizer took a seat opposite. "When did you lose sight of what music is?"

Kay raised her head, her green eyes clouded with confusion. "What do you mean?"

"When did making music become a job and not a joy? When did you stop looking for those perfect moments you described the other day?"

Kay's shoulders sagged. "It hasn't been fun for a long time."

"What do you do besides music?"

Kay pushed her thick hair away from her face. "Not a whole lot. Between travel and rehearsals, little time or energy is left to do anything else."

Dr. Keizer watched her protégé closely. "Kay, who are you?"

Kay rubbed her eyes, trying to hide the tears starting to form. "You've known me since I was sixteen. You probably know me better than anyone else except my father. What do you mean, who am I?"

"I know what you do. I even have a pretty good idea of why you do it. But, in a deeper sense, who are you?"

Kay had no answer.

"Think about it tonight. If you decide to continue, I'll see you at the usual time tomorrow."

Wednesday, April 26

Kay didn't sleep well. Between the prior day's conversation with Dr. Keizer and the lingering tension with Anna over their mother and uncle, she had tossed and turned all night.

By 5:00 a.m., she had given up on the idea of sleep. On her way downstairs, the third step from the top squeaked as always. Kay stopped, listening to hear if the squeak awakened Anna. She was relieved it hadn't.

Kay opened her computer and checked her email. Nothing but ads. *At least, no new cancellations.* She typed *St. Francis Catholic Church, Ellston, MN,* in the search engine and clicked on the first link. A picture of the church front appeared. She stared at the picture, remembering processions from the school behind the church and up those steps for Mass on special feast days. She shivered at the thought of the nuns and teachers marching them to confession, and the grumpy old priest listening to their pitiful little sins.

She moved the cursor over the *Contact Us* link and pulled her hand away from the mouse, as if an electric shock had run up her finger. She let the cursor wait for several minutes before clicking it.

When she clicked, a picture of her uncle appeared. She hit the email address below the image and typed a long-overdue request: *Father McDonough, would you have time to see me this afternoon?*

Typical for an early spring afternoon, the sun, high in the clear azure skies, warmed body and soul while the northwest breeze sent the clear message that winter hadn't relinquished all control.

Kay gathered her jacket more tightly and quickened the pace across the intersection. A glance at her watch told her she was five minutes early. If there was one thing she hated, it was being late for an appointment.

The large wooden doors at the top of the steps leading into St. Francis Catholic Church were wide open, extending an invitation she was unwilling to accept. Instead, she strode hurriedly around the side of the church to the rectory door; a door, she noted, that matched the entrance to the church.

A teenage girl greeted Kay at the door and ushered her into the rectory study. "Father McDonough has just returned from Mass. He'll be with you shortly. Please, make yourself comfortable. May I get you some tea?"

"Thank you. That would be nice."

"Ms. Malone," said the young girl shyly. "Excuse me for being, like, forward, but... may I have your autograph? My folks took me to your concert, and I loved it. Father McDonough told me you would be stopping by. I asked if it would be, like, okay for me to ask you, and he said he was quite sure you wouldn't mind. Is it okay? I mean, would you sign my program from your recital, please?"

Kay smiled warmly. "I'd be happy to."

She looked at the young teen after locating a pen in her purse. "What's your name?" The bright-eyed, innocent enthusiasm on the young girl's face surprised Kay the most. She had signed hundreds, if not thousands, of programs, but it had been a long time since she had felt as alive and energetic as the young girl standing in front of her project.

"Kristina."

"Are you a singer?"

Kristina fidgeted self-consciously. "I'm taking voice lessons and piano. I sing in the choir at school, and once in a while, a solo in church." Kay smiled and wrote on the young girl's program: *To Kristina, may the music in your heart always find a voice. Best, Kay Malone.*

The young girl's face lit up. "Oh, thank you so much! I'm sure Father McDonough will be here real soon." Kristina turned, bounced out of the room, and returned with two cups, a pot of tea, sugar, and cream. "Father McDonough likes a cup of tea after Mass. He likes it strong. I hope it's not too strong for you."

"It will be fine. I like it strong, too."

Restless, Kay roamed the room, stopping at a picture on the credenza. She picked up the framed portrait to see her grandparents, twelve-year-old Sean and Maarit, staring back at her.

"That was our last family portrait. Mom and Dad left for South America shortly after that picture was taken." Father McDonough stood in the doorway of his study. Dressed in his clerical black suit, he appeared as a silhouette, with the bright light of the hallway behind him.

Startled, Kay quickly turned. "Sorry, Father McDonough, I didn't hear you come in. It's been a long time since I've seen a family picture. I couldn't help taking a closer look."

Father McDonough smiled. "Kay, can we get past the formality of the 'Father' thing? I'm your uncle, and coming from you and Anna, that's a much more comfortable title. I also answer to just plain 'Sean.'"

"I don't think I've ever addressed a priest by anything other than 'Father.' If nothing else, twelve years of Catholic school drummed that into my head."

The priest laughed warmly. "Yes, indeed. Catholic schools are very high on drumming things into little girls' heads. However, family is still family."

"Where in South America?"

"Argentina. That was their last post overseas before they retired and moved back to Ireland."

Kay stood awkwardly, not knowing whether to hug him or offer a handshake. She did neither. "Uncle Sean, it's been a long time."

"Way too long, Kay."

Father McDonough led the way to the coffee table, flanked by comfortable, high-backed chairs in the corner next to the credenza. He gestured that Kay should do the honors and pour the tea. "A little cream and two sugars. I like it sweet and strong."

"These old-world rituals, like the proper way to pour tea, are somehow comforting," Kay said. The subtle aroma of strong black tea added to the peaceful ambiance of the room.

"Indeed, they speak to the continuity of pleasant things, even amid turmoil."

Kay put the cream in the cup, added the sugar, poured the tea, and gently stirred the light brown liquid before passing it to her uncle. Sean sipped the steaming liquid and nodded approvingly.

"You certainly made young Krissy's day. She was so excited, I barely made it in the door before she showed me your autograph. Thanks for accommodating her."

"Glad to do it. She's a delight."

"Krissy is one of four or five teenagers the housekeeper hires to answer the phones and do odd jobs around the church and rectory. When one of them is working, a group of friends usually hangs around the place. Better here than the streets, though it can get a bit noisy sometimes."

Uncle and niece looked at each other across the table, unsure how to begin the conversation. Sean spoke first to ease the tension. "To say the least, your email was quite a surprise."

Kay nodded. "I'm sure it must have been. Actually, I surprised myself a bit."

"Why did you reach out?"

Kay looked down, busying herself with folding her napkin. "That's difficult to explain, since I'm not entirely sure. Perhaps to bury the hatchet, declare peace, seek justification, or absolution. I don't know. Maybe a bit of each."

"Did you want to see the priest or the uncle?"

Kay raised her head and looked directly into her uncle's eyes. "Maybe both."

"Which do you want to see first?"

"I think that maybe, at this point, the uncle is the most important one?"

"That works for me," he replied with a nod. "I wasn't aware you and I were at war."

"I think maybe it was a one-sided war, waged within me. After Maarit left, you disappeared. My favorite uncle, who used to play tea party with me, tickle me, and give me big hugs, vanished from my life when my mother did. At the time, I didn't understand what was happening. I felt angry and blamed both of you for tearing my family apart. It wasn't rational, I know, but the feelings were real all the same."

"I tried to visit a couple of times, but it felt very awkward," Sean said, his eyes lowered. "Then I went away to college and…"

Kay went to the credenza, picked up the family photo, and returned it to its place on the table. She ran her fingers over the image of her mother. *She looked so young and alive. What had changed her?*

"Uncle Sean, from the beginning of this trip, event after event has pointed toward my mother. First, I dreamt of her while dozing on the red-eye flight from San Francisco. Then, after I ran into you at the hotel, Dr. Keizer revealed that Maarit had been her student. To say that I was shocked is an understatement. Still am, actually."

Her uncle sat quietly, carefully studying Kay's face. Behind Kay's professional demeanor, he could see the turmoil, the mixture of confusion, sadness, and anger she was trying to conceal.

"Even the psychiatrist I'm seeing thinks losing my voice may, at least partially, be the result of all the festering anger at my mother. It seems as if every time I turn around on this trip, my mother is haunting me." Kay paused and asked, "Uncle Sean, do you know why my mother left?"

Sean raised his head to look at Kay. "I was only sixteen or seventeen when she left. Like most teenage boys, I was more concerned with my adolescent quandaries and not observant of others. I do remember that she and your dad fought a lot. I was at their home for dinner one evening shortly before she left, and even I could feel the tension between them. They hardly said a civil word to each other. It became quite uncomfortable."

"They had to have loved each other once, didn't they?" Kay's raspy voice was barely above a whisper, and her eyes pleaded for an honest answer. "Didn't she ever love me?"

"Yes, I believe she loved both of you, but that was not enough. Her job as a translator had her traveling. That's always hard. But I always thought a more serious barrier existed between your parents. I couldn't figure out what it was."

Sean gestured at the portrait on the table between them. "I remember asking my mother, your grandmother, what happened during the split. She said that Maarit had always had a restless streak. She couldn't sit still and was always seeking more adventure and excitement. The grass always seemed to be greener elsewhere."

"Dr. Keizer told me she had a terrible temper and a magnetic personality."

"That's true. She was funny, witty, and warm if she was in a good mood, but she could cut you to the core with a few words when her mood turned dark. I loved her good moods and feared the bad ones. She only yelled at me once. It was when I told her I would become a priest; she was unhappy with that idea."

"Why not?"

Sean shrugged. "Not entirely sure. She hated the church. Couldn't get past whatever it was that had turned her against it."

"I can certainly understand that," Kay murmured as she stirred the contents of her cup. "Uncle Sean, did she keep in touch with you?"

A profound sadness was etched on the priest's face. "Not much. A few Christmas cards, an occasional phone call on my birthday, until the spring before she died. One day, out of the blue, she visited me and asked if, in the event of her death, I would officiate at a small wake. She also asked me to deliver a package to her attorney." He shrugged as if to say, *What can I tell you?*

Surprised at the revelation of a mysterious package, Kay shifted in the chair. "By any chance, do you remember the attorney's name?"

Father McDonough walked over to a desk, pulled out his phone, and checked his contact list. He then wrote a name and phone number on a small notepad.

"Her name is Allison Williams. Her law office is over on Wizzyington, off of Broadway."

Kay glanced at the paper before putting it into her pocket. "Williams? Do you know if she's related to Paul, the newspaper editor?"

"Yes, I believe she is."

"Small, small world," she mused. "Uncle Sean, an attorney representing my mother, came to see me in Atlanta. She gave me a letter from Maarit and had me sign several legal papers. My mother left a small inheritance that helped pay off some school loans. I was still so angry that she had abandoned me that I didn't even read the letter. I laughed and tore it to pieces. I think that attorney was from the Williams law office."

Sean returned to his seat and studied his niece's face intently. "Are you still angry at your mother?"

"Yes. That's what I'm trying to work through with Dr. Phillips."

"Are you making any progress?"

"I think so. But…" Kay paused. "Dr. Phillips asked me the strangest question the other day. He asked me why I became an opera singer."

Sean nodded. "That's a pretty standard question."

"It was weird because Dr. Keizer asked me the same question yesterday. She asked me why I had gotten my first major opera role."

Father McDonough watched Kay struggle with the question. "That's an interesting coincidence." *Is there a connection between the music and Kay's anger at her mother?*

"That's the confusing part. I started taking lessons from Dr. K. in high school. She knows what I've done to become an opera singer. To top it all off, she also asked me who I was. Why would she ask me that?"

Sean smiled. "Ah, yes, the existential questions. *Who am I? Why am I here? Who do I want to be?* She wasn't expecting you to answer the question for her, Kay; she wanted you to answer it for *yourself.*"

"The answers were always obvious to me. I wanted to sing opera, I wanted to be famous, and I wanted to be rich."

"And, are you all of those things?"

Kay chuckled, "I've managed two out of three. I haven't gotten rich yet. And now, the two things I have accomplished are in danger of falling apart, and the third doesn't seem all that important anymore."

Sean was silent for a moment, remembering a time when he wrestled with the same questions. "Over time, I've found that the answers to those questions change. Each age requires a person to ask them again. It's part of the personal journey through whatever this existence is."

Kay pointed to her head, "I understand that here," then pointed to her heart, "but not here." Her heart felt heavy, like an anchor that threatened to pull her under forever. Every part of her longed for the answer, the act, *the thing* that would relieve her angst.

Sean smiled lovingly at his niece. "I don't believe that the who you are question is nearly as important as who you want to be. Who you have been helps shape who you want to be, but it doesn't dictate it. It only puts you in a position to choose."

Kay put her fingertips together and gently rubbed her forehead. "Uncle Sean, I almost quit my voice therapy with Dr. Keizer yesterday."

"Why?"

Kay's eyes filled with tears. "Fatigue, frustration, lack of progress, fear."

"Fear of what?"

"Fear that my voice will never come back."

Sean leaned forward in his chair and asked, "Or, could it be fear that it will come back, and you'll be stuck doing what you were doing?"

Disconcerted, Kay tried to process her uncle's question. *That is ridiculous. Or is it?* "Is it possible that I'm afraid my life will have to continue along the same path?"

Father Sean's eyebrows lifted. "'Have to continue.' That's an interesting choice of words. Aren't you satisfied with your life?"

"I thought I was. But now...?" Kay's voice trailed off, revealing her confusion.

Her uncle continued. "Human motivation is rarely obvious, especially to the person trying to figure out who they want to be. It's all tied up in what we think others expect of us, who we've been, and what we want to be. Why don't you want to go back to the success you've enjoyed?"

Kay paused to think while absently twisting her hair around her slim fingers. "Sean, that question has never entered my mind. Since I was sixteen, the only thing I could see myself doing was singing. I've never even considered a different career. It's all I've ever wanted to do."

"It's a big world, Kay."

Kay smiled. Clearly, she needed to take some time to think. She glanced at the gentle man across the table from her. "Uncle Sean, for a priest, you sure seem able to see beneath the surface."

Sean threw up his hands in mock despair. "It's an occupational hazard."

Kay chuckled and stood to leave. She felt strangely lighter and more at peace. At the rectory door, she turned to her uncle. "I apologize for all the years I held a grudge against you. Please forgive me for the time I've wasted between us."

Sean took her hand in his. "Nothing to forgive. The important thing is not the time wasted. What's important is how we use the time we have left. Say hello to Anna for me."

CHAPTER THIRTY-FIVE

Friday, April 28

K ay sat at the piano in Anna's living room. Her fingers wandered over the keys, playing bits and pieces of various works that she had memorized.

Bored, she began to rifle through the piles of music stacked on top of the piano, looking for something new to play. She took several sheets of music from the stacks and began to play. She didn't recognize the song, but it was magical. Her fingers skipped expertly across the keys as the small living room filled with glorious music.

Intrigued, she played several more. The composer was clearly talented. And inventive.

"Anna," she called. "Do you know anything about this music? There's no name on it. I know I heard this recently, but can't place it."

Anna appeared in the kitchen doorway, a dish towel in her hands.

"I...uh...a friend of mine wrote it and gave me a copy." *Oh god, she found my music. I forgot to put them away.*

"They are very good. Are they studying music?"

"Yeah, with Dr. K."

Kay glanced at her sister over her shoulder before returning to the curious music before her. It seemed so familiar...

"That's it! Dr. Keizer showed it to me the other day. She said a student of hers wrote it. She wanted my opinion on it. This was one of several I saw."

"Really?" Anna tried to keep her voice calm even though her heart was pounding. *Crap!*

"I thought it was strange. Dr. K. wouldn't tell me who the person who wrote it was."

"Hmmmm, yeah. Umm. That's weird." Anna was unable to resist her nervous habit of twisting her hair.

Oblivious, Kay was studying sheet music intently. "Why would someone not want me to know their name?"

She started to play another of the pieces. She laughed again at the musical joke of the quartet singing in different styles simultaneously. "Come here, look at this one, it's a stitch. So clever and it works musically."

Anna slid onto the piano bench next to Kay. She studied her sister's face, surprised at the delight she saw there. Timidly, she said, "Maybe they feared you wouldn't like the music. Or, think they were terrible at it. Maybe they feared being embarrassed in front of the big star."

Kay pulled out another piece of music—a sweet lullaby, calm, serene, and gentle. She pulled out another one, full of rollicking tunes. Anna slid off the bench, afraid her trembling hand would betray her secret. Afraid of what the sister she idolized would say about the music.

"I suppose that could be it. Well, these pieces are very good. I'd like to know who..." Kay took a sharp breath, put her hand over her mouth, and swiveled on the piano bench to look at her sister.

"Anna, did you..."

Barely able to breathe, Anna only dared to nod.

"And the other pieces Dr. K. showed me?" Anna nodded a second time.

"Did you also write the choral and orchestra piece I heard them rehearsing the other day?"

Anna, in a small voice, answered. "Yes."

Kay motioned for her sister to rejoin her on the bench. She nudged Anna's shoulders with her own.. "These are very good. Why didn't you tell me you were writing music?"

Afraid to look at her sister's face, Anna shrugged and mumbled. "I was afraid you'd laugh at me."

Kay gave her sister a loving nudge. "I admit I did laugh at the just plain funny quartet. A great musical joke." Perplexed, she asked, "Why'd you think I'd laugh at you?"

Anna hesitated, her cheeks flushing pink. "You're so good, and I was afraid you'd look at my compositions and laugh, or worse yet, patronize me."

"When I told Dr. K. these were very good, she commented that she wished the composer thought so, too," Kay said.

Anna took a deep breath. The secret was out, and her sister was impressed with the music she had written. *Dr. K. won't be able to resist saying, I told you so. But maybe that wasn't such a bad thing.* "Dr. K. thinks I should go on to grad school and study composition."

"Ya think!?" Kay shot back with mock sarcasm. "That's a great idea. Have you picked a school?"

Anna twisted her hair. "I've applied to four programs. Julliard rejected me."

Kay nodded excitedly. "Where else?"

"Wisconsin, North Texas, and the University of Chicago."

"Those are three very different programs, all excellent, but very different approaches. Which one are you hoping for?"

Anna laughed. "Whichever one accepts me. Though I really want to go to Texas."

Surprised, Kay raised her eyebrows. "Texas!? That's a surprise. It's a long way from home."

Anna nodded, her face suddenly serious. "That's the scary part. But I love the campus, and the faculty are going in directions I want to explore. It's only for two or three years, I'll likely move back home when I'm done.

"My sister, the doctor." Kay grinned. "You know I will never call you Doctor Jensen."

"Not even once."

The sisters laughed and hugged.

CHAPTER THIRTY-SIX

Saturday, April 29

K ay turned over in bed to avoid the morning sunlight. "At last," she said to the pillow. "No alarms, appointments, expectations, a day to myself. Anna's off to Chicago, again. Dr. K. can't meet today. No one expects me anywhere. I can do whatever I want. A girl could get used to this."

Kay closed her eyes and pulled the covers over her head. An hour later, she woke, slid out of bed, and wandered down the stairs. Next to the coffee pot, she found a note:

Kay,
Thought you could use the sleep. Jim and I left early to get to the airport. See you Sunday night. Car keys are in the tray next to the kitchen door. Enjoy the weekend.

—A

Kay lingered over breakfast, picked up the car keys, and drove around town searching for old haunts and good memories. The city had both changed and remained the same. New shops had replaced many of the original stores on Broadway. An ugly box store had replaced the old elementary school on Main Street.

She stopped the car next to the park across the high school and settled on a bench near the playground. Three young mothers watched their children run and play, allowing them enough freedom to explore while keeping a close eye on them to ensure their safety.

Kay wandered away from the playground along the bike path around the lake. The frogs, engaging in a conversation understandable only to them, made the lake noisier than she had thought possible. The croaking, the ducks quacking, and the geese honking as they herded their goslings across the path created a joyful cacophony.

She followed the path around the lake back to the parking lot. From there, she could see the back door of the high school. She smiled at the memory of sneaking out of dances to make out with her boyfriend. *It was somewhere in this park that I had my first real kiss. Jeff was a sweet boy; I wonder what ever happened to him?*

Leaving the car in the parking lot, Kay walked a few blocks to Main Street. The post office hadn't changed. The hotel on the corner of Elm and Main was now a franchise that resembled every other hotel in the country bearing the same name. Kay laughed as she passed the bank where Paul had tripped over the alarm with his golf club.

"Kay! Kay!" called a familiar voice across the street. Turning, she saw her uncle waving at her and miming the act of drinking a cup of coffee.

"Sure," she yelled back. *Why not?* It was an easy stroll down the sidewalk to a small cafe around the corner.

They took a table inside the diner's front door and next to the large front window. On autopilot, the waitress brought two cups, a carafe of coffee, and a bowl with containers of cream.

"I like this spot," Sean shared. "The friendly waves from people walking by who recognize me make me smile. I come here often."

Kay had settled in the seat directly across from her uncle, but she still had a clear view of the bustling little community. Inside the diner, two waitresses got their daily exercise moving quickly between tables and the kitchen. The chatter of the patrons and constant buzz punctuated by the sounds of plates and cups being placed and cleared from the tables and counter.

"One of the reasons I like this place is that it reminds me of the five-and-dime store where I grew up. It had a long counter, with red stools, just like that one." Sean pointed to the counter and stools that ran almost the entire length. "When I was about eight, I'd sit on the stool and try to go around by waving only my arms and legs. Mother would let me do it, but never father."

"It's hard to imagine you as an eight-year-old," Kay said. "Did you make it all the way around?"

"Sure did."

"I suspect you spend a lot of time in places like this. Since I've been back, we haven't been anywhere that you aren't considered a regular."

Her uncle chuckled. "You're right." He poured some cream into his coffee and stirred it vigorously. "Besides the obvious problem with your voice, has it been good to be back home?"

Kay sipped her coffee and nodded. "I've spent the morning driving around town and visiting old haunts. Maybe old T.S. Eliot was right about returning home after a long absence to see it again for the first time."

Her uncle nodded.

"Uncle Sean," Kay said. "I've been thinking a lot about what you said the other day."

"As I recall the conversation, I started to get a little preachy. It's hard to break the habit when you have delivered as many homilies as I have."

Kay threw up her hands in mock horror, and her eyes sparkled with amusement. "You priests are all alike. You can't resist giving a sermon at any and every opportunity."

Father McDonough chuckled at Kay's good-natured dig. "What have you been thinking?"

Kay's expression turned solemn. "There may be a bit of truth in your question. I am afraid my voice will come back. I told Dr. Phillips about our conversation. He agreed it's an interesting question, but wasn't convinced it was the fundamental issue."

"But the anger at your mother is?"

Kay nodded and avoided looking at her uncle. This was not a topic she wanted to pursue but knew her uncle wouldn't leave it alone. She held her response as a waitress placed delicious-looking pastries on the table. After the customary small talk about the weather and how spring seemed to be early this year, she scooted off to seat a couple who had just come in.

After the waitress darted away, Father Sean resumed his gentle prodding. "Have you ever told your mother how you feel?"

Kay nearly dropped her coffee cup in surprise. Her answer was stiff and sarcastic. "Wouldn't that be a little difficult? As you recall, she's dead."

His voice was soft and gentle when he asked, "Have you ever visited her grave?"

A flush of anger coursed through Kay's body. It took all of her reserve not to snap at her uncle. "No, I haven't. What's your point?"

A group of people leaving the diner delayed her uncle's answer. An older couple and their adult children warmly greeted the priest and expressed their sympathy to Kay about her voice. Again, the obligatory "how about this weather?" came up before the group waved goodbye and went on their way.

The priest quickly picked up the conversation where he had left it. "Think you can stand another short sermon from me?"

The distraction had given Kay's anger a chance to dissipate, and her uncle's gentle voice further soothed her. She sighed and picked absently at her pastry. "I suppose. If you must."

"I think that large and small rituals are for the living, not the dead. We hold wakes and funerals to help the living come to terms with their loss. Most people have a very strong need for the ritual, while others have no use for it at all. I think you haven't finished grieving for the loss you felt at age six. You seem to have gotten stuck in anger."

Sean pulled a small notebook from his pocket and drew on it. "This is a map of Mercy Cemetery over on 9th Avenue West. Drive into the cemetery's south entrance, take the second right into the old section. You'll find your mother's grave in the third row, three-quarters of the way down. Go talk to her."

Kay took the map from her uncle and looked at it. "Frankly, the last thing I want to do is visit her grave."

"I understand," he said. "However, I don't think you'll be able to put your anger aside until you talk to her."

~ ═══ ~

Kay left her uncle at the cafe, not intending to visit the grave. She purposely steered the car in the opposite direction out into the country. The further she drove, the more intense sadness crept into her mood. She stopped to turn the car around at the end of a long farm driveway and sat in quiet contemplation.

Was it a place like this that she died? All alone. In the middle of nowhere?

Kay rested her head on the steering wheel as the thoughts and questions coursed through her head.

She must have been scared. Terrified. No one to help. What must have gone through her head? Did she know she was dying?

"Stop it," Kay cried out. "Stop it."

A knock on the car window brought her back to reality. Standing beside the car, a teenage girl asked, "Are you okay? Is everything alright?"

Embarrassed, Kay rolled the window down and looked into the worried face of a teenage girl. "I'm okay," she said. "Thanks."

"Are you sure? Is there anything I can do to help?"

Kay shook her head. "I'm fine. Really. It's been a tough day, and I was going to use your driveway to turn around."

The girl smiled with relief. "Not a problem."

Kay reached out of the car and squeezed the young girl's hand. "Thank you. It was very kind of you to stop to help a stranger. I'll get out of your way. You helped in ways you can't possibly know."

The teenager returned the squeeze. "I'm glad."

Kay drove out of the driveway and turned the car toward town and the cemetery.

She parked the car on the street next to the cemetery. It took her thirty minutes to summon the willpower to walk across the street to search for Maarit's grave. The car chirped at her as she closed the door.

Damn, I left the key in the car again. She retrieved the key and closed the door with more force than necessary.

She went to the third row of gravestones at the end, furthest away from her mother's grave, and slowly walked down the row. Most of the stones along the way marked a family plot with space for two inscriptions on each stone. Kay read the inscriptions as she passed.

GONE BUT NOT FORGOTTEN.
REST IN PEACE.
BELOVED GRANDMOTHER, WIFE, AND MOTHER.
GONE TOO SOON.

Most graves indicated that the individual had lived long enough to have experienced a life of some type: age 78, age 73, age 82. The hardest graves to look at were the young children: age 3, age 18, age 16.

GONE TOO SOON.

Kay walked very slowly up the row. Her pace was more an avoidance than any special interest in the tombstones. Regardless of the pace, the path led inexorably to her mother. The stone simply read:

McDONOUGH
MAARIT McDONOUGH MALONE
1950–1995

Room for one more on that stone. Probably reserved for Sean, she thought. I feel so foolish. Sean told me I should talk to my mother and tell her how I feel. He told me to talk out loud. Don't just think it, he said. Say it. What sane person talks to a gravestone?

The anger and bitterness began to rise. Her jaw began to tremble. Her hands became tightly clenched fists. Kay took a deep breath and yelled. "Goddamn you, Maarit! I've hated you for thirty years. I've hated you since I first realized you weren't coming back. I didn't even read your letter. I tore it to shreds. God damn you."

Kay choked on her anger, and the volume of her voice escalated. "You abandoned me! Tore my dad's heart in two. You were a selfish, inconsiderate bitch to leave us like you did. Why did you leave us? What was so horrible that you didn't love us—didn't love me? God dammit…"

Kay stopped and turned away, shocked at her language. "I'm sorry. I…I shouldn't have spoken that way. It's not…I don't know what it's not."

She slowly turned her back to the stone. Across the driveway, a full city block away in the new cemetery section, preparations were being made for another burial. A canopy had been placed next to the open grave, and several white chairs waited in a row under it. The sunlight, reflecting off the railing that would soon support a casket, seemed to point right at Kay, piercing her soul.

Looking around the cemetery, she noted, "Mom, see how neatly trimmed the grass is around all the stones. We try to make it look peaceful and dignified. Perfectly ordered. But all around us, buried in the ground and the hearts of the mourners, chaos and grief reign. Anguish surrounds these stones. Sadness. Standing here, I feel cold… empty…alone…angry?"

Kay turned back to look at her mother's headstone. "This is stupid. To hell with it."

CHAPTER THIRTY-SEVEN

Monday, May 1

K ay stared at her cell phone screen after taking Paul's call. *That's weird, he wants to meet in an hour. Down by the river. Said it was important.*

An hour later, Kay walked onto the plaza at the end of River Street; Paul was leaning against the railing, looking out at the river, apparently deep in thought. A tow pushing six barges was making its way upriver. As it rounded the bend, it went under the bridge from Ellston to Wisconsin, she saw Paul wave at the tow captain and heard the blast from the barge's horn salute him in return. *This place fits him, but not me.*

She watched him standing there, as usual in his reporter attire— field jacket, open-collar shirt, jeans, and boots—staring at the water heading downstream. *He'd wear that outfit to a formal dinner, and no one would think anything amiss—that's who he is.* She hesitated to join him for some reason, even considering skipping their meeting. She was about to turn and leave.

Paul turned, spotted her, and waved. He pointed at the stairway that led to the river walk. She nodded and joined him at the top of the stairs.

"What's so important?" she said. She felt ill at ease but couldn't justify to herself why.

Paul's impish grin greeted her. "Thanks for coming. Let's sit on that park bench at the bottom of the stairs." Once settled on the bench, he began. "I'm a journalist..."

Kay held up her hand to silence him. "If you're angling for a story and trying to get an interview, I'm going to be really pissed."

"Kay, we're off the record. You are an interesting story, but I couldn't sleep at night if I tried to manipulate you for a story. You'll tell your story to the press when you are ready."

Somewhat mollified, she nodded. "Okay, what's up?"

"As a journalist, when confronted with facts and events that don't add up, it becomes like a giant puzzle I have to solve. I've been trying to understand why your voice quit, but I keep running into dead ends. That leads me to think there is a missing piece that will make everything fall into place."

Kay sighed. She was already getting impatient. "Paul, I don't want to talk about my mother. It's bad enough I have to talk to Dr. Phillips about her, I don't want to talk to you about her."

"I understand," he said. "It's not your mother I want to talk about."

Kay stood to leave. "I'm really tired. Do we have to go into this now?"

"Please, Kay, hear me out. I think I've discovered something that you will find helpful." Paul reached for her hand and gently pulled her back to the bench. "Here's what I see. You come to town, a town you don't like, to do a recital for your mentor. Losing your voice in a concert is highly unusual. You run into an uncle you haven't seen in years; he can't shed much light on your mother—dead end."

Kay's eyes narrowed, her voice threatening. "Paul, don't go there."

"Bear with me, please."

She frowned and nodded.

You reunite with your sister, but there's not much information there—a dead end. It turns out that Dr. Keizer also taught your mother, but there's not much information available—a dead end.

Irritated, Kay snapped. "Thanks a lot, Paul. All you've found are a bunch of dead ends. Did you drag me here just to recite what I already know?"

Paul's voice was gentle and patient. "No, I have, however, found the missing piece that ties it all together. It's my mother, Allison Williams."

"Paul, I don't even know your mother. I don't think I've ever even met her. How could she fit into this?" Kay's pulse quickened. She could feel trouble coming, but curiosity was getting the best of her.

"My mother has been your mother's attorney for years, and they had been best friends since college."

Kay looked at him. Speechless. Confused. Unable to grasp what the connection was.

Paul sat silent, waiting for her to absorb what he had told her. A houseboat slowly passed, heading for a sand bar to camp for the weekend. They waved, but Paul's attention remained focused on Kay.

Kay spoke, "I'm confused. How is she the missing piece?"

"My mother and Maarit were close all their lives. You met her once, when Anna ran away and you and I were going to help search for her."

Kay nodded. "I remember that. And a few other things from that day."

They both smiled. Their minds wandered back to the golf club, the bank, and the kiss.

Paul continued, "Shortly after you went to Atlanta, one of my mother's colleagues visited you and gave you some documents related to your mom's estate. When I asked my mother about that visit, she would say it was covered by client-attorney privilege and none of my business."

Kay inwardly chucked at the thought of Paul being told, by his mother, to mind his own business.

"The point is," Paul said. "My mother knows Maarit's secrets. This morning, I spoke with my mother about this, and she agreed to meet with you to discuss your mother, but it's entirely up to you whether you want to talk to her. That is the missing piece; she's willing to talk, if you want to."

Kay stood and walked a few steps down the river walk. She put her hands on each side of her head, spinning from what Paul had just said. She turned to face him. "Did she tell you anything about Maarit?"

"Only that she was Maarit's attorney and her best friend. That's it."

"And she's willing to tell me about her?" Kay said.

"Yes, if you want to hear the story."

Kay returned to the bench. Her breathing was shallow, and it felt as if bile was building up in her throat. "I don't want to," she whispered. "But I must."

Paul pulled out his cell phone, dialed the Williams-Laughton office, and handed the phone to Kay.

She shook her head, rolled her eyes, and took the phone.

CHAPTER THIRTY-EIGHT

Wednesday, May 3

The elevator chime signaled the top floor of the downtown professional building. Kay stood still, staring at the Williams-Laughton Law office sign through the elevator doorway.

"It'll be okay," she said aloud, stepping forward as the elevator door closed. "You have to do this."

The lobby of the law office was comfortable and welcoming. Unlike the opulence of a metropolitan legal firm, the Williams-Laughton reception area modestly portrayed a successful, small-town practice. Three people sat in high-backed, winged chairs around a low coffee table, engaged in a quiet, semi-private conversation. In bronze letters to the right of the reception desk were the firm's name and a list of four attorneys. Allison Williams' name topped the list as senior partner in the firm.

The receptionist ushered Kay into a conference room. "Ms. Williams is expecting you. She's on a conference call that should be over in a few minutes. Please, make yourself comfortable."

Kay glanced around the room. Eight chairs, evenly spaced around the table, were plush, functional rather than decorative. The blonde oak bookcases along the side wall contained leather-bound volumes of Minnesota statutes, neatly arranged in chronological order. Interspersed between each bookcase were photographs taken at locations along the

North Shore of Lake Superior. A large photograph of Devil's Kettle caught her attention. *I remember hiking to this spot,* she thought. *Seemed like it took forever for Dad and me to climb to the Kettle.*

"That's one of my favorite places," said Allison from the conference room doorway. "I took that photo several years ago. Took me all morning to get the lighting right. The sun had to be in the perfect position to throw enough light into the Kettle."

Kay found it hard to envision this professional woman standing beside her wearing an elegant, cream colored satin blouse, trim black trousers, and climbing the steep path above the Brule River. Allison's slightly greying auburn hair, erect posture, and purposeful walk perfectly fit this office. A closer look revealed a resolve that would fit anywhere, including the hiking paths in the Lake Superior backcountry.

"The photographs are wonderful," Kay said. "Did you take all of them?"

Allison nodded. "It's my escape. Helps me maintain perspective."

The two women shook hands. "It's good to see you again," Allison said as she took her place at the head of the table and motioned Kay to the seat next to her.

"When I saw you standing in front of the photo with your hands behind your back and your head tilted to the side…I almost called you Maarit. From behind, you look just like your mother. I'm so happy you called. I hoped we'd have a chance to talk."

Allison paused and studied Kay's face. "I'm curious. How did you make the connection between Maarit and me?"

"My uncle, Father McDonough, over at Saint Francis, told me he had delivered a package to my mother's attorney. He had your card in his files. At lunch yesterday, Paul told me that you had been my mother's friend in college and suggested I call you. He dialed the number on his cell and handed it to me while it rang."

"That is not a surprise. My son can be direct and take charge when he wants to."

Both women laughed, but the laughter did not lessen the tension in the room. Both women were searching for a way to begin the conversation that both dreaded.

Allison, comfortable on her home turf, a legal office, patiently continued the preliminaries. "I've lost track of your father over the years. Is he still living in the area?"

"No, a couple of years ago, he had a mild stroke, which caused mobility problems. Last year, he moved from Arizona to an apartment near me in San Francisco. Seems to have adjusted, but I know it's hard on him, especially when I travel."

"I'm glad to hear he's doing okay."

Kay's nervousness began to show. She fidgeted, trying to find a comfortable posture. "It's been tough, but he can still maintain his independence with a little help."

"That's good." Allison nodded her approval.

The conversation lagged for a moment. *It's time to start.* Kay thought to herself. *For Pete's sake, just ask!*

As if she had read her mind, Allison began the conversation. "I was at the recital. It was quite a shock to you when your voice failed. Is it starting to come back?"

Kay nodded. "A little. At least my voice is understandable. I can hum a little, but can't sing yet. All that comes out is half a hum and half a vowel. I fear it will never fully come back."

Allison sympathetically shook her head. "I don't mean to pry, but Paul told me you were seeing Dr. Phillips. What's his prognosis?"

"Guardedly optimistic." Kay's voice wavered. "I'm afraid I don't share his confidence."

"That's encouraging."

Kay nodded. "We did have a bit of a breakthrough the other day. He thinks we've discovered what triggered the voice failure. As I started the encore, a young woman sitting near the stage leaned forward. Her long hair fell along her face."

Kay moved her hands in a pantomime of the falling hair. "I had a flashback to my childhood. My mother's hair would fall forward like the woman's hair in the audience did. It's one of my last memories of my mom. She kissed me goodnight, and her hair fell forward and tickled my ear. After that, I never saw her again."

Kay closed her eyes and tried to blink back the tears. The flashback picture of Maarit returned, and, for a fleeting second, she once again felt her mother's hair tickling her cheeks. Seeing Kay's eyes brimming with tears, Allison stood to retrieve an ever-present box of tissues from the center of the table.

Kay struggled to compose herself. She swallowed a sob and, in a shaky voice, continued.

"As I started to sing, it struck me that the encore was a lullaby my mother used to sing to me. That was the trigger. Then my voice just… quit…"

Allison shook her head empathetically. "I'm always amazed at the tricks the mind can play."

Kay took several deep breaths to calm herself. She tried to erase the pain she knew Allison could read on her face, but the pain would not go away. With one last deep breath, Kay leaned forward, resting her forearms on the table. It was time to get to the heart of the matter. "Paul said you would tell me about my mother."

Allison nodded and smiled at the memory of her college friend. "We were roommates in the freshman dorm; we became best friends. For a while, it was a joke among our crowd that Maarit wasn't far away wherever Allison was, and if you wanted to find Allison, find Maarit. First, in some ways, I think, I was her safety net. My job was to try to keep her out of trouble; hers was to ensure I didn't permanently hide in the library. At times, it was a bit of a challenge for both of us."

Kay sat silently, trying to picture Allison and her mother as good friends. It seemed a very unlikely combination.

"The friendship worked both ways; I was a bit shy. She was exciting and alive, a trait I envied. We moved into an apartment together at the end of our first year. After college, we remained friends. Didn't get to see her very often. She was too busy traveling the world, but we kept in touch. Over the years, I handled various legal matters for her."

Kay leaned back in the chair. "Ms. Williams..."

"Please, call me Allison."

"Allison...did she ever talk to you about me or Anna?"

"Yes, frequently. Remember, Maarit was my best friend, and I was her confidant. I was also her attorney. Often, it's difficult to separate personal conversations from those covered by privilege."

"I understand," Kay said. "And wouldn't want you to betray any confidence. But it seems that on this trip, I'm constantly reminded of her. The anger boils up each time. It's like she's been haunting me."

Allison studied Kay. "Is the anger that stopped your singing?"

"Dr. Phillips thinks it may be. Allison, I don't have anyone else to help me with this. You and my uncle are the only links that I have to her. Father McDonough has told me a little about their family, but Maarit left home when he was only sixteen. He didn't have much contact with her after the divorce."

"And, your father?" Allison queried.

"He will say, 'I loved your mother, but we couldn't live together.' He always avoids the subject."

Kay looked down at the conference table, tracing the wood grain pattern with her fingers. Her voice was soft but edged with steel. "Do you know why she abandoned our family?"

Allison reached across the table and squeezed Kay's hand. "Some things are best left buried in the past. I'm reluctant to dig up old skeletons."

Kay returned the squeeze, her eyes pleading. "Please, tell me what you know."

"Are you sure you want to know?"

Kay looked directly into Allison's eyes. "I have to know. It's the key to everything."

Allison hesitated. Slowly, she released the air in her lungs. The familiar aroma of shelves filled with books comforted her, giving her the strength to tell the truth to the frightened six-year-old hiding behind the eyes of her friend's daughter.

"Tell me what happened," Kay pleaded. "Why did my mother leave and never come back?"

Allison began. "Much of what I will tell you would be covered under attorney-client privilege. When your mother died, Father McDonough—by the way, I did know he was your uncle—delivered a package to me. In that package were several documents for the Jensens and the material my colleague gave you in Atlanta, including the letter you refused to read and tore to pieces."

Kay's body went rigid as if steeling itself from a hypothetical body blow.

Allison went on. "The package also contained a document that permitted me to answer any questions you, or Anna might ask. In essence, she released me from any ethical or legal considerations that would prevent me from disclosing information to you. She left the timing to my discretion, and clearly Atlanta wasn't the right time."

Kay straightened in the chair. Her fists were clenched.

"Kay, there is no way to sugar coat this." Allison continued. "Your parents fought a lot. During one of those fights, your mother yelled at Tom that you probably are not his biological child. He was stunned, furious. He told her to leave and not come back. She swore at him, packed a suitcase, and left."

Kay recoiled, stood, and leaned across the conference table. "Are you telling me that Tom Malone is *not* my father!"

"No, I'm telling you that your mother, in anger, told your father that he may not be your biological parent. That's a big difference."

"My birth certificate names Tom Malone as my father," Kay sputtered.

"Your mother lied."

"Lied? To whom?"

Allison shrugged, sat back in the chair, and sighed. "Kay, please sit down."

Kay remained standing and leaning on the conference table for support. *This can't be happening.*

"Look," said Allison. "I'm sure you must know she was pregnant when she and your father married."

"It didn't take a mathematical genius to figure that out," Kay snapped, her voice riddled with emotion. "I thought they were in love, got careless one night, and voilà, here I am. No big deal."

"That's not the whole story. Your mother was one of those people whom others wanted to be around. She was like a magnet. When she entered a room, a group almost immediately formed with Maarit at the center. For reasons which I don't understand, she desperately craved attention. It seemed to energize her."

Kay sank heavily into the chair.

"Your mother was always dragging me to one of the frat parties. Frequently, we didn't leave the party together. She got pregnant and wasn't positive who the father was. She told me it could have been Tom, but she wasn't sure. She told Tom she was pregnant; he assumed the child was his, and they married. She was genuinely fond of your father, but..." Allison shrugged as if to say, *What can I tell you?*

The blood drained from Kay's face. The shock and anger began to well up inside her.

"When Tom sued for divorce, it ended her hope for a reconciliation. She was devastated, wracked with guilt. Maarit had a history of being on an emotional roller coaster. She could go from extreme exuberance to a devastating low almost instantaneously. After the divorce, she was headed for a very bad low. I was afraid she was going to have a nervous breakdown. Against my advice, she signed the divorce papers agreeing that she wouldn't contact you."

Kay felt her breathing become shallow and erratic. She wasn't sure if she should cry or throw up.

This can't be happening...

Allison paused to utter a deep sigh. Her voice carried a deep sadness. "When the divorce was final, I asked Tom what he planned to tell you. He said he wasn't going to tell you much. I remember he said, 'Whether that little girl is my flesh and blood or not, I love her. She's

— 284 —

a sweet child, and I will do everything I can to protect her, to help her be happy.' And to keep Maarit away from you."

Kay sat motionless. The realization that her father had kept her mother away from her for all those years slowly took over her mind. She barely heard Allison's last sentence.

"That's the story." Allison sat silently, drained. *For better or worse, at last the truth, or at least most of it, is out.*

Kay buried her face in her hands. Her shoulders began to shake, the tremor gradually engulfing her. From deep within her, a wail began, rising in pitch and volume to fill the room and escape to the lobby.

The intercom on the conference table buzzed. Allison pushed the button and said, "Not now."

Kay rose from the table and lurched around the room, sobbing hysterically. Allison followed her, trying to reach out and console her. Each time, she was waved off. When Kay sank to the floor in a corner of the room, Allison knelt, put her arms around Kay's shoulders, and held her tightly. Gradually, the sobs diminished, and she stopped shaking. Allison helped her rise from the floor and settle back into the chair when she became quiet.

The intercom buzzed a second time. "Everything is fine," Allison said. "Bring in a tray of tea."

Neither spoke until the tea arrived and the pouring ritual was completed. Allison could only watch, wary, afraid the sobbing would resume. It seemed as though Kay would begin again several times, then catch herself and regain her calm.

Kay finally spoke. "This morning, I visited Maarit's grave. I yelled and cursed at my mother. I all but spit on her grave."

Allison waited quietly; there was nothing more she could say.

Kay wiped her tears. "All these years wasted and full of anger because of one angry retort, that might not even be a lie. I hated her for leaving. My father didn't set the record straight. He was hurt and sent my mother away. He did say a few times that I shouldn't hate her, but that didn't stop me. Over the years, I've buried that anger. I thought I had overcome it, but it was just below the surface, waiting to erupt."

She leaned back into the chair with a heavy sigh and pushed it away from the table. She folded her hands and rested them in her lap. She bowed her head and closed her eyes.

Allison moved behind her friend's daughter and gently massaged her neck and shoulders. "I know both Maarit and Tom loved you," she said. "We were all friends in college. He is a great guy. She hurt him badly. I hope you won't turn your anger on him."

Kay choked back a sob. "I know he tried to do what he thought best for me. At age six, I wouldn't have understood…who knows when I might have." She sighed deeply again, and the adrenaline drained away, leaving her exhausted.

"I'm tired," she said. "I don't want to hate anymore."

Allison returned to her chair and leaned forward to hold Kay's hands. "Nothing says you have to hate," she murmured gently. "No legal or natural law says you have to remain angry or assign blame. It won't be easy, but you can live with this. Letting it go will take conscious effort, but it can be done."

Kay took a tissue and gently wiped her eyes. "Does Anna know what happened?"

"I don't think so. The packet I delivered to the Jensens included a letter to Anna. With Anna's permission, John and Peg showed it to me. There was no mention of any of this in it. Some time ago, Anna asked me about the circumstances surrounding Maarit's departure. I told her that she would have to ask you. And, if you want to know Anna's story, you'll have to ask her."

Kay composed herself. "Thank you for telling me."

Allison nodded, "What are you going to do?"

"I'm not sure," replied Kay. "Try to make sense of all this with Dr. Phillips, I guess. I'll have to talk to my dad, though I don't know how to approach him. Dredging up the past won't do much, except cause him more pain."

Kay stood to leave. "Thank you again."

Allison reached out her arms. The two embraced.

"Keep in touch," Allison said. "I'd love to tell you many happy stories and memories of your mother."

Thursday, May 4

The receptionist at the St. Francis rectory buzzed Father McDonough. "It's Ms. Malone. Do you have a few minutes to see her?"

"Of course." Sean greeted Kay at the office door and ushered her to his favorite spot in the office, the round table in the corner. He noted a marked difference in his niece's face from their last meeting. Her eyes were sad, rather than the defiance and anger he had seen before.

After the usual pleasantries, Kay again conducted the tea-pouring ritual and addressed her uncle. "I saw Allison Williams yesterday. She told me why my mother left the family. Do you know the circumstances?"

Her uncle looked at her and carefully chose his words. "Yes," he said. "I do."

"Why didn't you tell me?" Kay asked quietly, more curiosity than recrimination. Her voice had notes of sadness but not anger.

"I couldn't. I was told the story under the seal of the confessional."

"Who told you?"

McDonough smiled gently. "After twelve years of Catholic school, you know I can't answer that question."

Kay's shoulders involuntarily shuddered. "It was quite a shock. I haven't completely processed it yet."

"It will take some time, but you will come to terms with it." Sean waited for her to continue. Teenage chatter in the rectory reception area seeped through the door to his private study. *The sounds of youth juxtaposed with the concerns of adults—both of equal importance.*

"I took your advice and went to the cemetery. Twice."

"Twice?" Surprised, Father McDonough looked at Kay over his glasses.

"Once before I found out the truth, and then again this morning," Kay said. She looked past her uncle's shoulder. Her gaze came to rest on the crucifix hanging above the small altar on the other side of the office. For a moment, her memory took her back to the night her mother kissed her goodbye, so many years ago.

Father Sean waited until her eyes returned to their conversation. "Did it help?"

Kay's voice became more vibrant, more animated, more confident. "Yes, I believe it did. I can't say that I felt her presence, like you and Anna do, but it did help me. The anger seems to have been replaced by sadness. Maarit didn't see any way out of the situation she had created. And, my dad had been hurt so deeply, he couldn't get past it."

"Will this become a problem for you and your father?"

Kay smiled. "I don't think so. Yes, we will talk about it when I get home. I'm sure some tears will be shed, but he raised me. We are very close. I don't blame him. They were two people caught in a situation they couldn't handle. The anger and the hurt deprived them of much happiness."

"It is a sad story," he nodded. "Over time, your sadness will soften."

"I hope so."

"It will," her uncle reassured her. "Have you talked to Anna about this?"

Kay shook her head; her mouth turned upward in a mischievous smile. "I haven't seen her for a couple of days. She seems to be spending a lot of time with Jim Teigen." She chuckled. "It wouldn't surprise me if something serious doesn't develop between them. He's a nice guy."

"That would be a wonderful thing. For both of them." Sean set his teacup on the table and said, "I have something I want to give you."

The priest arose and strode to his desk. Deep in the top drawer, he withdrew a small box and opened it. Gently and reverently, as if holding a sacred relic, he pulled an octagonal, silver locket from the box. The locket, a Saint Brigit's cross embossed on its face, was suspended on a delicately woven silver chain.

Carefully, he pressed a small button on the locket's side. On the left side was a picture of his parents, and on the opposite side was an image of Maarit and himself.

As he returned to the table, Kay rose to meet him.

"She was wearing this on the day she died. Mom and Dad gave it to her on her twenty-first birthday. I know it meant a lot to her. I'd like you to have it."

Kay took the locket and stared at the pictures for a long time. "I don't know what to say, Uncle Sean. Are you sure you want to give this to me? It's beautiful. It must mean a lot to you."

"It does, but I want you to have it. Besides," he quipped. "It would look much nicer around your neck than mine. I have many memories and mementos to remind me of my sister. I think it's time you had your mother and me closer to you."

Kay carefully closed the locket, opened the silver chain clip, and fastened it around her neck. "Thank you, Uncle Sean. I will treasure it."

CHAPTER THIRTY-NINE

Sunday Afternoon, May 14

For over an hour, Elizabeth Keizer sat center stage at the concert grand piano, bathed in a circle of light from the spotlights trained on her. She played her favorite compositions, a Bach three-part invention, a Beethoven concerto, and a medley of Gershwin tunes just for fun. The audience showed their appreciation for her music and her career at Milan with enthusiastic applause.

She stood before playing the final piece on the program, Chopin's *Valse Brilliante, Opus 18*. "I chose this waltz to end this recital," she said, "because beneath the joyful theme lies an element of melancholy that the dance must eventually end. But the music concludes with a powerful exuberance. It is a fitting end to my career here at Milan College."

Back at the piano, Keizer lightly caressed the keys before beginning to play. *I love this place, but it's time to stop.* She leaned over the keyboard, her fingers poised. She let them dance. The waltz ended with a flourish and full, beautiful chords.

She stood to accept the standing ovation, which was given not just for the music the audience had experienced but also in appreciation for her career.

Dr. Keizer signaled for the audience to sit. "Ladies and gentlemen, thank you so very much. Sharing my music with you for forty years has been a true pleasure."

A round of applause interrupted her.

She let the applause die down before continuing. "As a special encore tonight, I have a surprise for you. Many of you were here for the benefit performance by Kay Malone in March and will remember that her encore was cut short by the loss of her voice."

A murmur rippled through the crowd.

"Over the past two months," Keizer continued, "she has worked hard to recover. I'm pleased to announce that her singing voice has returned and continues to gain strength. She has graciously agreed to return tonight to finish the encore she couldn't complete then."

Wild applause thundered throughout the concert hall.

"And, accompanying Ms. Malone is her sister, Anna Jensen, another of my students. This is the first time the sisters have performed together. Please, welcome Kay Malone and Anna Jensen."

The audience cheered as a spotlight followed the sisters as they joined Dr. Keizer on the stage. The three hugged each other to cheers from the audience before Keizer exited to stand in the wings.

"Before we begin," Kay said, "thank you all for coming tonight to honor Dr. Keizer's career. It is our pleasure and honor to participate in this celebration. We dedicate this performance to Dr. Keizer, our mentor, teacher, and friend. We'd also like to dedicate the music to the memory of our late mother, Maarit McDonough Malone, from whom we inherited our musical talent."

Sitting next to Father McDonough, Paul thought he saw a tear in the priest's eyes. A tear, not only for his sister, but for the reconciliation with Kay and Anna's debut. Paul discreetly looked away as Sean wiped his eyes with his hand.

Kay continued. "This is the world premiere of a selection from a song cycle composed by Anna. The cycle chronicles the life and times of St. Urho of Finland. If you don't know the 'legend,' Kay made quotation marks in the air, "St. Urho drove the grasshoppers out of Finland, thus saving the grape crop and Finland's wine industry."

Many heads in the audience nodded in acknowledgment.

"Coincidentally," Kay winked, "St. Urho's holiday is the day before St. Patrick's Day, thus giving Finns and Irish worldwide an extra day to celebrate. The song is titled *Sinikka*. The opening shows her frustration with Urho."

Keizer stood, holding her breath, waiting for Kay to begin singing, hoping this would not be a repeat of the March recital. The two sisters nodded to each other. Anna began playing.

The introduction, a rollicking rhythmic tune, began softly, quickly gaining volume and speed. Faster and faster, the notes rolled out of the piano. Kay began to sing the forceful cry of Sinikka's frustration with her husband, who was late for dinner again.

After the applause died down, Kay took the microphone a second time. "There is one more song I'd like to sing for you. It was a lullaby that my mother sang." She turned to Anna, "Sorry, sis, *our* mother sang to me when I was a child. It was a memory of her singing it to me at my recital in March that played a part in my voice deciding to take a 'vacation.' It's the lullaby by Johannes Brahms."

Anna raised her eyebrows and mouthed, "Are you sure?"

Kay nodded. Closed her eyes and waited for the introduction to start. *This is for you, mother. Rest in peace.*

Anna looked at Dr. Keizer standing in the wings, just off the stage. Keizer nodded and held her breath.

Kay began to sing,

Lullaby and good night,
with roses bedight,
With lilies o'er spread is baby's wee bed.
Lay thee down now and rest,
may thy slumber be blessed.
Lay thee down now and rest, may
thy slumber be blessed.

Dr. Keizer released a sigh of relief. Kay's voice was back but had a new tenderness and gentleness.

After the lullaby, the audience was silent. No one wanted to breathe, for to do so would break the magic spell. It was the highest compliment an audience can pay to a performance. The breathing must begin again. When it did, the audience rose to deliver thunderous applause. Anna and Kay waved for Dr. K. to join them on stage, and the three women hugged and bowed to the audience.

After 45 minutes, the audience left the recital hall. Well-wishers swarmed Dr. Keizer, Kay, and Anna, heaping praise and thanks for the magical evening.

Finally, only Paul, Kay, Jim, Anna, Father Sean, and Dr. Keizer were alone on the stage. They gathered at the piano to bask in the afterglow. No words were left to be said. Almost all had been spoken.

Almost all, but not quite. Anna spoke first. "I, I mean, *we* have an announcement to make. Jim moved beside her and put his arm around her shoulders. "Last night, Jim asked me to marry him, and I agreed."

Kay hugged them both and said, "Well, it's about time the two of you finally figured out what the rest of us have known since you danced that first night at Luigi's." The rest of the group added their congratulations.

"Well," Kay said, "since it seems to be announcement time, I just accepted a position as Artistic Director of the San Francisco Opera Company. It's a new phase of my musical career. There is not much singing, but a lot of music."

Again, congratulations flowed from the group.

Anna said, "I have one more announcement, I'll likely be starting work on a doctorate in music theory and composition at North Texas University in Denton, Texas. I'm first alternate but have been told it's highly likely that I'll be able to start this fall."

Dr. Keizer clapped her hands and laughed. "Sorry Anna, I just can't resist. I told you so." The group laughed.

Finally, the rush of emotions faded, and the group began to disperse. Father Sean excused himself, citing an early morning Mass. Liz Keizer looked and felt drained from the evening's emotions, and it was clear that Anna and Jim wanted to be alone. The concert hall had emptied; the only ones left, besides Paul and Kay, were the custodians beginning their clean-up routine.

Paul loosened the tie he wore only on special occasions, folded it neatly, and put it into his sports coat pocket. "Ready to call it an evening?"

"Not really," answered Kay. "The adrenaline is still flowing from the concert."

"Remember that jazz trio from Luigi's?" Paul said. "They're playing at a quiet little lounge downtown. Perfect place to unwind."

Kay linked her arm in his. "Sounds perfect. First, a quick stop at the hotel to change."

The Riverside lounge, perched on the side bank of the Mississippi, is in sight of the bridge spanning the river to Wisconsin. The lights were dim but not dark, and the tables were nicely spaced so that conversation could occur without intruding upon the adjacent patrons.

They chose a small table on the outer edge of the lounge. Sitting next to each other at the table, they had a comfortable view of the stage and the small dance floor. They settled into a comfortable silence. The soft strains of dance music blended with the clinking of ice against glass and quiet snippets of conversation from nearby tables.

"Your life has taken quite a turn," Paul said. "Are you pleased with it?"

Kay thought about his question for a moment. Her eyes lingered on the swizzle stick she used to stir her drink.

"Yes," she finally answered, "More so than I thought I would be. I went after the San Francisco job, more out of desperation than anything. However, as I learned more about it, I became even more interested. I get to sing without the constant pressure, the coaching will be a new challenge, and I get to try my hand at conducting an orchestra. That will be the real challenge."

"The best of all worlds. Congratulations."

Kay looked at Paul. "So, what about you?"

"Well, we have a couple of other things to celebrate tonight."

Kay tilted her head to one side. "Okay, I'll bite. What are they?"

Paul's impish grin spread across his face. "First, Brad Quinn is moving on. He got a job in Atlanta as an investigative reporter."

Kay laughed and clapped, "God help the journalistic profession in Georgia."

"I don't know," Paul shrugged his shoulders. "He may have learned a couple of things from our little confrontation. He showed me a draft of a follow-up article on your career; the 'scandal' was not included. When I asked him why, he smiled and said it wasn't important enough to include. He'll contact you after your new position is made public. I approved the draft. Time will tell if he truly learned anything."

"There's always hope," Kay said.

Paul's grin returned, "There is one other thing. It'll be official next week. I'm leaving the newspaper."

"You are?" Kay's mouth opened in surprise.

"Yep." Paul grinned at her complete surprise.

"To do what?"

"What I love to do: *write*. I've been offered a position as a syndicated columnist based in Monterey."

The jazz trio announced a break; they would return shortly for their next set. The conversation in the lounge increased in volume as the wait staff hustled to refill drinks and deliver hors d'oeuvres.

Kay leaned forward and rested her arms on the table. "As in California?"

Even in the dim light, Kay could see the twinkle in his eyes.

"As in California," Paul said. "That's…"

"Two and a half hours south of San Francisco." Kay laughed. "That's convenient."

"Yes, it is." Paul reached over to hold her hand. She did not pull away.

Kay's face turned serious. Her voice was concerned. "What prompted the move?"

"Several things. Management's not for me. Too much paperwork and not enough fun chasing down rabbit holes."

"I'm delighted for you," Kay said. "And thrilled that you're going to be so close. But isn't going back to reporting going to put you face-to-face with evil again? That's what made you come home to hide in the first place. It's not going to go away."

Paul leaned over to gently kiss her. She gently caressed his cheek. They kissed again. Kay whispered, "This could become a very nice habit." A waiter interrupted a third kiss, asking if they wanted another drink. Kay ordered a second glass of wine and a cup of coffee for Paul.

"No, the evil is still there," Paul said. "But neither kindness nor beauty is going away. Sometimes, one has to look harder to find it, but it's there, nonetheless. That is what I havelearned from you since the recital."

The trio's return to the stage and the strains of Brubeck's classic *Take Five* paused Kay's reaction. The five-beat repeating pattern, innovative when the tune first appeared, now felt comfortable and familiar.

Kay cocked her head to one side, her eyes asking the question. "From me?"

"Yes. I watched the way you responded to losing your voice."

"I almost quit," Kay said ruefully.

Paul nodded. "I know, but you didn't. You chose to continue the struggle." Paul paused. "Remember my poster?"

Kay thought for a moment. "The two wolves?"

"Yes, Paul said. "Good and evil exist simultaneously. At the recital, before your voice failed, I was overwhelmed by the beauty of the music. I became focused on what was happening at that moment. Even though I knew they still existed, all the evil and ugliness were banished briefly. The good and the beautiful, overwhelmed the evil and the ugly."

Kay teasingly punched him in the arm. "You really are an idealist."

Paul leaned forward and nodded toward a couple, weaving their way between the tables to the dance floor. "Watch this," he whispered.

The man stood over six feet tall, and his dance partner was in heels, barely five feet. His hair had completely migrated from his pate to his face, leaving only a silver halo around the side and back of his head.

The hue of her hair matched the pure white of his full beard. He gently offered his hand. She looked up into his eyes and placed her hand in his.

Kay looked at Paul, a question written all over her face.

"Watch," he said.

The two melded into one as the music started and glided around the dance floor. They were a perfectly matched pair, each knowing exactly the move the other would make next. Neither was leading the other; they moved in perfect unison, achieved through years of dancing together.

"Someday," Kay whispered. "Someday."

Paul stood and reached out his hand. "Dance with me?"

Monday Morning, May 16

It was mid-morning before Anna and Kay stumbled downstairs in their pajamas, searching for coffee. "I'm getting too old for this late-night stuff," Anna groaned.

"*You're* getting too old? Add another decade and see how you feel." Kay wiped the sleep from her eyes.

"Ah, but it was a glorious day. A glorious day. We do have to perform together again someday." Anna said as she pushed the coffee maker's on button. "I'm glad I took the time to prepare the coffee last night."

The two laughed and settled at the kitchen table to watch the coffee maker gurgle and spew forth the life-giving brew. Kay looked around the room. "I love this room. It reminds me so much of your mother. You left the little touches when you remodeled. The red clock on the soffit above the sink, the old-fashioned bread box in the corner of the counter."

"Yeah, even though they don't fit in with modern kitchen decor," Anna said, "I just couldn't part with them."

"Ya done good, sis."

The coffee pot gurgled loudly, its job almost done.

"I didn't hear you come home last night. I was sound asleep," Kay said.

Anna laughed. "I could hear you snoring as soon as I walked into the house. It must have been about two." Her eyes twinkled with mischief. "Did you and Paul go out after the concert?"

"Yes, nosy." Kay turned a light shade of pink, remembering the sweet kissing like teenagers. "We went to the Riverside and listened to a great jazz trio."

Anna noticed Kay's complexion change. She was about to comment and ask about the developing relationship with Paul, but she let Kay choose the moment to discuss it.

"No one was surprised at your big announcement last night," Kay said. "But so happy for you, Jim's a great guy. Have you talked about wedding dates yet?"

Before the coffee maker on the counter stopped beeping, the sisters simultaneously chimed, "Coffee's ready!" and jumped from the table to fill their cups. Neither said anything until the first two swallows were taken, and they returned to the table.

"The wedding date is a problem." Anna took another sip of coffee. "He wants to get married as soon as possible."

Kay said, "That's understandable."

"I want to wait until I'm done with grad school." Anna wrinkled her nose. "The last thing I want to do is to try to plan a wedding from Texas."

"How does Jim feel about you going so far away to school?" Kay gook another sip and moved to refill her cup.

"That's another problem. He wants me to go to school in Chicago. I hate Chicago and want to go to North Texas U. I don't know, but we'll see how this long-distance thing works out."

The look on her face doesn't give me much hope for this relationship. Kay thought ruefully, *I won't start thinking about a wedding gift yet.* Instead of voicing her concerns, she changed the subject. "So, tell me about Texas.

Anna raved about the opportunities that she would have down there. She shared with her sister the excellent performance venues and the active arts community in Denton. She gushed about the campus itself and mentioned that she would likely stay in a dorm that resembled an apartment building more than a traditional dorm. Even the name of the place was iconic — Mozart Square.

"Wow," Kay said. "I'm going to have to come and visit you. I need to see this place."

"Any time, sis. Anytime at all." Anna smiled.

"Tell me about California," Anna said in between mouthfuls.

"Not a lot to tell yet. I have to be there on Monday, so I'll catch a flight home the day after tomorrow."

"So soon?" Anna pouted.

"I've been here almost two months; I don't want to wear out my welcome."

"Never happen," Anna said. "Anyway, tell me more about your new job."

Kay smiled. "I'll be the opera's Music Director, responsible for the season, and also manage their summer opera workshop. Occasionally, I'll get to sing, though probably not in a starring role. A few recitals and guest spots. My voice is back, but not as strong as it used to be."

"Sounds exciting," Anna said.

"Exciting and a little terrifying at the same time," Kay said. But it's time to move into a new phase."

"For both of us."

Anna went to the counter, held up the coffee pot, and silently asked if Kay wanted more. Kay shook her head, no. Anna searched the cupboard, found some cookies, and brought them to the table. "Not much to eat," Anna said. "But…"

Kay took a cookie. "My sister, the doctor," she giggled. "Who'd a thunk it. Will you be able to start in the fall?"

"I think so. The program director indicated the spot is very likely to open up. I should know in a few weeks." Anna put her elbows on the table to support her hands holding the mug level with her face. "Will you do me a favor?"

"Sure, what do you need? More coffee?"

"No. Will you go to the cemetery with me this afternoon? I want to put flowers on Peg and John's grave and Maarit's." Anna winced, waiting for her sister to explode like the last time she had asked for this favor.

Kay smiled. "I would be happy to go with you."

"Really?"

"Yes. My anger has dissipated with the help of Paul's mother and Uncle Sean. It's why I could sing at Dr. K's recital. We haven't discussed this, but I'll fill you in before leaving. The flowers are a good idea."

Monday Afternoon, May 16

Anna and Kay first walked up the familiar path to John and Peg's graves. Kay stood silently while Anna tenderly placed a bouquet of tulips, Peg's favorite flower, on the headstone marking their graves. Anna slowly ran her fingers over their names carved in the granite.

"Miss you," she whispered. When Anna stood, Kay linked her arms with her sister.

The two walked arm in arm, a short distance to Maarit's resting place. The warm sunlight, filtering through the spring tree leaves, cast a lattice-work shadow on the gravestone. Kay filled her lungs with the fresh aroma of the earth, awakening from its long, cold rest. Behind them, the quiet splendor of the red and white flowering crabapple tree brought a sense of peace to the place.

They each placed a bouquet of tulips, daffodils, and hyacinths on Maarit's stone. Kay stooped to pick up a small stone and placed it next to the ones Sean and Anna had already put there.

"I like that tradition," Kay said. "It's a nice way to say I remember you." *I wish it had been different, but I cherish the memory of you leaning down to kiss goodnight.*

A flurry of red caught their attention. A cardinal flew into the trees behind them and began to sing. Its mating call reminded them that life's circles continued.

Anna began to take short, quick, shallow breaths. A look of panic swept over her face, and she began to shake. "She's not here," Anna whispered. "She's not here." Her voice quivered. "Kay, she's not here. She's gone." Anna's whole body began to shake uncontrollably.

Kay moved to stand between her sister and the gravestone. "Anna, look at me. "Who's not here? What are you seeing? Snap out of it. Anna, look at me. Look at me."

"Focus on my face, look at me," Kay ordered. Anna regained control of the shaking and calmed down, but a look of panic remained in her eyes. "Kay, Maarit's not here. She's always here when I visit. Now, she's gone."

Kay smoothed Anna's hair with her fingers to try to calm the terror she saw in Anna's eyes. "Isn't that a good thing?"

"But, she's always here. I always feel her presence." Anna tried to hold back the tears.

"Maybe she's done haunting us. Maybe she doesn't think you need her anymore." Kay continued to stroke her sister's hair.

"I'm all alone. She's been with me for years. I'm really scared I'm alone. She's abandoned me again?" Anna could feel the bile begin to rise in her throat.

"Look at me," Kay commanded. "You are not alone. It doesn't matter how many miles are between us. You are not alone. We are sisters. We can't be separated by mere miles. Perhaps Maarit is telling us both that we no longer need her. Her death brought us together twenty years ago. Now she's setting us free. Maybe she's at peace at last."

Anna leaned her head on Kay's shoulder, just as she had done twenty years ago at Maarit's casket. Slowly, she nodded. "Promise we'll stay in touch. Kay, promise me we'll keep in touch."

Kay hugged her. "I promise."

ACKNOWLEDGMENTS

A special note of thanks to all those who have read this novel's early drafts and generously given their time to comment and offer suggestions. First, thanks to Rebecca Flansburg. Her encouragement and tireless efforts to turn this story into a readable novel are greatly appreciated. Any mistakes in the manuscript are mine alone.

I'm forever indebted to Wendi Levitt, Nancy Kay Peterson, Dan Eastman, Tanya Ryan, and the Rochester (MN) Writers Group. Your encouragement and suggestions helped immensely.

Notably, the contribution of Dr. Robert Morse, a retired psychiatrist, is also noteworthy. His willingness to share insights into mental disorders played a critical part in shaping this story.

The roll call ceremony is taken from a video, "The Hornet's Nest," by Mike Boettcher. The scene is used with his gracious permission.

I also want to thank Mark Yunker, Sergeant First Class, U.S. Army (Retired), who served in Afghanistan, for his background information on military life in that far-away place.

ABOUT THE AUTHOR

R on Elcombe is a professor emeritus at Winona State University (MN), where he taught various advertising and mass communication courses for 25 years. His eclectic career encompasses teaching instrumental music, as well as sales and marketing roles for multiple companies. He has been published in the *Lake Country Journal* and several professional academic journals and has attended seminars on fiction writing at the Iowa Summer Writers Festival. *The Legacy of a Lie* is the first book in a three-novel series. He resides in Rochester, Minnesota, with his wife, Sharon, and enjoys summers on the golf course and at the family cabin in northern Minnesota.